BONI

'By the devil!' Carlton glowered. 'You're the rudest damn nigger I ever met!' He slapped the whip stock against his thigh and stepped back to take aim.

'I'll do it for yer!' another of the sailors called. 'My arm ain't weak from pullin' all night.'

'Damn you!' he shouted, attacking Prince with rage. The first blow cut a stripe across his shoulders. It oozed blood.

Prince bucked, tugging at the ropes. Nat groaned loudly.

The second lash scored a line that crossed the first. It made the watching seamen wince.

'Mas Carlton!' shrieked Caspar. He tugged at Carlton's arm as he drew it back for the third stroke. 'Look, Mas Carlton. Look!'

The boy's scream penetrated his fury and he glanced where Caspar was pointing.

There, in a corner of the deck, emerging from a chest that was covered with ropes and canvas, eyes glaring, her bodice ripped and her brown bosom hanging bare, was Gwen.

Also by Richard Tresillian in Sphere Books:

FLEUR
THE BONDMASTER
BLOOD OF THE BONDMASTER
THE BONDMASTER BREED
THE BONDMASTER'S REVENGE

Bondmaster Buck

Being Book Six of the Bondmaster Saga

RICHARD TRESILLIAN

SPHERE BOOKS LIMITED
London and Sydney

First published in Great Britain by
Arlington Books (Publishers) Ltd 1984

Published by Sphere Books Ltd 1985
30–32 Gray's Inn Road, London WCIX 8JL

TRADE
MARK

Set in 9/11 pt Compugraphic Plantin

Printed and bound in Great Britain by
Collins, Glasgow

CONTENTS

AUTHOR'S NOTE

Chronologically, this book is the second in the series begun with *The Bondmaster*.

It appears now after six others because only recently have papers been discovered detailing the activities of Carlton Todd – The Bondmaster – after he sailed away from Dominica late in 1807.

This series could not have been written without the support and assistance of Abraham Browne, Augustus Charles, Edward Ellis and Tony Moise of Dominica; Cartmell Warrington and Ms Tino McCoy of the USA; and Neel Jayantha of Wordsman Ltd.

Richard Tresillian

'Roxborough Estate in the Layou Valley was the most productive of Dominica's sugar plantations until it declined at the end of the eighteenth century when the Todd family started the first slave warren in the British West Indian islands.

'The Bondmaster, Mr Carlton Todd, is reputed to have made a considerable fortune by his selective breeding of enslaved Africans for sale to the plantation owners of neighbouring islands.

'A Roxborough slave became renowned as the elite of that subjugated race, and it is said that many of today's native citizens of prominence have descended from the line begun by the Bondmaster of Roxborough.

'There has been speculation that this line stretched beyond the shores of the Caribbean, with black blood becoming mixed with the blue of English aristocracy.'

From: *A History of the British West Indian Islands* by Sir Verne W. Bisset, Bart. Published by Shankland & Box, London & Cambridge, 1913.

Prologue
Exiles, 1807

CHAPTER ONE

Carlton was eager for exile. He gripped the reins of his horse and glared at the slaves shuffling nervously in the shade of the blood-red flowers of the flamboyant trees surrounding the courtyard in front of the house. He had made his decision. He put his foot in the stirrup and prepared to mount his horse.

'Carlton!'

He scowled at the interruption. Ella was moving with her usual savage dignity toward him, her long dress sweeping over the flag-stones and her head held high and proud. Her face was like a shining ebony mask and showed no sign of what she was thinking. He was grateful for that. Tears would be unseemly and would be a loss of honor for them both.

'Carlton . . .' She spoke softly so the slaves, although they tried, could not hear. She was facing him, her eyes hard.

'Yes.' His curt tone betrayed his tension.

She glanced down at the boy standing beside him. 'Take care of our son.'

Carlton stared at her without speaking.

'When you return, happens there be a brother for him. I does be pregnate for you.'

'We must go, sir!' Caspar's anxious cry shattered the sadness that was threatening to overwhelm them both. 'De vessel does be ready to leave, sah!' In his excitement, the boy lapsed into slave speech.

'Go inside, Ella.' Carlton stepped away from his housekeeper and mounted his horse. 'If you make another whelp like Caspar, then the old master be proud.' He looked up at his father standing on the balcony, waved to him for the last time, and dug his heels into the horse's flank.

He did not look around again as he galloped down the hill, between the avenues of the Roystonia palm trees he planted the day Caspar was born. His long golden hair fluttered in the breeze, his shirt was open and his eyes watered.

Behind him, Caspar hugged Ella hurriedly, ran to the wagon driven by Marmeduke and jumped on to the tailboard. He clung to the two wooden chests and the casks of Roxborough rum that was all they were taking with them to England.

Ella had herself rigid lest her apprehension be noticed by the slaves and regarded by them as proof of her vulnerability. Without blinking, she watched the progress of the wagon as it followed Carlton.

At the fork in the trail by the broad sweep of the Layou River, Carlton and the wagon turned west where Captain Loring's schooner was waiting. Ella swung around abruptly and looked up at old Massa Hayes. She waited for his command.

The man's frail hands gripped the balcony rail and his eyes stared over the top of the flamboyant trees, beyond the coconut palms and fields of sugar cane, to the hills lining the plantation boundary above the river.

For a brief moment, Ella felt sorry for the old man so desperately seeking comfort in the range of hills that marked the edge of the kingdom he had created. These hills that protected Roxborough from the outside world were closing in, imprisoning him on the plantation forever. He was the only white man left, a living ghost of the tyrant he used to be when he was the Bondmaster.

Ella waited. Hayes still stared. The slaves shuffled uneasily.

Pip, the houseboy, stood beside Hayes, a pewter tray with a tankard of sangaree balanced on the palm of his hand. He was saying Hayes's name. Hayes looked at him, saw the tankard and took it. He raised it in trembling hands to his lips and sipped.

Ella walked with deliberation across the courtyard to the grand flight of steps leading up to the balcony. Those steps were the pride of Roxborough Hall.

The slaves, even the house slaves, were forbidden to enter the house by them. The back stair was for slaves, the front one for their betters.

Ella knew that all the folk gathered around the courtyard were watching her. The drivers were there, with their whips held half-heartedly in their fingers, wondering what to do. The field hands began to murmur, shifting around like a herd of restless cattle. The lowing sound rose mockingly challenging Massa Hayes to stop them. Mas Carlton was their Bondmaster and he had gone.

Ella reached the flight of steps and paused. She was aware that Massa Hayes had seen her. She waited for his shout, the reprimand that would destroy her in the eyes of every slave on the plantation. She would have been surprised to hear it.

She raised her head and stared her defiance at the old man. He blinked, held the tankard to his lips and swallowed.

Ella lifted her skirts and climbed the grand steps slowly. When she was halfway up she turned, let her skirts fall, and clapped her hands.

'What yo' all does be watchin'?' she said in a voice heavy with sarcasm. 'Ain' dere work to do on dis plantation?' The drivers jerked to attention and the murmuring stopped.

'Yo' all get back to yuh tasks. Mas Carlton ain't here but Miss Ella is! Wid yuh ol' Massa Hayes. We go'n keep dis plantation de best in Dominique. When de Bon'massa does return, he go'n know who be unworthy.' She paused. 'He sure go'n lash any nigger dat don't work. Miss Ella de one go'n tell him who bad!'

She glared at the slaves and was delighted to see them cringe under her gaze. Satisfied that she had succeeded in intimidating them, she gestured at Hayes.

'Don't fret none dat yuh ol' Massa does be wasted wid age. He wise an' smart to de nigger ways. Ol' Massa Hayes does own yo' 'cause de Bon'massa done go. He go'n see yo' all does 'bey Miss Ella! Yo' hear?'

Ella's stare of contempt cowered even Dutchip, Congo Venus and Mally Ibo, the formidable trio of old biddies who tended the nig-gerlings in the nursery paddock. They saw Ella's assumption of authority was complete when she raised her skirts and completed her ascent up the grand steps.

She crossed the balcony to Massa Hayes's side and stood with him, dwarfing the old man's bent figure into insignificance. There was not a slave in the courtyard who didn't vow silently to beware of Ella.

It was not the power of their white master's tacit support for her that alarmed them. It was the reminder that Ella was the daughter of a Royal Batutsi princess and was gifted with that power over life and death against which there was no defiance: *obeah*.

Ella was satisfied when the slaves began to slink away from the courtyard. She waved Pip back to the drawing room to bring the pitcher of sangaree to refill Massa Hayes's tankard. She slipped her arm under the old man's elbow and gently led him to his chair.

She noticed the slight stiffening of his body when she touched him. It reassured her. Hayes Todd, in his better days, hated to be touched by a slave. It was demeaning to him, and unnatural. To him, negroes were animals to be beaten to his will. If Hayes still retained a vestige of his contempt, Ella knew he was still capable of anger. It was his anger she intended to mold and use to enable her to rule Roxborough until Carlton returned.

'What a heap of *bagasse*!'

The highpitched shriek of scornful laughter caught Ella unawares. She stepped away from Hayes as Pip filled the old man's cup, and turned to face the woman who had spoken. Tita was dressed in an opulent gown that had belonged to her dead mistress. The white powder on her face, mottled in patches by perspiration, made her look grotesque. Her eyes flashed insolently.

'What nonsense, Ella!' She spat out the words. 'Yo' ain' de mistress here whatever yo' tell dat nigger trash.'

'Indeed?' Ella pulled herself to her full height and placed her hand on the back of Hayes's chair. The old man, sunk in reverie and his sangaree-induced stupor, didn't seem to notice. 'If I'm not to look after Mas Carlton's interests, who will?'

'Oy, oy, oy!' Tita rolled her hips lewdly. 'Ain' yo' vex', *Miss* Ella! Mas Carlton put me in charge his children. Young Hayes an' Laura does be mine 'cause de mam does be dead. Yo' ain' got no one.' She cackled.

'He go'n sell yuh half-breed brat in England. Yo' ain' go'n see dat yeller tyke again, yo' black snake!'

'Hush yer noise!'

The two women turned in amazement. Hayes Todd pushed himself from his chair until he was standing upright. Pip caught his elbow to steady him, but he jerked his arm free.

'I say stop that caterwaulin'.' The old man's face was red and he spluttered angrily. 'My boy ain't gone five minutes and you two bitches start quarrelin'. I ain't havin' it. There's been too much raisin' up of niggers here and now you don't know yer place no more. Mas Carlton be gone, but I ain't.' He shook his fist.

'Now get off my balcony, both of you, before I yanks up them fancy frocks and beats yer ass 'til yer hollers!'

Ella signalled Pip to help Hayes back to his chair and then faced Tita. 'Yo' see,' she hissed, advancing on her and shooing her along with her hands. 'Yo' upset Massa Hayes.'

'Get out! Both of you.' The old man sighed. 'Leave me be . . .'

He turned sadly toward the west where a schooner was waiting in the river mouth poised to race past the sandbar with the tide.

Roxborough Hall, as Hayes Todd in moments of grandeur was wont to call his ramshackle home, was not one of the Caribbean's Great Houses. The legendary mansions of the wealthy English planters were to be found in Antigua or Barbados, not in a wild and neglected island like Dominica. Here there were few resident planters like Hayes and his son, Carlton.

Most sugar plantations were run by attorneys and overseers on behalf of owners absent in England. The attorneys resided in Roseau, the island's run-down capital, while the overseers housed in makeshift dwellings represented white authority on the plantations.

Hayes had constructed his house at Roxborough when he arrived in Dominica as a refugee from the American War of Independence over thirty years before. With a carpenter who had cost him a hundred pounds even in those days, he built the house with a solid lower storey of river stone and a single story of seasoned timber above.

He planned to extend the house as he grew prosperous but with the death of his French wife, Monique, three years after Carlton's birth, the intention was abandoned. The house, which the slaves called the *cou*, was big enough for himself and his only son.

The kitchen, pantry, store and quarters for the house slaves were in the lower part. The stone walls kept it cool, aided by the breeze which flowed through the kitchen when the wooden shutters on both sides of the house were open during the day. Upstairs, the carpenter had built a magnificent balcony that girded the house on all four sides, holding in its walls like a fat whore's corset.

The house crowned a small hill and from the balcony there were views over the whole plantation. The slaves, whenever they paused in the cane fields and raised their eyes to the house, were constantly aware that they could be seen by their Bondmaster.

At the rear of the house, leading off the balcony, was a flight of wooden steps for the house slaves to use. The dining room was at the back, adjoining the drawing room, and had its own entrance to the back balcony to facilitate the serving of the whites when they dined. There was a bed chamber on either side of the dining room, one used by guests and the other occupied by Carlton's two children, Laura and Hayes.

The unusual layout of the house was deliberate. Access to the guest rooms was possible only from the back balcony. This was to enable visitors to have slave wenches in their chambers at night without disturbing the rest of the household. Now there were children in the house, old Hayes was grateful for those rooms to keep them out of his way. His own chamber, like Carlton's, was at the front of the house, with a dressing room and a separate slave entrance from the balcony.

Hayes relaxed as he heard a door slam and knew that Tita had retreated to the children's room to check on her charges. Ella, downstairs in the kitchen, would be venting her displeasure at the clash with Tita on the house slaves. Hayes snorted. He liked the two females; he had a grudging respect for Ella's ability and for Tita's care of Carlton's spoilt children. But he did not see the sense in Carlton's reliance on them. They were both negro animals, not to be trusted. And not to be treated as human beings.

Hayes had made Carlton the Bondmaster, with complete responsibility for the running of Roxborough and control of the slaves, shortly after his stroke ten years before. Carlton did well, cutting back on sugar and rum production and concentrating on slave breeding. The paddock was packed with a hundred healthy young negroes being reared for sale. In five or six years, they would be ready for the market.

Hayes cast his glance over the coast far below, beyond the fields of cane and the forest of trees that surrounded the riverine village of Layou. There was a wide sandbar stretching across the mouth of the Layou River, creating a natural anchorage much favored by droghers and schooners with cargoes to be unloaded out of sight of the revenue officers in Roseau. It was on one of those vessels, now tacking its way out to sea, that Carlton was quitting Dominica.

'I'm going away, da',' he had announced coolly on the evening after his wife had died.

Hayes had reached for the rum decanter and poured himself a large measure in the silence. It was dark, the lamps had not been lit, and fireflies flitted with their bright glow of emerald green in the branches of the flamboyant trees. He drank deeply and let the rum, his own brew seasoned with peppers to give it an extra kick, rouse his brain. His heart was filled with sorrow for his son but it would be pointless to try to change the boy's mind.

'Perhaps it's best,' he said at length. 'For a few weeks . . .'

'I want to go to England, da'. I want to learn.'

'Learn, boy! What can they teach you in England about running a plantation?' Hayes was offended. If Carlton had listened to him and treated the slaves properly instead of favoring them so much, his wife would still be alive.*

'I doubt I'll learn anything you ain't told me already, da'.' Carlton grinned ruefully.

'It's not that alone. It's quiet here now. We don't have trouble with the slaves, and the sugar crop is no longer important to us. The whelps in the pen aren't ready for market yet. This is a good time for me to go.'

Hayes eyed the boy suspiciously. He was a strong lad, lean and muscular, with a jaw set firm and eyes, the beguiling yellow eyes of the Todds, that were bright and determined. The horror of the last few days hadn't shown itself in his face, and his shock of sun-bleached hair made him seem younger than his twenty-seven years.

He scowled, aware that whatever he said would have no effect on Carlton's decision. The boy's mind was already made up.

'You could run Roxborough again, father, couldn't you?' His eyes pleaded. 'Ella knows everything I'm trying to do. She knows every slave on the plantation and they all respect her. They think she's an *obeah* woman.' He stood up, his drink forgotten, and paced the balcony.

'We can send to Roseau for a white overseer. You can have him to supervise the field work so you won't have to ride and tire yourself.'

Hayes had let Carlton prattle on. He knew the boy was talking himself into exile, trying to justify leaving the plantation in the care of an old man who had relinquished control ten years before. He wasn't angry, not with Carlton. Perhaps the boy did need more experience. He was born in the island and had never left it.

Hayes was English born, apprenticed in Georgia and married in

* See *The Bondmaster*

New Orleans. He had no desire to leave Roxborough.

'Carlton can say what he likes,' he muttered to himself, staring at the sails of the schooner as it scudded across the waves to the north. 'I ain't havin' no white overseer here!' He gripped the arms of his chair so tightly that the blue veins of his fists seemed ready to burst through the skin.

Pip was beside him immediately. He proffered another cup of sangaree. Hayes shook his head and waved him away.

'No!' he cried, and snapped his jaws shut. A sudden fury entered his eyes. 'By the devil!' he said, pushing himself up and glaring around the empty balcony. The sharp scrape of the chair on the wooden floor startled a slave sauntering across the courtyard. Hayes saw him and shook his fist.

'Get to work, you lazy cur!' he cried, his rasping voice strengthening to a shout of anger.

The slave took to his heels and dived down the path to the quarters, terrified by the sight of the old man who dozed on the balcony unexpectedly coming to life.

'By the devil!' Hayes said again, stepping up to the balcony railing. 'I can do it! I'll keep Roxborough safe for Carlton!' He paused and glared at the canefields.

'There ain't no one, white or black, going to do it for me. I'm the Bondmaster now. I don't need no help from any lily-livered white wastrel nor blood-sucking black bitch!'

Ella, standing silently by the open window under the balcony, heard his cursing and smiled happily to herself.

CHAPTER TWO

He lay on his left side. His ankle was shackled by a chain that ran along the ledge on which he and the other captives were confined. He couldn't sleep. The man who lay in front of him, and the one who pressed against him from behind, were both asleep. He was wedged so tightly between them that every movement of their bodies was like a shudder in his own. He envied them the regular rise and fall of their breasts that indicated the solace of dreams was theirs. He willed himself not to move and wake them.

He could not remember when last he slept. Now even that comfort was denied him.

The motion of the ship was no longer frightening. At night, fettered on the boards jutting out from the side of the ship like a shelf, he imagined the pitching of the waves was the motion of a cloud buffeted by the wind as it bore him through the sky to join his ancestors.

The discomfort of being closely stacked with these strangers, like arrows in a fallen quiver, had ceased to worry him. The shelf above his head was so low, he could sit up only with his shoulders hunched. When the man above puked, opened his bowels or discarded his waste water, it seeped through and dripped on him. When he and his fellows did the same, the men on the shelf below were befouled.

The stench in the ship's hold, the stifling heat, the stickiness and the pus-filled sores of his wasted body were no more than he deserved.

His eyes, open in the dark, could not see the lice-encrusted head of the man that lay in front of him. But he could see, in his mind, the shocked face of his father. His beard was gray, looking white and venerable against the shining blackness of his skin in the bright sunlight of the afternoon. It was the time when the tribe's women were preparing their meal and the men were alone.

His father's eyes were wide with astonishment and his mouth

hung loose showing his yellowing teeth. He was squatting in the dusty mud, his sinewy legs supporting his proud old warrior's body without a tremble. The only sign of his displeasure was in his eyes as surprise left them and was replaced by anger.

'No, father,' Ndja repeated in the long silence. 'I will not do this.'

He had been dreading that day for many moons, ever since he completed his manhood training and had been accepted by his father as an equal in his home and his tribe. His father was a leader, not only of the village where he lived but of countless villages spread throughout the great plain and in the hinterland of the jungle, mountains and rivers that constituted the kingdom.

The honor to Ndja, the first son of his father's seventh wife, was immense.

'No,' Ndja said again, his voice less confident. Three times he had refused his father's command. He knew the cost.

The old man's brow furrowed as he sought wisdom. He stroked his beard and Ndja heard him sigh. The breeze rustling the leaves of the bushes surrounding the hut seemed to echo his father's sorrow.

'Son,' his father said, shaking his head again. 'I have not heard.'

'You have, father.' Ndja stood up, compounding the insult to his parent by standing in his presence without permission. He towered over the old man and realized instantly that the gesture made his decision irrevocable in the elder's eyes.

'I will not marry my sister,' he said, no longer scared that he would weaken to please his father because he was heir to the old man's kingdom.

'You are no longer my son,' the old man pronounced, turning his head. 'Do not let your shadow fall on my kingdom again.'

'I am young,' Ndja had said, anxious to avoid the curse his father was composing in his mind. 'Do you not want to know why I have chosen to disobey you?'

His father was silent, his face set in a stare at the savanna where his cattle grazed. He had been his favorite son. He'll get over it, Ndja thought. The old man had many children.

'Sister is my mother's daughter as well as yours. I have known her since I was born. I cannot marry her and know no other. I am young blood and must breed with new blood.'

Ndja knew he should say no more but his tongue ran away with him. 'There must be other women who would be worthy of me . . .'

The old man seized his spear from the ground and hurled it away from him with such force it pitched into a *balata* tree and stuck there, its tail quivering as a symbol of his fury.

'You no longer have worth. You are not even the value of a dung-ant, a boy without grain, a . . .' The old man's love for his son overcame his anger and stilled the curse.

Ndja was grateful for it. He strode away from the hut, his tall frame unbowed by what he was doing. He reached the tree and pulled his father's spear from it. He turned and saluted his father, raising the shaft to his brow as warriors did when they left for battle with the warring tribe across the river.

His father stared back at him and Ndja could feel the power of his gaze following him as he broke into a trot and ran down the path that led through the tall grass away from the village.

From that day, two full seasons before, Ndja had been driven by a questing spirit that never left him until now. Here, in the hold of this ship crammed with sons and daughters of the jungles, mountains and savannas, the spirit abandoned him. For what he had done to his father, he was receiving his retribution.

He had been so proud when he left the village. He needed that pride to smother the shame of what he was doing. Fortunately, his manhood training had successfully instilled in him the ability to survive in the wilderness even if he had not been able to learn unquestioning obedience to his father's commands.

Urged on by his spirit, Ndja traveled throughout the lowlands. He avoided people, skirted around villages, and slept alone under the stars, dreaming of the day when he would take his first woman. She would become his wife and would purge the memory of his sister and his father's impossible command.

Some days, he traveled great distances; others he spent in hunting and resting to recuperate his strength. His father's spear was blessed, and he fared well.

He headed in the direction of the setting sun because that seemed the right thing to do. A range of mountains that day by day loomed closer became the barrier between himself and the unknown. His spirit drove him on to climb one of the mountains and he approached the summit cautiously, fearful of what lay beyond.

It was more wonderful than he dreamed: a shimmering void of deep blue where the sky joined the earth, many days walk away.

Jungle stretched below him right up to that void which, as he got closer to it during his long walk, became not sky but water with white foam dancing on it. That first glimpse of the sea was awe-inspiring. But the next marvel that he saw made him realize that his father did indeed curse him. He saw Death.

He was aware of the caravan before he came close to it. For days, dust hung over the horizon marking the tortuous progress of a long line of people through the dry bushland. At first, he assumed they were nomads moving from one grazing ground to another but as he drew close enough to study their tracks, he was puzzled. They had no cattle with them. Who then was this tribe? Where were they going? Why?

For many sunrises, he followed them, keeping his distance, ever aware that they were leading him close to that great void he glimpsed from the hill tops. He was cautious not to approach the caravan because the signs told him the people were a savage and uncultured tribe. They did not respect their dead, of which there were many, but left them beside the trail for the hyenas.

One of the corpses, that of a woman, bloated and ugly, opened its eyes while he stood regarding it with pity. He stepped back in surprise as the body – surely no longer a living being – moaned.

He rushed through the bush to a stream, gathered water in a gourd and brought it for the dead one. He held it to her lips and she sipped. There was a gash in her side from a spear; flies fed on the blood oozing from it and the smell of decay caused him to retch.

The dead one spoke with words similar to his own tribe's tongue. He listened while she told him of the caravan of captives, a coffle, being marched in chains and led by a White Man.

'A man who is white?' He pulled back from the living corpse in horror. 'How can that be?'

'He is.' The dead one uttered a last croak and fell back to resume her fate.

Ndja was intrigued. He had never heard of a man who was white. For him, white was the color of death. The witch doctor donned white ostrich feathers when the dead of his tribe were sent to join their ancestors. White flowers were entwined in their hair and gray river mud was used to cake their faces with white masks.

Could there be a man who had a skin that was white? If such a man exists, he must be Death himself.

Ndja saw the man after three more sunrises. The nagging of his spirit forced him to draw close to the caravan. He overtook it by wending his way through the trees, always downwind the way he would hunt antelope. Stealthily, he approached the coffle of captives, men and women and children linked with chains and yokes. Then, as he crouched behind a thick bush and parted its branches to peer through, he saw.

The man was surely Death. His skin was the color of the witch doctor's daubs. It was gray, it was pink, it was red and peeling. The man's hair hung in sweaty strands down his neck, under a broad-brimmed hat. Only his face and hands were visible, with his body swathed in cloth. His nose was bright red where the sun had burned it, and his jowls were gray. The rest of his face was pink and his hands were like a monkey's that had been skinned.

'Gotcha!'

The shout of a strange animal warned him too late. A noose was slipped over his head and pulled tight, binding his arms to his chest. He struggled and struck out with his feet and charged with his head, but there were three of these white creatures and they overpowered him.

He was pushed to the ground, an iron ring was clamped on his ankle and he was dragged feet first through the undergrowth to the trail. The men who were white were snorting with a noise similar to that uttered by his father when a young virgin was offered to him as appeasement.

Ndja could not understand the ugly sounds grunted by his captors when they took him to the white man in the hat. The man bared his teeth and tried to touch him but Ndja reared away. His spirit wilted. Because of his curiosity and his father's curse, he had been captured. He must conserve his strength until the opportunity came to escape. He allowed himself to be chained to the other men in the coffle.

They were a listless pack. If they talked, the guards clubbed them. They were forced to march at a steady pace along the trail. Those who became too weak to walk were thrust through with swords and left for the hyenas. The iron ring around his ankle chaffed his skin until it bled, but he bore the pain without complaint.

They marched each day until long after sunset. Then they were fed and watered and allowed to sleep, chained to each other on the ground where they fell. Gradually, Ndja learned from his fellows who spoke a tongue similar to his, that the coffle was bound for the coast. The white men were not Death's messengers but from an ill-bred race that lived over the water.

It was Ndja's nature to consider everything very carefully. He had arrived at his determination to defy his father after several moons of sleepless nights agonizing with his spirit. He never made spontaneous decisions. So he bided his time in the coffle.

He was fit, not like the other captives who had walked a great distance in heavy chains, and he loped along observing and thinking. He was curious about this race of white demons who desired people so highly they stole them from their tribal lands.

They reached their destination, a stockade beside a river mouth within sight of the vast blue water he had glimpsed from the mountain top. Ndja was confined there in a cage with the others. There were more of the vile-smelling white men in the stockade.

The leader was a man whose face was pitted with pockmarks and who wore a coat of bright blue, with white pantaloons and his feet encased in black leather he called boots. He was an extraordinary sight, with a high pitched voice and a habit of scratching his crotch as though infested with lice. He carried a stick with leather thongs dangling from it which he used to smite people when they did not do what he wanted.

This man, whom the whites called Keptin, seemed pleased when he saw Ndja. He was unshackled and brought out into the sunlight in the center of the stockade. For the first time since his capture, he was free of the fetter but the menace of the white men surrounding him detered his desire to escape.

Water from a wooden pail was tipped over him and he stood dripping in front of Keptin while the man showed his teeth and spoke excitedly to his companions. Whatever was said seemed to be favorable. Ndja was taken out of the sun's glare and made to sit in the shade of a long platform in front of a hut. He was chained to a post and left.

Keptin spent the day inspecting the captives and ordering them to be chained in different cages. They were brought feed and water, with a special gourd for Ndja. He ate carefully and considered his position. He thought that, if he were to be fed and treated tolerably, he would remain to see what he could learn from this strange race of white people.

It was Ndja's docility that saved him. He did not discover, until later, that Keptin recognized his distinctive bloodlines and resolved to keep him for himself.

Keptin, during the moons Ndja stayed with him in the stockade, trained him in the ways of white people. Ndja learned to interpret some of the barks and grunts made to each other like jackals, as the white men's language. He began to understand Keptin's commands and did the things demanded of him.

After two moons, he was released from his chain during the day although at night he was always secured to a post and obliged to sleep on the floor in front of Keptin's door, like a dog.

Keptin admired his body and used to stroke him with his hands, his fingers white like corpse-worms against the rich black bloom of his skin. Keptin's hands had a magic in them and he would grasp him until he was stiffer than a hunter's spear. The feeling made Ndja weak behind his knees and caused him to cry out but Keptin wouldn't stop until he swelled and burst forth like a river in flood, spilling himself on the ground in the darkness of the night.

The captives he had traveled with were taken away over the water in a huge pirogue with wings. There were many such vessels, as Keptin called them. Countless captives over the moons were loaded into them bound for a destination Ndja heard called the Karibees.

Ndja was often inspected by white men who came on those vessels but always Keptin refused their offers for him. Ndja was proud that Keptin valued him so highly. His father had been wrong; he did have value.

'Holy Mother of Mary, Olaf!'

The oath was uttered by a white man striding across the center of the stockade. He had arrived that morning to pick out captives from Keptin's supply. Ndja had been waiting for him to come to Keptin's hut for the strong brown water the visitors liked to drink. It was Ndja's task to stand by Keptin with a jar of this liquid and pour it into metal cups for the visitors.

'Olaf!' The white man who had a thicket of red hair bristling around his mouth and on his chin, addressed the big man accompanying him. 'Have you ever seen a brute like that?'

The big man shook his head, his tiny eyes narrowing to a squint that warned Ndja not to trust him.

'Keptin,' said the red haired one. 'I'll not tarry. The buck, how much?'

'He's special,' said Keptin.

'I see that. Name your price.'

Keptin said something, Red Hair spluttered, Olaf scowled. Ndja proffered the jar and the three men sipped its contents thirstily. Red Hair barked again and Keptin's eyes lingered sadly on Ndja. He patted his backside, nodded then scratched his own crotch.

Thus Ndja passed from one white man to another. After the moons of comparative tranquillity, everything happened hastily. Ndja was again chained to scrawny fellows not long arrived from the long walk through the jungle. He was shipped on board a vessel commanded by Red Hair who was called Keptin Delawnee. He was driven by men with whips and swords into the deep interior of this Keptin's ship, and made to lie on a hard shelf.

At first, Ndja's spirit consoled him, telling him that soon the dreadful rise and fall of the wooden vessel would cease and he would be released once again into the sunlight and steadiness of land. Instead, with each sunrise, he and the men chained with him were forced to climb up to the ship's deck. There, laughing white men with whips and cutlasses surrounded them while they were hosed with water and made to dance. After this exercise, they were fed slops from a wooden trough and confined again to the bowels of the ship.

After many sunrises, there were men who did not stir when the sailors tried to rouse them from the shelf. These men were dragged away and thrown over the side of the ship into the sea. Strange creatures with black fins, like horns sticking out of their backs, devoured the men, making the sea crimson with their blood. Ndja heard Keptin Delawnee complain about the Black Vomit that scourged his niggers. These strange words added to his confusion.

He did not know how many moons he had been on his shelf, being prodded up on deck to wash, dance and eat, then whipped down again. There were more empty spaces as the dead men were thrown overboard. Soon, Ndja knew, it would be his turn to join his ancestors. The white men were indeed Death.

He touched his chest, no longer hard with muscle but skeletal with wasted flesh. His thighs were like twigs, his arms that once threw a spear further than any youth in his village, were withered and useless. He was dead.

He lay unmoving when the sailors came to take him up on deck.

They prodded him twice, whacking a sword across his buttocks, but he was incapable of feeling. They left him and drove out the other men. Later, two seamen whose anger at their duties made them careless, came for him.

'Blimey,' said one. 'The big'uns croaked it too.'

'Come on!' His companion was choking with the stink of the hold. 'Let's get out of 'ere.'

They pulled Ndja by his ankles up the ladder to the deck. His head banged against each rung but he didn't feel the pain.

'Moof fast there!' Olaf, the mate, shouted.

Ndja was dragged to the side of the ship and bundled over the rail. He was gone before the voice of Keptin Delawnee shouted at the sailors to stop. He fell with a splash into the water and sank deeply, welcoming the embrace of his ancestors.

Something slid after him, a dark shape, lean and hard, cutting through the water and shadowing him as the ship sailed on.

CHAPTER THREE

'Prince . . . Prince . . . Prince!' she sighed, her voice rising when he thrust deeper. 'Oh, oh, oh!'

Her final shrill cry as she reached her climax was what he had been waiting for. He tensed, summoning his ardor, then thundered into her with a great show of passion. He relished his success, delighting in the feel of her nails clawing his shoulders and her tiny gasps of ecstacy.

He caressed her cheek with his long, sensuous fingers, to calm her down and make her feel loved. She clung to him hungrily. He was alert for a sign that she was finished so he could withdraw without disappointing her. He had learned that sometimes such women could be spiteful.

'How I shall miss you!' she said, stroking the tight curls of his hair. 'Aie!' She gasped. 'Don't leave me!'

'It is you who are leaving me, Helen.'

'My husband . . .'

'I know,' he said, silencing her with his lips pressed firmly on hers. He eased himself beside her and slipped his arm under her shoulder so he could hold her. It was important not to let her feel regret; guilt at their parting would be more profitable to him.

'What about me, Helen? What will I do?'

'You'll find another woman, silly.' She tweaked the lobe of his ear. 'That's funny. I never noticed how small your ears are.'

'Don't joke, Helen. I shall miss you too.'

She sighed again. 'In more ways than one, I'm sure.'

Prince was wounded by her tone. If she was so flippant, she might leave without suitable recompense. He touched her cheek again and was relieved to feel dampness under her eyes. He kissed the tears away while she squirmed.

'You're not making it easy,' she said. He knew he would be all right.

'When do you sail?' He kept his voice low to prove his unhappiness.

'In two hours.'

'Then this is the last time?'

'You know it is.'

'Will you think of me in England?'

'How can I forget you? Whenever I hear the West Indies mentioned at court, I shall have a vison of you. Oh dear,' she sighed. 'To think I will never see that darling little nose again.'

'Is my nose the only thing you'll miss?'

She pouted. 'This won't do. Cuthbert thinks I am calling on my dressmaker to bid her *adieu*. I am to meet him on board.'

'I'll escort you to the wharf.'

'Fie! Do you want every soldier in the island to see us together? What a farewell present for my husband!'

Prince released her and lay back, his head sinking into the pillow of down. He wondered what Helen would say if she knew that among the free blacks in Antigua, his affairs with white ladies were notorious. However discreet one tried to be it was impossible to have secrets in the island.

St John's was a small capital and gossip was the currency of the free blacks and mulattoes who were the town's shop keepers, tavern owners and clerks. It was his liaisons with women such as Helen, Marchioness of Witham, that made Prince a legend in Antigua.

He supposed she knew his reputation. Why else was she afraid to be seen with him? She claimed never to have known a man other than her husband, something he doubted very much from her experienced ways in bed. It would have been unlikely for her to have learned such things from the man she was married to.

The Marquis was a pompous, gout-ridden old man almost twice her age, attached to the army on some diplomatic mission in connection with the war with France. For six months, she had been living in Antigua while her husband conducted his duties. Prince had known her for four, entertaining her twice a week in the chamber he kept especially for such encounters.

She slid out of bed and darted behind the screen to dress. He frowned.

'Must you go?' He asked now he was certain she would not return to the bed and ask for more. He was still concerned lest she really had overlooked his farewell reward.

He got out of bed and padded across the floor. He was naked. A candle burned on the table by the closed shutters of the window and its glow lit up his athletic frame. He knew his physique was superb. He was slender with strong limbs and a face that was handsome, even to whites. His complexion was the color of burnished gold, his eyes a deep, sultry brown, and his teeth a gleaming white.

'My god!' exclaimed Helen when she stepped around the screen and saw him.

He grinned mischievously.

'For heaven's sake, dear, put some clothes on. It's bad enough that I'm never going to see you again without you showing me what I'll be missing.'

'Helen,' he said, walking toward her and holding out his arms. 'I will always remember you.'

She faltered in her determination not to cry, as he knew she would. He embraced her, letting her cheek rest on his chest as he patted her back. He waited for her tears and smiled to himself when her shoulders shook with her sobbing. He took a deep breath, his chest heaving to indicate the extent of his own sadness.

'A farewell is so cruel . . .' he began.

She did not want to hear his speech and pulled away abruptly.

He held on to her hand, puzzled that she had not mentioned a gift for him. Was she going to leave without giving him a memento? True, in four months she had given him sufficient for his living expenses, but nothing substantial.

He tried again. 'Do you have to go? Stay here, with me.'

'Fie!' She laughed and picked up her reticule. 'Alas, Prince, although I adore you, there is another Prince I must serve first. The Prince of Wales would not approve if I embarrassed him and left my husband to remain here with you. What a scandal that would be!' She sucked in her breath at the thought.

'Is that Prince more important to you than your husband?'

'Of course, my black Adonis. It was he who arranged for me to marry my Marquis.'

'I don't understand.'

'Perhaps it's better that you don't. It's of no importance.' She stood on tiptoe and kissed him rapidly on his cheek. He reached for her but she slipped away and walked to the door. 'I shall let myself out.'

'But . . .'

'Don't speak, you might spoil it. I shall always have in my mind a picture of you standing there like some dusky Greek god come to life. If only you could come to England . . . No, it's not possible. I must go.'

She opened the door and was gone before Prince could stop her.

'Damn,' he muttered under his breath as he reached for his clothes. 'She's fooled me.' He struggled to pull on his silk breeches, looking around for his coat.

Had he wasted four months on a woman who paid only in kisses? He loved women, enjoyed their embraces, but nevertheless this one was no longer a beauty. He was surely entitled to a reward for his services. It was expected . . .

His breeches tied, and his shirt tucked in, he reached under the bed for his boots. He was taking too long to get dressed. She would have time to walk to the harbor before he could catch up with her. He could not chase her without boots. He had his reputation to keep, even though he wished hers to hell for deceiving him.

His toe jammed against something solid in his boot. He cursed and turned the boot upside down, shaking it. An object fell with a thud to the floor. He peered at it distractedly while he struggled to get his foot back into the boot.

How could the hussy treat him this way? He would write to the Prince of Wales himself and let him know what his mistress did in Antigua.

The object on the floor at his foot did not look familiar. He paused in his rush to complete his dressing and stared at it. He reached behind him and unfastened the shutter, throwing it open to let in the light.

The chamber was above a dressmaker's shop, providing an excuse for ladies to visit him without arousing the suspicion of their husbands. It was not yet sunset and light flooded into the chamber revealing the chaos of the bed. He stooped to pick up the thing by his foot.

It was a leather pouch, heavy with promise. He held his breath as he hastened to untie it, not believing what he hoped was true. Yes! He shook the contents into his palm and jiggled the gold coins in his fingers.

'Helen!' he shouted, laughing with relief. 'I love you. I really do!'

In law, Prince – or Prince d'Anjou as he had been known to call himself when escorting impressionable English ladies – was a slave. His owner was the dressmaker over whose shop he entertained those white ladies of shaky virtue who, bedazzled by his looks and body and emboldened by their loneliness, were pleased to reward him for his favors.

Clothilda Harkness was the dressmaker and she was sewing in her usual place before the open window when he descended the stairs. The house adjoined the street and friends and customers would pop in their heads at the window for a greeting and a chat.

Clothilda had lived there for twenty years, since she was freed and set up in business by her father, an English planter. She was the result of a union between Master Harkness and his favorite slave. Her skill as a seamstress had won her fame and respect as a dressmaker to the island's society.

'Clo'?'

Clothilda raised her eyes from her sewing as Prince walked over and laid his hand gently on her shoulder.

'She's gone,' he said, keeping the sadness out of his voice.

'They al'as do.' Clothilda's mouth twitched but she did not give voice to the many thoughts racing through her mind.

'Here,' he said, dropping the purse into her lap.

She covered it swiftly with the petticoat she was stitching and glanced out of the open window in case someone had seen. 'You're a good boy, Prince,' she said, blinking.

'I know.' He grinned at his arrogance but Clothilda didn't look pleased. 'I'm going out.'

He felt her watching him as he walked to the street door. He shrugged his shoulders.

'Don't worry, Clo'. I'm not going to Lindsey's Rooms.' That was the gambling house where gentlemen and free mulattoes of quality played Hazzard. 'You have all my money. I think I'll take a stroll to the harbor.'

'She was a real lady, Prince.'

'Yes.'

'I hope you treated her right.'

'Don't I always?'

Clothilda pushed a stray strand of hair under her cloth bonnet. 'Prince, it's not necessary, you know. I have a good business here. The ladies want fine clothes and they pay me well.'

He strode back across the floor and bent down, kissing her cheek. 'Clo', don't worry. Can I help it if your customers like me? I like them. The purse, well . . .' He spread his hands in a gesture of mock helplessness.

'Why don't you settle down now she's gone? Let me find you a position in one of the English merchant houses.'

He shook his head. 'That would bore me.'

'You promised after the last one, she that called herself Belle Lugay, that you'd settle down. You ain't getting younger, Prince.'

He squeezed her chin in his fingers and smiled wryly. 'I'll think about it . . .' He opened the door and stepped out before she could say anything else.

St John's was an orderly, well laid out town with wide streets set at right angles to each other. The streets were paved with stones that stuck out at angles and caused agony to anyone riding over them in a John Bott, the one-horse vehicle that was the favorite mode of conveyance of Antiguans. The little town was neat and pretty, built on a hill that sloped up gradually from the harbor.

Prince sauntered down the street, waving to his acquaintances as the day's commerce came to an end. Most of those he hailed were mulattoes. Antigua had become renowned over the years for the laxity of morals of its white planters. The large half-breed population of the town was the outcome. The negroes, too, were more advanced than those of neighboring islands due to the dedicated efforts of the missionaries to educate them.

Prince himself had benefited from a missionary's patience during his early years in Antigua. Under the earnest man's guidance, he completed an education begun when he was the playboy to a white child before he arrived in the island. He had been deeded to Clothilda fourteen years before by one Captain Loring when that rambunctious seafarer had tired of him. Loring was reputed to have a wench in every port throughout the Caribees, but his special favorite was Clothilda.

Loring had told Prince that he was being deeded to Clothilda for one purpose: to look after her in case anything should happen to him. Loring was still alive and visited Clothilda whenever his inter-island schooner was in port. Then Prince had to vacate the chamber and sleep alone with the dresses and bolts of material downstairs in the shop. He feared Loring and loved Clothilda; they were the only restraints he recognized on his carefree nature.

It was Clothilda who had insisted on Prince getting an education from the missionary. His previous existence as a young master's playboy had smoothed away the rough edges of slavery. From Loring he learned guile and from the missionary came knowledge. Clothilda helped him develop an appreciation of ladies, and a love of style and elegance. She encouraged him so much to be independent that both of them had forgotten he was still a slave and not free. It was Prince's secret.

He bowed slightly as a carriage clattered past him on its way to the harbor. The sailing of a vessel for England always attracted attention and the departure of the Marquis of Witham and his wife was not an event to be missed. Prince chuckled to himself about the number of new dresses Helen was taking back to England. She made so many visits to her dressmaker, her husband must have thought she was buying for a whole season of balls, not for the sailing across the Atlantic.

'Good riddance to her, I say.'

Prince felt the hand slip under his arm and he beamed down at the girl who had sidled up to him and walked at his side. Gwen was a mulatto with dark hair that fell in long tresses over bare shoulders. Her breasts bulged atop her bodice and she wore a full skirt that covered her ankles and emphasized the trimness of her waist. She pouted.

'Now, Gwen – '

'Don't say anything, Prince. I'm glad she's gone! Maybe I'll see more of you now.'

'If you have the time . . .'

Gwen raised her skirt and kicked Prince sharply on his shin.

They had reached the harbor and stood at the back of the crowd clamoring to bid the vessel farewell. Most of the seamen had women in Antigua and the shouts of the females, some sad, some angry, drowned out the noise of the ship as it prepared to sail. Prince scanned the deck.

'She's gone below,' said Gwen. 'She won't want to see you.'

'Of course she will.' He put his hand around Gwen's waist and squeezed. 'It's her last chance.'

Gwen stared at him. 'Do you wish you were leaving too?'

'Why should I? This is my home. I've got Clothilda and I've got you.'

'Hah, that's what you think! Prince, I'm warning you now. If you get involved with another white woman, I'm going to . . .

'Gwen, don't get vexed. You know how I am. I can't help it. White ladies like me. I can't be rude and disappoint them. It's you that I love, though.'

'So you say.'

'Come here.' Prince had learned that action was the best way out of an awkward situation where a woman was concerned. He pulled Gwen to him and kissed her on her mouth. She parted her lips and returned his embrace, wrapping her hands around his body and clinging to him.

The crowd of people at the harbor edge took no notice – what more natural place for a fond farewell? – but on the vessel bobbing at its mooring, a lonely figure stood staring into the gathering dusk.

Helen did not expect to see Prince in the midst of the crowd, but on some vantage point where he could be seen. Her gaze wandered along the mound at the back of the quay, passing over the couple engaged in a passionate embrace.

She caught her breath. The color of the man's coat, a glimmering kingfisher blue, was familiar. She looked again as Prince held the girl in his arms. Helen bit her lip and cursed him from the bottom of her heart.

Prince waved as the ship hoisted its anchor and began to tack out of the harbor. Gwen left him to return home where he promised to visit her that night. He stared after the ship feeling a little piece of his happiness sailing away with Helen.

'Dam'me,' he said aloud. 'I love that woman.'

He turned and, as he did so, the sails of a ship limping in out of the sunset caught his eye. He studied the vessel carefully. It was an ugly craft, with tattered sails and an air of disaster about it. He sniffed. The breeze was light but he smelled the stench of a slaver. He shuddered.

The slave factors' compounds would be full tomorrow with near-corpses. The sight of emaciated creatures who were once men and women, resembling skeletons with raw black skin stretched over them was appalling. Their cries of despair, and the awful smell of excreta and decaying flesh, would pervade the capital for days. It would take time for the factors to fatten up the human cargo and get the wretches on their feet so they could sell them at auction to the highest bidder.

It occurred to Prince that his own ancestors must have come to the West Indies in the same manner. He knew nothing of his parents. He was bright-skinned enough to be a mulatto but his size and features marked him as a pure negro. Sometimes he wondered if he was a Fulani because they were a race renowned for their beauty and Mediterranean complexion. He shuddered again; at least he was free in fact, if not in law.

Prince watched the slave ship inch to an anchorage far out in the harbor. The darkness was almost complete. Skiffs were setting out from the quay to welcome the slaver and to make arrangements to transfer its cargo to the factors' pens. Already the low moan of helplessness associated with these vessels was to be heard across the water. He turned away, sickened, and in doing so missed seeing the lanterns on the vessel that followed the slaver into the harbor from the south.

It was not until later that evening when he returned to Clothilda's house to prepare for his visit to Gwen, that he discovered it was Captain Loring's ship that had dropped anchor close to the quay, far upwind from the slaver.

Captain Loring, Clothilda informed Prince, wanted to see him on board immediately.

'Oh no!' Prince sat down and ran his fingers through the tight curls of his hair. 'I'm tired.'

'If you weren't tom-catting at all hours and did an honest day's work instead, you wouldn't be tired. Go to him now.'

He grinned sheepishly at Clothilda. 'He's probably got some old English matron he wants to foist on me. I've promised Gwen . . . I don't want to go.'

'He said your freedom depends on it.'

The tiredness left Prince and the blood drained from his cheeks. There was a chill in his heart.

'My freedom . . .?' He stared at Clothilda and they were both aware of the threat contained in Captain Loring's message.

Clothilda began to weep.

CHAPTER FOUR

Carlton Todd loathed Captain Loring. For the duration of the four day voyage from Dominica to Antigua, he managed to conceal his dislike. The animosity was rooted in the Captain's first words to Carlton when his skiff came alongside while the schooner was at its mooring in the mouth of the Layou River.

'Another minute,' said Loring, 'and yer'd be swimmin' ter Antigua, young Todd.'

Carlton grimaced, biting back his retort. He hauled himself up the side and clambered unaided over the railing on to the deck.

'We leave immediately,' snapped the Captain, ignoring Carlton's outstretched hand. He strode the length of the deck shouting orders and curses at his crew. Slowly the ship's sails unfurled and the schooner moved out of the river into the sea.

Carlton cooled his temper by gripping the rail and keeping his eyes on the coast. Roxborough Hall stood out among the cane and coconuts like a beacon marking the river entrance. As usual, clouds capped the ridge of hills bordering the valley through which the river flowed. The sun slanted over the sea, highlighting the house he was leaving for the first time in his life.

Although he did not know when he would return, Carlton was confident that he would be back some day. His destiny was linked with that fertile plantation by the Layou River. He sensed that wherever he roamed, he would die at Roxborough and his progeny would make the Roxborough breed renowned throughout the islands.

Caspar was standing beside him and he rested his hand affectionately on the boy's shoulder. 'See your mam? There! Standing on the balcony waving.'

Caspar looked up at Carlton and grinned. 'She too far now, sir,' he said in disbelief. But he still watched the island receding into the distance as the schooner scudded through the waves.

'That's a fine mulatto slave yer've got yerself young Todd.' Loring stood behind them, leering down at Caspar.

Carlton stared at the Captain in disgust. Loring's face was weather-beaten and pitted with scars. His black beard was flecked with sticky gobs of saliva and sea spray. His eyes were blood shot and hard. He returned Carlton's scowl of disapproval without blinking.

'Slave, Captain Loring?' Carlton made a conscious effort to keep his anger in check. 'This lad is my son!'

'Heh, heh!' Loring sneered and his eyes glinted suggestively. 'Yer've got yerself a choice bedmate for those lonely nights on yer voyage to England. He's a spunky brat.'

A feeling of despair swept through Carlton as he recalled when he was thirteen and Loring first came to Roxborough. He had wanted to buy slaves then and left with the one boy Carlton valued over all the others. He had hated Loring ever since. Yet it was this Captain who suggested turning Roxborough from a declining sugar plantation into the successful slave warren it had become.

'Captain,' said Carlton, choking back his distaste for the man. 'Do you remember when you first came to Roxborough? My father sold you a slave, a bright-skinned youth. Know what happened to him?'

Loring scratched his beard, sending a shower of scabs drifting away with the breeze. His eyes narrowed and he seemed to be pondering what was behind Carlton's questions. 'Mayhap I do . . .'

'Where is he? His name was . . . Prince.'

Loring's eyes misted over and his ugly face softened with a smile that revealed the stumps of his rotting teeth. 'Aye, Prince,' he said, clapping his hand on Caspar's shoulder.

Carlton frowned.

'Prince d'Anjou he calls himself now. He's the darling of every wench and white lady in St John's.' Loring's hand slipped slowly down Caspar's back. The boy didn't move.

'He's in Antigua?' Carlton forgot his anger. 'He's alive?'

'Aye. No doubt he'll be on the wharf when we arrive ter see what pickings I've brought. No fancy ladies for him this voyage.' Loring's hand reached Caspar's backside and he squeezed it, pressing his finger between the boy's legs.

'I miss that buck,' said Carlton, gazing out over the waves.

'I understand . . .'

Loring's lecherous chuckle alerted Carlton and he swung around.

He saw the Captain's hand on Caspar's bottom. The boy was licking his lips nervously.

'Take your hands off him,' Carlton snatched Caspar to his side. 'This ain't a slave to be fingered.'

'Dam' yer blood, young Todd.' Loring scratched his crotch and his mouth curled into a sneer. 'Yer'd do well ter remember what a man needs at sea. There ain't no wenches on board in mid-Atlantic. Mark me words, young Todd, yer'll be wantin' his backside yerself soon enough.' He strolled away, guffawing loudly.

'Take not notice of him, Caspar.' Carlton's voice was shaky.

'Dat a'right, sah. He didn't hurt me.'

He will if he gets a chance, thought Carlton unhappily as he steered the boy below to his cabin.

Loring kept up his lewd innuendoes and banter throughout the voyage. He disgusted Carlton with his stories of boys and virgins he had mounted. What troubled Carlton was the way that Prince must have suffered at his hands. He learned that Loring kept his former playboy with him for two years before billeting him ashore.

Talk of Prince made Carlton yearn for those days of his innocence when he was a young lad romping around Roxborough with no thought for the future. The calamities that had befallen him since then were numerous. He wanted to put them all behind him with a fresh start.

His mind was unclear about what he would do next. First, he must arrange passage. Antigua, with its regular correspondence with England, was the best place for that. There was a strong army presence in the island and a large English population. He would enjoy the company of civilized society. One small matter troubled him and he realized Loring was right. What would he do for companionship on that long voyage to England?

After the death of his wife, Carlton had no desire to get involved with a white woman again. A black wench, on the other hand, was different. He was accustomed to mounting one nearly every night. It was sound sense. If the wench yielded a whelp, it increased his stock. He had no feeling toward them. They were fillies, and everybody knew that while a white man could take his pleasure with a black wench, he could not love her.

'Sir?' Caspar broke into his reverie as he stood by the taffrail staring out to sea. Dominica, the isles of the Saintes and Basse Terre lay beyond the horizon. The schooner was crossing the Guadeloupe Passage with Montserrat and Redonda in the distance.

'What is it, boy?' He shook his head to chase away his somber mood, looking down at Caspar.

The boy's eyes were gazing up at him trustingly, mirrors of his own; a yellow that caught the reflection of the sun. He was sturdily built for his age, his limbs toughened by his carefree existence roaming the hills and fields of the plantation. His soft, tawny complexion seemed to be glowing like gold beneath the dark and silky locks of his hair.

He was almost eleven and already Carlton could see his own determined features in the boy's face, blended with the beauty he inherited from Ella. He was a confident, good-looking youth, and Carlton realized how he could be regarded as attractive to men of Loring's goatish tastes.

'I was be t'inkin', sah.'

Carlton shook his head. 'You must learn to speak the King's English properly now, boy.'

Caspar frowned. 'Yes, sir.' He tried again. 'I was be thinking that you does need plenty clothes for England.'

'By the devil! Who gave you that idea?'

'My mam, sir. Miss Ella tell me make sure you does go to a tailor in Antigua.'

Carlton cuffed the boy's ears warmly. 'An' yo' does be sure yo' does go to school, Caspar. What will people think in England when they hear you talking like an ignorant Creole?'

'What's a Creole, sir?'

Carlton was annoyed by Caspar's curiosity. On the plantation he had been learning the duties of a house slave since he was born. He could mix a strong punch and waited on old Hayes and himself with intelligence. He slept on the floor outside Carlton's door and was ready to do whatever he was bid.

Occasionally, Carlton clouted him when he was stupid, but otherwise the attention he paid the boy was minimal. He had too many slaves to concern himself with Caspar.

Now he found his eagerness disturbing. On the one hand, a slave was not supposed to ask questions but on the other hand, Caspar was his first born son. If he was going to be any use as a servant in

England, he needed to learn more. It was a situation Carlton had not anticipated. Up to then, Caspar was no more than a shadowy presence who fetched and carried on command. Now, with his excited face staring up at him, he was becoming an individual.

'A Creole,' said Carlton impatiently, 'is someone who is born in these islands. I'm a Creole.'

'So am I?'

'Not really. You're not white.'

'But you does be my father.'

Carlton blinked at Caspar's unerring intuition that had made him give voice to the dilemma in his own mind. 'Think of me as your master, Caspar, not your father.'

'Yes, sir. Can I . . .'

'No! Take a walk around the deck. Don't bother me again.'

Caspar seemed unperturbed by his rejection and trotted away quite happily. Carlton shook his head as he realized he could get very attached to the kid if he wasn't careful. Old Hayes always maintained that treating blacks like human beings led to trouble.

It was difficult to remember that Caspar was as black and as evil as any negro with his skin so light and his hair so straight. There was a savage animal lurking in him somewhere, bequeathed by his heritage. On his mother's side, his grand father was from the jungles of Africa. The boy was an animal and, to protect himself, Carlton must never forget it.

Carlton managed to suppress his dislike of Captain Loring so that he was civil to him when they met. Of course, it was impossible to avoid him. They dined together on foul food but there was the consolation of fine Roxborough rum to wash it down.

Carlton was shipping several puncheons to England and deemed it politic to invite the odious Captain to broach one with him. He was obliged to match Loring's bawdy tales with some of his own. It helped him bury in his heart the sorrow that was driving him away from Roxborough.

Many hours he spent on the fo'c's'le peering at the sea, sorting out his problems and preparing himself for the thrill of the new venture. Sometimes, he scanned the horizon ahead and on the fourth day he stared at it eagerly as the outline of Antigua became clearer.

From its coast, the island was a contrast to Dominica where the trees still smothered the hills as unexplored as it was when Colombus came three hundred years before. Antigua was a much flatter island, without Dominica's majestic, cloud-shrouded mountains and vast rivers scouring through the valleys to the sea.

His view of Antigua was of a more tranquil, less-tortured isle than his home. There were white sand beaches glimmering in the sunlight as the schooner sailed past secluded coves. Sugar cane covered the gently rolling slopes rising up from the coast, with fine granite houses standing guard at the brow of the hills. Carlton sensed an orderliness to life on that island that would be at odds with his own restless nature.

Ahead of the schooner, as they began to run back with the wind toward the harbor, was another vessel. Its sails hung limply as though it carried insufficient crew to change them to benefit from the breeze. Carlton's nose twitched and the hackles of his neck tingled at the scent. He called Caspar to him.

'See that ship, boy. Do you know what cargo it carries?'

Caspar shook his head.

'Use your nose. What smell is that?'

Caspar's eyes widened with surprise. 'Why, niggers, sir!'

'Hah! You're no slouch, to be sure. Old Hayes says he can smell a nigger when he's sitting outside his hut at night and, by old horny, he's right. That's a slaver, boy. Bound direct from Africa, I shouldn't wonder.'

When Loring brought his ship toward the shore, they passed close to the slaver as it tacked to catch the wind. Carlton watched the activity on the deck with interest. Africans were being brought up from the hold to be washed.

'They're trying to get the niggers looking good for landing,' he explained to Caspar. 'Those poor creatures will need more than a bucket of water to make them fit for market.'

'Look, sir! They does throw one overboard.' Caspar leaned over the rail in excitement.

'Hold up, lad!' Captain Loring ran up and hooked his hand in Caspar's breeches to pull him back. 'You don't want to join him, do you?'

'The captain of that slaver thinks we're the revenue.' Carlton eyed Loring suspiciously. Caspar backed away.

'Huh, I doubt that. Getting rid of dead stock, more like.'

They watched as a man with a red beard rushed to the edge of the deck and peered over the railing where the African had been thrown. He shouted something they couldn't hear. Two seamen ran up to the side and tossed a plank of wood into the sea. The bearded man shouted again and his crew scrambled to haul down the sail and change course.

'What do you make of that?' Carlton turned to Loring but the captain was already shouting orders of his own. The helmsman pulled at the wheel and the vessel eased close to where the plank floated.

'Seems like that nigger has a price on his ass,' shouted Loring.

'That's Red Delawney there. Seems to want that nigger bad. Think I'll oblige him.'

Sailors lined the rail to watch for the African to appear. Behind them, Delawney's ship was struggling to come around in the wind. He was shouting across the sea but he was too far away to be heard. Loring scratched his beard and chuckled to himself.

'Now what's so special about that black corpse, I wonder?'

'He ain't a corpse, Cap'n!' Caspar tugged at Loring's sleeve, pointing to the water. The African had broken the surface close to the plank. Instinctively, he grabbed it.

'He soon will be.' Loring pointed at the fins of a shark gliding in from the open sea. 'Hook him, men! Grog for the one that gets him aboard.'

Sailors with boathooks stabbed at the water, straining to catch the African. He raised his head and watched them dolefully. Caspar pushed through to the rail and shouted.

'Hol' de hook, boy!'

The African heard his shout for his eyes flickered. He did nothing to save himself. The poles splashed around him. Every time the sailors tried to drive the hook into his flesh, it slipped off his wet skin. He was dazed, unable to understand what they were doing.

Without warning, Caspar leaped over the rail into the sea. He plunged in close to the African and surfaced immediately.

'Dam' the boy,' said Carlton aghast. 'He's gone mad.'

'Sure has.' Loring was eyeing the shark. 'Throw him a line, men. Get the muskets.'

Carlton had no time to analyse his anxiety for Caspar's safety. It was all over so quickly. Caspar caught the rope and tried to tie it around the African. The black man's hold on the plank was weakening and he slipped into the sea.

'Easy, boy,' begged Caspar, treading water beside him.

The African grasped him, struggling and pulling him under. The shark sped through the waves toward them.

Caspar clasped the African around his waist with one hand while he held the rope with the other. The sailors pulled and he and the black rose slowly out of the sea. Men leaned over and grabbed them, hauling them up the side of the ship as the shark snapped at the plank.

Carlton pulled Caspar to him as soon as his feet touched the deck. He was spluttering but raised his head to look at Carlton with pride.

'What the devil did you do that for?' Carlton struck him with the back of his forearm, sending him hurtling across the deck. Caspar blinked with shock, lying where he had fallen.

'Dam' fool thing to do, boy.'

He turned away from Caspar to look at the African stretched out on the deck. Loring was shouting at his men to stand away and give the nigger air.

'Beats me why Red Delawney wants to save this bugger,' Loring said. 'He's only a pack of bones. Not enough skin on him to make a purse. Red must have a stinking cargo if this one's so valuable.'

Carlton was still furious with Caspar. Not for what the boy did, but for the feeling of concern he had roused in him. Carlton knew he must be hard, ruthless, insensitive to his slaves as humans. Only that way could he be strong enough to survive.

'Yer see anything special in this *bozal*?' Loring kicked the African over on to his belly. 'Long prick on him, that's all. No jewels in his ass, I suppose?'

'He's very tall,' said Carlton, musing. Tall like Ella, he thought.

The black's eyes opened and his expression of bewilderment, not fear, struck Carlton as familiar. He did resemble Ella in a way! Carlton crouched down beside him and looked at his body closely. The African was too weak to wince when he pinched him.

Carlton stood up. 'What are you going to do with him?'

'Why, ransom him to Delawney, of course. Ain't no one else goin' ter buy this pile of dung.'

'I will.' Carlton spoke softly but his excitement couldn't be kept from Loring.

The Captain glanced from the African stretched out on the deck to Caspar crouching in a corner watching them in dismay. He walked over to Caspar and hauled him to his feet.

'Yer did well, lad.'

Caspar nervously smiled his thanks.

'Yer can have the nigger.' Loring beamed at Carlton but his eyes were cold and triumphant. 'I ain't goin' to charge yer, seein' as we're old partners, like.'

Carlton stared at the African again, and his heart leaped. There was a tribe in Africa who were legendary, so seldom were any of them captured and sold in the slave markets. They were highly cultured, the aristocracy of Africans. Their leaders were bred from the finest stock in Africa with a bloodline that generations had kept pure through centuries. They were the royalty of Africa; the bravest warriors, the swiftest hunters, the wisest leaders and the hardest workers.

It was Ella who told him about such people and the sign that was scarred on them at birth. It was a secret mark etched into the skin of the shoulder. Ella's mother, a Batutsi princess, had the mark. So had the black stretched out on the deck at his feet.

Carlton was determined to have the boy at any cost. He stared back at Loring's hard eyes. 'What do you want for him?' he asked slowly.

Loring shrugged. He squeezed Caspar's shoulder. 'Not much. The lad . . . for an hour.'

Carlton fell on his knees and grasped the African's shoulders, hugging him to make him sit up. He touched the scars.

He nodded his agreement, keeping his eyes down so he did not see Loring lead Caspar away to his cabin.

'You're safe now,' he said to the African, his throat dry with shame. 'You're mine.'

CHAPTER FIVE

Carlton was standing by his bunk when he heard his cabin door open. He was engrossed in wiping the African's body with a rag to clean away the filth that was encrusted around its sores. He didn't turn when the door was shut.

'Mas Carlton . . .' Caspar hesitated, as though unsure how he would be received.

Carlton steeled himself and turned nonchalantly. He was relieved that the lad wasn't crying, nor staring reproachfully. 'Here, take this,' he said with deliberate brusqueness. He threw him the rag. 'Wipe the nigger's face. Gently now. He's in shock.'

Caspar went to work on the African, swabbing the cuts clean. Carlton watched him, pleased that he seemed none the worse for his experience.

'You did me a favor, saving this colt. He's royal blood, the best there is.'

Caspar smiled with pleasure. 'Yes, Mas Carlton.'

'Never do that again, do you hear? What would become of me if the sharks got you?'

'I'm sorry, sir.'

'So you should be.' Carlton ran his hand down his face, scratching the stubble on his chin. 'Got to fix that Captain Loring somehow, Caspar, what?'

Caspar flushed, nodding his head vigorously to hide his shame.

It was enough. Carlton vowed then to deal Loring a blow he would never forget. In the meantime, he had the African. The black's eyes showed he was aware of his surroundings and Carlton was intrigued to see curiosity was replacing his bewilderment.

The creature was woefully thin. He would need weeks of rest and good food to build him up. Carlton's idea was to send him back to Roxborough so Ella could use him for breeding. In time he would produce magnificent stock.

He watched Caspar wiping the black's face tenderly. His swim in the sea had removed much of his stench but the foul odor of a body near death still clung to him.

'By the devil,' said Carlton, 'we'll be ashore in minutes. We must get him penned and fed as soon as possible. Mayhap I'll find a nigger doctor to look at him. We don't want to lose the brute after what you did.'

The African stared at Carlton. 'Thankee, sah . . .' he gasped.

'Dam'me, he speaks English!' Carlton frowned. 'What kind of creature is this? Ask him his name.'

Caspar leaned over and spoke softly into the African's ear.

'Nd . . . ja . . .' the boy replied painfully.

Carlton grimaced. The name meant nothing to him. 'Where's he from?'

The negro's lips moved but he was unable to say anything.

'He's exhausted, Mas Carlton.' Caspar held his hand over his chest, feeling for the faint beat of his heart.

'Give him some rum and water.'

So engrossed were he and Caspar in tending the African, they did not notice their ship gliding into the harbor and mooring close to the shore. It was dark when Carlton left the cabin and went on deck.

There was the usual bustle of activity as slaves swarmed over the ship preparing to unload its cargo.

On the poop deck, Loring was engaged in a slanging match with an ill-dressed man with a red beard as bushy and as lice-ridden as his own.

'It was yer own dam' stupidness ter throw the bugger overboard!'

'By the devil's balls! There's been so much sickness in my niggers, the crew thought he was dead like the others.'

'Look, Red,' Loring placed his huge hairy hand on Captain Delawney's shoulder. 'The sharks got him. Ain't nothing to be done.'

'He cost me . . .'

'What's money, Red?' Loring laughed. 'Yer'll make enough profit from yer voyage to buy a hundred more Africans. Slaves are sellin' at a premium now. No one knows when they will get new stock again.'

'He was . . .'

'Shut up, Red. Let's have a grog. I've got some fine Roxborough rum on board.'

Delawney's eyes narrowed. 'You sure you ain't got that black stowed away somewhere? I'll find out, you know. Then I'll . . .'

'Yer'll do what?' Loring drew himself up to his full height, a hand taller than Delawney.

'Give your guts to the sharks!' Delawney spun around and clattered down the ladder in a fury. He glanced across the deck as though expecting to find the African but instead saw only Loring's mate and Carlton watching him dourly. He hawked and spat on the deck to show his contempt, then scrambled down a rope to his skiff tied alongside.

Carlton walked up to Loring without speaking, determined not to admit that he was obligated to him. Loring grinned, his foul breath smacking Carlton in his face.

'I keeps to me deals, young Todd. Yer'd better get that bugger off me ship tonight. Leave a few puncheons of rum in his place, will yer.'

'I hope the rum rots you, Loring.'

'Aye.' Loring nodded his head with amusement. 'Yer learnin', young Todd. Mayhap yer'll be a man yet, when yer lose yer fancy for niggers.'

Carlton bunched his hands and took a step toward Loring. He wanted to smash the smug smile off his filthy face for ever. He swung up his fist but a hand caught it, locking around his wrist like a manacle. He struggled to break free.

Loring's smirk broadened into a guffaw and he stepped backward. Carlton writhed against the arms which pinioned him from behind.

'Who the devil . . .!' he gasped.

Loring was choking with laughter, clasping the rail to steady himself. 'See the Bondmaster now,' he spluttered, showering spittle over the deck. 'Dancin' to a different tune, ain't yer, me lad!'

Carlton dived backward, digging his elbows in his attacker's side and bucking his rear into the man's crotch. The grip on his wrists slackened. He wrenched his arms free and turned. He glared angrily when he saw by the light from the lantern swinging outside Loring's cabin, that it was a negro he faced, not one of Loring's crew.

'You set a slave on me, Loring?' Carlton reached for his pistol then gulped in dismay when he found it had been snatched from his belt. He looked again at the negro opposite him. He was holding his own pistol pointed at his chest.

'What's the meaning of this?' he demanded, panting to recover from the shock.

Loring's laughter reached a new crescendo and he signalled the negro to lower the pistol. Carlton tucked in his shirt, seething with a desire to kick Loring in his teeth and chuck him overboard.

'I'll thank you to call off that nigger and return my pistol!' Carlton was fuming. 'I'm warning you, Loring. This is not a jape for you to laugh up your guts.'

'But it is, young Todd!' Loring stood up, patting his stomach. Tears of mirth streamed down his cheeks channeling through the dried sweat and grime into his beard. The negro backed away, watching Carlton with awe.

'Don't yer see who stopped yer silly swipe at me? Look at yon nigger more closely, young Todd.'

The negro blanched when Carlton stared at him. In the flickering light he felt a rush of excitement as he recalled features that stirred a memory. The negro fell to his knees, hanging his head. He proffered the pistol and Carlton seized it, clasping it firmly in his hand.

He reached down and pulled the negro to his feet. He held him at arm's length, hesitated, peered at him again, then pulled him into a tight embrace.

'Prince!' he gasped. 'It's you!'

'Master!'

Loring hawked up a glob of phlegm and spat with disgust over the side of his ship. 'Yer too dam' soft ter be a slave holder, Carlton Todd. He's a nigger, that's all. If yer old dad saw yer hug the bugger, he'd weep for yer. Niggers ain't ter be trusted. They're animals. Treat 'em like humans and yer dead.'

'Take no notice, Mas Carlton,' said Prince, swallowing hard and pulling away. 'He's an old bag of farts.' He grinned mischievously.

'I'm sorry I held you. I thought you were going to hit my captain. If I'd known it was you, I wouldn't have done anything.' They both laughed.

'Prince, it's good to see you.' Carlton tried to ignore the prickling at his eyes. 'How smart you are. You'll have to introduce me to your tailor.'

'Get on with yer,' shouted Loring. 'Prince ain't free. I've still got a lien on him. But he's yer'n while ye're here, if yer wants him.'

Carlton shook his head. 'I don't want more of your style of

bartering, Loring. I'll pay for his hire in currency.'

Loring shrugged his shoulders. 'Suits yerself.' He turned to Prince.

'There's a half-drowned black rat in Todd's cabin. Get him off me ship right quick. Hide him until Red Delawney's put to sea again or that blackbirder will have me vitals!'

Carlton, with his hand on Prince's shoulder, steered him below to his cabin. 'I'm dam' glad to see you, Prince!' he said remembering the time they were boys together. 'You look like a buck in his prime.'

'So do you, Carlton.'

'What?' Carlton tugged Prince's shoulder and spun him around so they were facing each other. 'Am I your comrade so suddenly? Master Carlton, if you please.'

'I meant no offence.' Prince sucked his lips in surprise at the abrupt change in Carlton's manner.

'That's right, Prince. You must show proper respect for me. When we were children at Roxborough it didn't matter. I can be of help to you, Prince, if you serve me well.' He paused outside the cabin door. 'Go on, open it.'

Caspar was surprised when the grandly dressed negro strolled into the cabin behind Carlton. The two of them eyed each other speculatively. Carlton waited, enjoying the tension as each wondered about the status of the other.

'Prince,' said Carlton, growing impatient with Caspar and gesturing at the bunk. 'This is the wretch we rescued. We need a place to hide him until he's fit.'

'His name is Nadjer, Mas Carlton.' Caspar touched the African's hand. 'He told me himself.'

'Don't think much of that.' Carlton sniffed. 'Too savage. We'll call him . . .' he thought, turning over the negro's name in his mind '. . . Nat. That's similar and it's a good slave name. Yes, call him Nat.'

'Can he walk?' Prince inspected the negro and frowned with misgiving. Carlton was pleased that he didn't ask why he was so important. It showed Prince had learned discretion, a valuable quality in a slave so elegant.

'Nat, can you walk?' asked Caspar, pointing at his legs.

The negro tried to move and Carlton was pleased by his willingness. It proved that he was an exceptional creature.

'We must carry him,' said Prince. 'You, boy, help lift him off the bunk.'

Caspar eyed Prince disdainfully and made no move to do any such thing. 'I'm Caspar Todd,' he said firmly. 'Not your boy.'

Carlton nodded. He was relieved that Caspar's spirit had not been cowered by Captain Loring.

'Is that so?' Prince chuckled. 'You're a Todd, are you? Well, I'm the Prince d'Anjou . . .'

Carlton frowned and he grinned wryly.

'Well, call me Prince.' He held out his hand and Caspar drew himself up to his full height, which brought him level with Prince's chest, and shook it gravely.

Carlton watched the three of them: Prince, a fancy slave in his prime; Caspar, his lusty mulatto son; and Nat, the royal black foundling. It was an odd trio but . . . by the devil! . . . Carlton saw how these three bucks could be of use to him in England.

'Come on,' he shouted, 'haul up Nat's ass and let's get off this dam' tub. We've things to do.'

Book One
Nigger Dandy, 1807

CHAPTER SIX

Carlton carefully inspected the guest chamber on the first floor of the lodging house. It was a large room with two full windows closed with hurricane shutters. He gestured to Caspar to open one of them. When he leaned out he saw the room overlooked the harbor.

It was dark with the only light coming from the flickering of lanterns in the wharfside taverns. He listened to the sounds of schooners straining at anchor, to the drunken songs of seamen rolling along the wharf, and to the clatter of a horse on the cobbles below. He withdrew his head and nodded for Caspar to close the shutter.

At one end of the room was a wide bed, a solid piece of furniture with stout legs of mahogany and carved posts that supported a tester and drapes of red velvet. He sniffed to show his disapproval. There was a screen the other end and he peered cautiously around it.

'What the devil's this?'

The mulatto wench who was showing him the room glanced at Prince for help.

'That's a bath tub,' said Prince, strolling over to his side. 'You sit this end where it's shaped to support your hips, and your legs fit in the other end. A slave fills it with hot water before you get in and will douse you with more water from a pail while you're in it.'

'Disgusting! You expect me to wallow in my own filth?'

'A bath tub is the height of luxury, Mas Carlton. It can be very stimulating if you have the right wench to soap and scrub you.'

'Dam' cheek!' Carlton gripped the handle of the pistol stuck in his waistband. He missed the assurance of the whipstock that he carried when he was on his plantation. He wondered if Prince was joking.

'Never heard the like! Is this what you've come to? You're more pampered than a planter's whore. Do you forget how we used to bathe in the Layou river? That's how a man takes a bath, with free flowing water to wash away the dirt.'

Prince hid his smile behind his hand. 'No rivers in Antigua,' he said with a shrug.

'An English gentleman had these rooms, sir.' The wench showing him the suite seemed anxious to impress him. 'He was equerry to the Marquis of Witham. He used the tub once a month.'

Carlton sniggered. 'Are you the one who soaped and scrubbed him?'

'Oh no!' The wench stepped back and blushed.

Carlton's grin broadened. 'Glad to hear it. What's your name?'

'They call me Gwen, sir.'

'Then I shall call you Gwen, too.' He gazed around the room again. It's too luxurious for me. I'm a simple planter.'

'In St John's, Mas Carlton, someone as renowned as the Bondmaster should have no less.'

Carlton scratched his ear, wondering about Prince's seriousness. 'If it's the custom here . . .' He looked at the velvet drapes again and scowled. 'Where does the boy sleep?' He nodded at Caspar.

Gwen walked to the side of the room and opened a door. Carlton admired the sway of her hips and the sight of a dainty ankle beneath the full cut of her skirt.

'There's a chamber for your attendant here.' She fluttered her eyelashes as she smiled. 'It has its own entrance to the backstairs so you need not be disturbed by any comings and goings.'

Carlton heard the hint in her voice. 'You are to have your own quarters, Caspar.' He ruffled the boy's hair. 'See how them English pamper themselves.' He was watching Gwen over Caspar's head. There was a winsomeness about her smile that he found enchanting. She lowered her eyes under his stare.

'By the devil! I'll take the chamber. Prince, arrange for my boxes to be sent here.' Caspar was tugging at his sleeve. 'What is it?' He said irritably.

'The puncheons of rum, sir. They does be on board.'

Carlton struck his brow. 'Dam'me, I'd forgotten. That African's chased everything clean out of my head. Prince, have twenty of them unloaded and see that they are placed in bond until I'm ready to leave.'

'Sir?' Caspar was frowning. 'There does be twenty-four in all.'

'Oho, young Caspar. You have a good head for figures, do you? Figure this out. What does twenty-four stripes applied to one fresh slave give you?'

'Sir?'

Carlton ignored his son's upturned face and eager expression. 'It gives you one sore ass and a boy who no longer questions his master's orders.' He turned to Prince. 'Loring, blast his balls, gets four puncheons. He can have them as your hire price.'

A look of puzzlement crossed Gwen's face. Its real meaning was not clear to Carlton so he said, 'We'll drink your tavern's rum here, Gwen.' He bowed with mock gallantry. 'I could use a screw now.'

'That's how they call a shoot of rum on Mas Carlton's plantation,' explained Prince. He led the way to the door. 'I'll attend to everything myself.'

'Get a doctor to have a look at the African when you've got him bedded down safely,' Carlton called. 'Make sure you find a man who can hold his tongue. I don't want to lose that royal buck now we've got him safe ashore.'

Gwen closed the door with a lingering look at him. He pulled off his coat and flung it on the bed. Caspar scurried across the room, picked it up, shook it, and carried it to the dressing room.

In the center of the chamber there was a couch and Carlton studied it quizzically. It was like none he had ever seen before. There was half a side to it and a headboard with a bolster at one end, and nothing at the other. This oddity was upholstered with delicately woven brocade material in green and gold.

For some reason, the piece of furniture made him angry with its ornateness. He threw himself on it and stretched out full length, plunking his muddy boots on the end.

'Can I get you something, massa?'

'No!' Carlton sighed crossly. 'You can't! Just because we've left Roxborough, you don't have to pester me with evidence of your good intentions.'

'I does be sorry, massa. My mam said be sure to look after you good.'

'Ella's right!' The thought of her made him wonder about Gwen. The housekeeper, or whatever was her function in the lodging house, was an appealing wench.

She was soft where Ella was hard, and was blessed with a body clearly designed for pleasuring. She made the prospect of a prolonged stay in St John's while he waited for passage to England, much brighter. Caspar was hovering at his side.

'What ails you now, boy?'

'Beg pard'n, massa. Your boots.'

Carlton wearily raised his legs so Caspar could pull off his boots. He carried them to the dressing room but within moments he was back. A tray was balanced in his hand.

'What's this?'

'I'm not sure, massa.' Caspar looked worried. 'A boy brought it for you. You did send for rum.'

'Taste it.'

'Me, sah?' Caspar lapsed into dialect, nearly dropping the tray in his astonishment.

'Aye, yo' sah! It ain't the first sip of my rum you've had, I'll be bound. You've done me proud today, boy. Drink your share.'

Hesitantly, but glowing at the compliment, Caspar raised the cup to his lips. He took a small sip and grimaced.

'Well?'

'It ain't displeasin', sir.'

'You must learn how to drink your rum like a man, Caspar. Take a hearty sip, like this.' He filled his mouth with rum then swallowed.

'Savor it before you confine it to your belly. Get the flavor and the bloom. Feel it warm your vitals. Aye,' he smacked his lips. 'Not a bad brew.'

Carlton stretched out on the *chaise longue*, appreciating its comfort even though he despised its elegance. There were no such things as reclining couches, velvet drapes and tin bath tubs at Roxborough Hall.

What good fortune to discover Prince, he thought. The buck was going to be invaluable. Why, he could train Caspar in the ways of English gentlemen so that the boy could serve him correctly in England.

Carlton did not find it odd that his former playboy should know more about white ways than he did. He never mixed with white society in Dominica. Like his father, he was contemptuous of the English who arrived as landholders and then, when a hurricane or the French threatened, fled like startled rabbits home to England.

England wasn't home for Carlton. It was a foreign country with odd customs and strange ways, to say nothing of fancy furniture. Prince would be a help to him as well as to Caspar.

It did not occur to Carlton to doubt Prince's willingness to serve him. He judged from the slave's modish attire that he was well placed. He disapproved of his air of independence but he realized that customs were different in Antigua. Loring hadn't managed to break Prince's spirit.

The thought of Loring angered Carlton. As he watched Caspar moving about the room, he vowed again to get his revenge on the Captain. Caspar seemed none the worst for the incident. He was studying the furniture and ornaments, trying to understand the function of each one.

The boy had a strong sense of self-preservation and it impressed Carlton. Slaves usually were dependent on their owners to think for them and made no effort to use what few brains they had. He attributed Caspar's intelligence to his own white blood that flowed in the boy's veins.

An odd question slipped into Carlton's mind. If Caspar had been a thoroughbred white son, would he have bartered him for the African? He twisted on the couch and looked around for the rum goblet. Caspar passed it to him.

He gulped, reminding himself that Caspar was not like white boys. His mother was a slave so the boy was property and could be sold, or rented out, as he wished. He was his owner by law; he should forget those qualms that were troubling him. He cursed himself for this sudden feeling of weakness.

'Go to your quarters and sleep!' he shouted roughly.

Caspar did not move. 'Are you all right, massa?'

Carlton stared at him. 'What's that?'

'Ain't you havin' a wench tonight?'

'Get out!' He flung the rum into Caspar's face then dashed the cup to the floor. He stood up. Caspar looked frightened.

'I warned you once! I'm the master, Caspar. I'll tell you when I want something.' He faltered when he saw the boy bow his head to hide his tears. He put out his hand to comfort him but withdrew it before Caspar saw.

'Get out when I tell you, dammit!'

Carlton turned his back and walked over to the bed. Without bothering to remove his breeches, he flung himself on top of the velvet coverlet and buried his face in the pillow. His heart ached.

The lodging house was located in the same street as Clothilda's dressmaking shop. Prince was going to carry Nat there in a wagon. The African lay partly covered with sacks while Prince was showing

Carlton his suite. The wagoner, himself a slave and a friend of Prince's, was left to guard him.

Beside the lodging house was a crowded tavern. The wagoner, nodding with sleep on his seat while he waited for Prince, ignored the two men jostling each other in the street.

'Ho, there!' a man cried. The wagoner tensed but didn't move. He remembered Prince's instructions to let no one see or touch the African.

'You lazy black bugger, wake up!' Someone thumped the side of the wagon and the horse shied restlessly. Jack, the wagoner, gripped his whip and looked around at the two men.

'Take us to a whorehouse,' the burly, red bearded one said, staggering against his companion.

'Wait, sah!' Jack cried in alarm when the man tried to climb on the wagon. 'Ah ain' free, sah.'

'I know that. You're a slave, ain't yer?' The red man clapped his companion's shoulder and guffawed at his joke. 'D'yer hear that, Olaf? He ain't free.'

Olaf glared at Jack, his huge bulk unyielding as the red man bounced drunkenly against him. 'Ve can free him, Cap'n.'

'Yes, yes, Olaf. 'Xactly so.'

'Please, sah.' said Jack, biting his lip and praying that Prince would hurry. 'Ah does be 'gaged, sah.'

'You'll be knackered too if ye don't drive us to a whorehouse.' The red man lunged at the wagon, trying to find a foothold on its wheel. 'Give me a hand, Olaf.'

There was a moan from inside the wagon.

'What the devil's that?' The man fell back in surprise, checking his fall against Olaf.

'Oh sah . . .' Jack wailed, unable to think.

'Vat in de cart haf you, boy?' Olaf leaned over the side of the wagon and peered in. It was too dark in the street to see properly, so he prodded under the sacks.

'A drunken sailor, most like,' laughed his companion, tugging Olaf's arm. 'Come on, help me in.' He found a toe hold on the axle of the back wheel and hoisted himself up. 'Hey,' he said with surprise. 'There's a nigger on board.'

'Don't touch him, Captain.'

The man dropped to the ground and turned his head to see who was giving him orders. A negro in a blue frock coat was standing in the doorway of the lodging house.

'Who the hell are you?' he demanded angrily.

'Dr Greville's helper, sir,' lied Prince, thinking quickly. 'That slave in the wagon has the plague. You touch him at your peril, Captain Delawney.'

Delawney tried to focus his eyes. 'The plague? Hell's bells, what's he doing here?'

'We're taking him to the incinerator, Captain.' Prince bowed. 'I'm sorry if the driver has inconvenienced you.'

Delawney drew back, wiping his hands. 'Come on, Olaf. What do we want to ride for? A walk will clear your head.' He linked his arm in his mate's and led him hurriedly up the street. Prince let out a sigh of relief.

Gwen, who had been watching from behind the door, touched Prince on his shoulder. 'Why's that African so important?'

Prince frowned. 'I'm not sure. I'm just doing what Mas Carlton told me.'

'He's a strange man, isn't he?'

Prince looked at her sharply. 'What do you mean?'

'He's not like the other whites who come here.'

'That's because he's from Dominica.'

'How do you know him so well?'

Prince paused and took Gwen in his arms. They had been sweethearts for two years, ever since she came to St John's from the plantation near Boon's Point where she was born. He had soon charmed her into bed with him and, over the months, she became his regular companion, instead of merely another conquest to notch on his belt. He was fond of her and it hurt him at times when he neglected her to tend his white admirers.

'I was born in Dominica,' he said, hugging her. 'Mas Carlton is the same age. We used to play together.'

She nodded her head, apparently satisfied.

Prince sighed inwardly with relief. He had never told Gwen that he was still a slave. He was darker than she and he worried lest she leave him if she knew his true status.

Mulatto wenches aspired to men with fairer skins than themselves. Their ambition was to have light-skinned children because, in the West Indies, blacks could become white in three generations.

The same ideal governed Prince's thinking; the lighter skinned a partner, the more desirable.

'I must go,' he said, squeezing her hips. 'I've got to hide this wretch before anyone sees him.'

Gwen pouted. 'Are you coming here later?'

He shook his head. 'I've got to unload Mas Carlton's rum.'

'Do that tomorrow.' She pressed herself hungrily against him.

He frowned. 'You don't know Mas Carlton. He told me tonight, so I must do it tonight.'

'That's slave talk!' Her eyes blazed with scorn.

'No it's not. I do what Mas Carlton wants because I want.'

'You spurn me for him! That's what you always do when there's a *béké* to beckon you. When a white person calls you, you don't care for me at all.'

'Gwen . . .' he seized her shoulders. The wagoner coughed loudly. 'Don't say that. Sometime I'll explain, not now. Please?' He bent forward to kiss her but she turned her face and his lips brushed clumsily against her cheek.

'Don't come tonight, Prince. Nor any night!' She raised her skirts and flounced back into the lodging house, slamming the door in his face.

'Wild wench, dat,' said Jack dourly. 'Mixed blood. De white strain make dem contrary.' The wagoner wiped his face. 'We takin' dis *bozal* some place? Ma massa don' know ah be ou' dis late.'

'Dammit, Jack. You'll get your hire fee.'

'No need to get vex' wid me, Prince.' He tugged the reins and the horse moved forward as Prince jumped up beside him. 'It dat she-cat yo' mus' beat, not me.'

Prince laughed. 'She can be troublesome, but she's not serious.'

'Most wenches like dat if yo' don' ride 'em right. S'prised at yo', Prince.'

'It's because I do it right that she wants me so much!' The two men chuckled together as the wagon jerked over the rough stones of the street.

In the back of the wagon, the African heard the chuckling and was puzzled, until he remembered that laughter belonged to black men. His eyes were open and he gazed up in wonder. There were stars and a half moon in a cloudless sky; the night was balmy, like it was on the plains. He was soothed by the laughter of the man who wore white man's clothes, the man called Prince. He had a good heart.

The wagon lurched and Ndja was jolted on to his side. He groaned at the unexpected pain. The pitching of this wooden contraption was worse for him than the continuous rolling of the ship. His body ached.

The laughter ceased abruptly and Ndja sensed danger. Before, he thought he had heard the voice of Keptin Delawnee but when nothing happened, he supposed it was another of his spirit's tricks. He lay still in the wagon, drawing his knees up to his chest under the sacks that covered him. The wagon came to a halt.

He heard Prince's voice. 'Wait here, Jack. Don't let anyone see him.'

There was silence broken only by the wagoner sucking his teeth nervously. Ndja dismissed the man as a low caste fool not fit to be even a dung-carrier. His spirit urged him to raise his head from the wagon to see what was the danger, but his strength had gone. He closed his eyes in frustration.

There were arms around his body, pulling him off the shelf. He came to with a start and tried to raise his hand to push away the person holding him. He was lifted out of the wagon and launched over the shoulder of a strong man as if he was no more weight than a sack of maize. His head hung downward, bouncing against the backside of the man totting him.

'Lord have mercy!' A woman's voice screeched as he was carried over the threshold into a house. He felt ashamed at entering a female's presence in such a manner. He heard a door close and the sound of a bolt being driven home. Was he in jail?

'Come on, Nat.' The kindly voice of Prince sounded in his ear as he was placed on a chair. He flopped forward until Prince caught his shoulder and pushed him back. 'He's very weak.'

'You sure he ain't dead?' The woman's voice was stern. Ndja sensed she meant well.

'Not yet, Clo', and we not going to let him die. Mas Carlton values him too highly.'

Value! Ndja stirred and lifted his head. His father said he had no value, yet a white man had rescued him from the sea and valued him highly.

'He looks awful.'

Why did the woman say that? he wondered. Was she scared of him?

'You'd look worse if you crossed the Middle Passage in the hold of Red Delawney's old slaver.'

Ah! Ndja was pleased when he heard Prince speaking in his defence.

'Can you make some gruel for him? We've must fatten him up so he's fit again.'

'I'm not nursemaid to a nigger.'

'I know that, Clo'.'

The woman shrieked suddenly, happily, as Prince squeezed her.

'It's important to me,' Prince was saying. 'Mas Carlton will pay well.'

There was silence in the room so Ndja ventured to open his eyes. He was amazed at the sight. Prince stood with his arms around a woman whose complexion showed she was of the mixed race. They were both watching him sorrowfully but what drew his attention was the rainbow of colors that bedecked the room.

On every side, on shelves, on tables, on chairs, and on the floor, were swatches of brightly-colored cloth, bundles of material in every hue, and clothes of a richness he had never seen before. His eyes opened wide with astonishment. He decided that he must be in a temple.

He fell forward off the chair to worship at the feet of the woman who was undoubtedly a most powerful priestess.

'Lord!' screamed the woman. Prince's hands helped him up. 'I don't need Carlton's money,' she said. 'The boy needs help. He looks stricken out of his mind.'

The priestess hurried out of the room. From behind some curtains, Ndja heard the cheering sound of a ladle scraping the inside of a cooking pot.

'Nat,' said Prince, hunkering down beside him. He stared into his face with kind, honest eyes. 'Clothilda is my 'keeper. She's your friend. She'll look after you.' He was smiling.

Ndja liked Prince's face. It had a benevolence the white man's didn't. He liked his beautiful raiment, the clean smell of his body, and the firm hold of his hands on his shoulders. One day, Ndja's spirit told him, he too would be as handsome and as smart as this Prince.

'Nat? Do you understand?'

'Nat . . .' Ndja repeated the word slowly, 'Nat?'

'Yes, you're Nat. That's the name Mas Carlton has given you.

That's your slave name. It's easier than your African name. You've got to forget that now. My name's Prince.'

Ndja cocked his head on one side while he considered this. If he was to have another name, he didn't mind. The old one brought him only misery.

'Nat . . .' he said, louder this time, but his throat cracked with dryness and he began to cough.

'Give him this.' The woman passed Prince a bowl of steaming liquid. He watched it warily.

Prince dipped a spoon in it and sipped. 'It's delicious, Clo'. You have some for me?'

'Later.' The woman wrung her hands.

Nat supped the broth from the bowl while Prince held it to his lips. He felt the warmth of its goodness seeping through his bones, filling him with strength. The priestess has a wonderful magic, he thought.

There was a loud shout of anger outside the house and the street door shook when someone pounded on it.

'Clotty! Open this dam' door.'

Ndja flinched as he recognized the voice. He dropped the bowl and stared at Prince in disbelief. Was this some trap to return him to the ship? The woman was clutching her cheeks in dismay as Prince tried to pull him to his feet.

'Yer got some buck pesterin' yer in there, Clotty? Open up!'

'Keep quiet,' said Prince. 'Let him think you're not here.'

Clothilda straightened herself, smoothing down her bodice. She tucked up her hair underneath her bonnet. 'Why shouldn't he come in? I'm not scared of Captain Loring.'

'Thank the lord! Neither am I. I know how to deal with that brute. But he mustn't know Nat is here.'

They looked at each other helplessly while Loring smote upon the door, bawling drunkenly. 'Ahoy, wench! I'm going to drop me anchor in yer dock tonight, Clotty dear. Let me in.'

'He's my man, Prince. I've got to do what he asks.' Clothilda moved toward the door, her face set with a grim smile.

CHAPTER SEVEN

The hammering on the door continued. Prince was aghast when Clothilda pulled back the bolt. He believed she would help him as she always did. In the past, she had lied for him, delayed angry husbands to give him time to escape out of the back door, and taken his side in altercations with authority. She was like an elder sister, not a mistress. Why was she betraying him now?

He glanced desperately around the room. There was nowhere to hide Nat and the African was too weak to run out with him to the back yard. He was slumped in his chair with his eyes downcast. Prince put his hands on his shoulder and feigned confidence.

'Don't be scared, Nat. I can deal with Captain Loring.'

The door burst open and Loring swept into the room with the force of a small hurricane. He was laden with packages that showered to the floor as he scooped Clothilda into his arms.

'Clotty!' he bellowed, then smothered her face with kisses, knocking her bonnet askew and making her gasp.

Prince stood protectively in front of Nat. Loring glanced at him then turned his attention back to Clothilda.

'How're yer faring, wench?' He slapped her backside and she shrieked with pleasure. 'See these,' he roared, indicating his packages. 'Lace, silk, bolts of cloth. All from them Spaniards in Trinidad. I want yer ter make yerself a gown for me next visit.'

'Loring!' Clothilda squirmed girlishly in his arms.

'Aye, I'm too good ter yer,' he said, releasing her and scratching his beard. 'Where's the rum?' He turned to Prince. 'Come on, boy, where's me grog?'

'I'll get it,' said Clothilda, fussing around him happily. 'Sit down.' She led him to a chair.

'Is that Red's nigger?'

Prince had not expected such a casual reaction. He spread his hands lamely. 'I didn't know where else to take him . . .'

'Yer did right. Red Delawney ain't man ter come here but he'll raid every factor in St John's if he's a mind for it.' Loring peered across the room. 'Stand aside, Prince. Let's see the boy.'

Nat's head drooped forward. His body was pathetically thin, his rib cage sticking out like a skeleton's. His shanks were festering with sores where chains had chaffed him. In the dim light from the lantern, he resembled a black wraith.

'Lift up his head.'

Prince put his hand under Nat's chin and tilted his head back. It lolled forward again. Prince wondered if Nat was pretending to be unconscious. He felt a pang of pity for him. If he lived, his life was going to be wretched as one of Carlton's slaves.

'Don't understand Todd's interest, meself, eh, Prince.' Loring took his rum from Clothilda and sipped it thirstily.

Prince sensed that Loring was not as drunk as he appeared when he banged on the door. His breeches and coat were clean and his hair combed. The coarseness he exhibited in front of his crew was stilled. Prince wasn't fooled by his dress; for him Loring would always be an arrogant and selfish thug.

'Won't you take some broth?' Clothilda was unable to contain her delight at his presence.

'Eaten,' he grunted, shaking his head. 'Yer feed the buck?'

'Yes.' Clothilda was surprised by his concern. 'What am I going to do with him?'

'Do?' Loring grabbed her. 'Are yer stupid, woman?' He slapped her bottom playfully. 'Mother him, of course. Same as yer done to Prince. See what he's become. A black jackanapes with more broken hearts to his credit than me!'

Prince was puzzled. 'I thought you'd be vexed I brought him here.'

'What the hell for? Ain't yer learned anything from yer old Cap'n? How many times have I told yer the only one ter trust is Clotty.' He held her firmly, patting her buttocks. 'Known this wench since she was a virgin chit. Where else could yer take that *bozal*?'

'You knew I'd bring him here?' Prince was dismayed that Loring anticipated his action.

'Makes sense. It's yer home, ain't it? He'll soon put on weight with Clotty's cooking and yer'll be able to teach him English. Then I want ter see why young Todd thinks this black streak of piss is worth so much fuss.'

'Why is that important?' Prince was disgusted with himself for doing what Loring expected.

Loring laughed. 'I gave young Todd a drowned rat. If he be better'n that, I got ter be paid properly.' He scratched his crotch. 'Young Todd will do anything for this blackie. Could be very profitable . . .'

With a heavy sigh, Nat slipped out of his chair to the floor. He was like a forlorn marionette with his limbs trapped under him.

'Take him ter sleep, Prince.'

Clothilda clapped her hands. 'He'll have to sleep outside. I can't have my shop smelling of niggers when my ladies come for their dresses.'

'Kitchen,' said Loring with a grunt.

Clothilda relented. 'Give him rags for a pillow and show him where to shit.'

'Doubt he got bowel control yet, me dear.'

Clothilda raised her eyes to the ceiling. 'The things I do for you . . .'

'And the things I do for conny!' Loring stood up and caught her around her waist, lifting her off the ground. 'Let's go upstairs, Clotty. I can't wait a moment longer.'

Prince laid Nat out on the kitchen floor and returned as Clothilda and Loring were ascending the stairs. 'Captain Loring?'

'Can't stop now, boy.'

'It's Mas Carlton,' he said. 'He told me to unload twenty puncheons from the ship tonight. I'm to leave you four.'

'Four, is it?' Loring arched his eyebrow. 'Now that's mighty curious.' He paused. 'Go up, Clotty. I want to speak to Prince for a while.' He watched her backside as she waddled happily up the stairs, then he leaned on the balustrade and eyed Prince suspiciously.

'Is something wrong?' he asked. 'Can I go'n unload?'

Loring pursed his lips. 'Something ain't right, that's for sure. Why should that nigger breeder give me four puncheons of best rum? He chokes every time he has to give me the time of day.'

'He said it was my hire fee.' Prince flushed, hating to remember that he was Loring's slave.

'Hah! Yer ain't worth more than a ferkin, boy.'

Prince decided that this was the best chance he would have to ask a question that had long been troubling him. 'Sir?' he began.

Loring had a baleful look in his eyes. 'Yes!'

'Since I'm not worth much and I don't serve you any more, could you see your way to giving me my freedom. I could pay off the lien.'

There was silence in the room that was somehow more intimidating than the outburst of anger Prince anticipated. Loring was tugging his beard and seemed to be considering the request. Then he frowned with his bushy eyebrows joining together in a dark line over his bulbous nose.

'Freedom, is that it? Was that Todd's idea? To bamboozle me with his dam' rum so I'll give yer back ter him?'

'No, sir!' Prince was appalled. 'I belong here with Clothilda, not in Dominica. I wouldn't leave her. Just my freedom . . . There's a girl, a mulatto, I'd like to marry . . .'

'No!' Loring's face was puce with rage. 'Yer won't ever be free, Prince. I know yer sort too well. That's why I deeded yer to Clotty. When I die, ye're hers. Yer ain't fit ter be free, to be ruinin' respectable white women with that snake yer got between yer legs. They don't know it's filled with more poison than a *tête chien*.' He shook his fist.

'If yer free, yer'll be dead. That snake'll be chopped off by some angry husband whose wife it's bitten.'

His tirade made no sense to Prince. He walked around the tiny room impatiently, knocking bolts of cloth to the floor as he gestured to illustrate his point.

'She's not a white woman. She's from Boon's Point. I can't ask her to marry me as I am. She's a high-colored girl and, well, she doesn't know I'm a slave.'

'Then yer'll have ter tell her, boy.' Loring turned his back and went up the stairs, snorting with anger. 'Freedom! Whatever next!'

Prince sank to the ground, surrounded by lengths of dress material, bolts of yellow and blue and red. He churned over in his mind what Loring had said. How he wanted his freedom! If Loring really had willed him to Clothilda, she would free him, but Loring must die first . . .

Prince jerked up his head as a hand touched his shoulder. 'By god, you frightened me!' he exclaimed, gaping at the feeble figure that was reaching out of the shadows to grasp him.

Nat had crawled out of the kitchen on his knees and lay between two rows of dresses. His eyes were full of concern but that did not mask the pain that registered in his features with every movement.

'What do you want?' Prince moved away and Nat's hand slipped from his shoulder. He caught it and held it tenderly.

'That man . . .' Nat raised his eyes to the ceiling to indicate Loring. 'Very bad.'

Prince smiled wryly. 'You're damn right.'

'I think he kill you. The bad words . . .'

'Don't worry about me, Nat. I can take care.' He was touched by the African's concern. It was odd for a *bozal*, especially a newly arrived one, to show such an interest in others.

'He have bad heart, Prince.'

Nat looked so worried that Prince drew him close and let him rest his head on his chest. He stretched out on the floor, using a pile of petticoats as a pillow. With Nat beside him, he had someone to worry about. His own troubles were nothing compared with what this innocent African had in store.

'On the savanna, we hunt bad animals. We kill. I help.'

Prince was stunned. 'Why are you worried? You don't have strength to stand yet you want to help me with Loring? His bark's worse than his bite, Nat.'

'He's a dog?'

'Yes, maybe he is.'

'We poison bad dogs . . .'

'Go to sleep, Nat. I'll stay here with you. I'll go for Mas Carlton's rum at dawn.'

Nat's eyes closed immediately and Prince smiled as he settled down to sleep beside him. If Gwen saw him now, what would she say about this *bozal* in his arms instead of her?

It was after midnight, the time Gwen loved best. Her employer, the formidable Mistress Nesbit, had gone to her chamber. The cook and the scullery slaves were asleep in the kitchen. Gwen's quarters were in the yard behind the lodging house and she ought to be sleeping too. In the morning, before six, she would have to wake the household and set the slaves to their tasks.

Gwen sat on the stoop of her little shack and gazed up at the moon. The slave girl who shared the quarters was already asleep on a rush mat on the floor. The dogs were chained in the yard. From the tavern in the neighboring house, a few yards away, came the sound of revelers on their last legs. She liked this time because she could think after a day spent chasing slaves, fussing over her mistress and tending to the guests.

Gwen was worried. As a mulatto, her chances for improving her lot lay in her ability to catch a good husband. True, she was free, yet under Mistress Nesbit, her pay was so small she could never change her station without help.

St John's was renowned for the comeliness of its women. Beautiful mulatto girls were everywhere, the consequence of guilt-stricken English planters, their fathers, freeing them. For Gwen, it meant intense competition for every eligible male.

She was luckier than many in having Mistress Nesbit, an old friend of her father's, to give her a position. She served the old lady well and since she came to the lodging house, business increased. She met many English gentlemen staying in the rooms while on duty with the army or attached to the English merchant houses.

The attention these men paid her was flattering indeed, yet she soon learned their interest was only in how fast they could spread her legs. She wanted more than a few dubloons. For Gwen, a husband was the answer to her dreams.

She sighed as she gazed at the moon, seeing Prince's face as though he was standing beside her. She loved him, but why . . .? It was obvious he was a feckless womanizer who would never be happy with one woman alone.

She smiled lovingly at the thought of him. He was so weak. Whenever a white lady laid eyes on him, he lost control. He was like a puppy, mooning after them with lovesick eyes and romping when they demanded. Couldn't he understand that those white ladies didn't care for him the way she did?

Perhaps he wasn't the wisest choice for a husband. He was darker than she, and there was his reputation. Yet she adored him. He was always dressed so smartly and every girl in the town was a little bit in love with him.

She giggled. He claimed that since he met her, none of the local girls appealed to him. If he weren't with a white lady – on business, he said – then he was with her. So where, she began to wonder, was he now?

Gwen looked around the yard. All was quiet. The tavern keeper had closed his doors and there were no sounds from the wharf. She listened carefully. Prince said he was going to unload the rum for Carlton Todd. She was sure he had not done so because she would have heard the wagon clattering past the lodging house on its way to the bond store.

She got up, strode across the yard, walked down the passageway that separated the lodging house from the tavern, and stepped out on to the waterfront. The ships tied up at the wharf were dark shapes merging with the blackness of the night. She walked confidently along the cobbles. The dark held no fears for her. She could deal with any drunken sailor with a knee to his crotch and a stab in his guts with the knife she kept in her garter.

There was no one on the wharf. It worried her. The watchmen were asleep and at Captain Loring's schooner all was peaceful. Prince certainly wasn't there. Without a doubt, he was up to something. She was horrified that he might have believed what she said earlier in the evening and decided to find another woman for the night.

It was not far to Clothilda's place. She hurried there, stricken with remorse. The stone houses built close to the sides of the street kept out the moon, so she guided herself by instinct. The shutters were closed and she stood outside Clothilda's front door wondering what to do.

She listened carefully. Someone was moving in the upstairs room, the room Prince used. She noticed the shutter was partially open. There was a giggle.

Gwen's heart lurched at the sound. It was the unmistakable noise of a woman being pleasured. There were gasps, and whispers and muted shrieks of delight. Of the man – Prince – she could hear only deep grunts of satisfaction. Even the wooden walls of the upper story of the house were shaking with the rhythm of lovemaking.

Gwen held her breath, reluctant to believe what she was hearing. The noises rose to a crescendo and the woman squealed in ecstacy. Gwen ran blindly from the house, unable to bear it.

The proof that Prince was giving to another what he denied her, was too much. She was prepared to tolerate his weakness with white women, if it was rewarding. They came and they went, but he was still hers. Now, it seemed, he had a wench from St John's. She would be the laughing stock of the town.

She lay down to sleep that night with a heavy heart. Her pallet seemed hard and sleep wouldn't come although she felt desperately weary and alone. She hoped with the departure of Helen Witham to get Prince back. Now someone else had him. Damn, she thought, searching for someone to blame. Damn Carlton Todd for ordering Prince to serve him like a slave.

Carlton Todd? The image of the planter made her stop thrashing on her pallet. He was Prince's age, a fine looking man with a proud face, lovely hair – not black whorls like Prince – and he was a wealthy creole to boot. She sat up, stunned by the enormity of what was going through her mind.

If Prince could dally with white women, why shouldn't she play with a white man? That would put his pretty shabine nose out of joint and make him pay more attention to her.

Why, she thought as she lay back and began to drift off to sleep, Carlton Todd was recently widowed! Undoubtedly, he would crave female companionship. Who knows, he might even be interested in marriage. Wouldn't that be something to show the St John's whore who had stolen Prince fróm her?

Mayhap, she dreamed, she could even become Mistress of Roxborough.

CHAPTER EIGHT

Ella roused herself by instinct. It was not yet dawn. She groped her way along the passage to the kitchen and crouched in front of the embers of the previous night's fire. The taper in her hand caught alight and she lit a candle with it, blinking away the sleep that still stuck in her eyes.

She threw a bundle of kindling in the grate from the pile Pool had collected the day before, and raked over the embers. When the fire was burning brightly, she added some small logs and swung the *bom* of water over it. The cauldron hung from the support projecting from the middle of the brick fireplace and the flames danced under it.

That done, she began to wake up. She opened the back door. The dogs whined but knowing it was her, they did not bark. She crouched down in the mud by the balizier tree to relieve herself. Then she took a gourd of water from the open cask with its bamboo guttering leading from the roof, and splashed it on her hands and face.

Her head was bare and she shivered in the cool air of the morning. She retreated hurriedly into the kitchen and shut the lower part of the door. The top part, on separate hinges, she left ajar so she could listen to the plantation waking up.

She puttered about the kitchen thinking what she would serve old Hayes for breakfast and dinner that day, and wondering what she would need from the food store. The cauldron of water was soon boiling and she poured some of it into a smaller *bom*, threw in some ground coffee beans, and waited while it simmered until it was about to boil over. She poured the brew, blacker than herself, into a dish and added a dollop of molasses to sweeten it.

She sat down with a sigh. In a corner of the kitchen, on a pile of rags, the small boy she had brought from the nursery to be her kitchen helper now Caspar was gone, lay asleep. Pip and Pool were in one cell while the two girls who helped with household duties were asleep on the floor of their own chamber. There was no one else awake. The only other slave in the house, Tita, was upstairs with the children.

Ella frowned at the thought of Tita. She regretted that Carlton had given the slave so much influence over Laura and the baby. It boded ill for the future. She might poison their minds to her mean way of thinking.

Ella glanced at the charcoal marks on the white-washed wall by the pantry door. Every evening before he went to bed, watched by all the house slaves, Pip solemnly added another cross to those already there. She counted them. There were twenty-nine, the number of days since Carlton sailed away. Already it seemed like a year.

She thanked her spirits for blessing her with his child. The baby was an extension of him; it was Carlton throbbing in her womb.

She moaned softly as she stroked herself imagining Carlton's firm thighs pressed against hers, his hardness plunging in her again and again until he collapsed, limp and exhausted, with his head buried between her bosom. Her hand moved faster until she arched herself off the chair and shuddered with a spasm that drained her very soul.

'Aie!' she cried, gripping the side of the table, longing for Carlton. 'Aie!'

She slumped back in the chair and grabbed the dish of coffee, panting as she brought it to her lips. She paused and slurped it thirstily. She had never known such loving as Carlton's. He was brutal, demanding and then so tender, like a child in her arms. He spoke words of endearment such as no negro ever used.

She gazed at the charcoal marks on the wall and wondered how many more would be there before he returned.

She drained the coffee dish and glanced out through the open half of the door. The sky over the sea was black but she knew dawn was only minutes away. On the east coast, the slaves would be stirring already. On the west, they clung to sleep until a glow, like a halo, appeared above the range of hills on the plantation boundary.

The steady drone of a conch shell being blown by one of the Wagenie river slaves reverberated around the plantation from the slave quarters. It was the signal that another day was beginning.

'Marcus,' she called, getting up from the chair, shaking down her shift, and walking over to the boy sleeping in the corner. 'Wake up, *gahson*!' She prodded him firmly with her foot. 'De conch done blow t'ree times, boy.'

Marcus scrambled to his feet, clutching his drawers around his waist. He blinked at Ella in confusion.

'Wake Pip and Pool,' she commanded, 'and get those two girls up too. It be dawn a'ready.'

The routine at Roxborough was dictated by nature. Work began at sunrise so that not a moment of daylight was lost. Cattle had to be rounded up and milked, the fields tended, fish caught and, in the nursery, the babies and niggerlings fed and watered. Carlton left a structure of command under experienced slaves who knew their duties. Even though he was not there, as long as his slaves retained the will to work, the plantation functioned efficiently.

Fear, Ella was aware, gave the slaves that will. She had instructed all the drivers to be wise in their use of the whip. Fear of the raw leather tongue slicing into their backs drove the slaves better than any other form of persuasion. Yet a bullying driver would be resented and could lead to trouble. So she had reasoned with the drivers and got them to understand that life would go sweetly for them all if they kept their gangs contented and productive.

The back door was flung open with a crash shattering her thoughts. Tita stood on the threshold, her eyes wild and her long hair uncombed. Not for the first time, Ella noticed how evil she looked.

'Yo' does be 'wake early,' she said calmly.

'Ain' slept wid dat dam' chil'.' Tita was wearing a nightgown with roses embroidered on the bodice and hem. She walked over to the table at the center of the kitchen. 'Yo' got coffee?'

'Of course. In de pot.'

Tita's eyes flared. 'Ah ain' gettin' it mahself.'

'Den wait 'til de girl come.'

Tita peered around the kitchen. 'Yo' hab dem two bucks and two girls helpin' yo' an' ah ain' got none.'

'Three bucks now,' said Ella cheerfully as the boy walked back into the kitchen. 'Dis be Marcus.'

'Yo' so lazy yuhself, Ella, ah surprise' yo' out of bed before nine.'

'Only today yo' be up early to know dat!'

The chatter of the two girls as they sauntered into the kitchen prevented Tita's retort. The girls felt silent when they saw her.

'Say good morning to Miss Tita,' Ella scolded them. 'Cleo, pour a dish of coffee for her.' She clapped her hands. 'Marcus, run upstair an' open de shutters. Quietly now, so yo' don't wake Massa Hayes.'

Tita seized the dish of coffee and held it to her lips. Ella watched her out of the corner of her eyes. There was something about the woman she could not fathom. She was not a Roxborough slave. Carlton had bought her from May Gregg, the owner of the casino in Layou, when he needed a wet nurse for Laura.

Tita had suckled Laura and, when she had a baby of her own at the same time as Carlton's wife gave birth to young Hayes, she wet nursed him as well. It was this that made her think she was better than any of the other slaves.

She was a Fulani, born in Africa. She had hair that was long and silky and black, her most cherished asset that she flaunted at Ella whose own hair was distinctively African with its kinks and whorls. Her complexion was lighter than Ella's and she wore powder to lighten it still more, copying the tricks she learned from her late mistress. She was slender, with a figure like a young girl.

Ella, in contrast, was bigger and broader. Now she was beginning to round out with her pregnancy, she seemed much fatter than usual.

'That nightgown,' said Ella casually. 'Very pretty.' She smoothed down her own shift of osnaburg, a rough slave cloth. 'It suits you.'

Tita set down the empty coffee dish and spoke between clenched teeth. 'Yo' ain' havin' it. Mistress gave me all her clothes. 'Sides, yo' too fat to wear lady's things.'

'I wouldn't want to wear a dead woman's knickers.'

'Oy, oy, oy! Ain' yo' de big mistress wid all dese slaves to serve yo'.' Tita's eye fell on Pool emerging from the passage, his early morning maleness evident from the bulge in his breeches. She gloated.

'Ah does wonder what yo' does do here at night alone wid such frisky bucks.'

Pool winked at her as he followed Pip out to the balizier tree.

'Yo' welcome to stay down here with us, Tita, if those children of Mas Carlton are too much for yo'.' Ella's smile was sweetness itself.

'Hah! An' let yo' have mah chamber upstair! Ah ain't stupid like yo' t'ink, Ella.'

'Miss Ella!' Marcus tumbled into the kitchen from the back stairs. 'De baba does be cryin' an' Massa Hayes 'wake an' he cursin' me. It ain't mah fault, Miss Ella.'

'A'right, boy.' Ella stood up, shouting for Pip. 'Massa done wake.

Take he coffee quick. An' de 'canter of rum case he vex'.' She turned on Tita.

'Dis be yuh causin', Tita. If yo' tended de baba prop'ly he ain't go'n cry an' wake de Massa.'

Tita pouted. 'De brat more trouble dan a kitchen of lazy niggers. Ah does need help wid he an' Laura an' mah own Mingoson too. Yo' got fillies an' colts like a queen.'

Ella frowned. 'I'll ax Massa if I can send yo' a nice clean girl from de paddock to season.'

'Don' sen' me not'in. Ah go'n chose de girl mahself. Ah ain' havin' no tittletattle chit runnin' to yo' wid stories all de time.'

Ella was amused that Tita thought she had any secrets. All the house slaves saw through her attempts to improve her status, shirk her duties, and ingratiate herself with Massa Hayes.

'Maybe de Massa go'n lash yo' if yo' don't hush de baby!' warned Ella. 'I can hear he bawlin' plenty.'

As if to emphasize her words, there was a banging on the floor above her head. 'Oh lor',' she said, raising her eyes in despair. 'De Massa vex' in trut'. I ain't had no time to dress.'

'Yo' so black an' ugly, he won' notice!' Tita hurried out of the kitchen. Pool was shaking himself by the tree and she smiled at him coquettishly before dashing up the stairs to the children.

'He does be ragin' dis mornin',' said Pip, wiping his brow. 'He callin' for yo'.'

Ella reviewed in her mind the possible calamities that could have roused Hayes's temper. Carlton once told her that a successful slaveholder must anticipate what his slaves were going to do, even before they knew it themselves. She applied that principle to the whites in her care.

'What he say?' she asked while she buttoned her shift, covering her breasts. She tied her apron of red and white check material around her waist. A girl ran for her cloth cap which she put on her head without stopping to comb her hair.

'He say somet'ing 'bou' lazy niggers dat all ah hear.'

'Oh lor'!' Ella's lips twitched. 'Yo' see de fuss Tita done cause?' There was another bang on the floor and the slaves stiffened. Ella was scornful.

'He an ol' man, Pip. Cleo, warm de bread an' Pool, yo' prepare de table. Oh lor', how am I go'n do ev'ryt'ing today?'

She was still muttering when she swept into the drawing room. The door to Hayes's room was ajar and she pushed it open without knocking. 'Mornin', Massa,' she said, taking in the sight of the old man leaning out of the bed with his walking stick raised in the air for another blow on the floor.

'Where the devil have you been, Ella?' Hayes looked sulky.

She moved over to the bed and gently took the stick from him, placing it out of reach. She tucked in the bedsheet while she spoke.

'I does be sorry, massa,' she said briskly, smiling her best. 'Dat wench Tita come down for coffee an' we delay.'

'That's why them whelps was hollerin'?'

'I expect so.' Ella beamed. 'Would you like your breakfast in bed today? I have fresh eggs and a nice piece of ham I been savin' for you.'

'Stop treatin' me like I'm sick, Ella. I'm gettin' up same as I always do, 'less I'm dyin'.'

'That's fine.' Ella took up the empty coffee dish and waited. She had learned not to disagree with the old man. *We say la pay*: yes is peace, the slaves said in patois.

If ever Hayes wanted something she thought unwise or that might interfere with her management of the plantation, she used subtle methods to foil his plans instead of outright opposition.

'Tell Marmeduke to bring out the wagon. I want to ride to the quarters. See, sun's up already and not one slave at work in the fields.'

Ella was dismayed at the idea of old Hayes riding around the plantation. Slaves were creatures of habit and a regular routine encouraged their docility. If they were shaken up by the unexpected appearance of a querulous old man wheezing commands, their reaction could be more than she could check. Besides, she wanted Hayes alive until Carlton came back. Riding in his state of health would be a foolish risk.

Ella knew why there were no slaves in the canefield that day. She had ordered all of them to the provision grounds instead. Without the yams, dasheen and sweet potatoes grown by the slaves themselves, they would soon go hungry.

'While you're riding,' she said brightly, 'could you visit the nursery paddock?'

'What for?'

'Tita say she want a girl to help her with the children. She say that they cryin' so much 'cause she can't cope with all three of dem by herself.'

'Humph!' Hayes sucked his gums, then shrugged. 'You do that, Ella. It's woman's work.'

Ella breathed a sigh of triumph. Tita was going to be vexed at that. 'Yes, massa,' she said coyly. 'There does be another thing.'

'By the devil, nothing but problems this morning and I ain't even out of bed.'

'I been checking the stores.'

'Someone stealin' from us?'

'Oh no, massa. Supplies gettin' mighty low 'cause we don't order from Roseau since Mas Carlton done leave.'

'Why ain't you done that, Ella.'

'I was be waitin' for you.'

'Dammit, Ella. You know what's needed to feed this plantation, don't you?'

'Yes, massa.'

'Then order it. Kingston can help you with the ledgers.'

Kingston was the slave who kept the stock books on the slaves, the equipment, the supplies and the produce. Ella had already sought his help. She could read and write and knew Massa Hayes couldn't any more. His instruction was a gratifying confirmation of her status.

'I was be thinkin', massa. De slaves like ground provisions plenty and it more cheap than imported flour an' potatoes. When you ridin', if you go to de polinks, you see how I cut down expensives by sendin' dem dere since we ain't botherin' wid sugar no more.'

'Capital idea, Ella! I don't like fancy food myself. Local vittles the best for man and beast, what!'

There was silence in the room. Outside the sun was climbing to the other side of the hills, throwing long shadows on the house. Within an hour the heat would become intense. It was the time when Carlton, astride his horse, made the rounds of the plantation before breakfast.

'Well,' she said, waiting for the old man to speak. 'I call Marmeduke. You go'n be ready to ride before breakfast? It gettin' hot soon enough.'

'Huh?' Hayes shook his head. 'Mayhap I'll go tomorrow. You take care of them things.'

'Yes, massa.' She poured a rum from the decanter. 'I put dis here,' she said, placing the cup within reach on the bedside table. 'Case you need it.'

She backed out of the room while Hayes watched her with a bemused expression. She had got her own way again.

She walked out to the balcony and gazed across the plantation. Birds chirped in the flamboyant trees at the front of the house. Slaves strolled quietly along the main path. There was an air of tranquillity at Roxborough that pleased her. Yet it was a fragile peace. One day Massa Hayes might get out of control and introduce his old regime of senseless brutality. Or he might die.

'Watchin' yuh niggers?' Tita rounded the corner of the balcony and sneered at her. Laura held her skirt and she carried young Hayes cradled in her arms.

'Dey mah da's slaves, Mammy Tita. Dey ain' Miz Ella's,' Laura said indignantly.

'Yo' right, chil'.' Tita beamed. 'Dey ain' she own, she jes' t'inkin' dat.'

Laura shook her fist at Ella. 'Silly black bitch!' she said. 'Ah go'n beat yo' fuh dat.'

Ella's spirits sank. The child was six. Her mother never liked her and she had been brought up by Tita. Carlton ignored her and her only influence other than Tita, was old Hayes. He regaled her with stories of slave thrashings, instilling in her foolish mind the attitude that slaves were the enemy. She had a twisted face, a permanent pout of petulance, and a parchment white skin.

'Yo' can have yuh helper,' said Ella. 'Massa Hayes tell me chose one for yo'.'

'Ah done tell yo' a'ready, ah . . .'

Ella clenched her fists to keep her temper in check. 'I wouldn't force any slave to work wid yo', Tita. Yo' can chose yuh own. Jes' keep young Hayes from cryin' an' wakin' de Massa.'

Laura let go of Tita's skirt and ran forward. She pummeled Ella's thighs with her fists. 'Yo' a wanton hussy!' she screamed.

'Where yo' learn such words, chil'?' Ella stooped and seized Laura by her wrists. She felt sorry for the little girl because of the dreadful things she saw and heard under Tita's tutelage.

'Let go of me, yo' black cunt.'

Ella squeezed Laura's wrists with shock. At that moment, Hayes shuffled on to the balcony.

'Grandda'!' Laura shrieked, seeing him first. 'She hurtin' me. Stop de wicked wench beatin' me, please, grandda'.'

'Ella!' Hayes's voice was thick with anger. 'Don't ever lay a hand on that child.' He glanced around him. Tita started to cry and the baby joined in.

Ella released Laura. The girl ran to Hayes and wrapped her arms around the old man's knees.

'She say she go'n take down mah knickers an' beat mah bum, grandda'. Ain't it wicked for a nigger to beat a white lady?'

Hayes hugged Laura and walked with her to his chair. Ella saw he was furious from the way he clenched his jaw. If she spoke he would feel challenged. She hung her head contritely, praying that Tita wouldn't speak and aggravate him further.

'There, there,' he said, smoothing Laura's hair as she began to clamber up his legs to his arms. 'No one's going to beat you.'

'Wha' yo' go'n do to Ella?' Laura asked between her tears.

Ella was stunned. It was as if Tita was controlling the child and putting the words of viciousness into her mouth.

Hayes was frowning.

'Ella don't like Laura and young Hayes,' said Tita, bursting into fresh tears to show how she had been wronged.

Ella threw up her hands in despair and marched off the balcony not deigning to look at Tita. Alas, it seemed to her that there would never be tranquillity at Roxborough while that wench was in the house.

CHAPTER NINE

'The breeding of slaves is a business in the same way that growing sugar is a business,' Carlton said, pounding his fist into the palm of his hand. He strode one length of the chamber, swung around and paced the floor for another length.

'There are differences, I agree.' He nodded his head as though his listener had dared to interrupt.

'I have to wait longer for my profits than from sugar. D'you know, Grosvenor, it takes twelve years to raise a slave until he is productive and ready for sale? No other domestic animal takes so long before it's profitable. Who keeps a cow for twelve years before it gives milk?'

He glanced down at the man perched uncomfortably on the edge of the chaise longue. Grosvenor was head of the English merchant house in St John's that was associated with the Colquhorns, the agents in London for Dominica. It was a tenuous connection and Carlton was not impressed with Grosvenor. He was the kind of man he detested but he needed someone to handle his business in the island.

'I intend to build up a herd of prize negroes, Grosvenor, that will be sought throughout the Caribbees, and paid for handsomely too. I've started the breeding. Now, while the whelps are growing, I'm going to England.'

'Er . . . yes, sir.' Grosvenor looked startled by the sudden silence. He wriggled his shoulders under the heavy English coat of brown that he was wearing despite the heat. In his hand he clutched a handkerchief that he used frequently to mop the sweat off his brow.

Carlton stared at him with undisguised contempt. The man's hair was greasy and dull, his complexion blotchy, his stomach bloated and he had the stench of degeneration about him. He wore spectacles and Carlton wondered if he could see through them or whether they were an affectation.

'How long have you been living in Antigua?' he asked roughly.

'Fi . . . five years, sir.'

'You came from England five years ago?' Carlton was amazed. 'Ever taken off your coat? Ever walked along the shore with your shirt off? Grosvenor, old chap, you must adapt if you don't want to die here. Keeping English habits is the way to expiry in tropic zones.'

Grosvenor flushed. 'I am the chief representative of an old established company. I must keep up appearances.'

'What about me? Is my appearance worse than yours?' Carlton thumped his chest. He was dressed in a cotton shirt and breeches with polished boots. He was tanned by the sun, muscular, and moved with the agility of perfect fitness.

'What's your age, man?'

'Twenty-six, sir.'

'By the devil, you're younger than me but you look forty. Relax, man. Find a mulatto mistress, drink fine grog, ride in the countryside. Live a little.'

Grosvenor sniffed. 'If you'll excuse me, sir. I find your tone off . . . offensive. Mrs Grosvenor has three children, two very sickly. My pay is small, sir. I am not a planter, and life here is very hard.'

'Quite so.' Carlton beamed as he discovered the man's weakness. 'In a manner of speaking, you would not despise some extra income, old chap, would you?'

Grosvenor coughed.

'Good. I thought we would reach an understanding. Most planters ship sugar to England, right?'

The man nodded. Carlton was standing with his back to the open window where he could watch Grosvenor's face as the light fell on it. From his dealings with slaves, he learned to watch for the flicker of eyelashes or the throb of a vein in the neck, as signs of what a slave was thinking. Grosvenor was no different.

'If someone wanted to ship livestock to England, it would be unusual and could present a problem, right?'

'Not really, sir.' Grosvenor did not flinch, thinking he was on familiar ground. The possibility of a bribe had perked him up.

'It's unusual, yes. They would have to be chained on deck. Provision animals – pigs and chickens that are slain on the voyage to give fresh food for the passengers and crew – are transported in such a manner.'

'Indeed?' Carlton arched his eyebrow. 'I'm not having my slaves chained on deck. I want a cabin for them. They are to travel in comfort, sir, not below decks like Africans in the Middle Passage.'

Grosvenor stood up, fiddled with his handkerchief, glanced around the room as though seeking an escape, and sat down again. Caspar, who had been regarding him from the open door of his own room, came forward with a tray.

'Some punch, sir?'

Grosvenor shook his head.

'Drink it, man. It's dam' good. The boy mixes the best rum punch in the islands. Learned from my own father.'

Grosvenor wilted under Carlton's glare. He took a glass and sipped. 'It's impossible,' he said, shaking his head.

'Nonsense!' Carlton was irritated by the little man. He had expected this reaction. The idea of slaves traveling in a cabin in the manner of fare-paying passengers was intolerable to whites. Carlton would probably have felt the same if he didn't have a reason for his odd request.

'Here's what you do,' he said to Grosvenor. 'Find me a ship, an adequate one not some blackbooter's barque, that's bound for England, London in preference, with a full cargo. It can have two or more cabins but no passengers other than myself and my slaves.'

'Sir . . . ?' Grosvenor screwed up his handkerchief. 'Slaves? There's this new law about shipping slaves. Mr Wilber . . .'

'Who's shipping slaves? Passengers who are black, that's all.' He winked, which added to Grosvenor's confusion.

'The cap . . . captain, the crew, what will they think? They look forward to a lucrative voyage out of St John's. So many English ladies of noble birth . . .'

'Ballocks, Grosvenor! Go about your business. I've been here four weeks. I'd like to sail within five. You'll receive extra recompense from me for your trouble when we leave. Good day, sir.'

He turned his back and gazed out of the window over the harbor. Three ships bobbed at anchor but he took no notice of them as Caspar ushered the perspiring merchant out of the room.

There, the deed was done. It was an extraordinary risk to take not one, but three slaves with him. Yet the more he saw of Prince and Nat, who was recovering rapidly from the physical effects of his long ordeal, the more he was determined to make his scheme succeed. The problem would be getting Captain Loring to part with Prince.

Carlton turned when he sensed Caspar standing beside him. The boy was becoming quite the young gentleman. He wore a livery especially tailored for him by the best tailor in St John's. The tailor, who had also accoutered Carlton, was recommended by Prince.

Prince had shown an amazing knowledge of white mores, etiquette and fashions. He was invaluable. Carlton was determined to have him on the voyage. He looked down at Caspar who was grinning broadly.

'What's so funny, boy?'

'Mr Grosvenor, sir.'

He lashed out and struck Caspar across his cheek. The boy staggered back, recovered his balance, and lowered his head.

'I'm . . . sorry, massa,' he said.

'Sorry because you're hurting?' Carlton clucked his tongue. Caspar was learning fast. He no longer cried when he was hit but bit back his tears and apologized. Carlton gripped his shoulder and crouched down in front of him.

'I've got Ella to thank for giving me such a lively whelp, eh, Caspar?'

The boy nodded his head while his cheek flamed red.

'You're an intelligent youngster, so why do you laugh when you see someone who isn't? Especially when he's white.'

'I don't understand, sir.'

'It's simple. Mr Grosvenor may be stupid but he's white and he's going to be useful. It's not your place to mock your betters.'

'Yes, Mas Carlton.' Caspar's lips twitched.

'Don't get sulky, boy! Always have a bright smile on your face, however moody you feel inside. A smile is a slave's main asset, his sign of quality. White teeth framed by a black skin can charm the most irate master.' Carlton paused, his eyes twinkling. 'Or mistress.'

Satisfied that he had explained the difference in a smile of servility and a grin of mockery, Carlton released Caspar. During the weeks they had lived together in the lodging house, he had grown aware of his qualities. Ella had indeed given him a worthwhile whelp. He was responsive to his whims, eager to help and to learn. In time, he could make a stout breeder. That gave Carlton an idea.

'Hey, boy,' he said. 'I've never examined you, have I?'

'Like yo' does de wenches, sah?' Caspar's shock made him lapse into dialect.

'Ah go'n beat yo' like ah does de slaves, if yo' speak dat way wid me!' Carlton mocked the easy rhythms of slave speech.

Caspar flushed at his mistake. 'I'm sorry, sir.'

'Well, strip off your britches, then.' He sat in the chair by the window and opened his legs. Caspar rolled down his tight silk breeches, pulled them off and placed them tidily on the *chaise longue.*

'Shirt too,' said Carlton, pleased by his initial sight of the boy's body.

Caspar folded the shirt and placed it beside his breeches. He was barefoot and padded over to Carlton to stand naked before him. Carlton put his hands on his buttocks and pulled him so he was positioned between his legs.

'Hmm,' he said, sniffing. 'No musky smell. You wash regular, boy?'

'Oh, yes, massa. Mam very particular 'bout that.'

'More than whites, eh, Caspar? You could smell last Michaelmas on Grosvenor.'

Caspar tried not to laugh.

'That's all right, boy. I made the joke so you can laugh. It ain't your place to do the same thing. You know what I'm going to do?'

'Finger me, sir?'

'Why?'

Caspar licked his lips. 'To see if I'm pleasin'?'

'Hah! Mayhap you're right. You ain't a breeder yet, anyway. Now my first glance of you is important. It tells me if you look healthy and pleasant. You do. You've a fine color, sort of dark yellowish because you have my blood and Ella's mixed together. That's a good combination. Your mam is the finest stock, pure Batutsi.'

'Like Nat?'

Carlton nodded, absorbed in studying Caspar's body. He passed his hands over his chest, tweaking his tiny nipples. 'Pectorals well formed.' He punched his stomach. 'Flat and hard.' He pinched his thighs. 'Strong and muscular.' He smiled.

'Now let's see the prick.' He grasped Caspar's penis. 'Kind of thin yet, boy, though you have the length to rut so the seed don't slip out.' He fingered the end, drawing back the prepuce between his fingers and thumb while his other hand and knees held Caspar steady. The boy was tingling with excitement.

'It'll fatten, boy. You mustn't feel 'shamed. It's natural to be proud of such a fine body. Let people see it. Aha!' He felt the penis stiffening in his hand. 'The sap's flowing.'

He rolled Caspar's tiny testicles in his fingers and bounced them in his hand. Caspar buckled at his knees with the pain and Carlton had to pull him upright. 'Balls dropped. Turn around.'

He fingered Caspar's rounded buttocks, pleased by their tautness, not loose and droopy like a white boy. 'Touch your toes.'

Caspar hesitated so he helped him with a push. He spread his buttocks and poked his finger inside. It was tight. 'No piles,' he pronounced as Caspar lurched forward and sprawled on the floor at his feet.

The door opened and Gwen walked in. Carlton leaned back in his chair, enjoying the astonishment in the wench's eyes. She clasped her face with both hands and blushed. The reddening of her dusky cheeks struck him as very appealing.

'Beg pard'n, sir,' she said, not knowing where to look. 'I thought you had gone out . . .'

'Shut the door, Gwen.'

'Yes, yes.' She was flustered and welcomed the distraction. She pushed the door closed and peeked at Caspar. He was standing up, quite unabashed, to retrieve his clothes. 'I didn't know . . .'

'Didn't know what, Gwen?'

She gasped and he guessed what it was she was too shy to say.

'By old horny!' He slapped his knees with delight. 'You thought I was going to bugger the boy!'

He bellowed with laughter until an image of Captain Loring flashed into his mind and he stopped suddenly. He grit his teeth and his eyes hardened.

'I came to see if the maid has cleaned your room,' said Gwen, breaking the awkward silence.

'Aye, I suppose she has.' He waved Caspar to his room to dress.

'I breed slaves, Gwen. That one is going to be a fine buck when his sap is stronger.' He was intrigued to see her blushing again.

'You have a beau?' he asked.

'No beau, Mas Carlton . . .' Her words hung in the air.

'What . . .?' He felt himself reddening too, as though she could read his thoughts.

'You're a fine filly . . .'

She stiffened. 'I'm not a slave. You can't strip me down and finger me. I'm a free mulatto of respectable virtue.' Her bosom heaved, threatening to burst out of the confines of the fragile cambric of her corsage.

'Indeed?' Carlton grinned broadly. 'It's been my experience that when a wench protests about her virtue, her skirt will be raised soon afterward.'

Gwen didn't flush this time, but her eyelashes fluttered like the wings of a humming bird hanging over a flower. There was a tension in the room. Neither of them moved.

Carlton let his eyes feast on her. She was a proud female and held herself well. She had child-bearing hips with the full breasts and high bottom of her negro mother. Her eyes were the sultry brown typical of her kind and she was raven haired. She dressed more stylishly than her position as a housekeeper required.

Her lips parted expectantly as she returned his gaze.

'Well, I'll be damned,' he said, leaping out of the chair. He put his arms around her waist and pulled her to him. She leaned her head back to be kissed.

'No, Gwen, it's not like that.' He lifted her off the floor and carried her to the bed. 'I've got something better for you than wet kisses.'

He dropped her into the center of the mattress and clambered on the bed beside her. He was wearing his boots and they rucked up the coverlet.

In his haste he failed to notice her mood change. The pucker of anticipation became a pout of disappointment. She rolled away when he tried to put his hand under her skirt.

'Mas Carlton,' she said firmly. 'Not that.'

'Come here, wench. I know what you want. No means yes, don't it?'

'Maybe.' She thrust herself nimbly to the other side of the bed, out of his reach, and stood up. He was left grasping at nothing.

'I told you I'm virtuous. I'm a woman, not a slave.' She smoothed down her dress while he gasped, too stunned to be angry.

'I'm sorry,' she said, her voice deepening with a sudden flood of emotion. 'I'm not a harlot, you see.'

'By the devil's balls!' He sat up and drew his knees to his chest clasping them with both hands. He felt oddly exhilarated. 'I ain't been refused before.' He chuckled, his eyes on her panting breasts, knowing – even more than Gwen herself – how much she wanted him.

'You've got mettle, girl. You lead me on . . .'

'Oh!' She was close to tears. 'Don't you understand? I'm not a ten-bit whore or an easy lay because I'm a half-breed. I've got feelings the same as any white woman.'

'Like a white woman?' He was outraged. 'What feeling is that? It's shameful for a white woman to have a fire burning between her legs, craving for a man to tend it! White ladies are bred proper, they don't feel like you unless they're whores.'

'Perhaps that's why I don't want to.' She stared at him helplessly.

'But you do . . .'

'Yes . . . I mean no. Don't you see?' She bit her tongue. 'I'm attracted to you, Mas Carlton. You're handsome and dashing and I think you're a little lonely and I could share love with you. But not like this.' She gestured at the rumpled bedclothes.

'I see.' He stood up, smacking his lips. 'You want to be wooed. Your head's stuffed with some romantic notion. Well, you've come to the wrong man for romance, Gwen.' He glared. 'I'll have you one day, though, before I go. That's a promise.'

She rushed from the room before her tears started. He smoothed down his breeches and tucked himself back between his legs. He was surprised to find Caspar grinning at him when he looked up.

'Why you!' He lifted his arm but Caspar danced away to the other side of the bed.

'No, massa,' he laughed. 'Don't beat me. I done enjoy the lesson. Why she go, Mas Carlton?'

Caspar's smile was infectious. He scratched the back of his head and grinned too.

'That's her black and white blood quarreling. The black knows it's a pleasure, but the white thinks it's a pain.' He grunted scornfully.

CHAPTER TEN

St John's was a bustling town. The English garrison stationed in the island added to its importance as an entrepôt for goods destined for the other islands in the Caribbean.

Every day, the town's narrow streets were packed with white planters on a spree and soldiers on furlough. They mingled uneasily with the mulattoes and free blacks on the prowl and slaves hefting cargo and packages from warehouse to wagon.

Carlton picked his way carefully through the crush. Prince walked tall beside him, bowing to white acquaintances and joshing with mulattoes and blacks. He had words of encouragement for the slaves who grinned broadly in return. Meanwhile, Caspar dodged through the crowd to keep up with them.

'You behave like you're a candidate for the Assembly,' Carlton was amazed by the number of people who knew Prince.

'You've come a long way since you were my playboy slave at Roxborough.'

Prince glanced around him anxiously. 'People don't know I'm a slave here. They think I'm Clothilda's relative. She's well known.'

Carlton watched the eyes of the white men whom Prince greeted. They were amused, not offended. The women reacted in a different way. Some were shocked, or pretended to be, while others let their eyes linger on his face before lowering them to the bulge in his breeches.

By his appearance, Prince was a thoroughbred stallion, but was he a breeder? Carlton had only seen him in his fancy garb, dressed with more finesse that the English planters shrouded in brown suits and large hats. He would like to see Prince naked, to know if his physique was as good as it promised.

'Why do you laugh?' asked Prince, gripping Carlton's elbow and guiding him around a group of gossiping negro women.

'At you. The wenches seem fascinated.' He pulled his elbow free and glanced behind. Caspar was pushing through the crowd to keep up with them.

'They do?' Prince grinned, and a trio of mulatto wenches turned to stare at him. 'It must be my new coat. Clothilda likes me to be smart. I'm good for her business.'

'How's that?' Carlton's eyes missed nothing. There was a definite quickening of interest when people saw Prince.

'They go to her shop to gossip about me so they have to order new dresses. They long to know if all the tales they hear are true.'

They reached the shop. Carlton followed Prince inside while Caspar held open the door. He nodded at Clothilda who was seated by the window.

'I saw you coming,' she said. 'What a pair you and Prince make, one white, the other brown. You have all the ladies aflutter.'

Carlton would have been affronted if the remark came from anyone else. He had learned to respect Clothilda. Without her care of Nat, the African would have been lost.

'We were inseparable in our youth,' he explained, remembering those days fondly. 'I came to love Prince as a brother, not as a slave.'

'And now?' Clothilda's shrewd question probed too deep. He glanced around uncomfortably. Caspar was standing by the door and Prince was studying the bodice of a ballgown draped over a chair.

'Now?' He laughed to cover his embarrassment. 'Age changes us, doesn't it? How can Prince be my comrade now?'

'Why not? Because he's not bright in color? He's as bright as you in his head.'

'That's all right, Clo'.' Prince stepped forward and touched the dressmaker on her shoulder. 'Mas Carlton's busy. He's come to see Nat.'

'Why not?' said Carlton, raising his head to answer her. 'Because he's a slave and I'm the Bondmaster, that's why.'

'Labels.' Clothilda spat, sending the phlegm through the window into the street. 'Have you ever seen a slave like him?' She gestured at Prince and laughed. 'He should be free like you, Carlton Todd, to make his mark in the world.'

Carlton studied Clothilda, watching for a sign about her intentions. Was she serious or was she merely probing in a roundabout way to find out what he planned to do for Prince? He answered craftily.

'Isn't his liberty in your hands?'

'Not while Loring's alive,' she snapped, obviously wishing the matter closed.

'Indeed?' He stroked his chin. 'Well, there's nothing more to be done. Loring's hail and hearty. He's due in port in a few days. I hope he'll have news of Roxborough.'

He changed the subject. 'Where's Nat? I want to see how he looks now you've got him clothed.'

Prince brightened, pushing back what seemed to be on his mind. 'He's upstairs. He sleeps there with me.'

'Ain't no good to mollycoddle the boy.'

'I understand that,' said Prince. 'It's the only place we can put him. Clo's clients will see him if he's here. He's getting mighty restless.'

'Musky too, I shouldn't be surprised. About ready for a wench.' He chuckled as he followed Prince up the stairs.

Nat was on his feet when Prince pushed open the door. He bowed low with a flourish.

Carlton laughed. 'Are you making a nigger dandy out of him, too?'

'No.' Prince seemed relieved at his reaction. 'I've been teaching him to show respect for his master.'

Nat's face did not match the submissive respect his bow implied. His eyes were bright with curiosity, not humble like a slave's. He stood with his hands hanging loosely at his side, looking uncomfortable in the fine cotton shirt with full sleeves and his new pantaloons.

'I'll wager you had a problem to make him wear those togs?'

Prince nodded. 'I explained to him that females here aren't accustomed to seeing bucks naked. He must wear clothes to protect his manhood.'

'Hmm. Can he understand logic?' Carlton was intrigued. 'It's well known that an African's skin is especially suited to the sun. That's why clothes ain't necessary for a field nigger.' He stroked his chin thoughtfully.

'Yes,' he said after a while. 'You're right about protecting the boy's prick. At Roxborough, I keep my colts penned away from the fillies until I'm ready to pair 'em off to breed. He showing signs yet?'

Prince looked blank.

'Come on, Prince. You can tell if he's lively enough for a filly now he's fit. Do you think he's a breeder?'

'I couldn't say.'

Carlton was about to tell Nat to strip off his clothes when a thought occurred to him. 'What about you, Prince? How many whelps have you sired?'

'None!' Prince stepped back in horror.

'None? What answer is that? We're the same age, you and I. I have a daughter and a son by my dead wife, there's Caspar here, and his mam has another in her belly plus I don't know how many whelps in the Paddock. You can tell me what you've sired.'

Prince was staring open mouthed. This puzzled Carlton.

Nat glanced from one to the other and pawed the floor restlessly.

'No whelps, Prince?' Carlton was disappointed. For him, a negro's privileges were justified by the number of children the nigger sired.

The banning of the slave trade between British colonies, thanks to the activities of some meddlesome individuals in England, had recently become law. It was because of the demand for slaves created by this ban, that Carlton ran his breeding venture to produce island-born stock. As long as there was sugar, all the Caribbean islands needed a local supply of slaves.

Sophisticated societies like the wealthy planters in Antigua, also needed house boys, valets, coachmen. The demand for bright-skinned slaves – Fancies – who could be trusted and were pleasing to look at, had to be met too.

At Roxborough, Carlton concentrated on rearing stock for field work. His stay in Antigua had shown him the potential for Fancies as well. Prince was an ideal stud to put to his light-skinned females.

'I'll give you a chance to sire whelps,' he said suddenly.

Prince's carefree face screwed up with concern. He opened his mouth to speak, then shut it quickly.

'It's all right. You don't have to thank me, Prince. I'll make an offer to Loring he won't refuse. With your style, you'd produce whelps that would be real fancies. Yes, boy!'

'I can't!' Prince gulped and moved closer to the watchful Nat, as though the African would help him.

'Can't? By the devil, something ails you?' Carlton's temper, always eager to trigger to anger, was dangerously close to firing.

'I'm in love, Mas Carlton. I want to be married if Captain Loring frees me.'

'Marriage? No, I say no! What right have you to think like a white man? You are a nigger, a slave! Your duty is obedience to your master.'

'I'm sorry, Mas Carlton. In Antigua, we live differently from Roxborough. I mean no disrespect.'

Nat was behaving oddly. He was shifting his weight from one foot to the other, his hands clutching at his chest.

'What's wrong with the *bozal*?' Carlton was distracted by Nat's fidgeting.

'He wants to speak,' said Prince.

'Can he?'

'Yes, very well. The buckra who owned him in Africa told him never to speak unless he was spoken to first.'

Carlton grinned. 'Damned sensible idea. Wish some slaves I know were like that.' He looked pointedly at Caspar.

The boy pretended not to notice.

'Let's see what he has to say?'

Prince nodded at Nat.

'Sah . . .' Nat began nervously. 'Buckra, master, I'm yours.'

He fell to his knees in front of Carlton and laid his head on the floor. His hands grasped Carlton's legs and tugged at his boot.

Seeing no menace in Nat's gesture, Carlton rested his hand on Caspar's shoulder and let the African raise his foot into the air. He laid it on his neck, twisting it with his hands.

'By the devil! Does he want me to grind his head into the floorboards?' Carlton yanked back his foot and regained his balance.

'Get him up off the floor!'

'He's only showing you obeisance, Mas Carlton.'

'I'll show him the toe of my boot in his rump if he tries that again.' Carlton's glare confused Nat who stood up and hung his head forlornly.

'Now you've upset him.'

'The devil I have!'

Carlton did not know why he was so angered by Nat's gesture. He wanted obedience from his slaves, yet the African's meek dependence disgusted him.

'What he did is a compliment where he comes from.'

'Dammit! You must teach him our ways, Prince.' He pulled open the door. He was badly shaken and needed fresh air. He hurried down the stairs, followed by Caspar.

Prince wanted to run after him but Nat held him back. 'I'm sorry.' He sounded perplexed. 'I offended the master.'

Prince sucked in air between his teeth, making a sound that expressed his exasperation. It sounded like *chupes*.

'Don't worry about him. He's a moody bugger.'

Nat's brows furrowed.

'It doesn't matter.' Prince shrugged his shoulders. He had spent many years in the company of whites, especially women who suffered at their husband's hands.

'White men aren't logical,' he said, sitting on the bed and motioning for Nat to sit beside him.

'You must not expect them to behave like you or I. Whites can't think properly. Maybe they have a missing seed somewhere. That's why they're white.'

'Please explain.' Nat touched his knee.

'White people aren't the same as us.' Prince lay back on the bed, linking his fingers behind his head. 'They don't have whatever it is that makes us black. That's why they do things an odd way round. It makes them very difficult to live with.'

He smiled ruefully as he recalled some of the women he had known and how he had suffered as a result of their moods.

'In my tribe, white means Death.' Nat lay beside Prince. 'Here I see dead men all the time.'

Prince shuddered at Nat's tone. 'Don't ever tell Mas Carlton that. He'll say he's death himself because he has your life in his hands.'

'Don't be scared of him, or of any white man. They can only do what you want them to do.'

'White men brought me here.'

'Yes.' Prince closed his eyes, unwilling to talk anymore.

The morning was hot. The murmur of people moving along the street, clinging to the sides of houses to keep in the shade and to avoid the wagons trundling over the rough cobbles, was soporific. He did not sleep well at nights. In the evenings he stayed at Lindsey's Rooms wagering a few pistols at Hazzard until the early hours.

His frustration was caused by Gwen. Many women made it obvious to him that they welcomed his attention, but he had no interest in them. There was only Gwen.

He wondered why she was ignoring him. It had never happened

before. She seemed resolute in her determination to have nothing to do with him.

He besieged her at the lodging house, followed her up and down corridors, begging her to return to her senses. His persistence resulted in Mistress Nesbit banning him from the premises except when he was there at Mas Carlton's bidding.

He had lain in wait for her when she went to the market, pleading with her in the street until she threatened to make such a scene, he had to slink away in shame. He had apologized, explained, done everything he could think of to win back her favor. It was no use.

If he knew what was wrong, he felt sure he could succeed. Gwen gave him no hint, merely saying 'You know.' Yet, from that hurt look in her eyes, he knew she was still keen on him.

'Prince . . .' Nat's voice broke into his thoughts. The African's head was on his chest.

'Sorry, Nat. I was thinking.'

'Why are you troubled?'

Chupes. 'It's nothing.'

'A female has done this to you?' Nat's hand closed over Prince's crotch, squeezing him.

He was hard and wriggled uncomfortably at Nat's touch.

'Yes.' Prince frowned. Nat's eyes were on his, watching him.

'I have never known a female.'

'What?' Prince jerked away from Nat so his hand wouldn't rouse him so much. 'I thought in Africa . . .'

'We are honorable! I was being saved for my first wife.' Nat's hand returned to Prince's thigh and stroked him.

Prince rolled away, anxious not to offend the African. 'We don't do that here,' he said gently. He yawned.

'I'm damned if I know what's wrong with Gwen. When Loring arrives, he must give me my freedom! I want to marry that woman . . .'

Prince didn't notice the look of resolve that entered Nat's eyes as he closed his own in sleep.

CHAPTER ELEVEN

It fascinated Carlton to sit by the window of his chamber and watch the activity in the harbor below him. The afternoon was not the time to walk the streets of St John's, at least not until sunset when the air was cooler. There were some in Antigua who were disappointed in him for not gallivanting in the manner expected of visiting planters. Instead of frequenting the taverns and brothels, he was content to spend the time in his chamber, either preparing for the voyage to England, or in quiet contemplation.

Sometimes, his thoughts were on Roxborough, and at other times on what he intended to do in England. Of course, he missed his plantation; the daily activity, the sessions drinking rum with his father on the balcony, and the nights with Ella.

Strangely, he was in no hurry to find a substitute, even a temporary one, for his old bedwench. He had been living at an extraordinary pace for years, allowing things to happen that should not have happened, so he welcomed this period of inactivity while he waited for the vessel that would take him and Caspar to England.

He heard his door open slowly, but made no move to turn. He was watching the commotion around the schooner that had recently arrived. A score of blacks were gathered on the wharf, unloading its cargo in great haste as though in fear of the vessel's captain. He smiled to himself, his ears alert as someone moved toward his chair.

'Gwen?'

'I thought you were asleep.' She blushed as he raised his head and appraised her.

'Is that why you came creeping in like a slave about to murder me?'

'No, Mas Carlton.' Gwen looked shocked. 'I wanted to see you.'

He sensed her distress and was amused by it. 'Can't keep away, eh? Now all the house is asleep after dinner, what better time to sport, eh?' He made a grab for her waist and she stepped away.

'Aha! You've still got your tricks. A little game before we tussle?' His mockery was born out of anger. If she wanted him to bed her, why didn't she let him get on with it? What right had she to toy with him?

'I was hoping for your advice, Mas Carlton.' She stood just out of reach, by the window, glancing around the room. Caspar was in his own chamber, asleep.

'Advice, you call it, Gwen? My advice is to stop pretending and come and sit on my knee.'

'Please, Mas Carlton.'

The plaintive note in her voice penetrated his rising desire. He peered at her. 'By old horny, Gwen, what's this? Not tears already.'

'I don't know what to do . . .' She clutched her bosom and he wondered how much of this was an act to win his attention. He waited, his eyebrow raised quizzically.

'It's Prince,' she said, blurting out his name in a rush. 'He won't leave me alone.'

'Not surprised.' He sat back, no longer interested. 'His instincts are sound.'

'I don't want him. He's got so many women. I'm the laughing stock of the town.'

'Seems to me you put a dam' sight too much importance on yourself, girl.'

'I thought you'd understand, since he's your friend.'

'Friend?' Carlton snorted. 'I'm only renting him. He ain't my slave yet.'

'Slave?' Gwen put her hand to her cheek and took a step back. 'He's not a slave . . .'

'Isn't he? What's that black rakehell been telling you? He's a slave all right. Used to be mine until my father sold him to Captain Loring. Look.' He pointed out of the window.

'That's Loring's ship down here. As soon as I see the captain, I'm going to buy back that buck.' He ignored Gwen's outburst of sobbing.

'Be the best thing to happen to that dandy. Get him under control again.' He tightened his lips with satisfaction.

Prince's attitude had shocked him. It was difficult to understand that a slave, and a Roxborough slave at that, had become so corrupted that he imagined himself entitled to the privileges of whites.

Marriage, Prince had said. The idea was outrageous.

Slowly, Gwen's sobs registered on his mind. He turned away from the window. She no longer stood meekly in front of him but had sunk to the bed. She was crying shamelessly, her hands covering her face.

'Is it you he wants to marry?' He strode across the room and raised his hand to strike her. 'For the devil's sake, stop that row!'

She uttered such a cry of despair that Carlton hesitated. He sat down beside her. Despite his annoyance, he put his arm around her shoulder. She didn't flinch and pull away as he expected.

'Cheer up, wench,' he said gruffly. 'Is any man worth such a racket?'

When she raised her face to him and he saw the tears on her cheeks, he was surprised how close her lips were to his. Her lower lip trembled like a fluttering moth and he was seized with an urge to crush it.

He opened his mouth and leaned over her, placing his lips on hers. He gripped her head behind her neck so she couldn't escape. He pressed against her, driving his tongue into her mouth. She quivered, then her hands grabbed his back and she clung to him passionately.

Without a word, he lay her on the pillow and kissed her again, violently, punishing her until he, too, felt the pain. She bit his tongue, drawing blood, and she sucked on it until he shivered with the shared agony.

He tore at her bodice, ripping open the corsage and mangling her breast in his hands. She squirmed beneath him, bucking her body to meet his, writhing with the anguish tearing through her.

He felt the tremors as she lay under him and fought her with the same strength. Her dress was in tatters, and he tugged it away from her until she was naked. Her body, the color of fine cognac, gave off a bouquet of musk that sent his desire soaring. He tore open his breeches and fell on her.

He wondered if she had ever known such loving. He teased her with his fingers and tongue until she was shrieking with ecstacy, begging for release. He ground into her with a fury that set her weeping. Yet she matched him kiss for kiss and blow for blow. She had movements that pitched him to heights he had never known, thrilling him with an extraordinary feeling of mastery even at the point where he was totally out of control.

They rolled in a flurry of torn clothes, bed sheets and coverlets, from one side of the bed to the other. There was a despair about their coupling, a fear that it would end and that it would not end. Each played with the other, aware of the nuances of the other's passion, determined to extend it out of spite, not consideration for the other's feelings.

Time no longer mattered. The first rush rose to a prolonged encounter that neither would concede. They were so absorbed, neither saw Caspar fling himself on the *chaise longue* to mimic their thrusts with his own young body.

Gwen's legs were entwined around Carlton and he was lodged so deep inside her, only submission could separate them. Their rhythm rose again and again to that point and each time they paused to begin again.

He pounded into her with the enthusiasm raised by several weeks of abstinence. He was determined to punish her and to show her that no man – certainly not Prince, a slave – could better him.

He was not privy to her thoughts but her body exposed her base instinct and yearning. With perfect understanding of each other's need, the frenzy came to an end with a crescendo of yelps and shouts and a flurry that had the heavy mahogany bed skittering across the floor.

Caspar fell off the couch with a groan.

'Bravo!'

The shout, repeated much louder and followed by a cackle of raucous laughter, penetrated Carlton's bemused brain. He was exhausted. His shoulders were bloody where the wench's fingers had raked his skin. His breeches hung in shreds around his boots. He was still inside the woman as he twisted his head to see who was shouting.

'Bravo!' Loring clapped his hands. 'A devil's ride, in truth. Couldn't do better meself.' He swaggered across the room, unbuckling his belt.

'I'll try, by old horny, I'll try. Come on, young Todd, haul up yer anchor from that mooring or I'll have to ride yer ass instead.'

Carlton was dismayed as Loring advanced on him from the open door of the chamber. He shrank with surprise and twisted away from Gwen. She shrieked, but he didn't comprehend why at the time. He was hampered by his torn breeches binding his ankles together. When he lunged at Loring, he fell flat on his face to the floor.

Captain Loring paused in the center of the room with his own breeches pulled down to his thighs and his scab-encrusted penis in his hand. He roared with laughter as Carlton scrambled to his feet. He pulled himself with anticipation, his huge belly shaking and tears of mirth streaming down his cheeks.

Gwen sought refuge under the tangled pile of bed clothes, glancing with horror from the vile Captain Loring guffawing as he massaged himself, to Prince, his mouth agape with astonishment, standing in the doorway.

It was Caspar who made the first move. He leaped up from the floor behind the couch and dived, with head down, straight for Loring's crotch. His shoulder walloped the big man's testicles and Loring doubled up in agony.

Prince, venting his anger on Loring, attacked the Captain from behind. He kicked him squarely in the buttocks so he sprawled face down on the floor with a shout of pain. Carlton rolled across and smashed his fist into his jaw.

There was a strident cry from the door. Mistress Nesbit stood with her arms akimbo, staring at the melee. 'Gwen,' she said aloofly. 'Where the hell's my afternoon tea? I've been ringing the bell for five minutes.'

'Sorry, Mistress.' Gwen snatched up the velvet coverlet and wrapped it around her. 'I'll bring it come straight away.'

Mrs Nesbit sniffed with disdain and swept away from the goings on in the room.

'Gwen . . .' Prince reached out both arms to hold her.

'It ain't my fault, Prince. You do it too.'

'No I don't! Not since Helen left.'

'You lie. I heard you.'

Prince looked baffled. 'When?'

'The night you said you had to unload the rum.'

'Not me.'

'Yes. In your room. I came to Clothilda's to look for you. I heard you and a woman in bed. You can't blame me.' She pulled the coverlet tighter.

Prince looked stunned. 'That wasn't me. That was Clothilda and Loring. Ask him.'

Captain Loring was sitting up on the floor, rubbing his jaw. Carlton had pulled up his torn breeches and was waiting to thump Loring another blow. He was still shaken at the interruption.

Gwen glanced at Carlton and blushed but it was her anger at Captain Loring that stirred her. She turned on Prince.

'Why didn't you come sooner? she said. 'This wouldn't have happened – '

Prince took her gently in his arms, kissing her forehead. He tightened his embrace and guided her out of the room.

'Get up, Loring,' said Carlton, recovering in time to assert himself over the captain before he got his breath. 'You've caused a hell of a mess.'

Loring grabbed the side of the bed and eased himself to his feet. He glared at Caspar as the boy scurried out to his own room. 'Yer've got a terror, there, young Todd.' He wheezed, his face red.

Carlton held his fists bunched loosely at his sides when Loring weaved to the *chaise longue* and flopped down on to it. He was snorting and blowing like a beached whale and it was moments before Carlton realized he was choking with laughter, not rage.

'Ain't as young as I was,' he spluttered, rubbing his crotch. 'By Neptune's ballocks, that was worth it. Never seen a pair of niggers rutting like yer did with that wench. Fair raised me old anchor watchin'.'

'What do you want?' Carlton stared at him bleakly. He was longing for news of Ella but it didn't seem so important any more.

'What do I want?' Loring stopped shaking and returned Carlton's glare. 'A shoot of rum will do for a start.'

'Caspar.' Carlton's shout brought no reaction. He strode over to the door and flung it open. 'What are you doing, boy?'

Caspar was standing with a tray in his hand, and the decanter and two glasses on it. 'Coming, sir,' he said hesitantly. 'Don't let Captain Loring touch me.'

'No, I won't son.' He marched back across the room followed by Caspar who glanced nervously at Loring.

Caspar placed the tray on a table close to where the Captain was sitting and backed out of the room. Carlton noticed he left the door open so he could hear what was being said.

Loring poured a large measure, sniffed the rum first, then drained it down his throat. He wiped his beard. Carlton needed a drink just as badly but he took his time over it, swallowing it slowly and relishing the strength the fierce brew brought back to his weak limbs.

The two men stared at each other in silence and Carlton got the impression that Loring was measuring him for some kind of contest. He had a right to demand respect from the captain but the nature of the man was against it. Instead he curbed his impatience and waited.

Loring smacked his lips and took a deep breath. 'When I makes a deal, young Todd, generally I keeps ter it. If it's a fair deal and I'm not being a-swindled.' He paused. 'If I'm a-swindled, then I considers there ain't no deal.'

'What the devil are you talking about?'

'Don't put on yer sweet little boy face with me, young Todd. I know yer for a schemin', thievin' nigger trader. Yer'd buy low and sell high from yer own father, but yer ain't doin' that with Captain Lorin'.'

'What do you mean? Did you see my father?'

'Sure did. The old man's guzzlin' Roxbro' rum like a good'un. He's put down a puncheon for yer return. Told him yer has a nigger for him, I did.'

Carlton frowned. Something was wrong.

'Mighty interested in that nigger, old Hayes was. So was that black wench of yer'n who keeps for him. They tell me ye're mighty skilled in niggers. The wench – Ella? that's right. Nice rump on her. She say yer only buy the best so that nigger yer a-swindled from me bound ter be somethin' special. She set me thinkin'.' Loring stopped to refill his glass.

Carlton knew he was expected to say something, but he didn't. He gazed out of the window at Loring's schooner, wondering how soon Grosvenor would find him a ship for England. He wanted to be far away from the West Indies, and the filthy whites – the dregs of civilization – who peopled the islands.

'Young Todd, I hear yer have a plan ter ship that nigger ter England. Don't look surprised. I've been here more years than yer've had connies, boy. I know everything. I know that that blackie's a Royal Tootsie or some such. I know Red Delawney reckoned he'd sell for ten hundred. I know yer a-swindled that boy from me!'

Loring's eyes blazed with a rage that would have cowered a whole quarter deck. Carlton returned his stare, feeling the anger rip through him.

'I value my son Caspar at ten thousand, Loring. You've had all you'll ever get from me for that nigger or any other.'

Loring rose and threw his glass against the wall where it smashed, showering the room with splinters. 'I'm goin' ter break yer like that, young Todd,' he said, walking easily across the floor to the door. 'My men will be takin' that nigger back and there ain't nothin' yer can do 'bout it.'

'I'll have you thrown in jail.'

'What the hell for?' Loring guffawed.

'You stole one of my slaves.'

'What do yer mean?'

'Fourteen years ago, you struck a deal with my father for my playboy. You took Prince and promised to pay half the profit you made out of him. I'm claiming that debt now.' He advanced toward Loring.

'I want Prince.'

'Over my dead body, young Todd!' Loring laughed and sauntered out of the room.

CHAPTER TWELVE

Nat was in a trance. He hunkered on the floor by the open window. It was night and beyond the roof of the house opposite, the sky was alive with stars, each one sparkling like the eyes of his ancestors. He gazed at them, drawing strength. Below in the street, a wagon clattered on its way to the harbor. The shout of a passerby to the wagoner did not distract his concentration.

He delved back in his memory to the time when he was a child at his mother's breast, and listened with her to the white-daubed witch doctor chanting the magic words. He tried to recall them. It was too long ago. He tried instead to hear the voice of his instructor as he explained the ways of witch doctors. If only he had paid more attention! He was going to be king, a great warrior, so what need did he have of the power to perform magic and obi?

He remembered that faith was essential: if he believed, it would be. He saw in his mind his father's witch doctor, a terrifying man whose smell made people approach him with dread. He saw his face, those red-rimmed eyes peering through the awful pallor of his mask. He pleaded with those eyes – for Death.

Nat saw every white man as the same man. Their clothes, their beards, were like the witch doctor's mask: underneath they were the same. The man who had taken him in chains from the great plains was the same man who held him prisoner in his stockade. That man, Keptin, was the same one who carried him across the sea and the one with the black beard and the harsh voice was the same as them all. The black bearded one was feared by Prince, who was his friend. It was time for Death to call him.

Nat concentrated on the witch doctor's eyes. He did not know the words he must use, nor the signs he must make and the dance, ah yes, the dance was the most important of all. He swayed as he sat on his hunkers, hoping to attract the witch doctor's attention. He was naked with white paint from Clothilda's make-up box smeared on his chest in a sign similar to the witch doctor's own.

In his trance as he rocked on his heels, he saw the witch doctor's eyes flicker. He cried out to him and the man bowed his head. It will be. Nat rotated faster from his hips, sweeping his face down so it almost scraped the floor. Sweat poured off him as the music of the dance pounded through his brain, crying with each beat of the goat-skin drums: it will be, it will be!

There was a crash as a door was flung open, jolting the house. A voice bellowed gruffly and another voice, warm and friendly, answered it. The drumming ceased and Nat slowed to a halt. He opened his eyes and stared around the room in amazement. He saw the bed, the chests, the ponderous mahogany furniture and he wondered what had become of the witch doctor's hut in the savanna.

He looked up to see only the eaves of the house, hung with cobwebs, no open sky. Yet, through the window he could see the stars and he knew: it will be, it will be.

He sniffed, but even the smells had changed. The foul odor was the scent of white men; it drifted to his nostril as though he were down wind of rotting corpses. He smiled and rose to his feet. Walking softly to the door, he opened it. Loring was below.

'Where's Prince?' Loring's shout of rage made Nat hold his breath lest he be seen.

'He'll be here soon, dear.' Clothilda's soothing voice reassured Nat. He believed in her ability to resolve difficulties. Now he knew her, he understood that she wasn't a priestess but he still had respect for her powers. Prince adored her, so he did too.

'I'm taking that rascal with me.'

'Really?' Clothilda sounded anxious. Nat wished he could see what she was doing. Slowly, careful not to creak any of the stairs, he lowered himself so, by bending his head and keeping to the shadows, he could see the room below.

Loring sat with his legs thrust out in front of him in the old oak chair opposite the window. The shutters were closed and light came from a lantern hanging above the table. A large pair of scissors and the material Clothilda had been cutting for a dress, filled the table top. Clothilda stood by it and looked at Captain Loring with an expression of disapproval.

'Where are you taking him?'

'Ain't none of yer business.' Loring scratched his crotch. 'Yer won't see him again, that's for sure.'

'You gave him to me as my provider, my protector.'

'Bah! I'm takin' him back. I'll sell him, that's what.'

'You can't.' Clothilda bit her lip and looked around the room as though seeking help among the dresses and bolts of cloth.

'I can, woman!' He growled. 'Should've auctioned him in Jamaica when he was a striplin'. He'll still get a fair price. Some men like 'em older.'

'No!' Clothilda was nearly in tears. 'If you were half-way decent, you'd give him his liberty. Let him go to England. He has friends there. He'll be presented at court, he could earn royal patronage, some black folks have. He could become a great man.'

'Ye're crazy, Clotty. He's a nigger.'

'So am I!'

'Aye.' Loring tried to grab Clothilda's skirt but she stepped away quickly. 'Yer rattle like one, too. Come here, wench. If Prince ain't here, let me have yer while I waits. Sailin' with him tonight, I am.' He leered at her. 'Takin' that African with me as well.'

'Nat?' Clothilda clutched her face with shock.

'Aye. He's worth more than Prince, I reckon. Don't look so startled, Clotty. Yer should be pleased. Think what fine cloth I can buy yer with the booty those two blackies will bring.'

Nat saw Clothilda's bewilderment and he longed to rush down the stairs and hold her in his arms to comfort her. He watched Loring who was stroking his beard and feeling pleased with himself. His eye returned again to the scissors on the table, only inches from Loring's heart. He heaved a deep sigh.

Loring belched. 'Ain't yer got no grog, Clotty? Needs a little wind in me sails before I boards yer.'

'Yes, dear.'

Nat glanced at Clothilda again, puzzled by the sweetness in her voice. She was moving with determination, out of sight of Loring, to the tall wardrobe at the back of the room. He wondered why she no longer protested at Loring's plan. His eyes moved back to the scissors; he watched them longingly.

Clothilda opened the wardrobe and, from its floor, under the skirts of the dresses hanging there, she took a decanter. She raised it to the lantern then, with a quick glance at Loring, took another, much smaller, bottle from the wardrobe's depths.

She removed the stopper from the decanter, uncorked the bottle, and tipped the contents from the bottle into the decanter. She swirled the mixture around, replaced the stopper and carried the decanter across the room to Loring. There was a grim expression on her face.

Nat crouched down to wait.

'Here's a special rum I've been saving,' Clothilda said brightly, putting the decanter on a table close to Loring's elbow. 'I mixed in some brandy one of my customers gave me. She liked the dress I made for her, so much . . .'

'Glass,' growled Loring. ' 'less yer want me ter drink the decanter by its neck?'

'Oh, how silly of me.' Clothilda was flustered. She hurried out to the kitchen and returned with a glass.

'Yer not drinkin' with me, Clotty? A toast to Carlton's two niggers.'

'No.' She blushed. 'I've got colic,' she said hastily. She rubbed her abdomen and grimaced. 'Rum will set me off. It's you I want, not that.'

'Oho!' The idea pleased Loring and he beamed as he poured the drink. He held the glass up to the lantern and admired its amber sheen. He sniffed it. 'Smells powerful,' he said with a grin.

'Drink up.' Clothilda stood beside him and placed her hands on his shoulders.

Nat wondered if he could leap down the stairs and seize the scissors while Loring was distracted. He could plunge the blade into Loring's heart before the man could move. In the plains he had the speed of a lion; his spear could pierce the heart of a running antelope. He had never killed a man, but weren't these whites less than monkeys? Their skin was thin and their muscles feeble. One leap, one thrust . . .

Loring uttered a strange cry, a gasp like that of a strangled animal. Nat stared, watching his jaw drop open and his tongue, like a foul gray toad, flop out. With shaking fingers, he was clawing at his throat and his eyes bulged as though they would burst out of his head. The glass fell to the floor.

Clothilda stood at his side, clutching her cheeks in dismay. 'Oh, dear,' she said. 'What's wrong?'

Nat noticed she did nothing to help him.

Loring's head turned toward her and he seemed to be asking a question. Then he raised his eyes as Nat descended the stairs. When he saw his naked body emerging silently like a black snake from the shadows, he screeched with agony and fear. His hand smote his breast. He rolled off the chair and toppled to the floor, thrashing and writhing like a large fish with its head chopped off. Clothilda and Nat stood over him.

It will be.

'Lor'.' said Clothilda, grasping Nat's arm. 'Whoever did!'

Loring's body stopped twitching and he lay, a fat and ugly corpse, at their feet.

'I didn't know,' blabbered Clothilda. 'The brandy . . . I must have used rat poison instead.'

Nat held her, comforting her with his strength. She sobbed dryly against his chest, then withdrew her head and gazed up at him.

'It's better this way . . . for Prince.' She choked back her tears. 'Will you help me?'

'Yes.' Nat wondered how. The deed was done.

'We must hide him. Before Prince comes.'

'Where?'

She gazed around the room in panic. 'Not here, my ladies . . .'

In the great plains, there were animals and birds who devoured the bodies of the unwanted dead. Nat peered at the twisted body of Captain Loring, looking as grotesque in death as he did in life. On the voyage from Africa, the white men threw dead Africans into the sea. He smiled at Clothilda.

'It will be done,' he said calmly.

'Capital!' exclaimed Carlton when Grosvenor brought him the news.

'When do we sail?'

'Don't you want to see the vessel first? She's not the best.' Grosvenor stood in Carlton's presence and twisted the brim of his hat nervously in his fingers. His red face was already perspiring and it was not yet breakfast time.

'As long as she has a good master.' Carlton was excited. It was yesterday that Loring had come with his threats to take Nat. He should leave at once! He paced the room anxiously while Grosvenor said his piece.

'Captain Eradus is renowned for his seamanship, sir. He is considered a little eccentric and doesn't care to carry passengers, nor they to sail with him, sir.' Grosvenor began to crush his hat brim.

'Sounds just the man. I repeat, when do we sail?'

'The vessel is fully loaded. Captain Eradus says if you care to join him with your entourage, you should be on board at sunset.'

Carlton listened with half an ear while Grosvenor, in the prissy manner of a tradesman charging an exorbitant fee, detailed the work he had done and the money that had to be paid out. His mind was on other matters. He interrupted Grosvenor as soon as the final price was named.

'The mate on the vessel, is he reliable?'

Grosvenor was perplexed. 'I assume so – '

'Have him attend me at Lindsey's Rooms this morning.' He strode to the window. The vessel was not moored in the harbor. It was at a bay a mile from St John's anchored where the revenue officers would not assess it. The arrangement was perfect.

Carlton glimpsed Loring's vessel at the quay. There was no activity so he guessed Loring was ashore. There was plenty to be done.

'Caspar!' he shouted, turning around and starting with surprise when he saw Grosvenor still standing in the center of the room. 'Don't you have other business to attend to, Grosvenor? I don't want to keep you . . .'

'I know the price is a little high, sir, but there were all the special arrangements. I – '

'It's satisfactory, if you do as I say. The mate, Lindsey's Rooms! You'll be paid in full when we board this evening.' He put his arm around Grosvenor's shoulder and steered him to the door. 'I'll thank you not to mention this to anyone.'

Grosvenor nodded and scuttled out of the room. Caspar was waiting when Carlton turned back.

'We sail today. Call that wench Gwen to help you pack. I'm going to see Clothilda Harkness.'

'Captain Loring may be there, sir.'

Carlton was impressed. 'Caspar, you have a good head. Use it wisely. Do you think I overlooked that?'

Caspar was worried. 'He doesn't want you to take Nat away.'

'Exactly. If we act quickly, he won't even know until we've sailed. Your job is to attend to the packing!'

Carlton clattered down the staircase in great haste. Gwen was at the doorway to the street. She smiled at him adoringly but he brushed past her into the street without noticing. He was considering the final stages of his plan.

To outwit Loring he would have to be clever and secretive. He was lost in thought as he hurried along the street to Clothilda's. A hand touched his arm; he shook it off impatiently.

'Mas Carlton!' Prince's shout halted him. 'I've been calling you for several paces. Didn't you hear?'

'Thinking, Prince. Can't stop. Where's Loring?'

Prince grinned. 'How should I know?'

'He hasn't said anything to you?' They were at Clothilda's shop and she was leaning out of the window watching them.

'Come in, come in,' she called anxiously.

'Morning.' Carlton was gruff. 'Where's Loring?'

Clothilda hesitated for a second. 'I thought he had sailed. He isn't here.'

Carlton stepped into the shop and sat down. 'Prince, take Nat to the lodging house. Don't leave him. We're to sail this afternoon.'

'Oh!' Clothilda stood up and bustled around the room in a sudden burst of activity. 'So soon,' she said, waiting until Prince had gone upstairs to fetch Nat. 'Why don't you take Prince with you?' she whispered. 'He's a good boy. He's wasted here.'

Carlton was nonplussed. 'Nothing I'd like better. Do I have your consent?'

'Of course!'

'That's not enough, unfortunately. Loring holds the lien on him and he won't sell to me.' He frowned. There was another way.

'Clothilda.' He reached into his pocket and withdrew a purse. He pressed it into her hand. 'Please take this for caring for Nat. You made him strong again. He's not the rat we rescued from the sea.'

Clothilda's fingers closed around the purse and her eyes registered surprise at its size. She tucked it in her corsage but Prince, coming down the stairs with Nat, caught sight of it.

Carlton peered at Nat suspiciously and scratched his head. 'What happened to you, Nat? You look different.'

'He's put on weight,' Clothilda said proudly.

'No, it's his eyes. There's a sparkle to them.'

Nat nodded his head but he remained wary.

He was a fine looking creature. He wore his clothes with ease now he was accustomed to them. The cut accentuated his superb physique, the massive thighs and broad shoulders. His face had a sheen to it, the ebony of his complexion glowing as though polished. His eyes were no longer scared or shifty, they focused boldly, challenging anyone to make him lower them.

Carlton wondered what experience he had undergone that had restored his confidence. He glanced at Clothilda. She blushed under his gaze. Was it possible? Perhaps when Prince was out, she had taken Nat to her bed. He laughed.

'You'll be sorry to see him go, won't you Clothilda?'

She shrugged her shoulders but he sensed she was feigning her indifference. He smirked.

'I hope he keeps your secret,' he said, rising and heading for the door.

Clothilda gazed at him open-mouthed. He bowed.

'Have so much to do. Prince, keep Nat safe in my room until I come.' He ignored Nat's beatific grin and ducked out into the street.

He made several calls, finalizing matters. What he learned about old Captain Eradus intrigued him and he felt certain Grosvenor had chosen the right man.

It was nearly dinner time before he met the ship's mate, a humorless Scotsman with a scar down his cheek. He was a small man, cunning and cocksure. It took only minutes for Carlton to persuade him to agree to his plan. When it was settled, Carlton saw Clothilda again before returning to the lodging house.

Gwen was waiting for him. She accosted him at the head of the stairs. Her features were contorted with rage.

'You're going away!' She stood with her arms akimbo and showed no intention of letting him pass.

'I suppose the secret is all around St John's?'

'Why didn't you tell me?'

'By the devil!' He leaned on the balustrade, weary with walking in the sun and desperate for a drink. 'I'll give you thirty seconds to let me pass before I throw you down these stairs.'

'Try it!' Her eyes blazed.

He was too tired to think properly. He lunged at her only to crumple in a heap at her feet, bent up with the agony of a searing pain where her foot had driven into his crotch. He clutched himself while tears came to his eyes.

'I should kick you downstairs, Carlton Todd, but I won't. Have I hurt you?'

There was a sob of concern, not triumph, as she kneeled beside him. He raised his arm and she took it, helping him to his feet.

He leaned on her and then pushed her off balance. He spun her around his body and sent her tumbling down the stairs. She shrieked.

He gripped the banister and sniggered. 'At Roxbro', girl, you'd be hung upside down from the nearest branch and lashed till your hide was striped off your back.' He spluttered with rage. 'How dare you strike me!'

'I'm not your slave, Carlton Todd!' Gwen shouted back, as angry as he was. 'I'm a free woman. You can't punish me.'

He choked with amazement as she stood up and straightened her bodice. She picked up her skirt and hurried up the stairs two at a time. He darted along the corridor to his room, dashed inside and bolted the door.

CHAPTER THIRTEEN

No one told Carlton Todd what to do. He grit his teeth and glared at the horizon. The sun was descending rapidly, sheathed in clouds that hung poised over the water like puffs of smoke from the fires of runaway slaves over the Roxborough Hills.

With him in the skiff moving toward the schooner anchored in the bay, were Caspar, Prince and Nat. The puncheons of rum, their chests and their boxes had already been loaded under the eye of the mate.

Carlton stared angrily at the ship. He was still furious with Gwen. After hounding him to his chamber, she had disappeared. He expected her to besiege him until he was ready to leave, but she had gone and no one knew where, not even Mistress Nesbit. Prince tried to find her without success. Well, good riddance!

The incident upset him more than he allowed. He was finding it hard enough, without that extra worry, to retain an air of calmness in front of Nat and Prince.

The African didn't want to leave Antigua without Prince. Prince himself was determined to stay in Antigua with Gwen. Carlton persuaded him to pretend that he was sailing with them to keep Nat relaxed until they had him secured on board.

'Damn the wench!' Carlton cried aloud to the surprise of the others in the skiff. He clenched his teeth to prevent his thoughts blurting out again. No one in the skiff dared to speak while he was in such an uncertain mood.

Captain Eradus was a stout man with gray hair flopping over his ears, and a stomach that bulged over his breeches. His face was chubby and battered and he regarded Carlton with a stare devoid of emotion.

Carlton returned the glare coolly and inclined his head with the minimum of politeness. The Captain's eyes took in Caspar, Nat and Prince and he heaved a sigh that wobbled the flesh on his cheeks. He turned without a word and went below.

'We sail immediately,' announced the mate.

'I'll go now, Mas Carlton.'

Carlton ignored Prince and walked away from him. 'Caspar, bring Nat over here,' he called. Nat came obediently to the ship's side.

'Watch the sun, Nat.' He pointed to where the sun was poised above the sea on the horizon. It was a bright orange orb that was slipping out of sight, as though drowning in the sea. 'Keep your eyes on it, boy.'

Carlton put his hand on his shoulder, 'Don't blink.'

The sun dipped out of sight and there was a faint flash of green, like a sparkle from an emerald caught in a bright light.

'Mas Car – !' Prince's shout made Nat turn. Carlton's hand gripped his arm. He twisted it behind his back and up between his shoulder blades.

'Stay, Caspar!' he commanded. The boy was about to run across the deck to where four men had seized Prince and were hustling him below. The mate was following them.

'It's all right, Nat, they won't harm him.' Carlton's voice was soothing but he clung to the African until Prince was out of sight.

'We had to do that to make certain Prince comes with us,' he explained. 'He won't be hurt.'

Carlton was suspicious of Nat's passivity. If he wanted, the African could have broken free and rushed to help Prince. Yet he didn't move. He released him and Nat turned. His eyes were heavy with perception, peering right inside his mind.

'Now back off, boy.' Carlton stepped away. He had his pistols and his plantation whip but he felt inadequate beside this African giant.

'As soon as we sail, I'll release him. Loring hasn't a chance of catching us and Prince is too fancy to try to swim to St John's, even if he does love Gwen.'

How odd, he thought, that he should explain his actions to a slave. Loring had been right, he was going soft.

Nat shook his head but said nothing. His eyes held Carlton's as though the two of them were part of a conspiracy.

Caspar was jumping up and down with delight. 'I knew it,' he cried. 'I knew you'd bring Prince.'

'Shut your mouth!' Carlton hit him across his cheek, feeling easier now he had broken away from Nat's gaze.

Caspar rubbed his face and grinned. He accepted that the blow was his fault for coming within striking range when Carlton was tense.

The three of them watched the shore rapidly receding into the distance. Grosvenor, who had accompanied them to the bay to receive his commission, had departed as soon as they boarded the skiff. Carlton was puzzled by his eagerness to be gone.

Night was falling quickly as it does in the tropics. Soon not even the hills of sugar cane were visible. It was a sad moment for Carlton; his break with the Caribbean was complete.

He thought about Ella as darkness descended. Caspar, sensing his need to be alone, led Nat away.

Caspar had lots of Ella's traits. He was observant, atune to his moods and with a wisdom that belied his years.

Carlton could see Ella in his intense stare when he wanted to query orders without voicing his thoughts.

Did Ella miss him? Did slaves have human feelings?

He gazed at the sea, a mirror of shadows as the early light of the moon played on it. Oddly, at that moment, he thought of Captain Loring who spent his lifetime floating on such seas and who, in all probability, would spend his death the same way.

What would the goatish captain do when he discovered he had lost Prince and Nat together? Clothilda Harkness had repeatedly assured Carlton not to worry about Loring, but he did not know why.

No one had seen the Captain all day. Clothilda was not concerned. She helped willingly with the scheme to kidnap Prince since the boy refused to leave Antigua. She packed a chest with his clothes and hid her tears so that his suspicions would not be roused.

Carlton ceased staring into the darkness and groped his way below. Caspar was waiting with Nat outside the cabin where Prince was confined.

'Prince is cursing you, sir,' Caspar said eagerly, keeping a wary eye on Carlton's right hand. 'He blue vex'. He say Gwen go'n miss him.'

'Gwen!' Carlton burst out laughing. 'That wench is hot for me, not Prince. 'Sides, she's a wharfside whore. Let Prince wait 'til he gets to London and see the doxies there. He'll soon forget his Antigua strumpet.'

Prince's muffled curses could be heard through the closed door. Carlton sent Caspar to call the mate with the key. The Scotsman, scowling heavily, was soon with them.

'You did your job well.' Carlton pressed some coins into his hand.

The mate counted them, nodded his head without surprise that there were too many, and unlocked the door.

'Cap'n Eradus wants ye to sup with him. But na' ye darkies.' He leered at Caspar then hurried out of the passage.

'Mas Carlton . . .' Prince's tone was one of despair when the door was thrown open and Carlton faced him. Caspar ran to his side and embraced him around his waist. Nat stepped silently into the cabin and laid his hand on Prince's shoulder.

'You're coming with us,' said Caspar with excitement. 'We'll explore London together.'

'Get back!' Carlton grabbed Caspar's shoulder and flung him aside. Nat moved away too. Carlton slapped Prince rapidly on both cheeks. 'Snap out of that mood, boy.'

For a second, there was a flash of resistance in Prince's eyes. Carlton was shocked by it. He glared at Prince until he lowered his head.

'I'm your master, Prince. Don't forget that. You are still a slave and must do what I want.' He turned to see Nat crouched in the corner of the cabin like a black tiger waiting to leap.

'By the devil!' he exploded. 'I shall have to give both of you a taste of my tongue before long!' He pulled the whip from his waistband and waved the stock in Prince's face.

Nat pawed the floor, watching Prince for a sign.

'Prince,' he said, feeling nervous. 'Tell that nigger I'm master here. He is to obey me or he'll be lashed to so many strips –'

'Yes, Mas Carlton.' Prince's voice was wary. He walked over to Nat and whispered in his ear. Nat frowned. Prince whispered again, then Nat relaxed and squatted on the floor.

Carlton sighed. Sweat trickled down his chest to his crotch. He was worried at how close he had been to losing control over them both.

'I used to worship you,' Prince said with a shrug. 'When we were boys. Now you've stolen me from the people I love . . .'

'Nonsense! What do you know about love?' Carlton grunted. 'Do you know who told me to take you away from Antigua? Clothilda Harkness herself.'

'No!'

'If you don't believe me, then ask yourself who packed your fancy togs in that chest there?'

'It's true,' said Caspar grinning. 'She tell massa take yo' 'way from Antigua to make yuh mark in de world.'

Prince shook his head. 'She always did say that.'

'Fine.' Carlton sighed with relief. 'Be reasonable. No more contrariness, please. You have a comfortable cabin and it will be a pleasant voyage. I don't want to have to chain you below deck like a *bozal*.'

Prince sneered. 'Damn you to hell, Carlton! You deceived me.'

The accusation stung Carlton as much as the curse and Prince's familiarity did. He was speechless.

He clenched the whip in his fist for reassurance. He was still the Bondmaster even if he was on board a ship without drivers to beat his slaves into submission.

He glared at Prince's surly features, then backed to the door, stuffing the whip back in his waistband. If he let the remark go without comment, he would lose face in front of young Caspar and the African. Yet he had no energy to strike Prince. Or was he scared?'

Warn a slave of his punishment and you give him a chance to run away. The adage of slaveholders occurred to him in the silence. *Don't punish in anger* was another.

'Deceive?' Carlton was scornful. 'I am not your comrade, Prince, I am your master. You forget that at your peril.'

He beckoned Caspar and Nat to follow him out of the cabin.

'Stay here without supper to reflect on that!' He closed the door and locked it.

It was a meek gesture. The time for punishment was later, when Nat was safely confined so he could not interfere. For the punishment to be effective, it must be humiliating. Carlton wanted it to serve as an example to Nat to show he was omnipotent over him too.

'Trade in niggers, do you?'

Carlton jerked up his head. He stared at Captain Eradus who was addressing him from the doorway of his cabin. 'I prefer females.'

'Forgive me,' Carlton said, stiffening. 'I was thinking. I didn't see you.'

'Come in.' The captain stood aside as he stepped in to the cabin. His cheeks were quivering and he was tugging nervously at his gray locks. 'Since we'll be together for a few weeks you can meet my family.'

Carlton stared around the gloom of the cabin. A table was set up for two with chairs at both ends bolted down on the deck to prevent them rolling with the motion of the ship. The captain's bunk was opposite. There was a wardrobe bound to the side of the cabin with brass brackets. Some charts were open on top of a sea chest.

'This is Grace,' said Captain Eradus, pointing to the emptiness of the room. 'And this is our daughter, Henrietta.'

He peered anxiously around the cabin again. In all respects, it was perfectly normal. The lantern swinging from a beam as the ship rolled gently with the evening tide, threw shadows over him. It showed up every part of the cabin. He was certain that there was no one else there beside himself and Captain Eradus.

'Excuse me,' he said, holding his forehead. 'I've been so preoccupied, arranging my affairs. I thought you said your wife is here.'

'Aye, fair lass. Henny here is giving you such a curtsey.'

'Indeed?' He swallowed and looked again at Captain Eradus. He didn't know whether to humor or ignore him. Because his welfare until the ship arrived in London depended on the eccentric Captain, he decided on the former. The man himself looked harmless enough with his dumpy stature and wobbly jowls.

'An interesting family,' he said. 'Good companions.'

'They'll not take dinner with us.'

Carlton heaved a sigh of relief. He had no patience with charades.

'They'll serve us, though. Be seated. The soup is on the table. It's getting cold.'

He stared at the table. Apart from the cutlery, it was empty. Captain Eradus was waiting.

'Please forgive me,' he said. 'I . . . er . . . I have no stomach for supper this evening.'

Eradus's face quaked with disappointment.

'My apologies to your wife, and to your charming daughter.' He bowed to the right and left of the captain, edging toward the door. 'My slaves,' he said. 'I must punish one of them . . . insubordination, you know . . .'

Eradus sat suddenly in his chair and dismissed him with a wave of his hand. 'I was planning a game of cards for the four of us. Delights the wife, it does. Ah well, you have your business, and I have mine.' He lowered his head until it withdrew into his shirt like the head of a shy tortoise.

Carlton opened the door and stepped out with relief. The mate was waiting for him, his eyes grim.

'Ye didna upset the captain?'

'Of course not. I don't feel hungry, that's all.'

'They all says that. Not that we have passengers noo. Ye an' ye blackies are the first to sail wi' us for tae years. He won't trouble ye again. If he does, present ye compliments to his wife an' say ye na partial to dancin'.'

Carlton's heart sank with dismay. Too late, he recalled Grosvenor's warning.

He took the mate by his elbow. The man growled and pulled his arm free.

'My slave,' he said, 'the fancy one. I want to punish him. Detail two of your men to tie him to the mast, will you?'

The Scotsman's dour face broke into a grin. 'Aye, aye, sir. The lads like a little entertainment. Ye'll stand the grog?'

'They can have a cask of Roxborough's best.'

Carlton felt no qualms about the activity he unleashed. He strove to ignore it by reasoning that it was good for his slaves.

Two seamen bound Nat on deck so that he was powerless to interfere. They wanted to chain Caspar too and he was obliged to ask the mate sternly to restrain them.

Prince was dragged on deck protesting angrily. He was made to face the mast and put his arms around it. His wrists were tied together and his feet were bound so he was unable to dodge behind the mast.

All the crew came on deck to watch, except for the Captain who remained in his cabin with his ghosts. They were a jolly bunch, toasting Carlton in his own rum as a fine fellow, and enjoying Prince's hopeless struggles.

Some carried torches they held aloft to see better. When Prince was secured, Carlton walked over to him and tore off his silk shirt, exposing his back.

The sailors shouted lustily.

'Is this necessary, Carlton?' whispered Prince.

'By the devil, it is!' He was riled by Prince's blatant rudeness and it steeled his heart to the beating. 'I'll have your respect, Prince, if you please.'

'Yes, if I please.' Prince tossed his head arrogantly, straining against his bonds.

Carlton faltered for a moment, something inside him questioning why Prince was ridiculing him. He shook his head, angered by what he was being forced to do.

'Caspar, make sure Nat watches,' he called, 'He must know what happens when a slave is disrespectful to his master.' The sailors cheered.

'A master has to earn a slave's respect, Carlton. By honesty, not by the lash.'

'Get on with it,' shouted a sailor. 'You ain't hearin' confession.'

Carlton flushed, shocked that he was being mocked. 'It's not too late to say you're sorry, Prince.'

'I wasn't going to, Carlton. It's you who should apologize to me. I was going to wed Gwen, now I'll never see her again.'

'By the devil!' Carlton glowered. 'You're the rudest damn nigger I ever met!' He slapped the whip stock against his thigh and stepped back to take aim.

'I'll do it for yer!' another of the sailors called. 'My arm ain't weak from pullin' all night.'

'Damn you!' he shouted, attacking Prince with rage. The first blow cut a stripe across his shoulders. It oozed blood.

Prince bucked, tugging at the ropes. Nat groaned loudly.

The second lash scored a line that crossed the first. It made the watching seamen wince.

'Mas Carlton!' shrieked Caspar. He tugged at his arm as he drew it back for the third stroke.

'Go away, boy.' He shoved him aside but Caspar clung to his arm so he couldn't raise it.

'Look, Mas Carlton. Look!'

The boy's scream penetrated his fury and he glanced where Caspar was pointing.

There, in a corner of the deck, emerging from a chest that was covered with ropes and canvas, eyes glaring, her bodice ripped and her brown bosom hanging bare, was Gwen.

CHAPTER FOURTEEN

The line of slaves, their backs bent parallel to the dark brown Roxborough earth, hoed around the ratoons, harrowing the weeds from the cane roots and moving in a slow, wearying pace across the sloping field. The midday sun blazed down on them, scorching their black backs even darker. In the sparse shade from the gomier tree, the driver in his wide-brimmed *bakoua* hat, eyed them lazily. His whip was coiled in his hand.

Ella toiled up the main avenue to the *cou*, trying to keep to the shadow thrown by the palm trees and bushes. She felt the eyes of the slaves on her as they peeped surreptiously, willing her to stop and speak with them so they could rest from their numbing tasks. She was hot, sweat drenching her body under her loose tunic. She waved to the driver and called out to him so the slaves would hear and think highly of her.

'Yuh gang doin' fine, Mercury. Hardes' workin' *atelier* dere does be. Can't stop, dough. Massa Hayes bawlin' for me.'

She sensed the sigh of satisfaction passing through the fieldgang. It was good for them to know she worked just as hard as they did. She patted her *mouchoir madras*, the square of Indian cotton made with specially dyed and treated banana threads which she wore tied in two points in her hair.

'Yo' sweeten de massa,' called Mercury with a laugh.

That was good, she thought. At least the slaves realized that she was the one responsible for keeping old Hayes malleable. If he was more active, the hoeing would have to be done three times as fast. Now it was sufficient for there to be slaves in a field so Massa Hayes could see them from his seat on the balcony. It made him believe work was being done. It was foolish. The slaves were busy enough keeping themselves and the hundred whelps in the nursery paddock supplied with ground provisions, fish, fruit and food.

She had spent the morning in the mill house with Kingston, the old bookkeeper. He was in his sixties and nearly blind. He was Jamaica born, one of Massa Hayes's first purchases, and because he could read and write was made the bookkeeper nearly twenty years before. His tireless pouring over the ledgers by candle light after a day's work delivering rum to the plantation's customers, had weakened his eyes. He explained his ledgers to Ella and she inspected the casks of rum with him.

She was panting when she reached the courtyard at the top of the hill. She glanced anxiously up at the balcony to see if Tita was sitting with Massa Hayes. That could mean trouble.

Old Hayes was by himself, staring out to sea. She wondered what he saw when he was in those moods. Something must have disturbed him for him to send for her so urgently. She hurried across the courtyard and into the kitchen. All the slaves stopped work the moment she entered.

'Lor', Ella,' said Pip with relief.

She counted the slaves. It was an old habit. They were all there. Cleo was preparing the dinner and Pool was polishing the silver. Pip, she guessed from his glazed eyes, had been mixing a new pitcher of rum punch, and tasting it. Marcus and the kitchen girl were cleaning the wares. Whatever it was that had happened couldn't be serious.

'Let me catch my breat'.' She sank into a chair. Pool gaped gormlessly at her which she found annoying. He was too old for his job.

'Get me water from the filter, Pool,' she said to distract him.

He shut his mouth but made no attempt to move. Instead, he snapped his fingers and called Marcus. 'Ella does want water, boy. Make haste.'

She sipped the cool water while Pip explained that a messenger had arrived from Layou with a paper.

'What kind of paper?' Ella feared the worst.

'It white an' thick, folded like a square.' Pip ignored Pool who was smirking at him, trying to make him laugh. 'It had one red seal on it.'

She nodded with relief. If it was bad news, Captain Loring would have brought it himself. To entrust a letter to a boy from Layou showed its contents were of minor consequence. 'Massa Hayes seen it?'

'Oh yas, Ella.'

'He say anything?'

'No, Ella. He take de paper an' he stare at it an' he look a' de sea an' de hills but he ain' say not'in.'

'He can't read no more,' she said sadly. 'He too 'shamed ask me.'

'He don't know you can read words, Ella. He use Kingston for dat.'

'Tita can read,' said Sophie.

Ella looked in astonishment at the girl who had entered the kitchen. Sophie was the chit Tita had chosen to help her with the children. She was carrying a bowl.

'Gib me some brot' for Hayes,' she said holding out the bowl, unaware of the consternation she had caused.

'Does Massa Hayes know dat?' Pip asked to show his authority.

'Shut up!' snapped Ella. Sophie was a talkative brat and if Pip gave her the idea, she would soon tell the old Massa about Tita's talent. This was treacherous news.

'It can be dangerous for a slave to read,' Ella announced solemnly. 'Sophie, don't tell no one 'bou' dis. If white folks know dey go'n gouge out Tita's eyes so she can't read no more.'

Sophie's hands trembled as she held the bowl of broth. 'Ah ain't mean no harm, Miss Ella. Ah not tell no one.'

'Good.' Ella rose from her seat and clapped her hands. 'Come on, yo' lazy niggahs, we don't have time to sit an' prattle like we'se white women. Ah go'n to de Massa.'

She followed Sophie up the back stairs to the house. Tita was sitting on the balcony bouncing the baby on her knee. Her own child, the black one, Mingoson, was being held by Laura.

Tita's smile vanished when she saw Ella, and Laura stopped chattering to Mingoson.

'Good day, Tita,' Ella said coolly.

'Yo' bin wid de fiel' hands, dem?' It was an accusation.

'Why not, Tita? Dey does be workin' well.'

'Dat wha' yo' tell Massa Hayes?'

'It true.'

'Ain' no cane growin' dis season like when Mas Carlton here.'

Ella shrugged. 'If you feed de baba de brot' when it hot, he go'n burn.' She swung away from Tita and bustled around the side balcony to the front where Hayes was sitting.

She noticed that his glass was empty and she wondered how much punch he'd drunk already. His head was nodding as she glided silently beside him. The wad of paper was clasped in his frail hands.

'I hear you creepin'.' He raised his eyes and glared at her.

She stiffened, horrified that she had set him off in a bad mood. 'I'm sorry, sir,' she said contritely. 'I didn't want to disturb you, if you sleeping.'

'Eyes in the back of me head, Ella. A white man needs that.' Hayes relaxed but he still scowled heavily. He fanned himself with the parchment.

'Where you been? I know you weren't in the house 'cause Tita been fussin' 'round me.' He snorted. 'Don't know which is worse, you or she.'

This was bad. She wondered what Tita had been saying to get him riled. She couldn't look after the plantation and keep watch on the old man at the same time.

'I was be at the mill checking the rum wid Kingston.' She spoke calmly, not wanting to exasperate him further.

'Kingston? Aye, that slave can read. He was a fine buck when I bought him off the factor. Didn't want me to know he could read and figure, but I knew.' He looked at the parchment in his hands and was about to speak when Ella interrupted.

'He 'most blind now, massa I does help him with the ledgers.' She held her breath, waiting for his reaction.

He was a pitiful sight; his wizened body dried by sourness and mistrust during his years as a slaveholder. His prejudices had eroded the decency in him until he was no more than a wretched mockery of a white man. Despite his stroke ten years before when he was forced to hand over the plantation and slaves to Carlton, he refused to accept his disability. Daily he fueled his frustration with rum, seeking excuses for his failures but never blaming himself.

'Bah!' he said. 'Think you're better than a fine Jamaican buck, do you?' He scowled. 'You're Carlton's bedwench, not mine.'

Ella was tight lipped, waiting for his irascibility to cool. There was silence. 'More rum, massa?'

'Dam' you, Ella.' He struck her with the parchment. 'I can't stand a wench who fusses. That's what Tita doin' all mornin'. I know her game. Wants to get me drunk so she can wheedle somethin' out of me. Same game as yours.'

Ella drew back.

'Surprise you, did I?' Hayes wheezed triumphantly, slapping the arms of the chair with the paper.

''Course I know what you want. You forget who I am? Wasn't it me who taught you slaves to think? I know every thought in your empty head.' He shrugged. 'Waste of time, that is. Mayhap I'll hire a white overseer.'

Ella flushed. 'We can manage all right, massa. You don't want no strange buckra here.'

'Tita says I do. She tells me you're encouragin' the slaves to be slothful. She reckons there'll be no plantation for little Hayes when he's older, if you have your way. Maybe you are jealous of him? After all, he is Carlton's heir instead of your own child.'

Ella felt the blood draining from her cheeks. She put her hand out to steady herself against the verandah post.

Hatred welled up inside her. She cursed Tita silently for the vile thoughts she had planted in the massa's mind. Didn't Tita realize it would be worse for them all if she upset Massa Hayes? It was vital that the old man did not get beyond her control.

'You're a fine looking woman when you're angry, Ella.'

She was conscious of Hayes gazing at her with a strange look in his eye. She stiffened.

'Long neck, good bones and when you're vexed, your cheeks tense. No spare flesh on you, save the belly and that's the baby comin'. You've got good hips for whelps. Drop 'em without problems, I'm sure.' He nodded, sucking his gums.

'I remember the day Carlton fingered you. How proud you were until then.' He chuckled and plucked at his crotch.

Ella waited, uncertain what was happening. She sensed Tita had already done the damage and set Hayes off on a tack she could no longer anticipate. When he didn't speak, she tried to set things right.

'Tita ain't a Roxbro' nigger, massa. She evil. She don't care de children prop'ly. She jealous. That why she tell you lies 'bout me.'

'Aye.' Hayes nodded his head wisely. 'Knew you'd say that.' He fanned himself again. 'Want to see what Carlton says, don't you?'

'Carlton?' She stifled her gasp. So the paper *was* from him. She must send Pip to Layou at once to question the sailors from the schooner that brought it. She must find out what Carlton was doing in Antigua, how Caspar was behaving . . .

Hayes was fidgeting. 'Get me a punch. I been waiting long enough.'

She walked calmly to the corner of the verandah and clapped her hands for Pip. She was conscious of Hayes watching her as her long dress swept across the floor boards. She was barefoot and moved silently.

She turned in time to catch a glance of yearning in Hayes's eyes. One hand was in his lap, between his legs. It gave her an idea of what to do.

Her eyes met his. Instead of lowering them she kept her head raised and returned his stare provocatively.

'Dammit, Ella,' he snapped, soaring off into a temper again. 'Just because Mas Carlton favors you, don't mean I do.' He flung the letter at her.

'Go on, read it! But don't get ideas that you're better than me. I'm your master while he's away.' He snorted grumpily and turned his back on her, staring defiantly at the sea.

Ella retrieved the parchment from the floor where it had fallen. The seal was broken. She opened up the letter; it was a single page folded over into a package with the broken seal on one side and writing on the other. There were greasy finger marks around the edges.

Pip hurried onto the balcony with a fresh pitcher of punch. He poured a goblet and Hayes accepted it without taking his gaze from the sea. Pip glanced at Ella. She indicated with a nod of her head that he should wait in the drawing room where he could hear what she read.

He would be useful as a witness to support her when she related the letter's contents to her cronies in the quarters. If they didn't believe her, then Pip could tell them she spoke the truth. She needed as many slaves as possible on her side, in case Tita succeeded in stirring up more trouble than she could handle alone.

Carlton had taught her to read when she sat with him while he studied his books in the cabin that was his schoolroom. She shivered with yearning when she saw the familiar strokes of his writing. She studied the paper, trying to understand what was written on it.

'Go on, go on,' said Hayes. 'It's for me, ain't it, not for you.'

'Yes, massa.' She moved to his side and squatted on her haunches where he could see the parchment over her shoulders. She didn't bother to close her bodice when it gaped open. Flirting was Tita's tactic to mollify Hayes so she would try it too.

With care, glancing at him occasionally to emphasize her cleverness in interpreting the letter, she read it to him.

Carlton began by explaining that since Captain Loring had disappeared and couldn't be found, he was writing the letter to send by another schooner and he trusted Ella to explain its contents.

Hayes snorted with scorn. 'So you're the only slave he trusts, Ella? You bewitched him, didn't you?'

She continued. ' "We sail this evening. The vessel is bound for the Pool of London. I am taking two negroes with me as attendants; the African I rescued from drowning and a lively buck who is known to you because he was born at Roxborough. His name is Prince. He is very much spoiled and has a high opinion of himself." '

'Two niggers?' Hayes spluttered, gripping his chair. 'What does he want two for? He got Caspar, ain't he?'

Ella hid her concern for her son, and continued to read.

' "It is my intention to expose London society to my trio of "blackamoors," as niggers are called in polite society. You are aware that some politicians are engaged in a campaign for the amelioration of slavery. When they see the quality of Prince and Caspar, my pair of genuine Bondmaster bucks, and my Royal African, they cannot fail to view slavery in a different, kinder light." '

Ella paused, puzzled by the long words and wondering what Carlton meant. Hayes, too, was baffled.

'Seems like he's picked up some odd ideas in St John's,' he muttered. 'English politics! Don't know why he wants to go there. His place is here.'

'Yes, massa.' Ella wished he hadn't gone, but she knew it was for the best. She was proud of his mention of Caspar in the letter. 'Shall I read the rest?'

Hayes nodded. Carlton concluded by wishing him well and hoping that nothing was amiss. He promised to write upon arrival in London and urged him to entrust Ella with any communication he wished her to write for him.

Ella glowed with pride. How fondly Carlton remembered her! If only he were there and she could tell him what trouble Tita was trying to create.

'Give that to me!' Hayes snatched the letter from her fingers. 'Now call Tita.'

'What – ?' She got to her feet quickly. 'Yes, massa.' She stifled her misgivings, clapped her hands and told Pip to call Tita without delay.

'Don't you ever do anything for yourself?' Hayes asked gruffly. 'Always givin' orders. Worse than any white woman.'

'I has my place,' Ella said sharply in a rare outburst of temperament. 'The slaves have to know that.'

Tita, who must have been hiding at the side so she could listen, sauntered into view. Laura trailed behind her. The girl sneered at Ella and ran past her to Hayes. The old man patted her shoulder while he spoke to Tita.

'See this,' he said, thrusting the letter at her. 'Why didn't you read that bit about 'entrust any communication to Ella'?'

Tita stopped in her tracks. 'It's a lie,' she gasped without thinking.

'No, it ain't!' Hayes waved the letter. 'Look again.' He held it out in front of her. 'You think you're so clever, the pair of you. *I know* what Carlton's saying.'

Tita pouted. 'It a disgrace to 'trust anything to Ella. De mistress share her secrets wid me. Ah don' tell no one what ah hear, an' ah hear plenty.'

Hayes sighed. 'I'll wager you'll tell when it suits you.' He clutched his chest.

'Hush now,' said Ella rushing to his side. 'You've upset him.'

'She ain't, she ain't!' cried Laura.

'Devil protect me from wenches!' Hayes sat up and pushed his daughter away. 'Get out, all of you!'

He sat defiantly on the edge of his seat until Ella ushered Tita and Laura out of sight. He chuckled then and reached for the pitcher to pour more punch.

Ella, watching through the louvers of the drawing room window, was relieved. She decided to carry out her plan.

For a long time, she suspected Hayes was feigning his feebleness because he wanted to be pampered and to gain sympathy. She sensed, in his testiness, a certain fear of the power the slaves held over him.

Occasionally, she noticed a spark in his eye that made her think there was plenty of life left in him really.

With Carlton away, the old man had no company. She was worried that if he felt lonely, he would overcome his antipathy for whites and hire a white overseer to stay at the house with him. That must be avoided. She knew what to do!

Ella supervised the serving of lunch carefully. She gave Hayes the succulent claws of *cyrique* crab that he liked in his *calalloo* soup. She was a good cook and seasoned the food to his taste. He liked his broth with juicy yams and small bright orange peppers floating in it.

Pip waited on him carefully and poured enough rum to make him drowsy. After dinner with the sun hot and the air lifeless, he retired to his chamber. He was soon snoring peacefully.

Ella went to work with her plan while he was asleep. She sent Marcus to the nursery to call Congo Venus, the overseer of the young negroes in the paddock. The woman dragged herself up to the house with great reluctance. Ella was pleased that she obeyed the summons, however grudgingly, because it showed that the old curmudgeon accepted her authority.

The two of them huddled together in her room where none of the slaves could overhear them. When she left, Congo Venus looked spryer than when she arrived and was chuckling to herself with excitement.

Hayes spent the rest of the day unaware of what was being planned for him. He berated Pip for the quality of his punch, and blamed Ella for the noise the house slaves were making. His hearty complaints made her certain he was as fit as any other man of his age.

Laura spent an hour playing with him. By the time he had eaten some fritters for supper, he was ready for bed.

At Roxborough, the day finished with dusk, unless it was the cane season when the mill ground all night. Hayes's favorite pastime in the evening was to stand at the corner of the balcony where the breeze blew up from the slave quarters. He strained his ears to hear the noise from the quarters, and sniffed the air energetically.

'Can't smell none of them tonight, Ella.' He sounded disappointed when she approached him at the corner.

She smiled to reassure him. 'I'm sure them slaves too tired to be outside their cabins now,' she said. 'They been working hard in the *polinks* all day.'

Hayes smacked his lips. 'You're a shrewd hussy, Ella.'

'Thank you, massa,' she said, pleased. Her preparations were complete. Tita and her maid Sophie were out of the way, in bed with the children. Pool was chasing some wench and Pip was downstairs in the kitchen.

'I was thinking, massa . . .' She let her voice trail off to give Hayes the chance to guess what she was going to say. It made him think he really did know more than she did.

'Yes?' He sniffed suspiciously. 'The answer's no, whatever you want.'

'Not me, massa.' She wore a newly laundered gown that concealed her swollen figure. Her corsage was low cut and, with the light from the lantern highlighting the rouge on her cheeks, she knew she looked attractive.

'You,' she said softly.

'What?' Hayes caught his breath as he gained an inkling of what she was suggesting.

'I was thinkin' that mayhap you does feel a trifle discommoded at night, massa. It ain't right for a man in his prime like you does be, not to have a wench to drain him.'

Hayes stared at her, gripping the balcony railing. 'Dam'me, Ella. You sound like Mas Carlton himself.'

She smiled and clapped her hands. Two girls walked shyly from the other side of the balcony where they had been waiting. All afternoon, Congo Venus had instructed them on how to behave. They had been bathed at the river, powdered and perfumed, and given *bois bandé* tea to drink in case their desire should flag.

They were fifteen years old and stood naked in front of him with pink ribbons in their short plaits. Hayes gulped. Their breasts were like ripe mangoes and their curly body hair, pomaded and greased with snake oil, glinted in the lamp light. He swallowed and clutched himself.

'Virgins,' she said smiling. 'They're yours.'

The two girls giggled. They stood beside Hayes and touched him gently. One massaged his chest while the other stroked his thighs.

'By the devil,' he muttered as his tired old body began to stir. 'Ella, you sure are a damn witch.'

CHAPTER FIFTEEN

It was a privilege for a slave to sleep with a white man. There were the obvious advantages of better treatment and also the immediate movement up the plantation hierarchy. The bedmate of a slave holder became a person of influence both with the slaves and the planter.

However, the white master suffered from these liaisons. They eroded the division that enabled him to control his slaves through distance and fear. He became, in effect, slave to the slave, no longer able to run his plantation impartially.

Prince was intelligent and recognised these strictures, even if Carlton didn't. He lay on his stomach on the wooden slats that were his mattress and considered the odd events of the day. His back, with its two stripes like a cross over his shoulder blades, hurt him too much for sleep.

When Prince was a child, he was Carlton's constant companion. He slept with him on the same bed, played with him, grew and learned with him. Although he was a negro and a slave, it never occurred to him that he was in the same class as the black animals who labored in the Roxborough fields. He understood, gradually, that he was subordinate to Carlton, but he saw himself as Carlton's shadow. At first, he assumed that was why he was black.

Whatever Carlton did, Prince did. They discovered sex together, playing with each other behind the bougainvillea bushes when they were eight. They easily coerced slave children into joining their games. They were eleven when they shared their first female together, with Prince, whose prick and curiosity were longer, showing Carlton how it was done.

The disruption to their friendship caused by Prince's sale, saved him the disillusion that a boyhood companion of a white child always suffered. There comes a time when the white child becomes white and the black black. For Prince, his sale did not destroy his regard for Carlton, only preserved it.

He was not banished to the fields, or the stables, to be lashed back into slavery. The feeling instilled in him since he was a baby alongside Carlton, that he was someone special, stayed with him.

He was too used to Carlton's ways to blame him for the beating. The strokes on his back did not hurt deeply; it was his pride that had been wounded.

He had provoked Carlton deliberately, to see what would happen. He was angry for being duped by the people he trusted. Clothilda's part in the scheme to ship him to England dismayed him. He liked Antigua and wanted to stay there. Gwen's unexpected appearance on the ship changed that.

He smiled to himself in the darkness of the cabin. He could hear Caspar's gentle snores and the deep breathing of Nat as they slept peacefully.

When Gwen emerged from her hiding place under the canvas, Carlton had dropped his whip in surprise. The crew stared at her, with her breasts hanging free, as though she was the consequence of some magician's trick. Prince himself thought she was an illusion conjured up by the shock of the whipping. Yet Gwen was reality, standing on the deck and shaking her fist at Carlton.

Caspar was the first to recover. He snatched up the whip and ran below with it. When he returned, Carlton was receiving a lash from Gwen's tongue.

'What you thrashin' my buck for, Carlton Todd?' Gwen flung the canvas away. 'Is that why you stole him?'

She ignored Carlton and hurried to Prince. 'Untie him!' she commanded the two seamen standing guard. Her voice carried authority and as Carlton didn't contradict, they loosened his bonds. The other seamen stood and gawped.

Gwen's eyes were sparking. Her long hair fluttered about her breasts as she tossed her head angrily. Prince smiled his gratitude, still unable to believe she was real. He reached for her.

She slapped him soundly across his cheek. He staggered back to the mast, the blow causing him more anguish than Carlton's strokes. The slap broke the spell and the sailors jeered.

'That's for whatever you did to make Mas Carlton vexed.' She flounced away from him to Carlton's side.

'Carlton, dear,' she cooed in his ear, taking him by his arm. 'That's a good slave you have there. Now he knows you're master.'

Carlton tried to thrust her away but she wouldn't let go of his arm. 'What the devil are you doing here?' Prince saw how shaken he was.

'You'll see,' she said. 'Now you've shown Prince who's master, come and show me.'

The seamen hooted with laughter as she led him below. Caspar freed Nat while Prince marveled at his good fortune. The mate shouted orders and the crew disappeared, leaving the three of them to go below to Prince's cabin.

Carlton's whip was on the floor where Caspar had thrown it out of the way.

'You must give it back to him in the morning,' Prince warned him.

'Why?' Caspar stared at him with defiance. 'He lashed you for nothing.'

'No, he didn't. He had to whip me to restore his confidence in himself. He thinks I'm a danger to him.'

'Dat ain' no reason to return dat whip.' Caspar kicked it.

'It's Carlton's symbol of power over us.' He gestured at Nat squatting on the floor. 'He needs the whip to remind him that he's our master.'

'Don't you mind being his slave again?' Caspar cocked his head on one side and watched Prince's eyes carefully. 'You sassed him 'cause you didn't want to sail wid us.'

Prince sighed. 'Gwen's here now.'

'How does she change it. She wid Mas Carlton, in his bed, not yours.'

He smiled. 'Ah, yes, Caspar. But who does she really love?'

The boy stamped his foot on the floor with exasperation. 'I don't know 'bout love.' He shrugged his shoulders and turned his attention to Nat. 'What are we going to do 'bout him?'

'He'll sleep here with us. Share the bottom bunk with him. Gwen will stay with Carlton for the voyage.'

'I was supposed to sleep in Mas Carlton's cabin.' Caspar couldn't keep the disappointment out of his voice.

Prince cuffed him. 'You'll have a better time with us. What a woman she is, stowing away like that! She'll sweeten Carlton until he's dripping like honey from a comb.'

Nat rose to his feet slowly. He walked over to Prince and inspected his back. He pursed his lips, concerned about his pain. Caspar went to borrow some unguent from the mate.

'Do you understand?' asked Prince when they were alone.

Nat's brow furrowed. 'Does it change it if I understand?'

'You can forgive.'

Nat's ebony face creased in a smile. 'Mas Carlton has done me nothing. Did he steal me? Did he kill you?'

'You won't be contrary and get him riled when he wants you to do something?'

'He is my master.'

'Aye.' Prince sat down. 'It's easy now. You're not likely to be driven into the fields to cut cane with the sun burning your back and the lash slicing your skin.'

'Neither are you,' Nat smiled. 'Your pain is from a different evil.'

He considered the tall African. Nat was a mystery. He spoke English but he was from such a different world. His blackness was a mask that concealed his real feelings. When his full weight returned he would be an impressive sight, as dark as midnight, with a haughty bearing and handsome features unmarked by tribal scars. His eyes were like mirrors, disturbing and profound.

'What do you mean?' Prince asked anxiously. 'What pain?'

Nat shook his head. 'If a man in my tribe takes my woman he disgraces me. I could not share my woman with any man. That is the pain you suffer.'

'Hah!' Prince's laughter made him forget his stinging back. 'I'm accustomed to sharing my women with white men. It makes the women appreciate me more! Whatever Gwen is doing with Carlton makes no difference. It makes Carlton my brother.'

Yes, just as it was when they were boys together, he thought, finally drifting off to sleep.

The voyage to England was uneventful. When they became accustomed to the rolling of the ship, the ceaseless creaking of the ship's timbers and the noise of the unhappy animals and fowls kept on deck for their meat supply, the days passed pleasantly. Captain Eradus was seldom seen and the vessel managed well without him. The crew were a contented bunch being well rewarded by the profits, mostly illegal, from their voyages. There was an atmosphere of easy comraderie on board and it affected Carlton and his slaves.

He devised a routine to keep his boys fit. It would be against his interests to arrive in London with blacks of inferior quality. With

Prince and Nat stripped to their breeches, and Caspar encouraging them, they engaged in contests. They wrestled, they climbed the rigging, they shifted cargo. In the evenings, they danced for the sailors, jigging on deck to the sound of a fiddle and improvised drums. Gwen joined in too, but only under the watchful eye of Carlton who glowered savagely at any seaman who looked like making a pass at her.

The weeks passed rapidly in such congenial circumstances. Carlton scarcely had time to reflect on how Gwen had become part of his life. He was not in love but he was not going to let any other man have his way with her. He eyed her possessively when she walked the decks. At dances, he permitted her to jig only with Prince or Nat. For her part, she showed interest only in him.

'Up to now, I don't know how you did it.' They were three days sailing away from London, out of the calm and into the rough seas off the coast of France. The dances had finished, it took all their effort to keep on their feet with the pitching of the ship. Carlton was lying with Gwen on his bunk.

'Did what?' She smiled at him, smoothing back a wayward lock of hair from his brow.

'Got here.' He squeezed her. 'Got right into my bed. I had no need of a wench.'

'What nonsense the buckra does talk, *oui*?'

'You sound like Ella.'

'Is that why you like me?'

He sat up, pushing her away. 'Like you? I don't like you.' It was almost a shout. 'That's impossible.'

She ran her fingers across his naked chest, tweaking the hairs around his nipples. He shied back from her. 'I don't like you either,' she said.

'Then why did you stow away?' He was pleased with his retort.

'Because you used me and was going to leave.'

'We had no affair . . .'

'I told you I was not a slave.'

'It's impossible.'

He lay back on the bed as doubts assailed him. They were so close to England and still he had no plan about what to do with her.

She was eighteen and headstrong. A slave he could control but not a free wench as tempestuous as Gwen. She had been a diverting companion on the voyage but he had no intention of prejudicing his reception into society by continuing involvement with her in London.

'What's impossible? I'm here. I'm real.' Her hands stroked his flat, hard stomach.

'What am I going to do with you in London?'

She pouted. 'What you do here.'

He rolled away impatiently.

'I know,' she said, sounding serious. 'It's not difficult. Put me with Prince.'

He tensed. His relationship with Prince was strained still. Neither of them referred to the beating. The scars had healed with only a faint trace of the cross engraved in his back.

Prince was respectful, even friendly, and took willingly to the task of minding Nat and Caspar. He groomed the African well and his exalted status was evident to white men who knew nothing about blacks. Caspar, too, had matured under Prince's guidance. What would he do to Gwen?

'Would you agree to that?' Carlton was anxious. 'Prince is pining for you. I thought you loathed him.'

'I do . . . I don't forgive when I'm wronged. Yet if I have you, I'll tolerate him for your sake.'

'And when you don't have me?'

She licked her lips, her sultry eyes burning into his. 'Then perhaps you are dead,' she said wickedly.

'Or you are.'

He pulled her to him and kissed her full on her lips, something he would not have done when the voyage began. They had been thrown together by circumstances and if she expected their relationship to be the same, she was in for a shock. But she didn't. It puzzled him.

Her mouth, open beneath his and drawing on his tongue as it swelled within her, drove reason out of his mind. She shimmied her body against his, rousing him for the third time that day. Her appetite seemed insatiable and the response of his own body to her demands amazed him.

Free of the worries of the plantation, and lulled by the artificial cosiness of their isolation on board ship, he was a stud like his prime negroes. He expected her adoration and reveled in it, responding to her loving with the brutal selfishness that was the most he could give any woman.

He had been brought up by old Hayes to believe that there were two types of females – slaves and wives – and a relationship with either should be profitable. Every child he sired with a slave was a new slave. Many planters freed their slave offspring to spare the child the wrath of their wives. Old Hayes and himself had no wives to worry about and they were enemies of conventional behavior.

His relations with his wife, when he had one, were solely for profit, to beget an heir. A wife, being white and respectable, did not enjoy pleasure like a black one did. She engaged in it out of a sense of duty. White women were built differently, and it was against their nature to be aroused by passion.

He sighed as Gwen raised her mouth to kiss him again. He moved his lips away and buried his head in the pillow above her shoulder. He was hard within her and drove himself furiously to match her demands. But his heart as he felt Gwen tense beneath him, shuddering with excitement, was not in it. He thrust at her in a frenzy, straining to meet her, squeezing her shoulders. In a sudden rush, he slapped his hand across her cheek and collapsed, exhausted, on top of her.

'Dam' you,' he gasped. It was the closest he could get to saying. 'I love you.'

The next morning, Carlton locked Gwen in his cabin and joined his slaves in theirs. The voyage had slimmed Prince and fattened Nat. Now they were both prime. Prince's countenance was rested after so many nights away from the gaming tables of Lindsey's Rooms. His complexion sparkled and he looked younger and lustier than when he was a St John's nigger dandy. Nat had rounded out, the haunted look of his gaunt body had been replaced by a comfortable leanness. Carlton was pleased.

'The extra livestock and provisions I brought on the voyage have served you well,' he said, regarding Nat with pride.

'What about me?' Caspar pushed himself forward. His voice had lost its boyish squeak and become husky.

'Ho, my young squire,' said Carlton, chucking him under his chin. 'Getting to be a man, are you?'

'Not yet, sir.' Caspar grinned ruefully. 'No wenches.'

'Nat's been telling us how a warrior isn't a man in his tribe until he has his first wife.' Prince leaned easily against the frame that held their bunk bed shelves. 'Maybe Caspar's ready for his first wife?'

'Of course, he is. A Bondmaster buck is a breeder.' He eyed Prince pointedly. The boy was wearing a worsted shirt over his breeches because of the change in temperature. 'What about you?'

Prince shrugged his shoulders.

'Then shuck off your britches and let me examine you. Should have done that a long time ago.'

Prince sneered. 'That's slave games for Roxborough. We're in the English Channel now. We're not slaves here. I know the law.'

Carlton folded his arms. 'So do I, Prince. You're mistaken. You're mine and it's your duty to do what I say.'

'Why?'

He looked at Prince with disdain. 'To make me proud of you, of course. Do you want to shame me with your disobedience? Now take off your britches, there's a good fellow. Show Nat how it's done.'

He was amazed to hear himself appealing to Prince instead of ordering him to comply. He had mellowed under Gwen's influence.

'Nat,' Prince said mockingly. 'When a white man is proud of his slaves, he likes to show them off to his cronies. In that respect, he's like a herdsman who owns cattle in Africa. A prize bull wins admirers, eh?'

'Get on with it!' Carlton snapped, tiring of the delay. 'Britches!'

Prince rolled his eyes.

'You want me to shuck off too, Mas Carlton?'

'No, Caspar.' He lashed out but Caspar was too spry and dodged away.

Carlton sat down and contemplated Prince and Nat standing naked in the center of the cabin.

'Step forward.' He beckoned Nat with his hand.

The African's size was impressive. His limbs and his trunk were in perfect proportion to each other. His expression was one of disinterest, and it made Carlton feel invisible. He turned to Caspar.

'You know what I'm looking for, boy?'

'Defects, sir. Blemishes that mar a perfect nigger.'

Carlton smiled. He touched Nat tentatively but the African didn't flinch at his cold hand. He rubbed his hands swiftly over his body, confirming with his touch what he could see with his eyes.

He touched Nat's penis and the boy regarded him balefully. He held it until the prepuce slipped back; the testicles were large and heavy. He was perfect. The only marks on his body were the two scars at his shoulders, like epaulet buttons, that testified his royal birth.

'Nothing wrong with that, was there, Nat?' Carlton slapped his buttocks and the boy moved away. Prince swaggered forward in his place, flaunting his nakedness in Carlton's face.

'Ah does be a breedah, yassah!' he mimicked. 'Yo' gib me a filly an' ah get she full, sah.'

'Shut up, Prince.' He felt foolish. Prince's body was a burnished gold with the dark tinge of the pure negro. His physique was superb like Nat's with the added refinement of his age and a lifelong diet of white victuals that gave him a finesse Nat lacked.

'Yo' ain't go'n skin mah prick?' mocked Prince, holding himself out in front of Carlton.

He shrugged with an exaggerated air of disappointment when Carlton merely glanced and shook his head.

Suddenly, Prince turned around and bent forward, thrusting his bottom in Carlton's face. 'Finger me, sah! Mah backside does be on fire!'

'Prince!' Carlton pushed him away and stood up sadly. 'I had to do that,' he explained, forgetting for a moment that no explanation was necessary. 'How else do I know if you've got the pox?'

'Pox?' Prince stared at him dumbly. 'Am I to be auctioned?'

'No.' Carlton strode over to the door. 'Don't bother to dress,' he said sharply. 'Come with me. As you are.'

Prince hesitated, unprepared. Caspar tickled him playfully in his backside and he moved forward, followed by Nat and Caspar, down the passage to Carlton's cabin.

'Here's yuh wench, boy!' Carlton sneered at him with the gruff tones of a slave driver. He flung open the door. 'Ride her good.'

He kicked Prince in his backside and pushed him in the cabin. Gwen shrieked.

He closed the door on them both and locked it.

'Now, Caspar,' Carlton said, putting his arm around the boy and walking with him onto the deck. Nat trailed behind.

'See there?' He pointed to the coastline in the distance.

'There's the *white* cliffs of Dover. That's England.'

Book Two
The Darling Blacks, 1808–1810

CHAPTER SIXTEEN

The sky was gray with the damp chill of autumn. It was typical London weather with the drabness brightened only by the changing colors of the leaves with their tinges of copper and gold.

Prince huddled under one of the trees in the garden clasping his coat around him as he tried to keep warm. He stamped his feet and watched fascinated as his breath billowed out in the cool air like steam.

The square of garden was surrounded by tall terrace houses, gray with stucco. London had many of these square gardens isolated from each other by houses. It intrigued Prince that the white man's ingenuity enabled him to confine nature into architectural shapes as though he had decreed to the trees, you may grow here and nowhere else. In Dominica, people lived with nature as an unruly family member. In London, even the trees and plants were enslaved.

He glanced with impatience across the cobbled street to the house where he had been instructed to wait for Carlton. Through the long windows overlooking the street, he could see two men standing up and gesticulating. The glow of a coal fire illuminated the room behind them.

From his stance, Carlton was angry. The man with him strode nervously across the room. A woman, the host's wife, rose from an armchair in front of the fire and hurried over to him, laying her hands on the man's arm to calm him down.

Prince enjoyed the scene because it resembled a drama at Astley's Royal Amphitheatre in Lambeth. The man's wife was trying to persuade him to return to the conversation but he would not hear of it. He folded his arms and glanced across the room at Carlton.

Prince knew what they were discussing; it was Carlton's sole topic of conversation: slavery. The wife was clearly distressed, begging her husband and Carlton to shake hands and agree to differ.

Carlton raised his hands in the air, reminding Prince of the gesture of a slave pleading for mercy when he is about to be whipped. He saw Carlton drop his arms to his side and turn on his heels. Final words were exchanged and the wife hurried across the room to show him out.

Good, thought Prince, now his waiting was over. He had been there at least half an hour and felt the chill of the late afternoon biting into his bones. He crossed the street, dodging between two carriages that bounced around the corner of the square at a great pace.

He arrived at the house as the street door opened. A maid in a cap held the door for Carlton. He paused briefly and the woman's miserable face was transformed as he coaxed a smile from her. Prince grinned. Carlton knew how to sweet talk the servant even if her master resisted his rough charm.

'See you next week, Brady,' Carlton said, giving the maid's elbow a squeeze.

'Yes, Mr Carlton.' The woman attempted a curtsey, blushing with confusion at his familiarity. Prince waited at the foot of the steps as Carlton ran down, buttoning up his coat.

'Shall I find a carriage?'

Carlton raised his eyes to the sky and shook his head. 'I wonder when we'll see the sun again? It won't rain so let's walk. The cold will clear my head after that session.' He strode up the road briskly and Prince fell into step beside him.

Since they arrived in London four months before, Prince had seen little of the fashionable life that he expected. He was allowed to accompany Carlton to meetings but then had to cool his heels in the gutter until it was time for Carlton to return home.

Carlton rented a house in Chapel Street. Most of his time was spent in the house or in pursuing what was known in Parliament as the West India Interest group.

Vast fortunes had been made out of slave-grown sugar and the wealth would secure many English families for generations to come. These new dynasties were under attack and welcomed Carlton when he presented himself as an articulate West Indian planter prepared to speak in favor of slavery. It was at the behest of this West India Interest that he had been meeting James Stephens, an influential adviser to the Colonial Office.

'Stephens is a prig!' Carlton declared, gripping Prince's arm and causing passersby to regard him with curiosity.

'He refuses to concede that slavery can be beneficial to niggers. By the devil, I'll show him! Next week I'll take Caspar to his house and we'll see what he has to say then.'*

Prince kept silent. They had reached St James's Street and he was watching with awe the dandies who were parading its length. Carlton seemed not to notice those elegantly dressed young men in their flawless outfits, skin-tight trousers and starched cravats. They strolled the street in pairs, drawling languidly to each other. Beside them, Prince felt shabby; he was ashamed of Carlton with his ill-cut suit and rustic gait. He was sensitive to his impact on others and it was clear to him that he and Carlton were attracting some disdainful stares.

Carlton was still gripping his elbow. 'These people don't want to understand that without slaves there can be no sugar. If there's no sugar, where will they be?' He waved his hand at a couple of brightly dressed young men sauntering along the opposite side of the street. They looked startled and averted their eyes.

'The money those wastrels get from their fathers comes from sugar. If they don't grow it, they ship it, and if they don't ship it, they sell it, and if they don't sell it, they make money out of people who do. At the bottom of this pile of popinjays, propping up his whole fashionable pretense, is the slave.'

He clapped Prince on his shoulder adding to his embarrassment. The parading dandies within hearing distance, turned up their noses and sniggered loudly.

'Carlton,' he begged, 'Please don't. People are watching.'

'Of course they are. Can't mind their own business, any of them. This town thrives on tattle and scandal. They don't want to hear the truth.'

Do you? Prince longed to ask. Now was not the time to remonstrate and cause a scene. It was a slow process to enlighten Carlton. Since their arrival there had been some changes in his attitude. He now permitted Prince to call him by his name unless they were in company.

Carlton had learned that he could not exert the control over Prince, Gwen, Nat and even Caspar that he could do in the isolation of his plantation. Instead of being slaves, they were now his servants;

*See *Bondmaster Fury*

Caspar was his valet, Nat his steward, Gwen his housekeeper and Prince his secretary/companion.

When members of the West India Interest came to call, they all, including Carlton, played the roles assigned to them. At other times, they lived together as a family. They were all aware that Carlton's control over them could not be enforced with the whip. There was another bond. Carlton was being gradually drawn within an orbit controlled, not by him as he thought, but by Prince.

'Aren't you disgusted with the English?' Carlton spat out his contempt then lapsed into silence, glowering at any of the dandies whose amused glances he noticed.

Prince couldn't say he was disgusted with the English because he knew so little about them. He was familiar only with the tradesmen who called at their house and with the folk he met casually around Chapel Street. Apart from political acquaintances, no one called on Carlton or invited him to dine.

Prince had come to realize that in London, Carlton Todd was not the great man he was in the Caribbean. There were no invitations to balls or soirées. The haunts of the *beau monde* such as Almack's Assembly Rooms in King Street were closed to him.

This lack of entrée to the fashionable world of the Prince of Wales's London dismayed Prince. He knew so much about it from hearsay, listening to the gossip of the ladies he used to squire in St John's. He regarded having to live outside it as an indication of deficiency on Carlton's part.

Carlton claimed to despise social life. He became deliberately coarse whenever one of his political acquaintances invited him on a fashionable outing, and refused to go.

If Prince was disgusted with anyone, it was with Carlton not with the English. Instead of seeing him as a man he once respected, he seemed uncouth beside the sophisticated dandies of St James's.

'Carlton,' he said, drawing him aside, 'can we walk through Hyde Park?'

'What the devil for?' Again, heads turned at his oath for Carlton's gruff voice was used to shouting at slaves across the canefields, and it caused a ripple of disturbance in the tranquil surface of the afternoon promenade.

Prince hurried to lure him away. He guessed that the pair of them would be the object of ribald discussion in the clubs and coffee houses that night.

'Hyde Park is where people of quality ride in the evenings,' he said quietly. 'Stunning sight, I'm told.'

'Bah! What's the point of such frivolity?'

Prince grinned. 'Some of the ladies are reputed to be very beautiful.'

Carlton stopped suddenly. 'Prince! I know what's in your mind. You want to get me hooked so that you can have Gwen to yourself.'

Prince continued to walk which made Carlton annoyed because he was forced to run after him, or look ridiculous bellowing at his back.

'Why don't you stop when I stop?' he said, catching up with him. 'In Dominica, you'd walk two paces behind. Such a high opinion you have of yourself.'

'Perhaps you should have one too,' said Prince quietly, flushing with shame at the attention they were still attracting. 'We are in London, not Layou.' He held his head higher to control his temper.

'Aye,' said Carlton as his mood softened. 'There are times when I wish I was in Layou. Not even Ella shows such disrespect for me as I get here.' He clapped Prince on his shoulders as a way of showing that he was not really cross with him.

Prince's anger did not subside as easily as Carlton's. His personality harbored a hot temper that when roused could blow as long as a hurricane. He rarely lost control over his emotions, unlike white men who flew into a rage one minute and the next could be slapping their enemy's back and saying they didn't mean it.

His lack of confidence in Carlton had developed over the weeks as he noticed that Carlton was being shunned and snubbed. It was not lack of money – he had a fortune with his huge credit with the sugar importers – it was his behavior that put people off. Had he been less dogmatic about slavery, he might have been accepted by society as a creole eccentric from the Colonies.

Prince was piqued because he knew that beneath Carlton's bombastic manner, there was a pleasant individual who could be charming. His hope that Carlton would be his introduction to London's fashionable life diminished the more Carlton became convinced that society was frivolous.

'You're in a queer mood this evening, Prince,' said Carlton, banging his back again. 'Maybe it's my fault, eh? I've been so engrossed with my affairs, I haven't begun to do what I came to England to do.' He sighed.

'Yes, we must see the sights. Since we're walking, we'll take a stroll through Hyde Park.'

Prince seized Carlton's hand and shook it, to the delight of the dandies who had stopped parading to watch the spectacle of the creole and his nigger.

'It's this way,' he said, quickening his pace and leading Carlton down a street to the right.

Hyde Park was given up exclusively at that hour to persons of rank and fashion. The carriage company consisted of the celebrated beauties of the town. Some were ladies of quality while the connections of others with quality was through the patronage of such ladies' husbands. Dashing young guards officers cantered alongside the carriages, peering into them in the hope of obtaining a smile from the winsome ladies concealed within.

Prince gazed with delight at this spectacular display of wealth and intrigue. It was just as he imagined. He could not understand Carlton's disgruntled attitude in wanting to decry it. For him, this was the center of the world and it was easy to believe that every well dressed man on horse back and gracious lady in a carriage were grand people of great importance.

If only, he thought wistfully, Carlton had a horse to ride in such company.

'They say,' he whispered happily to Carlton as they strolled through the Park, 'that the Prince of Wales himself does ride here.' He had forgotten the cold and in his excitement turned his head this way and that to stare at the people riding around them.

He noticed that there was no one else walking through that part of the Park. Unknown to him, there was a tacit understanding among the lower and middle classes of London not to intrude themselves on the areas favored by the upper classes.

'You've seen enough, Prince,' said Carlton. 'I'm thirsty and I'm cold.'

'Don't you find it interesting?' He turned with reluctance to follow Carlton out of the Park. 'All these lords and ladies in their fine clothes.'

'Give me a coffle of slaves without any clothes and I'll show you people worth ten times as much as these fools.' Carlton strode down the path not caring about the horses riding toward him, and blind to the angry glares of their riders.

Prince began to wonder if they were committing a social gaffe by being in the Park. A carriage bore down and Prince pulled Carlton aside just before it could crash into them.

'By the devil!' exclaimed Carlton, waving his fist. He shook off Prince's effort to restrain him. 'You're not fit to drive a gang of niggers in my fields!'

Together they glared at the occupants of the carriage as two pairs of eyes blazed back at them.

'Heavens!' a voice gasped.

'By the devil,' growled Carlton again.

'A blackamoor!' shrilled a woman's voice.

Prince frowned, catching Carlton's arm as the carriage came to an abrupt halt. 'Let him come to us,' he hissed as the coachman turned to look at them. But the coachman didn't descend. Instead, a lady's head emerged from the carriage window, stared at them, then withdrew.

Carlton nudged Prince in his waist. 'Come on, boy, this is none of our business.'

There was an impasse. Neither Carlton nor Prince moved. The coachman faced forward and the carriage waited.

'We can't run off like footpads,' said Prince. 'Maybe you should present your compliments to the ladies . . .' He longed to go up to the carriage and introduce himself.

'I'll have no truck with them.' Carlton shook his head vigorously. 'So called ladies! They ride here in the hope of meeting the Prince of Wales.'

'They surely don't think you're him in disguise.'

Prince's exasperation made Carlton laugh. 'That's true, a fat old toad he is, I believe.'

'I say,' a voice called from the carriage. 'You there.'

'Huh!' Carlton turned his back and folded his arms.

'Let me go,' Prince begged.

'Who said "let him come to us"?' Carlton chuckled. 'Now it's a lady who calls, you can't wait to run to her. You're a natural slave, Prince.'

'She can't very well get out of the carriage and come here. A gentleman would go to her as well as a slave.'

'Go then.' Carlton shook his head, hiding his amusement behind a stern expression.

Prince sprinted up to the carriage and bowed before the open window. 'Yes, ma'am?' he panted, raising his eyes. He gazed into the face of the lady studying him through a lorgnette.

He could see only her bonnet pulled low over her face and the firm bodice of her brocade coat buttoned high to her throat. Of her companion in the coach there was nothing to see and only a whisper to hear as she directed the questioning.

'Ask him is he all right.'

'Are you all right?' the voice behind the lorgnette demanded with a trace of resentment.

'Yes, ma'am.' Prince grinned cheekily. 'And you?'

'Tell him we were concerned that he may have been hurt by the horses. That's why we stopped.' The whisperer waited while the remark was repeated.

'It's not the custom for people to walk on this path at this hour,' the lady with the lorgnette added, a hint of reprimand in her voice.

'Imagine,' she said under her breath, 'a blackamoor, here!'

'May I ask what is wrong with me walking here?' Prince asked, keeping his smile broad and friendly. His question was greeted by a giggle from the lady out of sight.

'Bid them good day and let's be gone!' shouted Carlton.

Prince nodded at him, pleading with his eyes for permission to wait another moment. He was enjoying the heady scent of perfume that exuded from the carriage. It was more potent than any smell from Clothilda's cooking pot. He longed to see the lady who kept herself hidden. She sounded much gayer than his frosty interrogator.

The coachman was keeping his eye on the horses, from which Prince assumed him to be a man of discretion. He also guessed that his passengers were in the habit of stopping to speak to strange men.

'If I have done something wrong, I apologize,' he said when there was no more conversation offered from the inside of the carriage.

He was standing on the path and whereas he had a good view of the coach's interior with its pink silk lining, he could see nothing of the occupants. The lady with the lorngette leaned out again and lowered it so he saw her eyes. They were gray and twinkled merrily in contrast to her formidable voice.

'My friend wants to know from where do you come?'

'Please inform m'lady that such confidences are not to be divulged to strangers.' He winked.

For a moment, it appeared that his boldness had been too much. The lady withdrew her head in consternation. He heard the hidden lady whispering insistently and a sudden reference to the Prince. He wondered if the royal guard was to be summoned to have him removed for insolence.

The lady returned to the window. 'Do you come,' she asked while her gray eyes regarded him with intense curiosity, 'from Antigua?'

Prince broke into a sweat; he felt his heart quickening as a tremor of excitement seized him. He stared into the inviting eyes of the woman and gave a shout of joy.

'Carlton!' he called, racing around the back of the carriage to the other side. He pulled open the door.

The lady who had been whispering put her hands to her cheeks in alarm. Her eyes met his. 'Prince?' she said breathlessly.

'What the hell are you doing?' demanded Carlton, taking hold of him by his collar and pulling him away from the coach.

'I apologize for my nigger,' he said. 'He hasn't long arrived from Africa and –'

Prince brushed Carlton's hand away. He bowed.

'May I present my friend, the Bondmaster of Roxborough, Mr Carlton Todd,' he said with a grin. 'Mr Carlton, this lady is the Marchioness of Witham.'

CHAPTER SEVENTEEN

' "The Marchioness of Witham has invited us to tea." '

Hayes was pacing the balcony as Ella read the latest letter from Carlton. She sat on the edge of an upright chair to take the weight off her feet of the child she was carrying. She was in the last few days of pregnancy and, being tall, seemed enormous. Hayes avoided having to look at her and grumbled aloud as his eyes swept restlessly over the plantation.

'What's my boy havin' tea with a marchin-whatever for? Is that why he left me alone with ten score niggers? To gallivant around London with nobility!' He spat off the balcony in disgust.

Ella ignored his outburst, continuing to read the letter, more anxious than Hayes for news of Carlton and her son.

' "I shall take Prince, whom ladies regard as *très amusant*, and young Caspar. We are all having new clothes made for the occasion as it is considered bad taste to be accoutered in anything but the latest style." '

'Has he gone mad?' Hayes gripped the balcony rail.

'He explains why, Massa Hayes. Shall I finish?'

'Yes, yes, if you must.' He glanced at Ella as though it was somehow her fault.

' "I know you will not approve," ' she continued. ' "I am somewhat astonished myself. I believe it is in the best interest of planters that their situation should be known in the highest circles. There is a great deal of ignorance abroad about the condition of slavery and certain individuals are agitating with considerable effect for its amelioration." '

Hayes strode over to Ella and snatched the letter from her hands. 'Did Carlton write this? Where did he find such words?' He stared at the page, biting his lip in fury.

Ella felt weak, unable to stand and face him. He had made such an astonishing recovery in the months of Carlton's absence, that she found it tiring to keep one step ahead of him. With her time drawing near, he constantly surprised her with his changing moods and new rages.

He was holding the paper in front of her face. She took it in trembling fingers, dismayed that he noticed her nervousness.

'It's not Mas Carlton's hand, massa,' she said, feeling wretched and not knowing why. 'I believe the letter is written by Prince.'

'His comrade is a slave!' Hayes twirled away and paced the balcony deck with his hands behind his back, accentuating the stoop of his shoulders.

'In London, he should have an English companion, a gentleman who will take him to brothels and introduce him to whores, not to simpering ladies in a fashionable drawing room.'

'Yes, massa. There is more.'

Hayes snapped his fingers for her to continue.

' "The ban on the shipping of slaves from Africa two years ago was inspired by these fellows," ' Ella read. ' "It is clear their influence must not be underestimated. However, as I have explained to the members of the West India Interest who are concerned for the continued prosperity of their holdings, it will be people such as ourselves on whom they may rely for fresh stocks of slaves.

' "I have endeavoured to convince them that purpose-bred Roxborough slaves will be far superior to any import from Africa. A Roxborough slave will be able to produce at a greater pace and at less expense of management and money, because he is especially reared for the cane fields. Needless to say, my representations have aroused considerable interest." '

Hayes shook his head and Ella studied the paper again to see if she had read it correctly. She did not understand all that was there and, judging by Hayes's bemused expression, neither did he.

'Does he say when he's coming back?' he asked suddenly.

She scanned the letter again. 'No, massa. There is only one more paragraph.'

'What does that say?'

She hesitated. She closed her eyes, but there was no way she could avoid reading it. Whether she did, or not, Hayes was going to ask Tita and then Kingston to read the letter. Visitors – often planters and traders looking for slaves stayed the night – would be obliged to read him Carlton's letters as well.

'He says, "I am pleased to hear your health improves and I pray that it will continue to do so. If you find Ella interferes too much in your restored interest in the plantation, please do not restrain yourself on my account. She is a loyal slave but, of course, has no authority that supersedes whatever you chose to do for our mutual benefit." '

She read the final words of salutation and held up the letter for Hayes to take. The gleam in his eye alarmed her.

'Hah! The boy is learning some sense in London!' He took the paper and stuffed it into the pocket of his clean shirt. He was wearing new boots, polished to a high shine and walked to the edge of the balcony.

'Be about your work, Ella. I'm going to the nursery.' He eased himself down the steps, clinging to the brick balustrade to lessen the pain in his knees.

She rose wearily from her seat and called out after him. 'Shall I send Pool with you, massa?'

He grunted and waved his hand in refusal.

She sighed. There was no more she could do. Congo Venus would give her a full account of everything Hayes said and did in the nursery. There was nothing the old man could do, no wench he could eye, no slave he could watch, without her being informed. Yet she could only feel dread when he wandered around the plantation alone.

She was concerned for his safety. Despite his renewed vigor, at times he was doddery, especially if Pip had been generous with the rum in his punch. If Massa Hayes were to have an accident and die while Carlton was away, it was unthinkable what chaos would ensue.

Ella's main concern was his temper. So far, she had dissuaded him from meting out any dire punishments, but the slaves were made nervous by his unexpected appearances.

Ironically, she was to blame for his recovery. It happened with the bedwenches.

Instead of draining the venom from him and causing him to collapse exhausted, the opposite happened. Once his virility, which had lain dormant for a decade, was fired, he was a new man.

No longer was he content to wallow in sloth; he was driven by an urge to prove himself. He began at first to walk around the courtyard aided by Pip and Pool. Soon, there was no restraining him. Ella was obliged to post Marcus on special watch in case he ambled off without her knowing.

Inspired by his new vigor, he began to take care of his appearance. Pip was summoned every morning to shave him. At night, he removed his day clothes instead of sleeping in them for weeks, as was his custom. Now he donned a night shirt. He took a bath once a month and was fresher and tidier than ever before.

The improvement in his dress changed his posture. He walked steadier and held himself better. He became so preoccupied with his return to health that he no longer spent hours in his chair sipping punch. He drank when he wanted but, to Ella's consternation, he no longer wanted so much.

If this revitalized Hayes was not problem enough, Ella observed that the old man was becoming partial to Tita. He saw her five or six times a day, often visiting her in her chamber, ostensibly to see how the children were faring. Thanks to Sophie, who was a natural boaster quite unable to keep a secret, Ella had a daily report on what Massa Hayes said and did to Tita. She knew when he pinched the baby's cheek and – oh lord! – when he pinched Tita's bottom.

At the very time when she needed to be active, constantly monitoring this impetuous old man, Ella was at her weakest. Her first pregnancy, with Caspar, did not cause her so much inconvenience, but that was over twelve years before. Now she was always tired and had only her belief in Carlton to keep her going.

'Wha' yo' doin' in de massa's chair, Ella?' The shout from Tita roused her immediately. She gazed around in confusion. She must have fallen asleep and it was true, she was lying back in Massa Hayes's chair with her feet stretched out on the balcony railing.

'Yo' does be like one fat old sow,' said Tita with a cruel laugh. 'Yo' ain' fit to run de house for de massa.'

'Tita!' She put down her feet and dragged herself out of the chair, pulling herself up to her full height. 'Yo' ever get cursed in yuh life?'

'Don't talk to me, Ella. If yo' curse me ah know how to fix yo' good.'

'I ain' go'n waste de obeah on yo', gal. I believe yuh mam done hex yo' to make yo' so mean.'

'Ah go'n fix yo', Ella! See if ah don't.'

She felt Tita's eyes burning with hatred as she walked slowly off the balcony. She swayed and held the rail to support herself. She was ashamed at being caught feeling so low. It was the strain of the baby, of running the plantation.

'Mayhap someone done do you' somet'in' . . .' Pip suggested when she complained about feeling out of sorts.

'Yo' ain' de only one does know obeah. In Layou, dere be one ol' lady dey does say be a *soucoyan*'. One day dey go'n catch she when she flyin'.'

Ella was sitting in her chair in the kitchen. She had sent Marcus to follow Massa Hayes to see he didn't get into difficulties. Pool was nowhere to be seen. Cleo and her helper were baking. It was after four, the sun was no longer bright and a breeze was beginning to stir.

'Who go'n do me dat?' she asked scornfully. 'De slaves know I help dem. I done keep Massa Hayes from lashin' dem an' causin' discontent.'

'Yes.' Pip nodded agreement, his handsome face creased with concern. 'Dey be grateful for dat.'

'Dere does be one . . .' Her heart sank at the thought. 'If she have de power . . .'

'Tita?'

'How can dat be?' She shook her head. 'She only talk plenty.'

'She hab plenty chance . . .'

It was a shattering thought. She felt the baby kick. If Tita wanted to slip a powder in her morning coffee or put something in her cocoa tea at night, she could do it with ease. The kitchen was a busy place, with field hands as well as house slaves passing in and out all the time.

'Quick, Pip. Help me up.'

'What nuh, Ella?' He supported her with his body held steady against her weight.

'My quarters, Pip. I go'n search.'

She swayed down the passage followed by Pip. She threw open her door and gazed around the simple room. She had a bed with a reed mat on it, and a wooden chest for her clothes. Other paraphenalia – pots, a mortar and pestle, jars of dried herbs, a candle, piles of rags, even some books – lay strewn around the floor. The room was dark for she kept the windows shuttered during the day. She peered at it carefully.

'Wha' yo' searchin' for, Ella?'

'See if she done put a 'figy here.'

An effigy, a crudely fashioned image of someone disliked, was an essential part of any malediction. Ella knew that for obeah to be successful, the victim must fear it. An effigy, or cock without a head, a powder wrapped in a dry leaf envelope, or a bottle placed in a certain way, were all signs that struck terror into the heart of a slave who suspected obeah was being used against him.

She searched her room thoroughly, her doubts growing greater with each minute. Finally, she sank on the hard bed and sighed. 'Dere ain't not'in here.' she muttered.

'Why don' yo' protec' yuhself'gainst she?'

'I can, Pip.' She grinned wryly. 'I need yuh help.'

'Me, Ella?' Pip backed away. 'Pool de one for dat. Ah does be a respec'able nigger. An don' know he danda conjure.'

'Tonight, Pip.' She stared at him. 'When everyone has gone to sleep.'

There was no moon that night. The house was still. The only sounds came from the leaves of flamboyant trees rustling together as softly as ribbons on a Lady's gown. Ella stood in the darkness of her room, with the shutter open to the night, and listened carefully.

There were slaves who said she flew out of her window at night and that she hovered in the shadows of the quarters listening to the slaves talking together. She sighed. How she wished she *could* fly. She prowled the slave quarters at night, but she walked there and back through the bush like any other mortal. It was that, and the strength she needed for the baby living inside her, that caused her to feel such fatigue.

She padded softly out of her cell to the kitchen where Pip was asleep, curled up on a mat on the floor, waiting for her. He jumped when she touched him with her finger on his lips to stop him crying out. She held his hand and led him around the kitchen table to the fire where the embers glowed faintly.

'Take that,' she said, pointing to the cauldron she had hung over the fire earlier that evening. It contained an assortment of herbs and powders, some pig's blood, a strand of Tita's hair, and some ash from the *boucan*, the fire, where Tita's mistress died. The secret was in the spell, in an African tongue she had memorized from her mother but which she didn't understand.

Pip lifted the cauldron reluctantly. It wasn't heavy and he held it out from his body lest a drop of its contents splash on him. He let Ella take his other hand as she guided him out of the kitchen and up the back steps. It was so dark he was unable to see the cauldron at his side.

Ella bade him wait at the stop of the steps. She glided away before he could protest at being left alone with the magic. They arranged that if anything happened to disturb them, Pip was to return to the kitchen and say he knew nothing. She needed him to carry the cauldron because in her present state she was too weak to lift it. For a strong woman that was unusual. Her baby was going to be a giant for the strength he was draining from her.

She trod softly around the balcony, guiding herself with her hand on the railing. The guest room adjoining Massa Hayes's chamber was empty and the window closed. She felt her way past it and listened outside Hayes's window. The sound of deep breathing told her he was asleep. She listened again and heard the noise of the wench lying with him. It was the new one he had found for himself in the nursery that afternoon. The air was rank with the odor generated by the coupling of the old and the young.

She passed Hayes's room and entered the house through the drawing room door. Her intention was to spread the contents of the cauldron along the floor outside the room where Tita slept with Sophie and the children. She wanted to isolate the evil there so it could not affect her or anyone else in the house. To do this, it was necessary to splash the mixture along the base of the outside of all the walls.

She sniffed the air in the drawing room. When she was convinced it was empty, she went back to call Pip. She was unhappy about making him follow her around the house. The old man was a light sleeper and a clumsy move from Pip would wake him immediately.

'Wait here,' she hissed, drawing a ladleful of the liquid from the cauldron resting by his feet. He opened his mouth to protest but she touched his lips gently then crept away, bearing the ladle before her.

Hayes was still sleeping soundly as she passed his window. She slipped into the drawing room, crossed around the floor, keeping to the outside to reduce the risk of the floorboards creaking unexpectedly, and into the dining room.

The room where Tita slept was on the right, although its entrance door opened on to the balcony at the back. She sprinkled her nostrum along the base of the wooden wall that divided the two rooms, repeating the ancient curse under her breath.

On her way out, she was careless and knocked against a chair. It scraped over the floor with a retort that seemed to her as sharp as a gun shot. No one stirred. She reached Pip and refilled the ladle. Now she had to do a complete round of the balcony to the door of the dressing room that adjoined the chamber where Carlton used to sleep. One wall of the dressing room was the wall of Tita's chamber. It was empty, so there was no danger if she was careful.

She reached the door and eased it open. Carlton always kept the hinges oiled so that his bedwenches could come and go at night without disturbing his father. She stepped into the room.

By touch, she found the wall and poured the liquid along its length. She turned to go, feeling for the doorway. The door was shut. She frowned to herself, wondering how it closed without her hearing. She knew she left it open. She tried the handle and gently pushed. It didn't move.

Sweat trickled down the inside of her thighs as she pushed again. The door was locked. From the outside.

She heard nothing in the darkness, yet her ears were usually as keen as a bat's. She turned to the other door, the one that gave access to Carlton's chamber, and moved cautiously across the floor. Her foot touched a table and she groped her way around it, careful not to make a noise. Outside a dog began to bark.

Pip, she thought to herself. He's heard something and gone back to the kitchen. That would have set the dog barking. But who had locked the dressing room door?

The door to Carlton's chamber was ajar and she eased it open. She had moved around this room many times in the dark and soon found the handle of the door that opened into the drawing room. She turned it and pulled the door toward her. It was locked too.

She didn't panic; there were the windows. Although she was big with her child, she believed she could ease through the one above Carlton's bed. The shutters were fastened on the inside. Perhaps it was a coincidence and she hadn't been discovered.

Her hopes died when she pushed open the shutter and found herself gazing into the barrel of Massa Hayes's blunderbuss.

'Whoah, wench!' she heard him say. He was wearing his night shirt and threw an ominous shadow over her when Tita came up behind him with a candlestick in her hand.

'What have we here?'

'Yo' see, massa!' Tita's lips foamed with excitement. 'Ah done say she prowlin'.'

'You caught her good, Tita.' Hayes prodded Ella away from the window with the musket barrel. 'Now close that shutter,' he said, 'and we'll fasten it from the outside. We'll keep this evil wench here until day break.'

'Please, sah . . .' begged Ella, falling back onto Carlton's bed. The shutter slammed above her and she was alone in the dark.

Judging by the creaks and crashes and excited voices, her capture roused the whole household. She wondered if Pip had been able to slip back into the kitchen unobserved. Lanterns were hung on the balcony and she realized that Massa Hayes had posted slaves to watch she didn't escape.

She didn't try. She was so weary. Tita had won. She lay back on Carlton's bed, cradled his pillow close to her breast, and wept herself to sleep.

The moan of the dawn conch shell woke the slaves. It didn't disturb Ella. There was a second call, an hour later, when Pool stood on the grand steps, raised the conch to his lips and blew lustily into it. Massa Hayes and Tita stood beside him.

The slaves, preparing to walk to the fields and provision grounds for work, heard the wailing and looked at each other in terror. This was the call to the *cou*; it only sounded when all the slaves were being summoned to the house because of some dreadful event. The house conch never brought good news: sometimes it meant death, a proclamation or some terrible punishment.

One by one, in groups and in gangs shepherded by their drivers, the slaves made their way up the trails to the house. They walked reluctantly, speculating among themselves about what calamity had befallen Roxborough. Congo Venus and the other old ladies in the Paddock, clutched each other for comfort. They drove the children up to the house, leaving behind only the babies.

Ella slept on, unaware of the slaves gathering in the courtyard, their hushed murmuring filling the air like the drone of mosquitoes. The sun was climbing up the side of the hills that hemmed in the plantation, and would soon burst over the top, flooding the valley with brightness and chasing away the shadows of the night

Hayes stood beside Pool on the top step and watched as the slaves clustered nervously below him.

The sight of their master fired new speculation and the lowing of the herd increased. Hayes stomped back to his chair, feeling threatened by the sound.

'Bring Ella,' he snapped at Pip.

Laura ran across to stand beside him, her tiny eyes bright with excitement. Tita was dressed in her best gown, her waist drawn in with a tight corset. Her hair, which Sophie had been brushing for an hour, glimmered in the morning sunlight.

'Wake up, Ella,' Pip begged, shaking her shoulder.

Sleep had been merciful to her. Was it from Carlton she regained her strength? She opened her eyes and smiled bravely. There was no longer any fear of Tita, nor of Hayes, nor of anyone. The baby inside her was her comfort.

She sipped at the strong coffee Pip had brought her. She watched him calmly.

'Don't be frightened,' she said. 'Did he see yo' las' night?'

'No.' Pip paused before the words came rushing out. 'Ella, some-t'in' terrible go'n happen. Massa summon all de slaves. He an' Tita plottin' somet'in for yuh wickedness.'

'I know,' she said sadly. 'He thinks he has no need of me. If he don't shame me today, he sure go'n shame me tomorrow.'

'Yo' ain' scared?'

She was scornful. 'Of buckra? No white man can change what I does be. My mam was a princ . . .'

'Dat ain' no help.' Pip led her out of the room. He was shaking. 'Ah done put plenty rum in yuh coffee, Ella. It make yo' boozy?'

She drew herself up to her full height and stepped onto the balcony. She was still wearing her night shift and nothing else. Yet she was more dignified than Tita tarted up in her dead mistress's finery.

There was a gasp from the slaves in the yard. It grew to an outburst of astonished chatter as they realized it was Ella who was to be punished.

'Shut up!' shouted Hayes, banging his whip down on the rail. The handle cracked loudly against the wood. The slaves hushed at the sound, their eyes on Ella and on the whip. It was a bull whip, the master of whips, with its short stock weighted with lead and its raw leather tongue plaited into six strands of varying thickness.

Ella stood upright before Hayes and stared at him haughtily. She no longer felt weary and weak. The blood of the Batutsi flowed in her veins and she would not cower before him.

'You were caught in Mas Carlton's chamber, Ella,' said Hayes, loudly so that the slaves closest to the house could hear. They would pass on the substance of her crime to the others.

'What were you doing there?'

Ella declined to answer. She gazed beyond him to where the sea shimmered. There, Carlton and Caspar were waiting.

'She done make obeah!' screeched Tita, unable to stand the tension. 'She try to put a spell on young Hayes so he come sickly an' die.'

Ella's eyes flickered as she wondered whether to answer the charge. No. It would give Tita too much importance. Instead, she raised her head higher, not deigning to acknowledge Tita's presence.

'Is it true, Ella?' Hayes was angry, determined to make an example of her. If he showed the slaves he could humiliate her, he would have their respect. He would be master of his own plantation.

He cracked the whip on the balcony once more, his frail arm burning with pain at the effort.

'It's not true,' she whispered so only Hayes could hear. 'You will do what you must do. I won't beg for mercy.'

'Take her!'

Pip and Pool shuffled forward reluctantly. 'Where, massa?'

'There!'

For the first time, Ella noticed Mercury standing in the center of the courtyard with two members of his field gang. They had hoes in their hands. They had scraped a small trough in the hard mud of the yard.

She was puzzled about its purpose. She was vaguely flattered that old Hayes had taken the trouble to devise a punishment for her that was unique. She expected to be strung up from a branch and beaten with a paddle.

She held her head high as she was marched down the grand steps. The black faces around her were a blur and she sensed their concern. They were relieved she was the one being punished, not them.

Pip squeezed her arm above her elbow to give her courage. She was grateful for it.

'Lor', massa. Hab mercy!'

Congo Venus waddled forward and stood at the bottom step, her gray hair in two plaits that stuck out of her head like crumpled horns. Her *mouchoir madras* was adrift and tears streamed down her cheeks from her rheumy, bloodshot eyes.

'She full, sah!'

'Aye!' Hayes nodded. 'Hence the trench.' He walked to the balcony rail and directed Pip and Pool to lay Ella on the ground. 'Let her belly rest in the hole.'

She kneeled at Pip's feet and he stood back. Mercury helped her.

'Lay yuhself in de hole, Ella.' He whispered in her ear while he steadied her, 'Ah go'n flick de whip so it crack. It ain' go'n cut yo'. Holler loud an' de massa go'n be satisfy.'

'Do it properly, Mercury.' she chided him. 'Let dem see I ain't 'fraid de lash.'

She lay with her stomach in the trench and her chin resting on the mud with arms spread out. Her legs were splayed apart, half in and half out of the hole. Her shift was rucked up to her shoulders and she felt the warmth of the sun seeking out her bare buttocks.

She sensed the slaves were puzzled, unable to know what to make of the woman they admired and feared for her obeah powers being stretched out half-naked and half-buried in front of them.

She didn't see Hayes toss the bullwhip to Mercury. He raised his hand for silence. The murmuring of the crowd died.

Hayes snapped down his hand, and the whip hissed through the air. It cracked above her buttocks with a sickening whistle that set the crowd wailing. She felt the tickle on her skin and remained motionless.

Tita leaned over to Hayes and spoke in his ear. He watched the second lash hiss over Ella.

'Mercury,' he shouted. 'Make every lash cut or I'll have you hung up by your grain.'

Ella heard. She twisted her head so she could see Mercury. She nodded her understanding.

The next blow hissed and sliced into her skin with a pain that made her rise out of the hole in shock.

Tita squealed with pleasure and Laura clapped her hands, gurgling with delight. Hayes's lip trembled. He leaned on Tita for support.

The second stroke fell close to the first, opening a cut that oozed blood as the tongue of the whip caressed it. The third splashed blood and sliced away flesh that plopped onto the mud beside the hole.

Ella's inside wrenched as the fourth blow seemed to split her apart. She bit her tongue, determined not to cry out. The fifth stroke drove her mouth open with a shriek of agony as blood spurted out between her legs.

There was another cry, not hers, and a shadow fell across her.

'Lor', massa! Hab mercy! De baby done burst.'

She slipped into a deep peace as Carlton cradled her in his arms.

CHAPTER EIGHTEEN

Carlton pretended to listen to the ancient lady sitting with him. He was perched on the edge of a couch, a tea cup balanced in his hand. He felt ridiculous. The lady, whose face was camouflaged with a pallet-full of paint and powder to conceal her advanced age, was conversing politely while he grew more and more impatient with her small talk. He longed to be out of the salon with its fashionable ladies and dapper men with braying voices and studied poses.

London's smart society, he thought, was not worth a nigger's toss compared with a fête in Dominica, or even an afternoon on the balcony with Hayes discussing matters of importance such as which colt to put to a filly in her first menses. As for fashion, Ella in a chambray shift was more attractive than any of the corsetted women chattering around him.

The Marchioness of Witham was *At Home.* This expression, so Carlton was informed by Prince when the card arrived, was an invitation for them to call at her home during the times and on the day indicated. Prince's assurance that it was a great honor to be invited, flattered him into agreeing to go. For status, he insisted that Casper should accompany them as their attendant.

The lady addressing Carlton lapsed into a meaningful silence. He jerked himself back to the present and faced her.

'I beg your pardon.' He sipped the dregs of his tea, which was cold, to cover his rudeness.

'I inquired whether you are married, Mr Todd.' The lady's eyes gazed at him reproachfully from the depths of her painted face.

'No,' he answered gruffly. With relief, he surrendered his empty tea cup to a passing servant. He regretted his unnecessary discourtesy and turned back to the lady with a smile of apology.

'My wife died last year.' He held up his hand to stall the woman's expression of sympathy. 'It was a blessing. She was quite mad.'

The old lady quivered and Carlton was pleased with the effect he was having on her. He hadn't spoken to anyone about his wife since her death. He felt detached. What seemed a disgrace at the time, wasn't important any more.

'It ran in her family.' He laughed, as though this explanation finished the matter.

'One should be careful when marrying a stranger,' the lady answered, placing her hand on Carlton's wrist. 'Of course, it is possible to make a perfect match.'

For a moment, Carlton wondered if he was being propositioned. The old lady's eyes were studying him intently although her jowls and wrinkled face were shaking out of control. He glanced around him.

All the other men were surrounded by beautiful women and, judging by the peals of laughter, had admiring audiences for their sparkling wit. He was the only one trapped on a couch with a lady who was gaga and nearly three times his age.

'I understand you have a considerable amount of property, Mr Todd. A gentleman with your looks and status will meet no end of personable young ladies this season. One could be your next wife. None of them mad, I assure you; from good families. Not heiresses, you understand, but with *background*.' She shut her mouth firmly and stared at him to emphasize the importance she attached to her last word.

He was alarmed. The old lady, he realized too late, wasn't dotty at all. Helen, the Marchioness, had introduced him to her on his arrival, and sat them together. He paid scant attention to her questions, being more interested in watching the other guests in the room and, when that became boring, in wondering how to extricate himself without causing offence.

Now it occurred to him that he had been placed with the old lady deliberately, to be interrogated as to his means and suitability.

He edged along the couch away from her. 'I'm sorry,' he said. 'I'm not looking for a wife this, or any other, season.'

'That's what you think, young man. Perhaps your bereavement has been too recent.' The old lady smiled to put him at ease, but to Carlton it looked like a leer for a condemned man.

'There are so few eligible bachelors this season. Oh,' she fluttered her hands to convey disgust, 'there are plenty of those worthless rakes who prance up and down St James's Street and think they're smart. Silly apes! I wouldn't match a healthy gal with any of them.'

He smiled as he recalled he had held similar conversations on the Roxborough balcony about his slaves and who to pair them with. Maybe life in the drawing rooms of London's nobility wasn't so different from slave rearing.

'You are amused?' The old lady sniffed suspiciously.

'I appreciate your concern for me, ma'am,' he said, bowing his head. 'An English wife would not be suitable for the rugged life of the tropics. It's the climate, you see. One needs to be born in it to live comfortably. So please do not go to any trouble on my part. Your efforts would be misplaced.'

'Permit me to know better than you, Mr Todd.' The old lady twisted in her seat. 'Who is that blackamoor?' she said, spotting Prince on the other side of the room. 'He seems to be a popular young man.'

Prince was surrounded by the most attractive women in the place. Those gazing at him with adoration were the daughters of the elderly ladies chattering behind their fans on the couches lining the walls. Others, the maturer and unmarried, fluttered their eyelashes energetically, vying for his attention.

'Blackamoors are fashionable,' the old lady said with a smile. Carlton was relieved that his interrogation was over. 'The dandies hate it, of course.'

'Why?' he asked, more to keep the lady company than out of interest. He was wondering what tales Prince was telling to keep so many beautiful women enthralled. His easy stance and glib tongue annoyed him, yet he was proud of his slave's success.

'Isn't that obvious? Just look at him. He is so handsome. His bearing, superb! His dress is smart, not exaggerated. A most attractive young man. I must ask Helen where she found him.'

'He's mine.'

'What?' The lady drew back, astonished.

'He's my slave.'

'Hush!' she said, raising her finger. 'You must not mention such a thing here, even if it's true.' She looked flustered.

'I shall forget I ever heard you. Helen would be disgraced. Besides, he is far too sophisticated to be anything of the kind. You only have to look at him to know that. Oh!' she sighed with relief. 'You're having a joke at an old lady's expense. It's because I made you cross.'

'I'm not cross. I have another one here.' He snapped his fingers at one of the liveried servants standing by the doorway. The servant regarded him haughtily.

'Come here, boy,' he called, ignoring the people who stared at him in horror at his behavior. 'Where's my slave?' he said when the servant sauntered over. 'Fetch him here.'

'Mr Todd,' said the lady anxiously. 'What are you going to do?'

'Show you another fine nigger, ma'am. My own breed.' He grinned as the lady twitched with consternation. 'Don't be alarmed, ma'am. I won't ask him to strip off. He won't disgrace our hostess.'

'It's most unusual,' she murmured, fluttering her fan and edging along the couch to the cushions at the end.

Carlton was pleased. Perhaps now the old woman would change her opinion of him as a marriage prospect for her spinster nieces. He had no desire to get married again. He believed white women were faithless and hypocritical. He needed wenches like Ella and Gwen who enjoyed him in bed and weren't shocked by their own instincts. Wenches who knew their place.

'Yes sir?' Caspar stood in front of him.

The boy was holding his head proudly. He wore silk breeches with white stockings and black, highly polished shoes with silver buckles. His coat was burgundy – colored and he sported a white cravat that was flawless in the way it was gathered at his throat. His outfit had cost Carlton as much as a young slave in Dominica. He wanted these English bigwigs to be impressed.

'What a darling black!' a voice shrilled from across the room.

Carlton looked to see his hostess and another woman bearing down on him. He grinned at the old lady. 'Someone likes him,' he said, preparing to stand up.

'That's Lady Norton.' The lady lowered her voice. 'We're related. Very good family. Husband killed in the war. Lively young woman, moderately wealthy . . .'

'Isn't he adorable?' Lady Norton clapped her hands with delight as she looked at Caspar. 'Is he yours?' she asked, her gray eyes fast on Carlton without any pretense at shyness.

'Aye,' he said, rising to his feet. 'His name is Caspar.'

Helen Witham bustled around them. He couldn't help noticing how the old lady was relieved to have her company. Dammit, he thought to himself, it's not my fault if these people are such bores. He bowed briefly to Lady Norton, pleased that someone his own age was showing some interest in him.

'How fortunate you are,' Lady Norton gushed. 'Blacks are quite the rage these days. Several of my friends keep them. As pets, you know.'

'Indeed?' He scowled to keep down his anger. 'This one is too precious to be a pet. He's fully house trained. Mixes the best rum punch in the Caribbean.'

'How divine!' Lady Norton sat in Carlton's place on the couch, overpowering the old lady with her exuberance. Helen Witham hurried back to Prince's side.

Carlton decided he liked Lady Norton. Despite her elaborate coiffure and formal gown, she had a breeziness he found refreshing beside the stilted behavior of the other guests.

'I don't think I've ever had rum punch. It sounds devastating. I'd love to try it.'

'You'd be welcome –'

'Don't be so bold . . ., Lydia!' The old lady interrupted him with a glare that implied priorities had to observed.

'Mr Todd is a stranger here. I must tell you something about him before you proceed willynilly. He's had a tragic marriage and his wife died last year. He has property in the West Indies. A large estate, isn't it, Mr Todd? Worth several thousand a year, I believe?'

'Now you're being bold, aunt.' Lydia laughed and turned to Carlton with a smile of apology.

'Aunt Hortense likes to see people are compatible. She's endearingly romantic and only content when she's pairing off people to their mutual satisfaction.'

Carlton returned her smile. 'It's a practical idea. At home I do it with my slaves. I never thought it would happen to me.' He waited for Lydia to make some comment. Instead, she turned to Caspar.

'How old are you, my dear?'

Carlton flinched. 'Pray call him "boy",' he said crossly.

'I'm twelve years, ma'am.'

'Oh, so polite!' Lydia turned to Carlton with excitement. 'Would you lend him to me, Carlton? I may call you Carlton, mayn't I? Aunt Hortense disapproves but you look an approachable man. I've never had a blackamoor. Do say yes. He's the sweetest thing I've ever seen.'

She leaned over and pinched Caspar's cheek. He squirmed with embarrassment.

Aunt Hortense was outraged. 'Lydia, do behave. What do you want a blackie for?'

'He would be so amusing, aunt. To take to the opera and so forth. My friends would be sick with envy.'

'Do you live in London?' Carlton tried to smother his amazement by changing the subject.

'Oh no, Carlton.' She smiled at his ignorance. 'No one *lives* in London. We only come up for the season. Parliament. You know. I'm staying in this house with Helen. My *home* is in the Channel Islands.'

'What do you think, Caspar?' He was pleased the boy had created a good impression. He was warming to Lydia's charm.

'Whatever pleases you, sir.'

'Then we'll consider it.'

Helen Witham's *At Home* was a great success. It was held in a huge drawing room with floor-to-ceiling windows overlooking the park. As dusk descended and more guests arrived, servants lit candelabra and the party became gayer. Outside, groups of spectators lined the road watching the throng of people within.

There was always a crowd around Prince. His wit entranced his listeners. Carlton, having escaped from Aunt Hortense, strolled around the salon with Caspar at his heels. He endeavored to interest guests in the fine qualities of his blacks.

He did not notice the amusement he was causing Lydia Norton who kept her eyes on him wherever he stood. She discussed him at length with Aunt Hortense after he left the two of them together, and then with Helen Witham. Eventually, she joined him when he was standing alone with Caspar by the fireplace. People were preparing to leave.

'I was serious, Carlton,' she said. 'I would like to borrow your *boy.*'

'May I call you Lydia?'

She raised her eyebrow. 'Why stand on ceremony?'

'Do you?'

'No.' She blushed. 'People do here, you know. Not just Aunt Hortense. That's why Prince is such a success. He's black and the ladies love his perfect manners. His tales amuse the men.'

Carlton scowled. 'I don't hold with such nonsense.'

'So I've noticed.'

'I'm a planter, Lydia. My crop is slaves. Strong creatures bred to work in the fields, to earn their price and their keep, and to make a profit within three years. I don't hold with fancy bucks.' He glanced at Prince.

Lydia Norton frowned.

He misinterpreted her expression as one of interest in his theories. He continued without regard for where he was.

'Of course, I realize that in England a buck like Prince, or even young Caspar here, might be in demand. Maybe I'll breed special slaves just for the English and American market.' He smirked.

'They could be dressed up like macaronies and serve ladies such as yourself. That's why I brought these two with me this afternoon, to learn. I've another one at home, as black as a sweep and as royal as the Prince of Wales himself.'

'Carlton!' Lydia stiffened. 'Do lower your voice. He's over there.'

'Who is?'

'Prinny, of course.' She touched her cheek anxiously. 'Your Prince is keeping him amused. That's why Helen's so happy.'

He stared across the room to the circle around Prince. There was a portly man with a face like a sausage, pink and fat. He was chortling loudly and put his arm around Prince and hugged him.

'By the devil! I must get him away.'

'No!' Lydia restrained him with her hand on his arm. 'Poor Prinny has so little opportunity to be himself. He's enjoying this so much, thanks to your blackamoor. Every house in London will be open to you and your darkies when people hear how the Prince of Wales has accepted them.'

'I didn't know . . .'

'Then keep quiet, I beg of you. Do you see that dour-faced man at his side. The one dressed like a tailor's dummy? That's Beau Brummel. He's furious at your Prince's success. Oh, Helen's so clever to have asked you. It's made this quite the most talked-about afternoon of the season. You'll be on Almack's list in no time. Aunt Hortense will see to that.'

Carlton missed the scheming look in her eye. He was too busy considering the enormity of what was happening. That his breed should be favored by royalty! What a fortune he could make out of selling Prince's offspring.

He was thinking prematurely. Prince didn't seem inclined to

breed. The fool. Even though he had given him Gwen, he had made no progress with her.

The royal party was leaving. Carlton stood anxiously by the fireplace with Lydia at his side, wondering if he would be presented. The gaze of the group was being directed toward him. He braced his shoulders.

Prince called, 'Caspar!'

The boy left his side and strode forward. He swept his right arm across his waist and fell down on one knee in a deep bow. He was rewarded with a great guffaw from a delighted Prince of Wales.

'By the devil!' muttered Carlton aloud. 'Where did he learn that trick?'

'Don't you claim all credit for your blackamoors?' Lydia's friendly sarcasm was lost on him. She gripped his arm as he stepped forward. 'You mustn't go unless he calls you,' she hissed frantically.

He halted. He longed to hear what the Prince was saying. There was a raising of eyes in his direction. Beau Brummel leaned across and said something in the royal ear. There was another gust of laughter and the Prince of Wales turned and swept from the room.

'Bloody Beau!' murmured Lydia to his surprise.

'What's the matter?'

She shook her head. 'You were very nearly presented but for him. It's not important I suppose. Your success is assured thanks to your darling blacks.' She smiled brightly and slipped her arm under his so they could walk across the room to where Helen was standing with Prince.

'Congratulations, dear Helen,' she cooed, clinging to Carlton's arm.

'Thanks to Prince,' said Helen, gazing up into his eyes with rapture. She patted his chest, her hand lingering on his heart.

Carlton was dismayed by the display of intimacy.

'Come on, Prince,' he said gruffly, tugging at his arm and breaking the bond he sensed existed between them. 'We must go.'

'Must you?' cried Helen. 'A glass of champagne first, surely.' She smiled at Prince. Carlton felt disgusted at such outrageous flirting.

'My husband will be here soon,' said Helen, unaware of the anger she aroused in him. She led Prince to the couch where Aunt Hortense was sitting.

'Come and talk to my aunt, dear Prince. You've had such a

success. Who would have dreamed it when we met in Antigua.'

The tension building up in Carlton was deflected by Lydia squeezing his arm. 'Is Antigua an amusing place?' she asked with forced brightness. 'Do tell me what it's like.'

He grunted. 'Another time. Prince, say goodbye. We're going.'

Lydia pouted and toyed with the buttons of his coat. 'Of course,' she said coyly, 'if you've got another engagement . . .'

'We haven't.' He pulled away from her. 'There's been enough high life for these two for one day. Caspar, call our carriage. Prince, take me home!'

He bowed to Aunt Hortense, to Helen and to Lydia, and walked stiffly from the room.

'Oh dear,' cried Lydia to Helen. 'What's upset him?'

Helen blushed. 'I think I know.'

Prince seized her hand and kissed it, bowing low. His eyes smoldered with promise. He bid farewell to Aunt Hortense and Lady Norton then swaggered from the room. The three ladies sighed.

'Carlton Todd is right,' said the old lady, rising slowly to her feet. 'Too much excitement for one day. I'm going to lie down.'

'Aunt Hortense,' said Helen. 'Are you all right?'

'Yes, yes. You did very well, dear. I'm sorry your husband wasn't here to meet your black Prince . . .' She weaved from the room helped by a servant. Helen and Lydia collapsed on the couch.

'She's evil,' said Helen.

'Heavens!' said Lydia, not hearing. 'What a pair!'

'Prince and Caspar?'

'No, Caspar and that divine man, Carlton.'

'I find him rather a bore.'

'Oh no, Helen. A little unpolished, that's all. He's so used to dealing with savages, he must find society rather a strain. So do I, really.'

'Are you saying Prince is a savage?' Helen reached for her fan and fluttered it in front of her bosom.

Lydia heard the note of excitement in her voice. She, too, had seen the glance between Helen and Prince, and noticed how it disturbed Carlton. She was intrigued.

'He is a savage, isn't he?' she said deliberately to provoke her cousin.

'How can that be, dear Lydia?' Helen fluttered her fan even faster which only heightened her agitation. 'He's so charming. You saw how he amused Prinny.'

'So would an organ grinder's monkey.'

Helen drew away. 'What are you saying?' Her eyes blazed with anger.

'Nothing, my dear Your face tells me all. You are somewhat attracted to that darling black, are you not?'

'Me? Whatever makes you think so?'

'No one could blame you, my dear. He looks, well, so manly.'

'You said he's a savage.'

'That's what makes him so *interesting*.'

'He's a gentleman. Kind and considerate.'

'Were you *often* in his company in Antigua?'

'Oh, Lydia!' Helen lost control and laid her head on her cousin's shoulder. Lydia held her firmly, murmuring words of encouragement.

'It was difficult. In Antigua. I never dreamed I'd see him again. He's such a godling, isn't he, and what a success! I feel awfully proud. I tremble when I think of him.'

'I understand.'

'Do you? He's not a savage or a monkey at all. He's so tender . . .'

'Other ladies have loved blackamoors, my dear. You are not the first. I think it's rather touching. To have come all this way to seek you out.'

Helen pulled away and stared at her through her tears. 'Do you think so? Do you really think he did?'

'Of course. He didn't meet you in the park by accident. Why else is he in London?'

'We haven't spoken. There's been no opportunity. Do you think . . .' She was speechless.

'That he loves you? Of course, Helen. I knew it the moment I saw his eyes on you in the park.'

'Heavens!' She clasped her bosom. 'What can I do?'

'What would you like to do?'

'Lydia, it's not that easy. There's Prinny . . .'

'And your husband.'

'Cuthbert doesn't care what I do so long as he doesn't know.'

'I'll help you, Helen. We can make a foursome.'

'Foursome?' She stared.

'I have a fondness for Carlton Todd. Why shouldn't he ask me to dinner? You come as my chaperone and I'll ask him to bring Prince as his companion. We can go to the best places without fear because Prinny's given the black his blessing.'

'Dare we?'

'Of course. I'm intrigued by your Prince, dear. Tell me, what was he like . . .'

'I told you. Very gentle.'

'His body . . . one hears things. Weren't you a little terrified at first?'

Helen swallowed then sighed. 'I don't know what came over me. I was so lonely. It was so hot, I felt I was melting.'

'I'm sure I would do the same, Helen. Is he, well, er, too much? The cut of his breeches, dear. Such a codpiece!'

'Lydia, dear, that is not a codpiece.'

'Oh!' Lydia gasped. 'Do tell.'

CHAPTER NINETEEN

The house in Chapel Street was in a terrace, a row of houses joined to each other by shared walls. It was narrow and large. The basement door opened on to a flight of steps that led up to street level. This was Gwen's domain, assigned to her as housekeeper.

It was Carlton's plan that Prince should sleep down there with her, but Gwen resisted that idea with such a rage that Carlton was obliged to change his mind. Prince was assigned the top floor of the house instead, and had Nat with him as companion.

Carlton slept in the main bedroom on the middle floor. Caspar had the room adjoining it. The first, or ground, floor, was given over to a narrow dining room and a small salon adjoining the passageway from the front door.

Although small, the house was a lonely one for Carlton. He was used to the intimacy of Roxborough where slaves were always within earshot. It was also confined, with no view except for the houses on the opposite side of the street. Prince, however, saw the house differently.

'We could have a grand *soirée* here!' he exclaimed with enthusiasm. He pranced around the small dining room. Carlton, slumped in an armchair by the window, regarded him morosely.

'Haven't you been to enough parties without wanting one here?' He waved at the mantel. It was covered with invitations, most of them unopened.

'Ten,' Prince said. 'It would be more if you weren't a . . .'

'What!' Carlton rose from the chair and glared at him. 'Do you forget who you are? Have those white ladies fawning over you gone to your head? I ought to tell Nat to take a strap to you!'

'Carlton . . .' He draped himself elegantly beside the fireplace. 'Do calm down. I'm only doing this for you.'

He grinned, amused at the way he could wrap Carlton Todd around his finger. He could control whites with ease, especially the women. So many of them!

'It's not my fault I'm in demand. I want to make you proud of me.' He cocked his head on one side and looked contrite. 'It could be good for your prestige to hold a *soirée* here.'

'Don't get coy with me.' Carlton waved his finger at him. 'I'm not having a *soirée* here. To hell with my prestige. Prestige is no good without whelps to capitalize on it.'

Prince sighed. It was always the same. Carlton's obsession with breeding was spoiling his enjoyment of London. 'I'm sorry,' he said sarcastically. 'I can't give Gwen a child just because you order it.'

'In Antigua, you wanted to marry her.'

He flushed. It seemed so long ago. 'I still do.' His voice dropped. 'She won't let me. It's you she wants.'

'Nonsense!' Carlton swung around to stare out of the window. 'You're not treating her right. Stop chasing those society ladies.'

'They chase me! I don't ask them to call here.' He studied his reflection, smoothing down his cravat. He was pleased with his appearance. It had taken time to convince Carlton that he needed enough new coats and breeches to wear a different outfit to every party.

'What are you doing with yourself, eh?'

The question shook him and he straightened away from the looking glass, his pleasure at his looks evaporating in this new blast from Carlton.

'Don't gawp at me like a stupid field slave, Prince. You know what I mean. You're a buck. If you're not mounting Gwen, what the devil are you doing? Pumping yourself?' Carlton paused and stared at him.

'By the devil, you're not jumping Nat, are you?'

He wanted to curse Carlton. But for him, Gwen would have been his long ago.

'I'm not an animal!' he cried. 'See these fine clothes you've bought me. I'm a respectable gentleman.'

'Hah!' Carlton smacked his fist into the palm of his hand. 'You may look like a St James's beau but under them togs you're still black. I know what you need. Your blood's different . . . it's hot. There's sap oozing in you that has to come out. Gwen should drain it from you and give me a whelp.'

Prince shook his head sorrowfully. 'Tell her that.'

'By the devil, I will. I've seen you mooning after Helen Witham.

You're not going to any more of those damn frolics until you and Gwen start rutting.'

Prince was used to Carlton's bluster but his excitement at the evening ahead and the chance of seeing Helen again had made him handle him carelessly. It was time to swallow his pride.

Yet he was damned if he was going to! The Prince of Wales himself had told him he was a fine fellow, a credit to his race. What made Carlton Todd think he was any better than him? What right had Carlton to treat him as a stud to mount Gwen at his command?

'No, Carlton,' he shouted, amazing himself at his outburst. 'You can't tell me who to lie with. This is England, not Roxborough.'

Carlton sat back in his chair, his expression showing his shock.

A demon drove Prince on. 'My life's my own, Carlton! People laugh when you talk about Roxborough and how you breed slaves. In England you must behave like the English if you want them to respect you.'

He brushed his hand along the mantel, sweeping the invitations to the floor. 'You see these? They're all addressed to me. It's me they want, not you!' He paused, wondering what was making him speak, hating himself for telling Carlton the truth.

Carlton closed his eyes. He clenched his fists and banged them together impotently. 'Is it right,' – he enunciated each word carefully, – 'for a black man to lie with a white woman?' He opened his eyes.

Prince glared his defiance. 'Yes! In England there are blackamoors wed to white ladies.'

'Is it right,' Carlton demanded more emphatically, 'for a black man to lie with a white woman who has a husband?'

He shrugged his shoulders, dismayed at the trap he had fallen in to. Carlton sneered. 'I had a slave who lay with my wife.' He paused and stared at Prince. 'I killed them both.'

'I . . . I . . .' he was speechless. He glanced around the room, at anything, to avoid meeting Carlton's eye. He stooped and picked up an invitation. It was for that evening – Lady Norton's. He let it fall on the floor and dashed out of the room. Slamming the door behind him.

Gwen was standing in the hallway, attracted by the sound of their raised voices. Nat peered out of the doorway to the basement.

'Prince,' she said sternly. 'Have you been sassing Mas Carlton?'

'You!' He groaned with despair. 'You're the one to blame!' He brushed past her to the front door. 'I'm going out.'

'Without Mas Carlton?' she lunged for him and grabbed his sleeve. 'No!'

He tried to shake her off. When she would not let go, he punched her. She fell against the wall and stared at him with hatred sparking from her eyes. Nat hurried along the passageway.

'Dam' you, Gwen,' he sobbed, opening the door and rushing out.

He ran down the street toward the park without looking back. His heart was heavy despite his anger. Was it his fault he was behaving so strangely when Carlton and Gwen made no effort to understand him? Not like Helen and her friends. They saw him as a human being with feelings like their own. They admired him, laughed at his jokes, and thought him a splendid fellow.

He slowed down when he became aware of people watching him and took a deep breath to compose himself. Damn Gwen, he thought again. Every time he tried to woo her she pushed him aside. Well, let her wait. Mas Carlton too.

He straightened his stock, smoothed down his coat, and strolled toward the Park.

He wandered blindly in the spring twilight. He ignored people who greeted him and walked by instinct to Helen's house where Lady Norton was holding her *soirée*. He was assured of a sympathetic welcome there.

'What a surprise!' said Lydia when he was ushered into the salon. She glanced anxiously over his shoulder. 'Is Carlton not with you?'

'He's staying at home tonight.' He tried to sound casual. He watched the crowd of guests in the drawing room, wondering where Helen was.

'I do hope he's all right. Not sick?'

'No.' He shook his head without attempting a lie. Lydia gestured to the throng in the salon, said something he didn't hear, and left him to greet her next guest.

Prince adored these parties with beautiful women in splendid gowns, diamonds ablaze at their bosoms, gossiping gaily in cliquish groups. He enjoyed the pomp of the men, in uniform or the latest fashions, chuckling exclusively together.

From the ballroom came the sound of a small orchestra adding to the excitement. Servants flowed through the throng of guests with trays of champagne and canapés. Everybody was laughing loudly or talking with a great sense of their own importance.

The men in the room were members of government, admirals, influential bankers and businessmen and wealthy young men about town. The ladies were their wives, daughters or mistresses. It was a glittering occasion and Prince, although he was the only negro in the room, felt completely at home.

A hand slipped under his arm and he turned. Helen was gazing up at him in rapture. He bowed.

'Helen . . .' he breathed.

'Prince!' She smiled. 'Lydia says you are alone . . .?'

'Carlton's staying at home. He's not one for damn frolics, he says.'

'Thank god! Now we have a chance. Go up the stairs, second floor, third door on the right. I'll be there in ten minutes.'

His loins tingled. 'Your husband?' He remembered Carlton's warning.

'He's in the smoking room with the Prime Minister. This is Lydia's party, not mine, so he won't find it unusual if I'm not here.' A group of young blades joined them. She introduced them to Prince and left without another word.

The heat within him would not die. It was like Antigua. This would be their first opportunity since he had met Helen in the Park eight months before.

'You appear distracted tonight, Black Prince,' taunted one of the young fellows surrounding him. 'You haven't made us laugh.'

'Forgive me,' he said with a mock bow. 'Wit is like the bullwhip. It has a heavy handle and can cut sharp yet it is useless in the hands of a beginner.'

'Bravo!' another blade cried. 'Nicely put.'

'Sometimes,' Prince added with a smirk, 'the noise of the lash is more painful than its cut.'

His listeners frowned at this. He excused himself and edged away while they tried to work out if he was insulting them or not. Lydia Norton's eyes were on him as he reached the double doors into the hallway. He winked and she blushed, turning her head.

The servants saw him leaping up the stairs, two at a time. He didn't care. He bounded onto the second floor and strode to the third door on the right. He hesitated, wondering if he should knock. He pushed open the door and walked in.

The room was in darkness. Heavy brocade curtains were drawn across the windows, blocking out the view of the Park and the watching crowds. A whisper of air, a touch at his waist, and Helen's hands found him.

He held her in his arms, eager to tell her what had happened. Her lips stopped his before he could speak. She kissed him with an ardor that roused him immediately. He squeezed her passionately and returned her embrace. Her fingers crept under his coat and clawed at the small of his back.

'Prince,' she said with a sigh when he lifted his mouth from hers. 'We don't have much time.' She led him in the darkness to a bed in the center of the room.

'Wait,' he said, breaking away from her hands. 'I must remove my coat. It's so hot.'

'Be quick.' Helen sat on the edge of the bed and put her hands on his hips. She stroked him as he slipped off his coat and let it fall to the floor.

She lay her head back on the pillows and pulled him onto the bed with her. He fell heavily.

'Shhh!' she cautioned. They both lay without moving to see if they had been heard. The noise of the party drifted up to them.

'Prince, I have waited so long!' She fumbled to unlace his cummerbund and reach inside his breeches.

'So have I.' He removed her hands gently and lay beside her. He stroked her breasts until she shivered with ecstacy. He moved so that she was cradled in his arms while his hand explored under her gown.

She sighed again. 'Why haven't you visited me before? I wanted you so much.'

'Carlton,' he said, feeling his strength weaken at the thought. 'He's old fashioned. He doesn't understand.'

She shuddered. 'He must never know! No one must know. This isn't Antigua. I would be ruined.'

'So would I.'

'What? Oh yes.' She stirred, writhing as his finger probed. 'Prince,' she said again. 'Please hurry.'

'We've waited nearly a year,' he said, preferring to create the right atmosphere. 'A few minutes more . . .' He was not a man to be hurried. For him, lovemaking was an art to be enjoyed for as long as possible. 'I'm not a –'

She kissed him hungrily, forcing her tongue into his mouth and rubbing her hands in a frenzy over his body. She pressed against him, spreading her legs apart and drawing him into her.

He hesitated, shrinking at the fury of her need. She was choking him and he pulled his face away.

'My darling!' she cried, returning her lips to his mouth.

He withdrew his head. Her lips brushed against his cheek, chewing on his flesh until she found his ear. She sucked on it greedily.

'Helen!' He tried to calm her, lifting her hand from him and laying himself gently between her thighs. 'Please, let me . . .'

'Yes, yes,' she said, beating the back of his shins with her heels.

'Let me do this in my time. It's better.'

Her hand gripped his softness and he shuddered. 'What's wrong, Prince?' She fell back in dismay.

'Do you have another, is that it? I saw you in St John's, when I left. There was a wench in your arms then.'

'No, Helen!' He laughed at the thought. 'There's no other. By the devil, I've been a saint since you left.'

'Then what's happened to this?' She squeezed him roughly.

'Don't be angry.' He was bewildered by this new side of her. Was this the same woman who loved so leisurely when she was in Antigua? Now she was a virago, demanding him without any thought for his feelings. He had never failed before, with anyone, even ladies older than she. As long as there was an atmosphere of romance . . .

Loving couldn't be bolted like a meal. He tried again. 'You are so beautiful, Helen! I declare I want you so much. Let's not hurry. We must take our time . . . like in Antigua.'

'I don't have time.' She rolled her thighs. He felt insulted by her mood.

'Do you want me to treat you like a whore?' he asked sharply, ashamed for saying it.

'Whatever you like, but do it!'

He pulled away and sighed. He wanted her, of course. He knew his body. He could harden to take her brutally, but why? The memory of those moments in St John's would be wiped out by a few frantic minutes.

She groaned and thrashed her body across the mattress. He touched her and found her fingers massaging herself where he should be. He was shocked.

'No!' he shouted, throwing himself on top of her and snatching her hands away. He thrust his own fingers into her until she squirmed with agony.

She was breathing heavily and clawing at his silk shirt. He drew himself up and opened her, plunging in as though he was driving a stake into the ground. He hammered his body against hers until she screamed his name and begged for release.

The dry, loveless act was done. They lay exhausted, panting like dogs. There was no feeling of satisfaction for him. He lay without moving when Helen sat on the side of the bed and rearranged her hair.

'Come Wednesday,' she said, standing up and pulling her gown back into place. 'At two. I am always alone then. I'll tell the butler you are to be allowed in. He's trustworthy. Come on Sundays too, at the same hour. My husband sleeps then. You will be reimbursed.' She walked out of the room without another word.

He got slowly to his feet. He pulled up his breeches and tried to smooth out the creases. He was amazed to find he still had his shoes on. He tucked in his shirt and reached for his cummerbund on the floor. To help him see in the darkness, he opened the curtains.

The bed was in disarray and he decided to leave it. If Helen didn't care, why should he? He struggled back into his coat and tried to get his stock, no longer stiff with starch but badly crumpled and wet with sweat, back into shape. He opened the door, peeped out to see no one was about, and crept to the stairs.

He descended stealthily to the next floor and peered down from the landing to the hallway below. It was empty. He was dishevelled and ashamed and couldn't bear to meet anyone. He slunk down the last flight of stairs, keeping to the shadows, ready to make a dash for the door and out into the street.

'Prince!' Lady Norton, who was positioned at the entrance to the salon, cried with delight when she saw him. 'Have you had a rest, you darling black?' she shrilled. 'Here, let me straighten your cravat. You do look a little bedraggled.'

'I'm sorry,' he said. 'I'm not feeling well. Something I ate.' He raised his eyebrow, begging her to release him. 'I really must go.'

'Of course,' she said, gloating as her voice dropped an octave. 'I understand. So will Helen.'

He was startled by the implication. 'You know?'

Before she could reply, the footman admitted more guests. He withdrew into the shadows and stood, just like a slave, behind Lydia's shoulder. Helen, who didn't see him in the hallway, wandered over as the guests joined the others.

'Lydia,' she gushed. 'Has he gone? I must tell you . . .'

Lydia moved away to welcome more arrivals, leaving Prince and Helen staring at each other.

'Aha! I thought I'd find you here!'

Prince jumped at the sound of Carlton's voice. He and Helen gasped simultaneously as Carlton sauntered across the hallway. Gwen held his arm and Nat and Caspar were at his side. They were all dressed in the latest fashion. Prince recognized the coat Nat was wearing as one of his own.

'Hello, Lydia,' said Carlton breezily. He took her in his arms and kissed her on both cheeks. She was too shaken to protest.

'Knows you like blacks, I do.' He stepped back and pushed Gwen forward. 'I brought all my blackamoors for you and your friends to meet.'

He bowed to Helen to include her in his introductions.

'This one is Gwen. Called that because her father was Welsh. Pretty, ain't she? Offspring of a white man and a black slave wench.' He winked at Helen.

'This is the wench Prince is pining for. Wants to marry her, ain't that so, boy?'

Prince darkened with shame, wishing the floor would open and swallow him up. He dared not look at Helen. Her eyes were burning with hatred.

Carlton, who seemed oblivious of the stir he was causing, pushed Nat forward to the center of the circle. Several guests gathered around them, eager for scandal.

'This one is Nat. Fresh from Africa, never worked in the cane-fields. Now ain't he pretty too? He's a royal nigger, blessed with a pedigree that goes back a thousand years. Some English princes can't say that, can they?'

Silence greeted Carlton's remark. There was a rapid intake of breath and all eyes were on Lydia, wondering how she would deal with the insult. Carlton didn't give her time.

'He's a lusty nigger,' he said, patting Nat on his shoulder. 'Hasn't lain with a woman yet. Interested?'

The front door burst open and a party of men strode into the hall, led by two who were chatting animatedly together. Finding their way blocked by Carlton and his negroes, the man in the lead stopped.

'Your highness . . .' gasped Lydia.

The Prince of Wales belched. He looked from Nat to Caspar to Carlton to Prince and to Gwen. He ignored Lydia and Helen and the crowd gaping from the doorway. The sound of the orchestra swelled in the sudden hush.

'Beau!' he said to the man at his side. 'I declare we've crossed an ocean, not a threshold.'

'Oh, yes. Ha ha!' Brummell tittered, waving his hands behind the Prince's back for the rest of the party to laugh at the royal joke.

Carlton scowled. Gwen gazed at the Prince wide-eyed, her bosom heaving, about to burst out of her lowcut gown.

The laughter died. Every eye was on the Prince. People held their breath as they tried to gauge his mood.

The Prince puffed out his cheeks and looked bored, ready to turn away and leave. Lydia was distraught. Suddenly, his eye returned to Gwen.

She smiled slightly, passing her tongue from one side of her mouth to the other, its pink tip showing up like a ruby against the dark velvet of her lips.

'I say,' said the Prince, stepping over to her and offering her his arm. 'Since it's a black and white night, why don't you and I show these buckras how a black wench can dance?'

A path opened through the astonished crowd and the Prince of Wales led Gwen with a cheerful grin and a twinkle in his eye through the salon to the ballroom.

Carlton pushed Nat over to Lydia. She seized his arm gratefully and guided him through the crowd to join the Prince and Gwen on the dance floor.

'Well, my boy,' chuckled Carlton. He slapped Prince between his shoulder blades. 'Mayhap I'll get a royal whelp out of Gwen from the Prince instead of a black one from you.'

CHAPTER TWENTY

The beat of horses' hooves on the cobbles disturbed Carlton. He tossed uneasily in his sleep, wondering who was visiting Roxborough so early. Perhaps it was someone to buy slaves. Ella must say there are no more for sale. He had disposed of the weaklings, the lazy and the rebellious. Now he was going to breed the best: negroes with dark skins to withstand the effects of the sun, with thick thighs and strong arms for work, and with an obliging disposition. A negro was for toiling in the fields, not for languishing in a house as a servant in a flashy livery.

'Ella,' he called in his sleep. 'Where are you?'

The door opened and Caspar walked in briskly. He held a tray in both hands so as not to spill the dish of black coffee perched on it. He placed it on the table beside the bed. Walking over to the window he half-opened the curtains. Light spread into the room and he saw that Carlton had slept fitfully and the covers had fallen to the floor.

'Mas Carlton!' Caspar shook his shoulder. 'It does be after ten.'

Carlton was bewildered. 'Ella . . . Caspar?' He blinked. 'I was dreaming.' He yawned, twisted in the bed and looked at Caspar again. 'What . . . what day is it?'

Caspar passed him the dish of coffee. 'I'm not sure, sir. Gwen ain't awake yet. I made the coffee myself. Nat helped me.'

'Oh?' Carlton sipped the scalding liquid. He tried to focus his thoughts for he still had that nice feeling of being with Ella on the plantation. Ella took care of everything. If she was with him in London, she would see his slaves did what they were told.

He glanced at Caspar again. He flinched as a horse and carriage lumbered by in the street below, the shouts of the link boy jarring his head.

'Did I have a heavy night, Caspar? To wake so late.'

'Yes, sir. You cursed me soundly for taking so long to pull off your boots. Nat helped me undress you.' He laughed.

'What's funny, boy?' Carlton placed the dish back on the tray. He had no energy to clout Caspar for his rudeness.

'I wasn't laughing at you, sir. Last night, Prince tried to get in the kitchen with Gwen. She was so cross, she emptied a bag of flour over his head. Then she chased him out and said even though he was now a white prince, he still wasn't going to bed her.'

Carlton shook his head. 'Since she danced with the Prince of Wales, Gwen is more contrary than a wife. Why won't she take him, Caspar?'

'She wants to make him suffer.'

'She's making me suffer! Four times this week I've taken her to balls and fêtes because the Prince of Wales might be there and her presence is requested.'

'Isn't that an honor?'

'Simple folk think it is.' He swung his legs over the edge of the bed and groaned. 'See how I did the wrong thing?' He aimed himself into the chamber pot that Caspar held in front of him.

'I thought when I took her and Nat and you to Lady Norton's, we'd cause such a ruckus we'd never be invited again. How was I to know that people would react different?' He shook himself while Caspar replaced the chamber pot under the bed.

'Imagine!' he mused aloud. 'They call my slaves darling blacks and send carriages for them. What nonsense! It's gone to the heads of Gwen and Prince. How will Nat behave when I get him to Roxborough and put him in the fields?'

Caspar held the basin of cold water while Carlton splashed his face and hands. He wiped the sleep from his eyes and stretched. He felt better.

The night before had been like the others. At the society ball, Prince and Gwen were in demand as dancing partners. Carlton's time was monopolized by Lydia Norton. She was a personable woman and he enjoyed being with her.

'What did you and Nat do when we were out?' he asked suddenly, catching Caspar unawares.

'Nothing, sir.'

He saw the boy's eyelashes flicker uncertainly. 'Did you go out? I told you not to walk the streets at night. A smartly dressed buck like you could be stolen and shipped to auction in Savannah. They have ships waiting in the Thames for half-white niggers like you.'

'No, sir.' Caspar shook his head vigorously. 'We didn't go out.'

He sniffed suspiciously. 'If you didn't go out, did someone come in?'

Caspar hung his head, moving away in case he tried to strike him. 'Yes, sir.'

'Tell me.' He strode over to the window and peered out. The sky was overcast, its grayness depressing for someone used to the sun. Was it time to think of returning to Roxborough, he wondered.

Something Caspar said made him realize he wasn't listening properly.

'Black did you say?'

'Yes, sir. That's why we asked him in. Nat saw the negro from the window. Not so much walking, more sliding. He looked helpless.'

'You invited in a strange black off the street?' Carlton didn't know whether to be angry. There were hundreds of negro beggars roaming London, although they were not often found in Chapel Street. Many of them were runaways or had escaped from ships.

'He wasn't a beggar,' Caspar laid out Carlton's breeches and shirt on the bed. 'He was looking for the American Ambassador.'

'Don't joke with me, boy.' He picked up the shirt and began to dress.

'He was a slave, sir. Escaped from Virginia and come to London.'

'He's still a slave then,' said Carlton. 'The law don't say that a slave gains his liberty when he reaches England. That's a rumor.'

'Yes, sir.' Caspar stood stoutly in the center of the room. 'He was seeking the house of the Ambassador to ask for employment. He had no money and was hungry, so Nat and I shared our supper with him.'

'Very noble of you.' He struck out quickly and caught Caspar a blow on his ear before the boy could dodge it. 'Don't let any stray nigger in my house again, do you understand? I'll catch the blacks we want.'

Caspar waited until he was pulling on his breeches before he moved back. 'Tom, that's his name, said he's a prize fighter in America.'

'What!' Carlton made a lunge for Caspar but he was handicapped with his breeches around his knees. 'You said he was helpless. You're too soft, Caspar. You'd believe any hard luck story.'

'It's true! He was as tall as Nat and much broader. He looked out of sorts, of course, having not long come off the ship that brought him here. He had a bout with Nat in the kitchen.'

'By the devil! Is that what you do when I'm being fêted by royalty? Have fist fights in my basement!' He paused and grinned. 'I believe I'd rather have been here.'

For many weeks, he had been wondering what to do with Nat. There must be some way to exploit the African for profit. Nat was not a success with women. He was too solemn and his gaucheness caused embarrassment. As a house slave, he was morose and tardy.

'Fighter, you say . . .? How did Nat fare against him?'

'Tolerably, sir. In fact, Nat was the nimbler but Tom is more experienced.'

'You know where to find this nigger again?' He watched Caspar's face intently. The boy turned away.

'Come on, Caspar, don't hide it from me. You asked him here tonight, didn't you? You think I'm going out and you took pity on him. Just like your mother!'

Caspar's expression of amazement told him he was right. 'You know, boy,' he laughed. 'I can read every thought in your head.'

Tom Molyneaux was a huge man. He overflowed from the tiny kitchen stool and made every object in the room seem puny. The mug of rum that he clutched in his paw was like a thimble in his hand. He was not impressed by Carlton descending to the basement to meet him, and glowered at him from under great black brows.

Caspar and Nat sat at the table to put him at ease, but he was the one who was intimidating. Prince accompanied Carlton below stairs; his eyes were on Gwen, not on the visitor.

'I hope it ain't your intention to turn my kitchen into a club for idlers,' Gwen grumbled as soon as Carlton stepped into the room. 'One's enough.' She tossed her head in the direction of Prince.

Carlton ignored her. Judging by his size, what Caspar told him about the stranger was true. 'Stand up,' he said to the black man.

Tom rose to his feet slowly, casting a doleful glance around the room. He was nearly a hand taller than Nat; his prodigious size dwarfed them all. Carlton was impressed by the man's height and his belligerent expression. He longed for him to shuck off his togs so he could examine him. The black's surly manner showed he would do nothing of the kind.

Carlton gestured for him to return to the stool. 'My boy here says you're a fighter.'

'Champ'n of Virginie, marse,' the man growled.

'I once had a giant,' he said to Prince for want of someone better to talk to. 'He became the Dominica champion.'

The relationship between him and Prince was easier now. He had noticed that there was tension between Prince and Helen Witham. The marchioness no longer pursued Prince and he took pains to avoid her. Because of his humbler attitude, Carlton was disposed to overlook Prince's rudeness. His revenge was in seeing the jealousy in Prince's crestfallen face when the Prince of Wales had swept Gwen into his arms.

'There's an academy for black fighters near Leicester Square,' Prince said casually.

Carlton sat down and beckoned Caspar to give him a rum. 'You see,' he said in a voice stinging with sarcasm, 'this mungo macaroni knows everywhere in London.' He swallowed the rum while the others watched him.

'How do you know that extraordinary information?'

'I can't remember,' Prince said. 'One hears so much in polite company. I was asked if I've been there. Gentleman John Jackson had a similar establishment in Bond Street but that's for noblemen to learn the Fancy.'

'The Fancy, is it?' Carlton scoffed.

'That's what the enthusiasts call fist fighting.'

'You know too much,' said Gwen. 'I don't approve of such gossip in my kitchen. Aren't you going to keep company with your *fancy* white ladies tonight?'

Prince shook his head. 'I'd like to stay here with you.'

Caspar was getting impatient. 'What are you going to do for Tom now you've seen him, Mas Carlton? You believe he's a fighter, don't you?'

'Aye.' He regarded the hulking black man perched on the stool. 'Do you know of this black academy?'

Tom Molyneaux shrugged his massive shoulders.

'He's only been in London a few days,' said Caspar. 'He's been looking for the Amb –'

Carlton raised his hand threateningly, 'Call a hackney carriage. Prince, you think you can locate this place?'

'Certainly. It's the Horse and Dolphin in Martin's Street, run by Bill Richmond. He's a black boxer from America too. Tom should get on well with him.'

'I'm thinking of Nat.' He stood up. 'Come,' he said to Nat. 'We'll see if Bill Richmond can make a champion out of *you*.'

Tom Molyneaux traveled on the box with the coachman while Prince and Nat rode inside with Carlton. When he arrived in London, Carlton was annoyed that people stared at him when he walked along streets accompanied by his negroes. A single slave following two steps behind a white gentleman was considered rather grand by the populace. A man surrounded by well-dressed black attendants was an object of curiosity. After a year, Carlton was accustomed to the attention he attracted. He thought of himself as quite a swell.

At the Horse and Dolphin, however, no one took any notice of him. Bill Richmond was famous as a pugilist. Of his fourteen major fights, he lost only three, one of which was to Tom Cribb who became the Prize Ring Champion of England. Richmond's inn and boxing academy swarmed with blacks; young hopefuls, old seafarers, and wise housemen. Carlton was bewildered when Prince pushed open the door and ushered him inside.

The dimly lit room was packed with negroes shouting and pushing one another. The aroma of cheap gin hung heavily in the smoke-filled air. In vain, Carlton looked for a white face; the closest was a half-breed who grinned drunkenly at him as he followed Prince into the depths of the crowd. He held his coat tightly to secure his pockets, and bid Nat stay close behind him. Tom Molyneaux's sullen features transformed at the sight of his fellows.

Prince procured a glass of cloudy liquid and thrust it into Carlton's hand. 'Blue ruin,' he grinned. 'Richmond is in the back.' He indicated with his head that he should follow him.

There were three pairs of blacks sparring in the back room. Spectators leaned against the walls with glasses in their hands. Bill Richmond, attracted by Carlton's white face, bustled over. He ignored him and walked up to Tom Molyneaux.

'By all that's holy,' he exclaimed. 'Who are you?'

The two burly negroes fell on each other like old friends. Richmond hurried Tom over to a corner where he questioned him enthusiastically.

Carlton sniffed and pointed out the sparring pairs to Nat. 'You think you could do that?'

Nat stared haughtily at the prancing men pawing each other. 'What is it?'

'The fancy,' grinned Prince. 'Fist fighting for prize money. You need a lot of bottom for that.'

Nat touched his backside uncertainly.

Prince laughed. 'Bottom means courage. Mill, that's a fight. You have a mill with an opponent and hit him with your fists until you knock him down. If he stays down, you win the prize.'

Nat shook his head slowly.

Carlton wondered why he was puzzled. 'It's a sport, fun,' he said to encourage him.

Nat was unhappy. 'Men do this for pleasure . . .?'

Prince laughed again. 'For money, not pleasure. The fighter gets the prize, and his backers made a packet.'

'Will you try, Nat? Prince, ask Richmond to give him a trial.'

There was a wait while Bill Richmond listened to Prince, glanced over at Carlton and Nat, and consulted Tom Molyneaux. He called over a tough looking youth who was lounging in a corner and spoke to him.

Carlton agreed Richmond's fee, paid the few pence required, and sat in the chair a boy brought him. He accepted a second glass of the coarse gin and settled back to enjoy the encounter.

Nat watched his opponent remove his shirt and did the same, giving his coat, shirt and cravat to Prince.

'Tap him with your fists and try to stop him hitting you,' advised Richmond in a fatherly way. 'Boy,' he said to his own fighter. 'Let him get the feel of you. He's never fought before so don't punch him hard.'

Nat's partner was proud of his physique and strength. He was shorter than Nat with a solid torso and a huge fist. He moved into Nat slowly at first, each blow scoring on Nat's body as the African tried to understand what was required of him.

'Hold up your fists,' Richmond shouted to Nat. 'Keep them in front of your face to stop him hitting you.'

Nat copied his partner's stance and by aping his thrusts began to get the feel of it. Carlton chuckled when Nat's fist penetrated his opponent's guard and smashed against his chest. He was dancing around the man and leading the attack. Sensing something of interest was taking place, a crowd surged into the room to watch.

'He's livelier than you,' Richmond called to his fighter. 'Give him a couple of blows to tame him.'

'Nat's good!' Carlton drained the gin and grimaced. 'I've got a fighter there, Prince.'

He was impressed by Nat's agility; his opponent was lumbering slowly beside him. Nat threw a punch that landed on the other's nose. It angered the fighter and he lashed out. He caught Nat on the side of his head with such force that Nat stumbled backward, lost his balance and fell over.

The small crowd jeered. 'Fine punch,' Richmond told his fighter. He raised his fist proudly.

Nat sprang to his feet, a wild gleam in his eye. Carlton spotted it. 'Get ready,' he whispered to Prince. 'This will be interesting.'

It was over before Prince knew what Carlton meant. Nat stood very still in the center of the room, his hands at his side. Richmond, who hadn't noticed the change that had come over him, shouted at Nat to put up his guard.

Nat ignored him; he was waiting for the fighter to strike him again. The boxer shrugged his shoulders at Nat's foolishness and moved in, his fist churning as he aimed for Nat's jaw.

Nat's response was so fast that even those who were watching closely failed to see Nat's clenched hand shoot up from his side and strike the negro under his chin. He was lifted off the ground with the force of the punch. He tumbled backward. His head banged into the wall with a sickening crack.

Nat walked away. Bill Richmond rushed to his fighter. The crowd gathered around to see what had happened.

'Come on, Prince,' said Carlton, grabbing hold of Nat by his arm. 'Let's get out.' He pushed frantically through the drinkers, out into the street. A hackney carriage was waiting and they jumped in.

'What's the hurry?' gasped Prince.

'You don't know?' He looked at Nat and patted his knee.

'I did what you wanted, Mas Carlton,' Nat said softly. 'He shamed me, so I killed him.' He held up his fist.

Carlton smiled happily. 'I always knew you were a killer!'

CHAPTER TWENTY-ONE

Ella's baby was a year old. She bounced the child on her knee, and looked toward the *cou*. She wondered if Massa Hayes knew it was a year since she gave birth to his grandchild. The violence and agony of the birth had left its mark. She was bound to her baby by the lash of the bullwhip; Hayes by his shame at what his lust for punishment had wrought.

The child was born robust, bursting into being with the help of Mercury's blows and Congo Venus's grimy fingers. Had she given birth to a son, its destiny would surely have been to free slaves from their white oppressors. Her child, when the process was completed and she lay semi-conscious on the blood-stained mud in front of the *cou*, was not a son, but a daughter. She called her Miranda.

Miranda gurgled happily. She was a peaceful child, content to wait whenever Ella lay her down to perform her tasks in the nursery where she was confined. The barbarity of her birth did not affect the child; she was blessed with serenity and seldom cried. The old women who worked in the nursery doted on her, but none more than Ella. Here, in her arms, was proof that Carlton was still with her.

In Miranda's face, she was sure she could see Carlton's features. The child was fair, although her eyes were dark and her hair was Ella's. She was beautiful. Carlton would be proud when he returned. She had promised him a son but she was confident Miranda would enchant him.

Massa Hayes never enquired about the baby, nor about Ella. She made no attempt to ease the pain that was on his conscience.

After the child's brutal birth, she was helped to the nursery by Congo Venus and Dutchip. Massa Hayes, from his vantage point on the balcony, declared that she must not enter the house. She did not mind. The old man had chosen his hell; he must live with it just as she would live with hers.

The women in the nursery cared for her lovingly. Congo Venus had birthed hundreds of whelps and her skill saved Ella. She took time to recover from the birth, from the lash, and from the smashing of her prestige. Strangely, instead of losing her power over the slaves with her banishment from the *cou*, she increased it.

Before, because she was the slave closest to the master and able to influence his commands, she was feared and hated. Now, as someone who had suffered and been humiliated, she was liked and respected throughout Roxborough.

She lost no time in letting it be known that her fall from Massa Hayes's favor was to be regarded as temporary. The slaves could still depend on her.

With the resilience of her race, she turned the misfortune to her advantage. In the nursery, she was in touch with the slaves and could sense the undercurrents of restlessness. It was her intention, whatever Massa Hayes and Tita did, to preserve Roxborough and its slaves until Carlton's safe return.

Tita was trying to exert her influence over the Massa. The old man was resisting with a determination that fired him to take a greater interest in the plantation. He made his rounds, slowly and with frailty, accompanied by Pool. He discussed the plantation with the drivers and was sufficiently impressed by their competence to let them continue without interference.

If Tita thought that with Ella out of the way, she would become Mistress of Roxborough, she was wrong. Old Hayes loathed being forced to do anything. Tita lacked the subtlety to achieve influence over him, the plantation or the slaves.

'*Doudou*,' Ella crooned to Miranda, 'some day yuh da' go'n come den yo' go'n lib in de *cou*.' She laughed as Miranda tried to smile. 'Dat chil' so good,' she said to Mally Ibo who was sitting in the shale under the wooden nursery building watching her. 'She don't bawl like young Hayes an' Mingoson all de time.'

Mally Ibo sucked her toothless gums and sighed. The day was hot and not a breath of wind stirred the trees. Above her head the wooden boards of the floor of the nursery creaked as children romped over it. The noise of children screaming, shrieking, shouting and laughing was so loud around her ears that Ella no longer heard it.

The nursery paddock was an acre of land fenced with bambo stakes. Bougainvillea and flamboyant trees overhung it. There were children of all ages, shapes and shades playing in the open or lounging under the trees. All of them, even the eldest in their teens, were naked.

The kitchen for this nucleus of the Bondmaster breed was an *ajoupa* adjoining the nursery. It was an open-sided shelter where the cooking was done in big cauldrons over a wood fire. There was always something on the boil. Ella's duty was to see that the children were adequately fed and cared for.

The trough alongside the kitchen was filled from the cauldrons three times a day, with broth, cocoa tea, and sometimes with meat and dumplings. The youngsters scooped with their hands as much as each could grab. Dutchip switched the naked bottom of any child who was too greedy to eat calmly.

It was a tranquil existence for Ella. She had time to spend with Miranda and to hunker down under the nursery and natter with the old slaves.

Mally Ibo cleared her throat, disturbing Ella's contentment.

'D'yo' t'ink he go'n come back?' she wheezed with great effort.

'Mas Carlton? Of course he will.' She rocked Miranda. 'Maybe next year. He ain't been gone long.'

'Ain't he?' Mally Ibo considered. 'Doubt ah go'n see de buckra 'gain.'

Ella was horrified. 'Don't say dat!' It was bad luck to pronounce on fate. She swung Miranda out of Mally Ibo's view in case she said anything against her.

'Yo' hab news of de buckra?'

'No.' She was ashamed to admit that she hadn't. Since she was banished from the house, it was Tita who read Carlton's letters to Massa Hayes.

'Ah know he comin', dough!' She hitched her shoulders defensively as a plan formed in her mind.

That night, when it was dark and not even a star's glitter was to be seen through the trees, Ella scratched on the kitchen door. It was opened immediately and she slipped in. Pip held her in his arms but she pushed him away. In the glow from the embers in the hearth, she saw the outline of Marcus curled up asleep on the floor. She pointed at him.

'He 'sleep,' whispered Pip. 'So's ev'ryone. De massa snorin'.'

'Yo' give him de powder?' she asked softly.

'In de punch. He don' know. He 'sleep 'fore he have time to sen' for a wench.'

'Wish I could give Tita one.'

'No need. Pool wid she.' Pip grinned philosophically. 'Tita ain' go'n leave Pool les' Sophie jump him too.' From his deep chuckle, Ella realized he was drunk.

'Hush yuh noise, yo' great *makak*.' She opened the kitchen door. 'Stay here. If de Massa wakes, I done for.'

She knew the risk she was taking, yet there was no other way. Mally Ibo had planted the seed of doubt in her mind. She wanted to know what was in Carlton's letters. Pip was well-meaning but too clumsy to steal them for her. The letters were kept in a cabinet in the drawing room.

She climbed the grand staircase swiftly. She relied on a sixth sense to guide her because a light, even a candle, was too risky. Despite the reports of the *nègres marrons*, runaway slaves, camped on the upper reaches of the Layou Valley, none of the house doors were locked. No attacks had ever been made on a west coast plantation.

She stepped silently on to the balcony, paused to listen and to sniff the air for the scent of anyone out of bed. She heard the deep rumble of Hayes snoring. Her powder, herbs dried and ground fine with a pestle and mortar, were as good as any white man's medicine. She was confident that Massa Hayes would sleep until daybreak.

She opened the door to the dining room and felt her way slowly around the furniture, careful not to creak the wooden floor and wake Tita or Sophie.

The door to Hayes's room opened without a sound. She groped for the chest of drawers where Hayes placed his keys. She was lucky, her fingers touched them immediately. She took up the bunch so it didn't clink and moved out of the room.

She located the cabinet, found the lock with her fingers and began to try the keys. There were a score of them and it was a long process finding one that fit. The cabinet was an odd piece of furniture, a kind of bureau, acquired by Hayes in Savannah before he came to Dominica. It was in two sections divided by a single pair of drawers, with doors to the upper and lower parts. She concentrated on the upper doors.

It seemed she tried every key in the bunch before she found the one that opened the door. How she wished for a light. She fumbled frantically inside and then paused, summoning patience. She began again, very slowly, feeling the floor of the cabinet to judge what was in it. Her fingers touched a handle. Suddenly she was struck a blow in her waist.

She drew back in fright. There was no sound and no one moved. She stared into the darkness, holding her breath. Gradually, she became aware that it was a thing not a person that had struck her. She touched the cabinet again; a hidden drawer had sprung open at waist height. Inside were leather pouches stuffed with coins. Slowly, she closed the drawer and resumed her search.

There were some ledgers in the cabinet, and rolls of parchment. She found papers and, by feeling for the broken seal, was able to determine that they were letters. She stuffed two of them in her bodice and closed the cabinet, locking it. She returned the key to Hayes's bedroom.

She hurried down the steps to the courtyard and took a deep breath, relieved to be out of the house. Pip was waiting for her by the kitchen door. He ushered her in and lit a candle from the embers. Marcus was sleeping soundly as she hunched on a stool and peered at the two papers.

'One be from Carlton,' she whispered with excitement. Pip swayed, trying to see over her shoulder.

'What he say?' he demanded hoarsely.

'Wait!' She laid her hand on his arm while she studied the letter. 'He say he livin' well in London an' all dat.' She was scanning the lines for references to Caspar. 'Ah,' she breathed, reading slowly.

' "I have become friendly with a lady of noble birth who is much attached to me. Now the season has ended, London is dull and the lady, whose name is Lydia, has become my regular companion. We visit the country together, accompanied by Caspar who looks very smart in his English clothes and shoes. He attracts considerable attention. Lydia has several times asked me to lend him to her but I find the boy invaluable and I am not disposed to part with him." '

She looked at Pip proudly. 'Shoes!' she said.

'He like de boy,' Pip nodded with approval. 'Who de lady? Mayhap Mas Carlton go'n marry?'

She shrugged and continued, ' "My menage, or *menagerie* as Beau Brummell, a friend of the Prince of Wales, chooses to call them, fare well. Prince does me credit by being received, frequently without me, in the best places. His knowledge thus gained is assisting me in my own endeavours. My housekeeper, Gwen, and Nat, my steward, serve me well. I have no complaints." '

Pip frowned. 'Dat steward don' sound no good. Mas Carlton always complainin' 'bout me.'

'Listen to this,' said Ella. ' "I was wrong in my assumption that my negroes would breed here, and I could sell their whelps for a profit. It must be the climate, which is abominable, for it serves to *freeze* the inclination, even in me. My African shows no interest but I expect his attitude to change in the atmosphere of Roxborough when I assign him a suitable wench. I had hopes of an alliance between Gwen and Prince but she resists him. The demand here isn't for whelps but for mulatto playthings of Caspar's age to dance attendance on wealthy ladies." '

'Caspar like to dance,' said Pip.

She scanned the rest of the letter. It contained comments on Carlton's negotiations on behalf of the West India Interest, and his discussions with eminent gentlemen about slaves.

' "Several people," ' she read aloud, ' "have inspected my African. I might put him to Ella when I return. I'm advised to breed him with the purest stock to preserve his blood line and I have none purer than she. Treat her well, father, for she is of even greater value to me than before." '

'Mas Carlton a wise man,' Pip announced happily. 'He go'n gib yo' a buck dat tame yo'.'

She sniffed. 'I hope Tita done read dat to Massa Hayes,' she said, folding up the letter. She glanced at the other one. It carried the official seal of the island's Lieutenant Governor, Colonel Barnes.

'Dat pretty,' said Pip when she showed him. 'A soldier done bring dat for Massa las' week. English man. No manners, drink rum straight. Dey talk 'bout 'surrection.'

The paper was a notice advising planters to take precautions against attacks from maroons and possible insurrections among disgruntled slaves. It reported that confrontations between the maroons and the authorities were increasing. The legislature had been asked to take measures to break up the encampments. Colonel Barnes was proposing to make use of the Regular troops stationed on the island.

Ella thought of the wisps of smoke that drifted skyward from the hills surrounding the plantation. These marked the encampments of runaway slaves who lived in the island's interior. None of them were from Roxborough. Maroons, as they were called for the hopelessness of their cause, were viewed with suspicion by the slaves.

'Ain't go'n be no 'surrection here,' she said, handing the two papers to Pip. 'Our niggers are too scared of jumbies in the dark to join de maroons.'

Pip looked blankly at the papers in his hand. 'How yo' returnin' dese, Ella?'

'Yo' do it, Pip. I stay here too long a'ready. Pool go'n tire of Tita an' come soon. Put de papers on de floor in Massa Hayes's room. He t'ink he drop dem himself.'

She blew out the candle and headed for the door before Pip could protest. She slipped out silently. Like a spirit, she glided across the courtyard and down the main avenue, turning off toward the slave quarters. The air was cool and refreshing and she was used to walking in the dark.

The quarters lay between the nursery and the river. The slaves were housed in cabins built in lines. The canefields were opposite and the hills and the provision grounds behind.

She mused on Carlton's letter as she sauntered easily through the darkness. Suddenly she heard the cough of a man close at hand. She halted, her heart leaping at her carelessness. She was a hundred feet from the first cabin in the slave lines. She sank down on her haunches, holding her breath, and listened.

The silence worried her. Perhaps the man was waiting for her. She strained her ears. A door closed, its noise reverberating dully in the bush. Her ears became accustomed to the burble of night insects, the crack of creatures by the river, and the splash of water coursing over stones. She felt the vibrations of the footfalls of someone striding along the path. She edged deeper into the vegetation.

A voice, only five paces away, spoke softly. 'Pool?'

The person walking the path stopped. 'Ah don' see yo'.'

'Here, man.'

Ella couldn't see Pool and the stranger even though they were close enough that she could feel the heat from their bodies. She wondered why Pool was not at the *cou* with Tita.

'Dey willin'?' the voice whispered. The two men were hunkered down. She drew further back into the bush so she wouldn't be observed.

'Dose niggers *sot*.' Pool was angry. 'Too stupid.'

'Yo' tell dem we go'n hab guns?'

'Sure. Dose slaves don' want no 'surrection here. Dey say de massa ain' pesterin' nor starvin' an' lashin' dem so why dey want join yuh camp?'

'Yo' tell dem so dey does be free?'

'Dey say dey better'n free a'ready.'

There was a sigh of exasperation. 'We need 'em, Pool. Jacko say when de slaves run'way an' join us, de plantations go'n fall.'

'Ah know dat, Quashie. Ah wid yo'. Tita too. Dat why ah come 'cause she say yo' here.'

Ella stiffened.

The maroon, Quashie, snorted with disgust. 'We does want men to fight, Pool, like yo'. Tita too white.'

Pool grunted. 'She hollerin' for me if ah stay longer.'

Quashie stood up, stirring the branches overhanging the path. 'We tell Tita when ah come 'gain.'

Ella had butchered pigs many times, slicing the knife across the animal's throat while it squealed like a baby. Slaves who killed maroons were rewarded by Governor Barnes. Slaves who were caught helping Maroons were punished.

She didn't know Quashie; whether he was big or small. He wasn't from Roxborough which was why he inveigled Pool to do his recruiting. She suspected he was one of Tita's lovers whom she met when she went to the village at night.

Ella quietly drew out her knife. The blade was sharper than a razor, and harder.

She was strong, silent, and fast. She bided her time until Pool walked clumsily up the path to the house, causing a ruckus in the night sounds. She waited for Quashie to follow. When she smelt him and saw him looming over her in the darkness, she struck.

The knife sliced into the softness of his crotch. He reached out, gurgling with shock, and tried to grasp her.

She drove the blade deeper, twisting upward. He toppled forward. She left the knife inside him and fled into the bush.

The next morning, the Wagenie river slaves found the naked negro dead by the river bank. The maroon had pulled out the knife and spilled his guts out with it.

The plantation slaves clutched themselves to ward off the evil lurking around them when they heard of the mysteriously slaughtered man. They all knew that there was only one person at Roxborough with the power for such obeah.

In the nursery, Ella smiled and dismissed Congo Venus's questions about where she was that night. She played calmly with Miranda, tickling her belly to make her laugh. Behind her dark eyes, she was brooding about Tita and Pool, and the threat they were to Roxborough.

CHAPTER TWENTY-TWO

Wednesday was the evening for Almack's. For two years, Carlton sought admission to the subscription ball held once a week throughout the season at Almack's Assembly Rooms in King Street. Although he affected a cavalier attitude to society, he was anxious not to be dismissed as an eccentric creole from the Colonies. His acceptance at Almack's was vital.

He maintained his relationship with Lydia Norton during that two year wait. The woman was almost too persistent, yet he found she was entertaining company, not shallow like the society beauties. When she left for her estates in the Channel Islands, he was surprised that he missed her. He filled the time by visits to the brothels around Covent Garden with Prince. That drained off his anger although it left him depressed and longing for her return.

He was sitting gloomily before the fire, a book open on his knees, thinking of Roxborough and wondering what Ella was doing. There was a gentle tap on the door. He hated to be disturbed by his slaves. They were trained to move in and out of a room silently, like shadows, without him noticing. The knock on the drawing room door annoyed him.

'Nat!' he shouted. 'What the devil are you doing? Come here.' He glared into the fire and waited. There was no answering bleat of apology but he sensed someone enter the room. He didn't move.

Hands covered his eyes and a voice giggled, 'Guess who?'

He jerked himself out of the chair in panic, swinging around with his fists ready and his senses alert.

'Oh Carlton! Can't you take a joke?'

'Lydia! Dam'me, why d'you do something so foolish?' Sheepishly, he dropped his hands to his sides. 'I could have hurt you.'

'Aren't you pleased to see me?' She swept around the chair toward him, waiting to be embraced.

'What? Oh yes, of course I am.' He held her in his arms and kissed her hurriedly. Nat, who was watching from the doorway, closed the door and withdrew. 'You surprised me, that's all.'

She pouted. 'You look as though you were going to kill me.'

'Not you, Lydia. I'm a slave breeder. At Roxborough, I have to be on guard all the time. Why, only yesterday I received news of an uprising in Dominica. On the east coast, far from my home. It's the maroons, they stir up the slaves.'

'My goodness!' Lydia removed her bonnet and looked around the room. 'You do lead a dangerous life. Where shall I put this?'

He walked past her to the door and opened it. 'Caspar!' he shouted then turned back to her.

He was astonished at her loveliness. She was abloom with health, her gray eyes sparkling with excitement and her cheeks glowing. Her hair with its copper luster and curls graced her face with stunning effect. Her cloak, as she unfastened it, revealed a dress cut low to her bosom.

Caspar bounded in, saw Lydia and bowed. He stepped straight to her side, took the bonnet and helped her with her cloak. 'Welcome back, m'lady,' he said.

'Caspar, you're so sweet.' She patted his head. He bowed his way out of the room, blushing with pleasure.

'It's so hot in here, Carlton. A fire in June?'

'You look radiant, Lydia.' He returned to her side and embraced her. She stroked his face.

'It's the sea air, Carlton. Away from London's drawing rooms, I'm a country maiden.'

He laughed. 'In Dominica, a lady does all she can to preserve her pallor. If she has to walk in the open she has a slave holding a parasol over her to keep off the sun.'

'That would be no use. In Guernsey, it's the air not the sun. You don't find my colour too coarse, too ruddy, do you?' She was anxious. 'Perhaps it's not ladylike enough for you?'

'For me? It's enchanting!' He hugged her. 'Now you look like a wench, a woman, not some wilting widow . . .' He hesitated at his familiarity.

She sat in a chair away from the fire. 'I enjoyed being at home, but what a relief to be back in London. Did you miss me?'

'Did I?' He threw himself into a chair, wondering if he should tell her how he yearned for her company during the long winter evenings. 'Sometimes . . .' he said instead.

'Would you like a punch? In Dominica, we wait for sunset but since it sets so late here in summer, we could begin now.'

She giggled. 'I don't know if I should.'

'Nonsense! Caspar,' he shouted again.

'Don't you have a bellcord to pull?'

'Better to shout. Makes me think I'm in Dominica.' He noticed the glint in her eye but he ignored it in the pleasure of seeing her. She had changed somehow, not just in her rude good looks, but in her temperament, too. She seemed more boisterous, lively. She reminded him of a white version of a black wench. The idea intrigued him.

By the devil, he thought when he glimpsed her ankles as she raised her skirt to sit more comfortably in the chair. I'll have to go to Covent Garden tonight. He crossed his legs to hide the rising in his crotch.

'Yes, sir?' Caspar beamed at Lydia from Carlton's side.

'Make a real Roxborough punch, Caspar. Use our own rum.'

'For two, Mas Carlton?' He pretended surprise.

'Of course, boy!'

Caspar's smile broadened as he trotted out of the room.

'Have we shocked him?' asked Lydia. 'Don't ladies drink punch at Roxborough.'

'What does it matter what he thinks? You're here, that's what's important.' He leaned forward. 'Will you stay for supper?'

'Oh, Carlton! Even an hour is too long. You know how people gossip. My coachman is outside.'

'Don't worry. He's probably in the kitchen being entertained by Gwen. Will you stay?'

'Another evening, Carlton. I have to dine with Helen tonight.'

'Who else will be there?' The sharpness of his question surprised him. Was he jealous?

Lydia glanced at him with that odd glint in her eye. 'We're dining at home. Aunt Hortense will be there.'

Caspar entered proudly with two glasses of punch on a silver tray. He served Lydia then Carlton, and hovered at the door while they took the first sip.

Lydia eyed Carlton speculatively over the rim of her glass. Caspar slipped quietly from the room, and closed the door.

'That's very . . . well . . . bracing,' she said, placing her glass on the table beside her chair. 'I'm not used to a concoction so strong.'

'It's like me,' boasted Carlton with a grin. His eyes met hers and he felt himself stirring. 'Dammit, Lydia! I'm pleased you've come back. London's been damned dull without you. Only Prince to keep me company.'

'Yes . . .'

'Is something wrong?'

'No, Carlton.' She hesitated. 'Aunt Hortense has got you on the list for Almack's. She wants you to take me there next Wednesday.'

'Indeed?' He tried not to let his enthusiasm show.

'Do you know what that means?' Her lower lip trembled.

'I have an idea. I'll wear my best suit and won't drink too much. I'll be on good behavior, I promise.'

She sighed. 'It's not that, Carlton. Besides, they don't serve drink there.' She reached for her glass and swallowed the contents in one gulp.

'Being on Almack's list means something. It's not only status that's implied. If we go together . . . well . . . it is a *marriage* market, Carlton, and it's such a hothouse of scandal and gossip.' She paused, then rushed on.

'When people see us together, they are going to *say* things.'

'Let them talk!' He finished his drink and wanted to call for another. By jove, he felt good! He slapped his knee and was about to speak when he caught sight of Lydia's crestfallen face. 'Have I said something wrong?'

'No . . . no, you didn't say anything wrong. Nothing right, either. Oh dear, I must be going.' She stood up.

He was aghast, standing up and shielding himself with his hand. 'You've just arrived . . .'

'Forgive me.' Her bright cheeks were darkening. 'Perhaps it's the punch. I feel so hot.'

'You do look rather red.' He strode to the door so his back was to her, and pulled it open. Caspar tumbled in. 'Hah! Thought you were listening!' He struck him a blow on his ear as he rose to his feet.

'Don't hit him!' Lydia cried.

'He's a scamp. I know slaves.'

'Better than you know women?' She looked at him coyly.

'Aye, I suppose so.' He put his arm around her now that the heat in his loins had subsided. 'I'm not stupid, you know.' He kissed her cheek.

'You are a wonderful woman, Lydia. I'm uncouth and a bit slow at times. I've never met a woman like you. We'll go to Almack's together. We'll go whenever you like. I've no one else. Have you?'

She pulled away from his embrace, shocked by his question. She lifted her hand and slapped his cheek.

He bunched his fist by instinct and raised it to hit her. Prince who was standing behind him caught his wrist. He held it securely. Lydia burst into tears.

'Take her in your arms,' urged Prince in his ear. 'Tell her you love her!'

'You do it!' Carlton turned angrily and stormed out of the room.

As much intrigue was practiced to gain admission to Almack's as went on in the government of the nation. It was the high temple of the *ton*, the seventh heaven of the fashionable world to which all London craved admittance. Only a select few ever gained the privilege.

It was too much at stake for Carlton to ignore. For days, Prince was engaged in carrying messages between him and Lydia. Neither would speak directly to the other. In vain, Prince explained the reason for Lydia's outburst to Carlton. He refused to apologize.

The slap on his cheek had wounded his pride. For her part, Lydia was deeply shocked at his attitude. How could he be so insensitive when she was offering him not simply an entrée to Almack's, but herself as well?

With his natural charm, Prince patched up the quarrel and Carlton arrived at the Rooms a few minutes before Lydia. It was the first time he had seen her since the evening at Chapel Street. He was stunned when she stepped from her carriage. She was radiant with the allure of a woman who sought fulfillment, and was confident she would find it.

Passion burned brightly in her eyes when she confronted him. He seized her hand, fuming with anger. The couples crowding the stair-case leading to the ballroom, sensed the tension.

He spoke first, to gain the advantage. 'Have you taken more boxing lessons from Gentleman Jackson?'

She dug her fingers into his palm. They ascended the stairs together toward the doorway where Lady Cowper was waiting.

'If you weren't so pig headed, my dear,' she hissed, 'you'd know you deserved it.' She smiled brightly at the people who turned to stare.

'Lydia!' Lady Cowper exclaimed. 'So this is your Mr Todd? How kind of you to come.'

Carlton compressed his rage long enough to bow in a perfunctory manner. It didn't hide his sulkiness.

'What a dreadful man,' he heard Lady Jersey whisper to Lady Sefton. 'However did he get here?'

He shook off Lydia's hand and barged past the reception committee, pushing through the dancers until he reached the other side of the ballroom. Lydia followed him unhurriedly, nodding gracefully to her acquaintances as though nothing was amiss.

He stopped a steward and demanded refreshment. His harsh voice made the ladies nearby wince. A pair of them moved away, fluttering their fans.

'Tea or lemonade is all you'll get here,' said a voice laughingly in his ear. 'Bread and butter and stale cake. Exceedingly dull fare for such bright company.'

He turned to scare away the man he thought was mocking him. He was surprised by the fresh faced youth, soberly dressed, who smiled at him. He wasn't one of the Beau Brummell's fashionable louts.

'Fourth time I've been here,' the fellow said with a yawn. 'Pleases my mother, don't you know.' He waved his hand at the crowd. 'Isn't it awful? She wants me to be married, to one of those . . .'

'And you?' He was intrigued by the youth's accent. It wasn't the affected drawl of the smart set. He seemed to come from the Midlands. He was obviously a newcomer to London although he was more at ease than Carlton.

From the corner of his eye, he saw Lydia worming her way through the throng of bejeweled and monstrous ladies toward him.

'Marriage? My dear, my career comes first.'

It served his purpose to talk to the young man so he didn't appear to be waiting for Lydia. He put his arm on his shoulder and drew him closer. 'What career is that? You look young to be so dedicated.'

'Not only young, brilliant too. In twenty months I'll be qualified as a doctor.' The youth grinned. 'If I can escape Mother's plans.'

'A doctor?' Carlton pretended to be impressed to encourage the youth to keep talking. The steward served him a glass of lemonade which he sipped. It tasted vile.

'I would think this bunch has need of a doctor.' He gestured at the mass of fashionably dressed men and women seething around the ballroom. 'An unhealthy lot, aren't they?'

'My dear, this is the *cream*. Just to be *seen* here is something. Those seven sisters rule London whatever the Tories may think.'

'What seven sisters?' He drew the man aside. Lydia had seen him and was moving closer.

'You don't know? Where have you been? There's Lady Cowper, the one who greeted you at the door. She's *so* popular. Lady Jersey is a bitch although Lady Sefton means well. Those two *très grandes dames* over there, you see, that's Lady Castlereagh and Mrs Drummond-Burrell. Princess Esterhazy's a *bon enfant* but the haughty one with her, Countess de Lieven is *very* exclusive.'

Carlton sighed wearily. 'It's dam' complicated.' He dodged behind the youth as Lydia advanced on him.

'Carlton,' she said softly. 'I'm so glad you've made a friend.' She waited to be introduced.

'George Tyndall, ma'am,' the young man said with a flourish.

'He's going to be a doctor,' Carlton growled.

'How nice. Do you have need of one, dear? For your *niggers*, perhaps?'

'Niggers?' The youth's eyebrows rose in alarm.

'Mr Todd has a plantation where he breeds slaves, Dr Tyndall. Hasn't he told you? The welfare of his blacks is his abiding concern, above all others. He knows *so much* about them.' Lydia's eyes flashed.

Carlton stared back at her. George Tyndall was aghast and tried to move away. Carlton clapped him on his shoulder.

'There's an idea! Come and tend my slaves when you're qualified. You'll be with much better company than here.' He grinned triumphantly at Lydia.

'Yes, yes, I'll consider it.' Tyndall drew back. 'Forgive me, perhaps you two need to be alone . . .'

'He's right,' said Lydia, biting her lip. She touched Carlton's arm and he tensed. 'We're behaving like children.'

'I wasn't aware of that.'

'I am,' she said. 'I'm sorry I hit you. I don't know what came over me. You sounded so smug and I've been having a dreadful time, I suppose I took it out on you.'

He lowered his head, putting his arm around her waist. 'How do you think I've been feeling?'

'It's more than that, Carlton.' She looked around. 'Oh dear, this is nowhere to talk. People are watching. We mustn't make a scene. I can feel people dissecting me.'

'Don't worry, Lydia.' He sighed. It finally occurred to him what a cad he was. He was beginning to realize that women were different from slaves. 'Tell me what's wrong.'

She shrugged her exquisite shoulders, bare in her sleeveless gown. The pathetic gesture filled him with a desire to protect her. It was curious when only minutes before he was so cross with her.

'My brother,' she said, 'is Hex De Quesnel.' She uttered the name softly, as though it was a curse. It meant nothing to him.

'He's a lot like you. In appearance, you're more handsome. He's tough and ruthless and used to having his own way. He doesn't have any good qualities.'

She sounded so close to tears, he refrained from answering the gibe. He prepared to listen patiently. George Tyndall was eyeing them, obviously relieved that they weren't causing a scandal by coming to blows in his presence.

'Hex is my sister's guardian and he's rather cruel to her. She's terrified of him.

'Why don't you bring her to London with you?'

'I'm hoping to do that. Hex agrees and she'll come with me at the end of the year.' She smiled, putting aside whatever it was that was worrying her. 'Oh, don't concern yourself on my account. Shall we dance?'

He looked at the couples waltzing together. 'I'm not sure I can do this new dance.'

'It's so simple.' She laughed and tugged his hand. 'Do let's try. It will give Lady Jersey a fit.'

The idea of shocking the gawping cabal of dowagers appealed to him. He winked at George Tyndall and led Lydia onto the floor. He put his right arm on her waist as she instructed, and held her right hand with his left.

'Relax, dear,' she urged. 'Now take two steps forward and one to the side.'

He was determined to do it right, to please her. He picked up the movements quickly. Several couples were practicing the new dance and neither of them felt selfconscious.

'I enjoyed that,' he said when it was over. 'Holding you close . . . May I have another?'

Lady Jersey's disapproval of him was obvious by her frown. He nodded at her cheekily as he swept Lydia around the room.

'Oh no,' she giggled. 'You'll be struck off the list.'

'I don't care,' he said, the soft notes of the violin filling him with joy. If he was a romantic man he would have recognized the spell being cast on him by the music. His defences were trained to resist the obeah cunning of slaves, not the sophisticated magic of a ballroom, a waltz, and a beautiful, vibrant woman in his arms.

They drove home together, to Chapel Street. 'It's not late,' he said when she agreed to come in. 'Dismiss your driver. Caspar will call you a hackney when you're ready.'

They entered the house in silence. The fire was lit in the drawing room and he helped Lydia remove her cloak as she stood in front of it. He handed it to Caspar who was grinning with delight at seeing them together again.

'It's always so hot in here.' She fanned herself.

He noticed her nervousness. 'I feel it too,' he said, removing his coat without thinking to ask if she objected. 'A little punch?'

They both laughed. 'I promise, no more slaps.' She sighed, settling down on the couch beside him.

'Caspar,' he said sternly. 'Mix a pitcher of punch and bring it here.'

'He's cute,' she murmured as he nuzzled her neck with his nose. 'He's growing.'

'So am I,' he said. 'How objectionable I must have been when I arrived in London. So full of myself with my brash, slave master ways.'

She laughed, tweaking his nose with her fingers. 'Have you changed?'

He squeezed her, placing his lips on her mouth and kissing her passionately. She returned the embrace without hesitation, feeding on him. He felt her need and held her tighter.

Prince, who stood at the door while Caspar slipped in with the pitcher of punch and two glasses, viewed Carlton's technique with the eye of an expert. Caspar hesitated, wondering if he should announce his presence in the room with a cough. Prince beckoned him away. They closed the door so that it was ajar, and both crouched down to peer through the crack.

Carlton eased Lydia out of his embrace. Their eyes were so close, their eyelashes touched. They smiled at each other with contentment. He was pleased it was like this. Never had he had a woman as an equal.

'Lydia,' he said, remembering Prince's advice. 'I love you.'

'You're a liar, Carlton Todd.' She reached over him and took up the pitcher, pouring punch in both glasses. 'And not even a good one.'

She drank eagerly, and he followed her example. The rum had never tasted better.

'Come,' he said, taking her glass from her and placing it on the table. 'I'll show you if it's a lie.' He held her in his arms and kissed her again, sliding with her from the couch to the floor.

CHAPTER TWENTY-THREE

Lydia's influence mellowed Carlton and he welcomed it; so did Prince and the others. The months passed rapidly and more doors opened for him as Lydia's friends accepted him. Caspar accompanied him on the visits to the grand country houses. He was an engaging boy, petted and spoiled wherever he went.

From the house in Chapel Street, Prince conducted his *affaires de coeur* despite his passion for Gwen. Carlton, under Lydia's spell, turned a blind eye to what he once disapproved of. Having tired of Helen Witham, Prince was favoring society's belles with more than his wit. It amused Carlton that Prince was so successful. He created no scandal and preserved his dignity.

From time to time, there was news from Dominica. It gave Carlton no cause to think anything was wrong. Hayes employed visitors to write his letters in exchange for rum and a bedwench. The young in the nursery were thriving, the slaves were busy in the fields, and there were no signs of discontent.

From what Carlton gleaned between the lines, Hayes seemed to be enjoying his restored status. He claimed to be inspecting the plantation which meant he was fitter. Of Ella there was no news and he expected none. She would be busy tending the cantankerous old man. His children, he was told, were well under Tita's care.

When winter chilled London and the sky was forever gray, he thought of returning home. If he did, what about Lydia? He refused to admit the extent of his fondness for her. Yet the prospect of returning to Roxborough and his grumpy old father was no longer attractive.

One evening in December, Prince joined him as he relaxed before the fire in the drawing room. He sat down in an armchair and warmed his feet. Carlton no longer resented Prince's familiarity. On an evening such as that one, when Lydia was at some dinner to which he was not invited, he welcomed the man's company. Lydia's notorious brother was in town and she was meeting him.

Prince filled Carlton's glass with rum and water and passed it to him. 'Do you remember that big negro who was here last year? The one you took to Richmond's boxing academy with Nat?'

Carlton was used to Prince's stories that began on one tack and finished on another. His tales were usually a ruse to extract currency for roistering with his cronies, so he replied cautiously, 'What if I do?'

'His name was Tom Molyneaux.'

'I remember.'

'He's very famous now.'

'Indeed?' He sipped his rum. 'Those black beggars are everywhere.'

Prince ignored the ridicule. 'Bill Richmond took him under his wing that night. Started to train him and before long Molyneaux announced he came to England especially to have a crack at Tom Cribb.'

'Cribb? He's the English champion!'

'It's caused a great outcry. Cribb calls him The Ebony Imposter.'

'It's unthinkable.' He toyed with his glass. 'Even if Molyneaux was a champion in America, the sport isn't the same. He couldn't hope to take on an Englishman. He was a slave and a beggar only last year!'

Prince grinned at his outrage. 'Richmond was a slave too. He fought Cribb.'

'He didn't win though, did he?'

'Maybe not but he's been training Tom Molyneaux every day and the buck's become a hard fighter. He's proved himself against two of Cribb's best challengers.'

'That ain't the same.' Carlton swallowed the rum and held out his glass for Prince to refill it.

'On the tenth, that's next Monday, we shall see. Cribb's agreed to fight Tom. It's in Sussex, place called East Grinstead. Please, Carlton,' Prince composed his face in the expression of innocence that so moved the ladies. 'May I have a small allowance so I can go?'

'By the devil!' Carlton leaped to his feet. 'No, you may not! What ideas do you have in your head, Prince? I suppose you'll want to take Caspar and Nat. Why not Gwen? Make it a family outing. What of me? Am I to stay here alone?'

Prince blanched.

'No sir!' He shouted, dancing around Prince, stabbing the air with his free hand. He paused to gulp down his drink which was spilling on the floor, then resumed again. 'You may not have an allowance.'

'But Carl –'

'Shut up! Am I not your master?' He was amused by Prince's disappointment and laughed heartily at his woebegone face. He jabbed his chest with his fist when Prince stood up to quit the room.

'So, the black Tom challenges the white one, eh, Prince? What a fight that will be.'

'Can't I –'

'Prince!' Carlton hugged him. 'You shall see your fight. Let us all go together.'

'What?' Prince stared at him in astonishment.

'Why not? Of course, it won't be like the fights we have in Dominica but it may be amusing. We'll take Caspar and Nat.'

The Monday dawned with the kind of weather Carlton loathed. Out of London and into Sussex, there was cold, biting wind and driving rain. The four of them huddled together for warmth inside their carriage. Carlton didn't have the heart to make Nat and Caspar ride with the coachman. His boys were dressed like dandies with heavy top coats and hats to keep them dry.

The fight was to take place at Coptoll Common, near East Grinstead. It was to be fought in the open on grass. There were close to five thousand spectators when they arrived.

Prince plunged into the crowd leading the way to the front. The spectators assumed Prince was connected with Tom Molyneaux and let them through without incident. The banter at the sight of the three blacks was good humored. Carlton was proud of his boys.

Prince secured a position with a view of the ring. The four of them huddled together in the rain. There were no other blacks to be seen. Carlton watched the spectators with interest. He recognized Gentleman Jackson because of his school in Bond Street. There were three other men with him.

'They're all former champions,' said Prince whose excitement wasn't dampened by the rain bouncing off his hat. 'The Jew is Dan Mendoza and the one laughing so much is Jem Belcher. The man with the thoughtful look is John Gully. Cribb's beaten them all.'

'How do you know so much about it?' Carlton was identifying other figures at the ringside whom he had met with Lydia. The Marquis of Queensbury was there but he ignored him when he waved.

'The Fancy is so much talked about, I can't help knowing.'

Carlton looked around the crowded arena. Some of the spectators had their carriages drawn up at the outside perimeter of the crowd. It would be dry within them but they were such a distance away, it would be impossible to distinguish the action in the poor visibility. He pulled his collar higher and patted his hat firmly down on his head, prepared to stand for the duration despite the cold and the rain.

There was a hush in the crowd as a chaise arrived at the ringside. A bystander near him identified it as Lord Barrymore's. A wit cracked, 'Barrymore for a blackamoor!'

Tom Molyneaux stepped out of the carriage with a studied arrogance and defiantly flung his cap into the ring.

Prince and Caspar cheered lustily. Carlton tried to hush them but their noise was drowned by the jeers of the crowd.

Tom was accompanied by Bill Richmond and another negro as his seconds. 'He's Paddington Jones,' said Prince without being asked. 'Sir Thomas Apreece is going to keep the ring.'

A burst of cheering resounded through the crowd as Tom Cribb arrived. He climbed into the ring and waved at his supporters. He stripped off his shirt and posed for them, flexing the muscles of his massive torso. He stood 5′ $10\frac{1}{2}$″ and scaled 190 pounds.

Beside him, Tom Molyneaux was a black animal. The rain bouncing off his skin made his blackness seem like a tough hide. His arms were extra long and he swung them at his side in an apelike stance calculated to arouse the crowd. He was two inches shorter than Cribb and weighed the same. His hair was cropped close to his head and his battered negroid features were devoid of any human attractiveness.

'He looks brutish enough,' said Carlton with a thrill as he realized the negro could win.

The crowd tensed when the two fighters shook hands. They closed in and a gust of rain slammed across the turf. There was too much at stake to cancel the fight because of the weather. They shrugged off the rain and circled each other warily.

Molyneaux lashed out first, his tight fist landing a stunning blow on Cribb's throat. Cribb staggered backward, feinting with his straight left. He stopped abruptly and Molyneaux walked straight into a succession of rapid punches pounded to his body.

'What a way to fight!' wailed Carlton. 'Go for his ballocks!'

Prince laughed. 'This ain't Dominica. Different rules.'

Molyneaux winced with pain at Cribb's blows but he bore them bravely. He raised his long arms and moved closer, grabbing Cribb around his waist. The Englishman resisted. Molyneaux strained to lift him, until Cribb suddenly shifted his feet, gave Tom the crook and hurled him heavily to the ground.

'Now his blood's up,' chortled Carlton. 'We'll see some action.'

Tom Molyneaux's style was brutal and basic. In the next round, he advanced with both arms raised in front of him. As soon as Cribb was within reach, he rained his fists down on his head with a fury that was intended to pound him into the ground like a stake. One blow split Cribb's lip.

'Ah,' sighed Carlton. 'First blood to our buck.'

Cribb darted away, wiping his lip, and returned to the frenzy of blows with which Tom was trying to hammer him senseless. He kept calm and jabbed straight lefts to Molyneaux's face. He followed these with a quick right to the negro's flat nose. Down Tom went for a second time.

'Get up, you dam' nigger!' shouted Carlton. Caspar was jumping up and down with excitement. Nat stared unhappily as the rain dripped from his hat and the cold made his teeth chatter. Prince tried to encourage him but his expression remained dour at the folly he was being made to watch.

Another round began with Molyneaux rushing out of his corner to continue his graceless tactics. As soon as he got close enough to Cribb, he beat his fists on his head without stopping. Cribb dodged, bided his time, then landed a blow squarely in Tom's face. Molyneaux sank to the wet turf for a third time.

'Is it over?' cried Caspar.

'No, boy,' said Prince. 'Tom's going to win.'

'Not like that, he ain't.' Carlton frowned. 'He's got no technique. He needs more than brute strength. He should use his knees.'

'Not in English fighting,' said Prince.

Molyneaux came up to scratch – the line scraped into the turf where the two boxers faced each other at the beginning of each new round – and the fourth round began. Tom continued to use his fists like a battering ram.

'He's too reckless,' moaned Carlton with despair. 'Hasn't he got more cunning?'

'Cribb's on the run,' said Prince.

Round and round the ring the fighters went, Tom always pressing and attacking. Cribb was milling on the retreat although occasionally he pushed his left past Tom's guard.

The crowd wailed as they realized Tom Molyneaux's tactics were turning Cribb and overpowering him. Cribb's blows brushed lightly off Tom's face. His guard was no longer effective in staving off Tom's hammering. He began to slip and frequently fell to the grass, rising to his feet more reluctantly each time.

The rules of the match allowed a fallen fighter half a minute to get to his feet and come up to scratch. Cribb was beaten so badly at the end of the twenty-eighth round that Carlton saw no way the Englishman could return to the fight. Time was called and Cribb was still lying flat in his corner like a drowned rat.

'He can't get up!' shouted Prince, throwing his hat up in the air with delight. Caspar retrieved it from the mud and passed it back to him. 'He can't start the round!'

'Tom's won,' shrieked Caspar.

'Wait and see.' Carlton sensed the profound dissatisfaction of the crowd.

The referee shouted 'Time!' again and still Cribb did not move. He tried once more. Tom Molyneaux stood proudly on the mark, glaring at the crowd and waiting for the referee to declare him the winner.

'That's it!' shouted Prince. 'A black's beaten the English champion!'

John Gully and Jem Ward were Cribb's seconds. They rushed across the ring and shouted at Molyneaux. He put up his guard to take them on.

'What's happening?' cried Caspar. 'I can't see.'

Prince sighed. 'They say Tom's got lead weights in his fists.'

Carlton shook his head in disgust. 'Of course he ain't. It's a trick to gain time.'

The dispute lasted several minutes until the seconds were satisfied that Molyneaux's fists were free of weights. They waved good-humoredly at the crowd who roared with delight. Time was called again and Cribb, who had recovered in the extra minutes, ambled up to the mark.

The incident unnerved Molyneaux. He lost his pace. He continued to chop at Cribb but he was shaky and slipped often on the wet grass.

'What's wrong with him?' Caspar pulled Carlton's sleeve.

'The rain, boy. He ain't used to this cold, and the damp. The chill's got him.' Carlton had lost interest now. Cribb's followers had shown they were not going to let the negro win, whatever happened.

The fighters staggered on until the fortieth round when Cribb laid a light blow on Molyneaux's chest and he collapsed sinking to the ground, shivering and spluttering. He had been beaten by prejudice, not by Cribb.

'He was cheated!' Caspar was horrified.

'Aye.' Carlton patted the boy's shoulder. 'Let's find our carriage. You have a flask of rum there for us, I hope. Look at Nat. He's turning white with the cold.'

'Tom's the real champion,' said Prince bitterly, when they were safe inside the carriage out of the rain and the wind.

'England's honor is saved, Prince. That's important for them, not how it was done.'

'All the rum in Roxborough couldn't wash away the cheating I saw.' Prince drank deeply from the flask.

'Give the rum to Nat,' Carlton said. He was worried about Nat. The African was silent and stared blankly out of the window at the torrents of rain. He took Nat's hand.

'The boy's chilled to his marrow. He needs a fire to warm him.'

Prince held the flask to Nat's lips and persuaded him to drink. His cheeks were frozen and he sat motionless. 'How now, Nat?' he chided. 'No word?'

As the carriage lurched through the town of East Grinstead, Carlton spied an inn with several coaches parked outside. 'We'll stop here,' he said, 'so we can dry out.'

The inn was packed with people from the fight. Carlton took no notice and led his negroes through the crowd to the fire. He sat Nat on a box in front of the blaze and called a boy to bring four hot toddies.

The boy was surly and scuttled away without a word. Carlton removed his wet coat and held his hands out in front of the fire to warm them.

'They ain't servin' the likes of you in here,' said a voice. Someone pushed Carlton in his back so he nearly fell into the fire.

'Indeed?' Carlton turned around slowly to size up his challenger. He was in no shape for a fight. He was cold, wet and hungry, and worried about Nat. He was angry at the way the English supporters had treated Tom Molyneaux. A scrap with a pompous Englishman would suit him nicely.

The man leering at him had a black beard and stood with his coat open and his arms akimbo. He was taller and older than Carlton and had the stature of a seaman, bowlegs planted firmly on the stone floor, as though riding out a gale. Conversation in the inn died as the man glared at him. He stepped aside so his back was no longer to the fire.

'Since the sweat from Tom Molyneaux's brow tastes sweeter than English gin, I'm not insulted!' Carlton bowed, ready to plunge his head in the man's stomach and make a dash for the door.

The man guffawed heartily, breaking the tension. He extended his hand. 'Carlton Todd! What say you?'

This was a puzzle. He scrutinized the man, peering at his beard, his heavy brows, his wild eyes, and wondering if he had met him before. He glanced at Prince who shrugged his shoulders.

Carlton kept his hands to himself. The man snapped his fingers and the surly boy hurried forward with four tankards of steaming toddy.

'Drink!' said the man. 'You're my guests.' He glared around the room to see if anyone cared to contradict him. He thrust his hand out again, and this time Carlton took it. The handshake was firm.

'You agree with the referee's decision, don't you?'

'Do you?' Carlton was intrigued by the stranger. His brash manner was a contrast to the usual English diffidence. The people in the tavern feared him, or were his cronies, for they returned meekly to their drinking.

'It was the right verdict,' said the stranger. 'Who cares if it was just?'

'Tom Molyneaux might.'

'And you?'

Carlton was impressed by the man. He sensed he would make a formidable enemy. 'I had no money on the outcome,' he said to avoid the issue.

'Hah!' The man slapped his shoulder. 'Finance over principle, eh, Carlton Todd?'

He was grateful for the toddy. It warmed his frozen fingers and restored the color to his cheeks. His brain began to function again. He glanced at Nat. The African was showing an interest, his eyes unblinking as they watched the bearded man to see if he was going to harm him. Prince, too, was watching the stranger warily.

The man took no notice, hugging Carlton. 'One day,' he said, softer now, 'a negro might become the champion of England. Why not? Blacks are natural gladiators. They are superbly built and have bottom born out of recklessness. We have to see if they have brains too, Carlton, eh?'

Was it the toddy that made him warm to the man? He was cautious, realizing that the man's apparent friendliness could be a ruse to draw him into a brawl. He drank to gain time.

'Are you an expert in blackamoors?' he asked.

The man brushed aside the question with a laugh. His eyes lighted on Caspar and he was studying him eagerly. 'What a likely lad!' he said with enthusiasm. 'A buck to be proud of.'

'Thank you.' Carlton removed himself from the stranger's embrace and placed his empty mug on the mantel. He was feeling ill at ease and wondered where this encounter was leading. He was aware that he was alone with his three boys in a tavern full of half-drunken Englishmen eager for a brawl. 'We shall be on our way now.'

'Aye.' The stranger turned. 'I'll escort you,' he said in a loud whisper so everyone could hear. He barged his way roughly into the crowd, pushing aside people with his massive arms. Carlton ushered Caspar and Nat in front of him then brought up the rear with Prince.

The rain had stopped and the toddy protected them from the cold. The stranger waited while they boarded the carriage and then closed the door on them. He winked at Carlton.

'You owe me thanks for gettin' you out of there,' he said, his fiercesome expression melting into a grin.

'Really?' Carlton wondered why.

'Are you dumb, man? If I hadn't rescued you, you'd have been beaten to a pulp by those jackasses. That's a white Tom Cribb crowd in there! You can be thankful you walked out and weren't dragged out by your feet.'

He guffawed again, suddenly reaching through the window and squeezing Caspar in his crotch. 'I like that one.'

'By the devil!' Carlton slapped his hand away. 'I may owe you thanks but you can keep your hands off my niggers. Who the hell are you, anyway?'

'You don't know?' The man's mouth gaped open showing a set of decaying yellow teeth. He beamed, his eyes glittering with mischief. 'In a manner of speaking. I'm your brother-in-law.'

He smacked the rump of the horse closest to him and nodded his head for the coachman to drive off. 'Hex De Quesnel's the name.'

His laughter followed them up the road until they were out of sight of the inn.

Nat opened his mouth and spoke for the first time that afternoon. 'That man,' he said in his deep voice. 'He bad!'

CHAPTER TWENTY-FOUR

Carlton watched Nat closely on the ride home. The boy said no more. The hostility that blazed in his eyes towards Hex De Quesnel became blurred. He seemed to be in a trance and ignored Prince and Carlton when they spoke to him. Gwen was appalled when they helped him down the steps to the basement of the house in Chapel Street.

'Ain't you hab no consid'ration for the boy, Mas Carlton?' she railed, sweeping him into her arms. 'Take his togs off, Caspar. He soaked to the skin.' She bustled around the kitchen, taking a cauldron of boiling water off the hob and filling a bowl with it.

Carlton was relieved to have the problem of Nat taken off his hands. Gwen's competence had expanded with her size during the time in London. He was amazed that he once let her share his bed. She was still attractive in a blowsy way but it was hard to believe that he found her worth pleasuring. When he compared her with Lydia, the idea of bedding her was revolting. He wished she would forget her infatuation with him and settle down with Prince.

'We're wet too, Gwen,' said Prince plaintively.

'You go'n be bruised too, if you don't get out of my way.' She pushed him aside and made Nat put his feet in the bowl of hot water. 'Caspar, bring me a warm towel.' She turned to Carlton. 'I want some rum to rub this nigger.'

He nodded his approval and Prince flourished his key to emphasize his authority over Gwen. He unlocked the cabinet where the rum was kept and pulled out a bottle. Gwen scowled and snatched it from his hand. She splashed rum on Nat's naked, shivering body and rubbed him vigorously.

'When you done starin',' she snapped at Prince, 'stoke up the fire.' Caspar hurried in with a large towel which he placed over Nat's shoulders.

'Fill that pan with hot water.' She pointed to a copper bedwarmer.

'Put it in his bed.' Caspar rushed to do as she ordered.

'Put the rum inside Nat,' said Prince. 'That will do him more good.'

'Mas Carlton!' Gwen turned sharply and raised her arm to strike Prince. 'Take this black lummox out of my kitchen.'

'Come on, boy.' Carlton grinned. 'Bring a bottle of rum for us. We'll take our medicine our way.'

Gwen's ministrations warmed Nat but did not revive his spirit. He had never been zestful in the manner of Prince and Caspar. He rarely smiled and his countenance was frequently despondent, reflecting his brooding for his lost Africa.

For five days he stayed in bed, in a darkened room, staring at the ceiling. Gwen tended him with broths made from whole chickens and vegetables. She moaned about the lack of herbs to physic him properly.

'He don't seem to change, Mas Carlton,' she complained. 'He lyin' there like a babe, 'cept he ain't cryin'. Not with his eyes.'

'How's his appetite?'

Gwen sighed. 'He does eat some, not that he a big eater like young Cas or that idle Prince.' She scowled. 'I don't know,' she said. 'I ain't see a negro *cold* before. I hope he ain't go'n die.'

'By the devil!' He sat up. 'D'you think that's possible? I haven't got a whelp out of him yet. He can't die!'

Gwen sniffed and returned to her kitchen, leaving him to pace the floor of the drawing room while he wondered what to do. If he was at Roxborough, Ella or Congo Venus would take care of Nat. There was no doctor for the slaves. It set Carlton thinking.

Slaves were valuable; if they died young, his capital was lost. He had so many slaves at Roxborough. Lydia's idea spoken in jest about engaging a doctor to tend them now seemed a sensible one. He shouted for Prince and gave him instructions. George Tyndall arrived within the hour.

'Can't think why you've sent for me, Mr Todd,' the young man he had met at Almack's said, looking flustered. 'It's rather exciting, though; just like a real emergency.'

'Didn't Prince tell you I've got a sick slave?'

'What do you expect me to do? I'm not qualified. I only came because your moor was *so* persuasive.'

Carlton turned to Prince. 'Call Caspar to take Dr Tyndall to see Nat.'

'I'm *not* a doctor, Mr Todd.'

'Nat's *not* a white man, Tyndall. What does it matter? Look at the boy, you'll know what's wrong. It'll be practice for when you get to Roxborough. I've a herd of two hundred there. You'll be busy.'

'Roxborough? Are you serious? I don't think I see myself as a slave doctor.'

Caspar burst into the room. When he saw the stranger, he halted and bowed. 'Yes, sir?' he asked brightly, gazing at Tyndall from under his long lashes.

'Who is *this*?' Tyndall took a step back.

'Just one of the herd.' Carlton smiled. 'Wouldn't you rather examine and cure such creatures instead of those fat bags of wind at Almack's?'

'Well, *yes*, dear . . .'

George Tyndall spent nearly an hour with Nat. Carlton, sitting downstairs with Prince, wondered why he was taking so long. Caspar was with him, and he heard Gwen climb the stairs too, to give her advice.

If Nat should die, he thought, it would be a waste. He was young and must have a score of whelps in him. Think of that! Twenty royal black siblings. He would have to buy females of top quality for Nat as soon as he got back to Roxborough.

George Tyndall entered the room and he glanced at him anxiously. Caspar was at his side looking pleased with himself.

'Is he going to die?' he demanded.

'Not yet.' Tyndall flopped into a chair. He was shaking.

'What kept you so long?'

Tyndall drew a deep breath. 'My dear,' he said, 'I know I must try to *behave* like a doctor. I suppose you don't have a drink, do you?'

Caspar scuttled from the room before Carlton had time to snap his fingers.

'What do you mean he's not going to die yet?'

Tyndall stopped fluttering. 'You must understand, Mr Todd, that I'm not used to this. It's not a matter of my training. He's a blackamoor. I've never *touched* one before.'

'The smell washes off, Tyndall. That one's an African. He's a good boy. I don't want to lose him.'

Tyndall swallowed. 'I'm *sure* you don't.' Caspar returned with a glass of punch. He took it and sipped eagerly.

'There now,' he said, relaxing. 'I must consider this case medically.'

Caspar hid behind Carlton's chair but Carlton was too concerned to think of sending him away. Prince leaned forward to hear what the doctor was saying.

'I examined him completely. That's why I took so long. Testing for reflexes, heart beat and so on.' He sighed.

'I must say, he is the most *perfect* example of a human being, albeit a black one, that I've ever seen. I'd love to take him to the medical school. He'd be a sensation. Well, it was a privilege. Parts of his anatomy, I've only seen in illustrations. White people just aren't developed that way.'

'Ain't nothing wrong with his prick.'

Tyndall flushed. 'His body is sound. His breathing is good, no wheezing; his pulse regular. I opened the curtains, of course. Your woman told me he's been lying there in a trance. A sulk, I'd call it. With the curtains open and me taking an interest in him, he soon perked up. He's got an alert brain, Mr Todd. We had a fascinating natter.'

'By the devil! You went to physic him, not for cocktails.'

'Just practising my bedside manner.'

'So what's wrong with him?'

Tyndall shrugged. 'Absolutely nothing, as far as I can see. Maybe he's pining a bit; the dreadful weather here in London. He doesn't like it.'

'Aye.' Carlton peered at the fire. 'The cold is bound to tire him.'

'It's not so much that. He's tough, tougher than you or I. That's his nature.'

'That's why niggers make good slaves.'

'He told me he's from the jungle, like our countryside I suppose. These streets and the buildings and the carriages and the people . . .' He waved out of the window. 'All this can be so *enervating* to someone not used to it.'

'Bah! We've been here two years.'

'Exactly. My prescription is a change of air.'

'Is that all?' Carlton wondered if Tyndall was trying to make a fool of him.

'Oh, I'll send some medicine that will brighten him up. Do you know,' he said draining his glass. 'I found this quite exciting. I'm so pleased you asked me.' His eye fell on Caspar.

'Your young steward was most helpful. If you send him to my lodgings tomorrow, I'll have some medicines prepared.'

Carlton was satisfied. He let the conversation continue in a desultory way until Tyndall talked himself out and left.

At Roxborough, if a slave said he was sick, he was usually lying. A whip was the best cure. Was that what Nat needed? Carlton shook his head. It was curious how he had changed. Yet that was why he came to London, to learn. Now instead of a lash for a sick slave, he was consulting a doctor.

The next day, he sent Caspar with Prince to George Tyndall's lodgings for the promised medicines. He was keen to maintain the young medical student's interest in coming to Roxborough. It would be worth the expense to keep his slaves in fine fettle. If he got Tyndall when he was newly qualified and keen, the outlay would be no more than it cost to feed and clothe a slave for a year.

He guessed that Caspar, with his winsome smile and bright eyes, was an attraction for the young man.

Caspar returned later with some bottles and a message that Dr Tyndall would call the next day to see his patient. Carlton inspected the bottles dubiously.

'He's numbered the medicines,' Caspar explained. 'He told me which to give Nat before meals and which ones afterward.'

Carlton scratched his chin.

'He asked me if I'd like to help him when he qualifies and comes to Roxborough.'

'Fine!' Carlton beamed. 'Dose him carefully, the way you were told.' Nat's malady, he realized, settling back in his chair before the fire, was fortuitous. George Tyndall was committed.

Lydia was due to call that afternoon. Carlton dressed carefully, trying the new skintight trousers that were coming into fashion. His shirt was starched and he wore a coat cut narrow at the waist.

The tailor had complimented him on his build and said how trim he was compared with Londoners of his age and status. At Roxborough, he never worried about his clothes and appearance. In London, a combination of Prince's eye for elegance and Lydia's gentle insistence that he dress well to escort her, served to change his ways.

When Caspar ushered Lydia into the drawing room, there was another lady behind her. He scrambled to his feet and bowed low to the newcomer. She blushed and hung her head shyly.

She looked fragile and ill at ease. Her face, despite its thinness, bloomed with color and her fair hair shone in the light as she removed her bonnet and cloak and handed them awkwardly to Caspar. He smiled so she would forget her nervousness.

'This is Stephanie, my sister,' said Lydia. 'Forgive her shyness. It's her first time in London.'

'Then I'm honored to receive you in my house.'

Prince danced forward with a chair which he held out for the girl.

'I wish you had told me.' Carlton said with a wink at Lydia, 'how pretty your sister is. I would have entreated you to introduce us before.'

'Don't try to be gallant, Carlton. Stephanie won't be impressed.'

'Indeed?' He studied Stephanie from the corner of his eye while Prince helped her to be seated. She was about seventeen, with the wide eyes and timorous lips of innocence. She was overawed by Prince.

'The first negro you've seen, Stephanie?' he asked, expecting her to blush with embarrassment.

'No.' Her answer was prompt, even curt. 'The first I've seen who acts so grand.'

He was amused. 'Prince fancies himself as the grandest blackamoor in London, Stephanie, so you've said the right thing to win his heart for ever.'

'Oh dear,' she said, clasping her hands together nervously. 'I've no wish to do that.'

'That's enough, Stephanie.' Lydia frowned. 'Caspar tells me Nat is sick?'

'It's nothing,' Carlton shrugged. 'A medical man recommends a change of air.'

'Does that mean you're thinking of leaving?'

'Lydia! You'd be the first to know.' He wondered why she looked so concerned. 'I'm not going to uproot myself because a nigger's indisposed.'

'Are you sure it's nothing serious?'

'Of course! Why don't you see him?' It was an odd suggestion but he was irked by the startled look she gave him. She seemed so obsessed by his negroes that maybe she would change her mind if she saw one of them at his worst.

'Dammit, yes!' he said, springing to his feet. Stephanie quivered.

'Visit the buck and let him feel ashamed. Perhaps that will get him out of bed.'

He sent Prince to prepare Nat, brushing aside Lydia's protests. Stephanie had gone pale and was watching him with alarm.

'What ails your sister?' he was moved to ask. 'Tell her I'm not an ogre. My blacks won't eat her.'

'Please, Carlton . . .' Lydia put out her hand to restrain him. 'She lives with my brother and he bullies her. Don't you start too.'

'That reminds me,' he smirked. 'I had an odd encounter last week. Someone claiming to be my brother-in-law. D'you know what the devil meant?'

Lydia exchanged glances with Stephanie. 'Hex?' she said with resignation. 'So you've met him?'

'Don't sound so alarmed. He did me a favor. Got me out of a post house without a fight.'

'I'm sure it was only because of him that there was any likelihood of one. He has a habit of attracting trouble.'

'He was pleasant enough to me.'

'I'm *sure* he was.' From Lydia's stiff manner it was obvious she didn't want to continue the conversation. Stephanie stood up.

'May I see the negro too?' she said. Carlton was surprised at her enthusiasm. 'I've heard so much about your blackamoors.'

It was dark in Nat's room with the curtains closed. A small candelabrum burned by the bed. Gwen had tucked Nat in so that only his head was visible. He was a startling sight against the newly laundered white pillowcases. Gwen had warned Nat to be on his best behavior, to speak only when he was spoken to, and not to show even his bare shoulders while the white ladies were in the room.

Lydia uttered a cry of despair when she saw him. 'Nat!' She swept across the room to the bedside. 'You look quite out of sorts.' She turned to Carlton.

'It hadn't occurred to me that a black could be pale, but he is!'

'Sorry sight, isn't he?' Carlton turned to Nat and raised his voice. 'Say good evening to Mistress Lydia.'

Nat lifted his head slowly. His eyes met Stephanie's and he stared at her without speaking.

'Nat!' Carlton guessed the thoughts going through his mind.

'Dammit!' he said, swinging around to Gwen and Prince watching from the shadows. 'This boy's not sick at all. He's in musk! Look at him!' He strode across the room to pull the covers off. Gwen jumped in front of him and threw herself on the bed.

'Mas Carlton,' she said. 'The boy naked!'

'Then get into that bed and drain him! I'll not have a buck looking at white ladies like that.'

'He's done nothing,' said Lydia, clasping Stephanie to her side.

The girl was transfixed, her eyes fastened on Nat's. Lydia drew her away and Prince escorted them both out of the room.

'Take no notice,' he said. 'Sometimes Carlton sees things none of us do. That's his way. Hey, Miss Stephanie,' he joked. 'Are you catching Nat's malady?'

'No.' She refused to smile. 'I was thinking, I mean, I've never . . .'

'Never what, Stephanie?' Lydia paused on the stairs to look at her sister. 'Is something wrong?'

'It doesn't matter, you wouldn't understand.' She turned to Prince and managed a smile. 'You're very kind.' she said. 'Mr Carlton won't do anything cruel to Nat, will he?'

'Why should he?' Prince grinned. 'Do you know, you're a very beautiful young lady, Miss Stephanie. When you smile, that is. You should do it more often.'

'Even though you're right, Prince,' said Lydia, 'Stephanie's head is not going to be turned by your flattery. I've told her about you already.'

'Only the good points, I trust.'

'Are there any?' Lydia looked serious. They reached the foot of the stairs and stood waiting for Carlton. Prince went to find their cloaks.

'What do you think of him?' Lydia asked anxiously in a low voice.

'He's adorable.'

'Carlton? I didn't think you liked him.'

'Not Carlton,' said Stephanie, a faraway look in her eyes. 'Nat.'

Carlton emerged from the brothel and smoothed down his coat. It was a clear night, bitingly cold with the sky alive with stars and a half moon lighting up the rubbish-strewn streets of Covent Garden. He pulled on his gloves and stamped his feet to keep warm while he waited for Prince to conclude the unsavory business of payment.

The loud laughter that resounded behind his back made him turn sharply to see who was mocking him across the street. He cursed as he recognized the bulky shape and rolling gait of the bearded man strolling toward him.

'So that's where you spend your time when you're not squiring my sister!' the man said, breaking into an outrageous guffaw. The urchins and beggars who were patrolling the street watched him hopefully. Carlton was relieved when Prince hurried out of the brothel.

'Come,' said Hex De Quesnel, assuming command and linking his arm under Carlton's. 'I'll show you where you can find a decent whore.'

Carlton extricated himself from De Quesnel's grip. 'I'm not certain,' he said, 'that I want a *decent* one.'

The remark struck De Quesnel as funnier than it was. He shook with mirth while Carlton watched him with disgust.

'It's late,' he said, attempting to move away. 'We must go home.'

'Aye.' De Quesnel's mirth vanished immediately. 'My carriage is coming. I'll take you to Chapel Street.'

'You know where I live?' Carlton sniffed suspiciously. He resented the way Hex De Quesnel seemed to know everything about him.

'Of course, Carlton,' he said gruffly. 'Lydia told me. Is your African better yet?' A carriage lurched to a stop beside them and De Quesnel held the door open for Carlton to enter.

'I suppose you wouldn't mind if Prince rides outside?' De Quesnel said. 'Proper place for slaves, ain't it?'

Prince smiled smoothly and scrambled up beside the coachman without a murmur. He left De Quesnel to shut the carriage door for himself.

'What's this about?' Carlton sat at the far side of the seat and stared out of the window to show he was unconcerned.

'I've been hoping to get you alone.'

'You could have called on me at home since you know where I live.'

'So your slaves could listen to every word?' De Quesnel's laughter no longer sounded mirthful. It was a dry, harsh grunt of scorn.

'My negroes are to be trusted.'

Carlton peered in the dark interior of the carriage at De Quesnel's profile. The man exuded an extraordinary self-confidence. He reminded him of Captain Loring and also – what was it Lydia said? – of his own self.

'Your reputation with slaves is famous,' said De Quesnel.

Carlton sniffed, suspecting mockery. 'My opinions don't generally meet with approval. Mr Wilberforce has a wide audience. I find it better now to keep my views to myself. I *know* slaves, Mr De Quesnel.'

'Of course you do!' De Quesnel rapped his finger on Carlton's knee. He shifted away. 'I've sailed the Caribbean, Carlton. I've visited Layou. I know your reputation there, not *here*.'

'You do?' He forgot his doubts. 'When? Did you go to Roxborough?'

'Hah! You feel better disposed toward me now, don't you? Come, Carlton, am I not close to being your brother-in-law? You can trust me. You do intend to marry Lydia, don't you?'

So that was it! Now that he knew what it was De Quesnel wanted, he no longer felt at a disadvantage. He sat back and smirked. 'Are you worried about your sister's honor, Mr De Quesnel?'

There was that evil guffaw again. 'Call me Hex, Carlton. No need to be so pompous. What do I care about Lydia's honor?'

Carlton sat forward. He was puzzled. 'Then why did you ask my intentions?'

'Lydia is a woman of the world. If she wants you, your intentions will make no difference. Stephanie is my concern. She's an innocent, Carlton, led a sheltered life, and I cherish her. She looks on me as a father since our parents died.'

'Is that all you want to tell me? I assure you Stephanie is in no danger.' He pushed back his hat and scratched his head. The carriage was making good progress in the moonlight and would reach Chapel Street in a matter of minutes.

'Got you intrigued now, haven't I, Carlton?' De Quesnel chuckled. 'I like to tantalize a man. Softens him up.' He sniggered. 'It's not Stephanie I want to talk to you about. It's slaves.'

'My slaves? They're not for sale.' He recalled how Lydia often asked him to lend her Caspar. Was she closer to her brother than she allowed?

'I'm not parting with any of them, and definitely not Caspar, De Quesnel.'

'Hex, Carlton, call me Hex.' He muttered his name defiantly. 'We're friends. I'm your ally!'

'One needs allies in time of war.'

'Aha! Well, we're at war with the French, aren't we? What about Napoleon's Berlin decree? And the Milan one? No trade with Britain. The Tory blockade?'

'I find politics a bore.'

'Money don't bore you, does it?'

A frisson of interest stirred Carlton. 'Hex,' he said, 'why don't you tell me what you have in mind?'

De Quesnel turned in the seat to face Carlton. His eyes, caught in the flickering light of a lamp swinging on a passing coach, flared with evil.

'My friend,' he grinned wickedly. 'These are the times to make a fortune. I have an estate near Guernsey, on an island in the Channel, close to France.'

'Ideal for smuggling, I suppose? You beat the blockade by buying from the French and flout Napoleon's continental restrictions by selling to the English.'

De Quesnel flinched at his understanding. 'In a nutshell.'

'Tell me more.'

'Since you're not as naive in such matters as you pretend, Carlton, I'll be frank. I have a cargo of slaves, one or two hundred, who knows how many will survive. They are at sea on their way from Africa.'

'I'm not buying.'

'Wait! Lydia said you were short fused.' He paused and contemplated him before continuing. 'My ships are well known in the Channel, we have a certain neutrality. In my uncle Philip's name, I lease an island close to Guernsey. It's isolated, just like Roxborough.'

'That's of no interest to me.'

'I think it will be. I want you to come to the island, Carlton. Season my cargo of slaves for me.'

'It's madness.'

'I have some Batutsi wenches in the cargo. Pure breed.'

'I'm not interested!' He choked, angered by De Quesnel's sure knowledge of his weakness.

'We'll see, Carlton.' The carriage jolted to a halt outside the house in Chapel Street and Prince jumped down and held open the door. Carlton scrambled out with relief.

'I think I know what will make you change your mind.'

De Quesnel laughed heartily and drove off in the coach without another word.

CHAPTER TWENTY-FIVE

Christmas Day in Dominica was the slaves' own time. There was nothing Hayes could do to prevent it. He distrusted religion for the unsettling effect it had on slaves but the religious meaning of Christmas was lost on them.

Christmas as a tradition in Dominica began with the white settlers. The first of these were peasants and farmers from rural France. They were accustomed to providing their own entertainment and regarded Christmas as a fine opportunity to enjoy accordian music and dances. The custom soon spread to their slaves who knew nothing of the festival's religious origin.

The steady beat of the drums and the shouts of their laughter made Hayes angry. It was mid-morning on Christmas Day and he was sitting on the balcony with a visitor. Jean Beautour was a Frenchman who worked on his family plantation in Colihaut, a few miles up the coast from Layou. He had stayed the previous night at Roxborough.

'They've started feting damn early,' Hayes grumbled, gesturing with his tankard of sangaree in the direction of the quarters. 'Those drums will be pounding in my head the whole day.'

'All night also.' Jean Beautour shrugged his shoulders. 'Christmas is a good time for slaves. Give them a pig for a *boucan* roast and a cask of rum. They are grateful. They love the master more.'

'Bah!' Hayes sipped his sangaree.

'It's true, my friend. Christmas is a very useful time. It relieves the pressure. You don't want your slaves to run away, do you?'

'Our breed don't run.'

'I hope you are right! If you take away their Christmas, stop them beating *lapeau cabrit* drums, then they would surely pack their bundles and join Jacko in the hills.'

Hayes scowled. 'Those slaves are too lazy to run.'

'But no, my friend. Carlton is so proud of his Bondmaster breed.

They work hard with direction, I assure you. I have some at Colihaut, diligent beasts.'

'You recommend my own slaves to me?'

'Perhaps you are too close to see their value?' Jean Beautour swept his arm in a gesture that encompased the panorama from the hills in the east to the sea in the west.

'You have a fine plantation; it is well kept. Your slaves smile and they are obliging. Even if you had ten overseers, you couldn't achieve that if your slaves weren't willing.'

'I don't have *one*!' Hayes said proudly. 'I ride out now and then but there ain't much for them to do . . .'

'Just so. What superb slaves to work without an overseer. Don't begrudge them a little drumming and dancing. It is Christmas.'

'Never held with it myself.' Hayes spat. 'But then you're a Papist.'

Beautour flushed at the insult.

Hayes snorted. He had enjoyed the young man's company but he wasn't going to admit it. Jean's mother had been friendly with his wife. It was at the old lady's insistence that her son was visiting him because, she said, Christmas is a terrible time to be alone.

'There goes another of them.' Hayes sat upright and pointed to a boy darting acros the courtyard into the cane piece. They watched the sugar cane waving as the boy threaded his way through it, trying to keep out of sight.

'That's the kitchen boy, I'm sure. Dammit! I'll be mixing my own punch before the day's out.'

As if mocking him, the drum beats increased to a crescendo and a great shout rose up from the quarters. There were answering cries from the nursery and children shrieked with delight. The slaves were marching in procession up the path from the quarters to the children's paddock.

The men, pounding their drums made from goat skins stretched over hollowed-out tree trunks, led the parade. Women danced beside them, resplendent in brightly colored full length skirts they had made themselves as a change from the drab chambray of their working clothes. Some of them sported white cotton chemises trimmed with lace and wore kerchiefs wrapped around their heads. With a cotton triangle draped over their bosoms, their resemblance to French provincial women was complete.

Marcus, the boy Hayes had spotted running from the house,

clapped his hands at this extraordinary display. Children ran from the paddock to meet the parade, leaping joyfully around the drummers. Ella held up Miranda in her arms to watch and she swayed in time to the music.

'*Doudou*,' Ella whispered happily in her baby's ear. 'We go'n remember today. Aie!'

She was pleased because the parade was her idea. With the maroons camped on the hills around the plantation, periodic attempts were made to persuade the Roxborough slaves to join them since Jacko, the leader, knew Hayes was alone. To distract from the attraction of becoming maroons, Ella interested the slaves in celebrating Christmas in a grand style.

They planned this day for weeks. Material was bought and dresses sown. The men made drums. In the evenings, they practiced their dances. No one had time to consider the maroons.

She was taking a risk doing so much without Hayes's consent. Pip did tell him the slaves were going to hold a dance. They kept secret that it was going to be in the paddock for the children to enjoy.

She was thrilled with the slaves. Their perspiring black faces were bright with smiles. Everyone was happy. The children laughed delightedly at the gay colours and dancing parade. The beat of the drums stirred them. They chased across the paddock to join in.

Congo Venus and Mally Ibo were standing with Ella on the veranda. 'Dat de bes' Kissmass ah see,' the old midwife cried with excitement.

'Dinner ready?' asked Ella, ever practical.

'When de dancin' done. Mercury brung more yam an' de pig smoke juicy. Kingston find a cask of rum he ain't ledgered. Dis go'n be some fete, *oui*?'

Mally Ibo grunted. 'De *tambou* beatin' too fast for me! Mah legs too slow to dance.'

Ella laughed. 'Wait 'til night, Mally Ibo. The *lavway* go'n hold yo'. When yo' hear dat chorus, yo' feel young 'gain.'

Mally Ibo wiggled her fat hips in fun. The slaves were gathering in a circle. Men were drifting to the back of the nursery where Mercury was dispensing rum in calabash cups. Women squatted on the ground in the shade of the flamboyant trees, laughing with their children.

Congo Venus nudged Mally Ibo and they both looked at Ella, who was crooning happily to Miranda without a care in the world. The two old ladies beamed at her contentment.

The deep booming of a drum rolled across the paddock as the lead drummer slapped it with the flat palms of his hands. 'Hear de *tambou bélé,*' said Ella. 'I feel I go'n be de first to dance.'

'Yo' go!' Congo Venus took Miranda from her. 'Show de children de way.'

The bélé dance, or bellaire, was the most important part of any slave festival. Its origins lay in the mating and fertility dances of Africa. The drummer crouched with his drum between his thighs. He was encircled by a crowd of spectators who sang the *lavway,* or chorus. The *chantuelle,* a woman with a strident voice, sang the short simple words of the song while the spectators accompanied her with high, resounding notes.

Ella thrust her way through the throng, drawn by the music. Mercury saw her go and left the rum cask to dance with her.

Traditionally, one person dances at a time in bélé. Ella let Mercury, the *cavalier,* dance first while she, the *dam,* stood at the side. He danced with agility despite his age, following the routine known instinctively by every male slave. It was based on a display of physical style and prowess. The crowd sang and shrieked encouragement as he leaped and pranced.

When it was Ella's turn, the drummer kept his eyes on her feet, pounding the goat skin vigorously in time to her steps. She raised her skirt to her waist and beat the ground with her bare feet as though possessed. She followed the customary pattern of the dance, showing her approval of the *cavalier* and making gestures to tempt him.

Mercury sprung into the ring, pitching and dipping to display his dexterity and enticing Ella to join him. She resisted until the last piece when, to show her willingness, she entered the ring for the most heated dance of all.

She was caught up in the throb of the drum. She sprang and dived as the *chantuelle's* voice rose and fell. The *lavway* soared with excitement and the drum beat grew more frenzied.

None of them heard the first crack of the whip. The lash slid off her shoulders without her feeling it.

Hayes turned his attention to the drummer, pushing aside the slaves to reach him. He kicked the man on his shins and beat him around his shoulders until he stopped.

The moment the drumming died, Ella and Mercury collapsed to the ground like discarded marionettes.

Hayes swung the whip in an arc and the slaves scrambled out of his way. 'What the devil are you doing?' he shouted. 'Get back to the quarters, all of you.'

Tita and Jean Beautour stood behind Hayes. The Frenchman disapproved of what Hayes was doing and seemed more interested in the children. Congo Venus waddled across the paddock, still holding Miranda in her arms.

'Please, massa, sah,' she wailed at Hayes. 'We does be sorry, sah. It does be Christmas. *oui*?'

'Christmas, be damned! What are all these slaves doing in the paddock? They should be in the quarters.'

Ella raised her head to watch him. She had no strength to stand. She saw Tita and wondered what part that evil wench had played in getting Massa Hayes to stop their fete. She kept quiet. The slaves were already retreating out of harm's way.

Congo Venus begged Hayes, 'Can we dance in de quartahs, sah?'

'Yes, yes,' he said reluctantly. 'Not here! Too close to the house.' He looked at Jean Beautour for his support. 'That infernal racket gets on my nerves.'

Beautour was still casting envious glances at the children. 'I've never seen so many infants,' he said. 'Mama would love one of these.' He tickled the child in Congo Venus's arms.

'We got too many damn brats here. Carlton's idea. Breed niggers, he says. He don't have to put up with them!'

'This one is charming.' Beautour squeezed Miranda's cheek and she gurgled happily.

Hayes peered at the baby without interest. Tita sidled up beside him. 'Dat noisy brat be Ella own,' she whispered in his ear. '*M'sie* Beautour like she plenty . . .'

Hayes grinned. 'Fine child that,' he said, clapping Beautour on his shoulder. 'One of Carlton's gets. Tell you what, take the whelp to your old mother with my compliments.'

'*Mais* . . .' Beautour stood back baffled.

'Why not? No charge. She's being raised for market so you can have her. I'd like to give Madame something, she was so good to my wife. Take her. It's Christmas, ain't it?'

He nodded at Tita who grabbed Miranda from Congo Venus's

arms. The old slave watched speechlessly as Tita carried Miranda away in triumph.

Ella howled with anguish. She pulled herself from the ground and dashed at Tita, reaching for her baby. She felt dizzy at her sudden movement after the dancing. Her legs faltered and she collapsed, fainting at Hayes's feet. The old man kicked her, laughed, and followed Tita and Jean Beautour out of the nursery. Miranda, in Tita's arms, cried for her mother.

George Tyndall strode into the drawing room twirling his cane. He gave it and his hat to Nat with a cheerful nod, and then sat himself comfortably in a chair beside Carlton. 'Well,' he drawled without waiting for Carlton to welcome him. 'Aren't you going to congratulate me?'

'What for?' Carlton looked at the young man and frowned.

'Nat. He's on his feet. A bit peaky perhaps. Moving about though, and working.'

'No credit to you and your cures, Tyndall.' Carlton hated to see someone so happy when he was feeling depressed.

That morning, he heard that Lydia was on her way to the Channel Islands. Prince discovered the news from his cronies. She had left in a great hurry, taking Stephanie with her. He could not understand why she had left London without telling him.

'Come now, Mr Todd. Don't deny my talents because I'm not qualified.'

Carlton had forgotten Tyndall was in the room. He scowled at him. 'The buck's in musk, wants a wench, that's all. I should have known.'

Tyndall blanched. 'I've never heard the like.'

''Course you haven't. He's a nigger. A white man controls his urges. This one's an animal. He saw a wench, a white one, and was roused.' He slapped his hand down on the arm of his chair. Tyndall jumped.

'It's the sap in him. The only way is to drain it off. At Roxborough, I'd put him to a filly and get me a whelp.'

Tyndall looked embarrassed. 'How . . . how do you know when . . . what's wrong . . .?'

'There are signs.' He knew by instinct, but how to explain that to an eager medical student. '*You* know when you're attracted to someone, don't you?'

Tyndall's face lit up. 'Of course.'

'It's the same with a negro. I know it before he does.'

'Do you really know what your blackamoors are thinking?'

He laughed dryly. 'Since I'm the one who taught them what to think, it's not hard.'

'It must be a useful talent.'

Carlton glanced at him to see if he was serious. 'I wish I could do it with whites,' he said moodily. He wondered if he should ask Tyndall's advice about Lydia's unexpected departure. The young man was fidgeting.

'Mr Todd, I have a favor to ask.'

Carlton's heart sank. Was the man going to ask for money? 'Yes?' he said brusquely.

'Your boy, Caspar. May I take him for a walk? It's a sunny afternoon, although it's bitterly cold. He could wrap up properly. Since it's a holiday, I thought you might let him have some free time.'

'Holiday?' Carlton sat up and looked puzzled.

'Yes, it's Christmas.'

'Oh, that!' He sat back and stared at the fire. Prince was out, Nat and Gwen were in the kitchen if he needed them. He was going nowhere. He scratched his head. It was Lydia's departure that worried him. He wanted to stay at home and brood about it.

'Sure,' he said. 'Get the boy out of my way.'

'Thank you, Mr Todd.' Tyndall stood up. 'I'll take him to Astley's Circus. They have all manner of entertainers – tumblers, rope dancers, clowns and horse riding. It's great fun.'

'By the devil, doctor, you make me feel quite sick.' He turned in his chair and shouted loudly. 'Caspar!'

Tyndall rubbed his hands together anxiously, blushing under Carlton's stern glance.

Caspar peeped around the door. His eyes brightened when he saw Dr Tyndall. 'Good afternoon, sir.'

'Merry Christmas, Caspar.'

Carlton scowled at him. 'Why didn't you tell me it's Christmas, boy? I could have given you an extra beating.'

'Yes, sir.'

'I'm lending you to the doctor this afternoon.' He sat back in his chair. 'Have him back by eight, Tyndall.'

'Thank you, sir.' Caspar jumped with joy and ran out of the room for his coat.

George Tyndall bid Carlton farewell. Nat was waiting with his hat and cane. He took them, looking askance at the slave and moving away from him hastily as he sniffed for the smell of musk.

'Caspar!' Carlton's cry shattered the early morning calm of the house. He groped his way across the darkened bedroom and flung open the heavy curtains. Dawn, which came so late in the English winter, was stretching itself lazily across the gray sky.

'Dammit, boy! Where's my coffee?' he shouted holding the counterpane around him to keep warm. He opened the door and called again. 'Caspar!'

Prince poked his head out of his own room rubbing sleep from his eyes.

'Where the devil's that boy?' Carlton demanded.

Prince yawned. 'I don't know.'

'Then find out! I want my coffee. Because I let him go out yesterday don't mean he can sleep late.'

Carlton paced his bedroom floor, working himself up into such a pother he was ready to thrash Caspar. It wasn't only Caspar's absence that made him angry, it was Lydia's departure, the cold, Nat's broodiness, even Hex De Quesnel's pursuit of him.

There was a knock at the door. He opened it crossly and was surprised when Gwen walked in with his dish of coffee on a tray. He ignored her greeting.

'Where's Caspar? Can't he get up? I'll get him out of bed with my strap.'

'We don't know.'

'What?'

'He ain't here.'

He paused in his rampage. 'Not here? Where's he gone at this hour?'

'Carlton,' said Gwen patiently. 'Caspar didn't come home last night.'

'By the devil! That doctor! I'll have the man's grain if he's buggered my boy.'

He was furious. Why had he let Caspar go with the man? So much for Christmas, disrupting his regular behavior. Damn Lydia! If she hadn't left without a word, he wouldn't have been so preoccupied.

'Prince done go to the doctor's lodgings. He go'n bring Caspar home.'

'Hah!' He seized the coffee dish and raised it to his lips, scalding his tongue. He glared at Gwen.

'That boy won't be able to sit down for weeks when I've finished with him. Whoever does he think he is, gallivanting around London all night. I've been too soft on him. I told him eight o'clock! It doesn't matter what bribes the doctor gave him, he knows his duty.' He sat down on the bed.

Gwen laid her hand on his shoulder. 'Don't be vexed, Carlton. He's young, it's Christmas . . .' She stroked the nape of his neck until he slapped her hand away.

'Get off, wench,' he said. 'I'm not having it.'

She left the room and he dressed hurriedly, muttering to himself about Caspar's disobedience. It was time to make an example of the boy so that Nat could see. He was stumped for what he could do about Tyndall. Perhaps get him thrown out of medical school. If he did that, though, he would have to look for another doctor to tend his slaves.

He was cross, not for what might have happened to Caspar, but because he had let him down by not coming back when he was supposed to.

Carlton sat at the dining room table, pushing a mash of porridge around his plate while he tried to calm down sufficiently to eat it, when he heard voices outside the room. He listened carefully for Caspar's. Nat popped his head around the door.

'Doctor Tyndall here, sir.'

'Come in, come in.' He banged down his spoon and stood up. George Tyndall hurried in, followed by Prince and Gwen. Carlton glanced at them all and realized that Caspar wasn't with them.

'Where is he?' he demanded.

'Mr Todd, I'm most awfully sorry.'

'What have you done with him?'

'I don't know.' The man's voice rose hysterically. 'I brought him home by carriage last night, at ten minutes to eight, just as you said.'

'That's a lie! He didn't come home.'

'It's true,' said Prince wearily. 'Hear the doctor out.'

Carlton flushed, but held back his rebuke.

'I dropped him on the step,' said Tyndall. 'I didn't want to disturb you so I drove straight off.'

'I done hear the carriage,' said Nat flatly.

Tyndall glanced at him with relief for the support from an unexpected quarter.

'As the carriage turned out of Chapel Street,' he said, 'I turned to wave. Caspar was speaking to a man in a cloak. He waved at me, so did the man. I assumed he was a friend of yours about to pay you a visit.'

Carlton sat down heavily in the chair at the head of the table. He studied the group opposite him. George Tyndall was sweating yet he had come from the cold outside. Prince's face was grave. Nat's eyes returned his stare blankly. Gwen was flexing her fingers as though preparing to kneed pastry.

'This man,' he said sharply. 'What did he look like?'

It was Prince who answered. 'He had a beard, Carlton, and a laugh they heard in the basement next door. The servants there saw him.'

'De Quesnel?'

'I spoke to a friend who saw them together. One of De Quesnel's ships was anchored in the Thames. It sailed at midnight.'

Carlton slumped forward on the table, cradling his head in his hands. 'Dammit! He's stolen the boy to get me!'

Nat's eyes, as Gwen explained the reason for Carlton's distress, narrowed murderously.

Book Three
Slave Island, 1811–1813

CHAPTER TWENTY-SIX

The island of Jethou is situated at the geographical center of the Channel Islands. Within sight of its highest point, a hill not half as high as those on the Roxborough boundary, is the coast of France. Although Guernsey with its 16,000 inhabitants lies only three miles away, it is an isolated place.

The island was leased by George II in 1890 to Phillip De Quesnel who used it as a base for his operations as a privateer. As he grew older, he preferred the luxury of his residence in Guernsey and abandoned his homestead on the island to his nephew, Hex.

It was to Jethou that Carlton came in 1811. When it was confirmed that Hex was holding Caspar, he quit the house in Chapel Street and sailed for the island with Prince, Nat and Gwen. His anger at Hex for stealing Caspar was bolstered by his fury at Lydia's behavior. He could not abide a runaway. He wanted to punish her for betraying his trust.

Hex, Caspar and Lydia were waiting on the island's shore when he jumped from the dinghy. Lydia flung her arms around him with rapture. He had difficulty pushing her off. Her words of welcome were whipped away in the stiff breeze. There was spray, or tears, on her face. She was hysterical.

'Carlton!' she blathered when he pushed her away and walked up to where De Quesnel was watching his arrival. 'Hex made me do it! He said it was for the best.'

Lydia's whimpering, combined with Caspar's whoops of delight and De Quesnel's triumphant laughter confused his mind. He was already reeling from the effects of the voyage in the winter seas. He refused to shake Hex's hand and curbed his anger until he recovered.

Prince, Nat and Gwen joined him and they followed De Quesnel along the cliffside path to where they were to be quartered. There was a house for Carlton. He insisted that the four of them be left alone in it to sleep off their seasickness, tended by no one but Caspar.

After a night rolling on his bed as though still at sea, Carlton assessed his situation. He was in a solid, stone-built, four roomed cottage with a kitchen at the back. It was furnished simply with a trestle table and a few chairs. His room had a bed with a mattress; the beds in the other rooms were of dry fern raised two feet off the ground. The floor of the house was bare earth with a sand carpet and a covering of bracken.

'At last, Caspar!' he said when the boy brought him a dish of coffee and opened the shutters.

There was a view of the ocean from the bluff on which the house was built. He looked for the sun; there was only the dim light of daybreak and a wall of clouds lying heavily on the horizon. The wind gusted around the house.

'You look well, son.' He caught Caspar around his neck and ruffled his hair affectionately. 'This island life agrees with you.'

Caspar's cheeks were rosy-hued. He wore a waistcoat knitted in thick, dark blue wool; it was squarely built, meant for hard wear, and looked very warm.

'The women in Guernsey make these,' Caspar said brightly. 'Stockings too.' He showed Carlton his outfit. 'Mas Hex has warm clothes for you and the others. Mistress Lydia had them sent over from Guernsey.'

Carlton cuffed him gently before he sipped his coffee. 'Tell me, boy,' he said anxiously. 'Did he treat you well?'

'Yes, sir. Mas Hex wouldn't dare do anything else. He respects you.'

He took stock of Caspar. The huskiness in the boy's voice had deepened and his eyes, although as alert as ever, had shed the trusting innocence of childhood. In his woollen vest, worsted breeches and woollen stockings, he seemed to have filled out.

'You're a spunky lad,' he said proudly. 'If I didn't meet you fit like this, I'd kill Hex immediately.'

'He did me no harm, Mas Carlton.'

'Hmm.' He wasn't so sure. There were some things that Hex may have done that Caspar didn't care to mention. 'Mistress Lydia?' he asked. 'What was her role in stealing you?'

'None, sir! She was already on the vessel. That's why I went with Master Hex. He said she had something for you for Christmas. When I was on board, the ship upped anchor.'

'You were nicely tricked.'

'Mas Hex said you would be coming to Jethou on the next sailing, so I was content to wait. This island is better than London. It's only a mile big. There is a donkey for riding, and rabbits to hunt –'

'Slaves?'

'None, sir. Mas Hex has seamen to serve him.'

Carlton dressed in the woollen garments Caspar laid out for him while he considered the situation. Escape seemed impossible. On the other hand, he had his own slaves and the accommodation was tolerable. What rankled was that Hex had trapped him so craftily. He decided to bide his time while he planned how best to exact revenge.

Hex lived in the granite-built house at the other side of the fruit garden, opposite Carlton's cottage. This was the *seigneurie*, or Government House of the island. It was overshadowed by a giant mulberry, a gnarled tree at least a hundred years old.

The *seigneurie* was built strong enough to withstand a seige. It's front windows looked out over a lawn to the sea. Those at the back opened on to the walled fruit garden and the venerable tree.

Hex greeted Carlton warmly when Caspar took him to the house. He was shown through to the long parlor overlooking the sea. Waves splashed spray on the windows. The view was magnificent.

'That's Guernsey yonder.' Hex pointed to the coastline barely visible through the mist of the morning. 'If it weren't firm beneath your feet, you'd believe you were on a ship.'

Carlton was impressed with the view but he scowled and turned away. 'De Quesnel,' he demanded. 'I'm here under protest. What for?'

'Hex, do call me Hex, Carlton. Since we are now partners, we must be friends.'

'I'm no partner of yours, nor friend either.' He swung back to the window and folded his arms, ignoring Hex's invitation for him to be seated.

Hex clapped his hands. Caspar hurried into the room bearing two pewter tankards on a tray. Their contents were steaming.

'Mulled wine,' said Hex. 'A Guernsey speciality. Caspar's become as good at mixing these as he is at preparing your Roxborough punch. Try some, it's perfect in this chilly weather.'

The aroma of the wine stirred Carlton and he responded to the plea in Caspar's eye to try it. He sipped slowly, feeling the warmth seep through his body, filling him with a sense of wellbeing, despite his reluctance to show cordiality toward Hex.

'How's it made, Caspar?' He winked at the boy. 'Looks like I'll have to drink this until we leave for Roxborough.'

'It's ampurdam, a port, and claret. I put in spices, a little hot water and sugar. Mas Hex is partial to it any time of day, sir. In Guernsey, it's usually drunk at evening receptions.'

'We make our own rules here, Carlton.' Hex waved his hand to dismiss Caspar. The boy left the room as he was bidden.

'You treat my boy as your own?' Carlton was riled by the gesture and slammed down his tankard. 'I'll thank –'

Hex interrupted with a loud snort of scorn. 'No boy's ever had a grander time, Carlton. He sports all day, eats and drinks with me, and sleeps late. He's a likely lad.'

'He's mine. When the next ship calls, I'll thank you to arrange passage for us all. I'm taking Caspar back to Dominica.'

He felt better now he'd stated his terms. He remained by the window, gazing out at the restless sea, his arms folded resolutely across his chest.

'Of course, Carlton!' De Quesnel smiled wickedly. 'Not the next ship, though. That's bringing my niggers, and the Batutsis. You remember?'

'Why do you want slaves?' He was curious. 'You run this island with your crew. Judging by the way you've spoiled Caspar, you don't know how to handle a slave.'

'Exactly, Carlton. I *knew* we'd agree famously.' Hex strode over to his side. '*You* shall handle the niggers. I can't. Break 'em in, we'll sell 'em and share the profits, after expenses, of course. I'll provide all you need.'

It was an odd proposition. Despite the way he had been lured into it, now that he was actually in Jethou, it intrigued Carlton. The thought of the Batutsi females was too strong to ignore. In the summer, when the seas were calmer, he could sail home, maybe taking some of the wenches with him. He glanced at Hex. The man was watching him intently.

'Aha!' He chuckled. 'You agree?'

Carlton scowled. 'I'll consider it. I will need your agreement not to interfere in the way I treat them. A slave sees kindness as weakness.'

'I've never been called kind.'

'No interference? I punish them, not you. A slave can't serve two masters at one time. You must tell your crew, all the men here, not to touch them. When they're seasoned, it's a different matter. After that voyage . . .' he glanced with horror at the churning sea, '. . . they'll be more dead than alive.

'It will take months to get them over the voyage and properly responsive. Slave masters generally break in new slaves by beating them until they comply or die. Not me. I aim to revive a nigger and make him tractable and willing to work, not querulous.'

'Yes, yes!' Hex moved to put an arm around his shoulder but he stepped aside. 'Whatever you say, Carlton. I *knew* you wouldn't let me down. Caspar!' he called. 'Two more of your mulled wine.'

Carlton realized his enthusiasm was getting the better of him. 'The boy serves me, not you,' he said angrily.

'Let us share him, Carlton. You shall take your meals in the *seigneurie*. Your wench can be the housekeeper and cook under Lydia's direction. Let Prince be our vintner as well as your aide. Nat's our steward.'

Carlton drank deeply from the fresh tankard Caspar handed him. A close association with Hex De Quesnel was unavoidable now. The man was a rogue, yet his prosperity and influence suggested he was good at whatever knavery he specialized in.

The combination of the mulled wine, the warmth from the log fire and his relief at finding Caspar safe and Lydia blameless, served to relax Carlton. He joined Hex before the fire and listened while Hex continued the process of softening him up.

'Please don't get the wrong impression of me, Carlton. I don't cheat my partners. We'll work well together. I can see that. You're like me, an expert. I'll not interfere in your affairs . . .' he winked, '. . . and I shan't tolerate your interference in mine.'

'Your affairs?' asked Carlton, emboldened by his drink and the knowledge that Hex De Quesnel needed him. 'Just what are your affairs?'

'Hah!' Hex laughed loudly and slapped his knee. 'You think I'm a pirate, don't you? With conditions as they are between England and France, there is no need for piracy. I'm a privateer, licenced by the government, under letters of marque. Do you realize what that means?'

Carlton shook his head.

'A privateer is a vessel of war owned and equipped by private persons to seize and plunder enemy shipping. This war is wonderful. I have ten ships carrying eighty guns and over five hundred men. Can you imagine it? I can make a hundred thousand pounds in a year through the capture of French shipping.'

Carlton sipped at his third tankard of mulled wine and raised his eyebrow. 'This wine,' he said, 'is courtesy of the French?'

Hex's burly frame shook with laughter. 'Free trade is Guernsey's leading industry. Wine and brandy matures so well in our caves.'

'Free trade? Some would call it smuggling.'

'Carlton, we are the same. We are both engaged in enterprises that the law discourages, to our benefit. The banning of the slave trade is to your benefit, is it not?'

'Planters need slaves. No slaves, no sugar, no taxes, no progress.'

'Exactly.' Hex De Quesnel smiled smugly. Carlton's heart missed a beat as he realized he was trapped in more ways than one.

He returned to his cottage, staggering across the fruit garden under the force of the cold wind blowing in from the open sea. Prince was waiting for him. Gwen and Nat were sitting in the parlor. They made no effort to rise when he entered. He collapsed in a chair and gazed at them a little blearily, conscious of Nat's eyes studying him.

'Prince,' he said, waving to him to sit down. 'What do you think?'

'Not much amusement here.'

'Amusement? What about Lydia? She'll miss society more than you will.'

'I would imagine your presence here will sustain her.'

'What? Yes. Well, I'm not sure about that.' He stared at Nat. He was swathed in Guernsey woollens and beaming proudly.

Carlton was surprised. Nat had been the sickest on the voyage across the Channel yet now he was alert. Even his usual moroseness had vanished. His eyes were sparkling with zest that was rooted deep within him.

'Extraordinary,' he said to Prince. 'Perhaps Dr Tyndall was right. Nat did need a change of air.'

Prince looked skeptical. 'Has the mulled wine dulled your senses?'

'What do you mean?' He swayed in his chair, bothered by the criticism.

'Didn't you enquire of our host who else is living here?'

He stuck out his lips peevishly and shook his head to show Prince it did not concern him.

'Nat hates Hex De Quesnel,' said Prince. 'That's enough reason to revive him. There's someone else: Stephanie.'

At the mention of the girl's name, Nat lowered his head shyly.

Gwen, who had been crouched over the fire without speaking, chipped in, 'De Quesnel is a man's man, Prince. Not like you. I like him myself.'

Carlton let the banter pass over his head. Slave talk was always nonsense, based on ignorance and misconception. He knew they would all fit into their new surroundings with ease. Blacks possessed a flexibility unknown to whites.

Nat's revival, for whatever reason, was welcome. If Stephanie served to inspire him, so much the better for when he put him to one of the Batutsi wenches that were coming. Prince's despair at no amusements could be put to good account by involving him in the management of the slave shipment.

He considered his situation was not intolerable. It was the management of Lydia that presented the problem.

The weather changed overnight. The winds dropped, the sea calmed, the clouds rolled away to England and the sky had a vivid blue clarity that, were it not for the accompanying cold, could have belonged to the Caribbean.

Lydia suggested a walk. Bundled up in blue woollen vests under their cloaks, Carlton set off with her after breakfast the next morning. Caspar was keen to go with them but at the corner of the house, by the well, Carlton sent him back with a cuff around his ear.

'He likes it here,' said Lydia, leading him to the flight of stone steps through the walnut trees. There was a pigeon-tower on the right and pigeons and doves swirled around their heads, cooing with concern.

'Do you?' he asked brusquely, pulling his arm away from Lydia when she tried to hold him.

She ignored his churlishness. 'I do now.'

'Huh!' He strode out up the path leaving her to follow. Now was the time to get to the bottom of this mystery about her, but he wanted to think of it first. The path climbed gradually, past an outcrop of rock on the left. To the right was the sea, Castle Cornet close to Guernsey, revealed clearly in the morning's bright sunlight.

He walked briskly, invigorated by the breeze and working up a heat under his woollens. He knew that Lydia, scrambling along behind him, was bursting with eagerness to talk. Let her wait, he thought, let her wait for the injury she had done to his pride.

The path rose and fell around the island's central hill. There was a path down to the sea where a small inlet could serve as a secret landing. He glanced at it briefly then hurried on past terraces cut into the side of the hill, covered in bracken and brambles.

He reached the south side of the hill overlooking a small sand strip. This beach gave access to another island, an outcrop of rock that was the preserve of squawking sea birds. He relaxed his pace for Lydia to catch up with him. She was flushed with the exercise.

'At last,' she said. 'We are alone!' She twisted in a full circle with exhilaration. Behind them, the island rose to its flat peak. 'I thought you would never come.'

'You took Caspar. You knew I'd come.'

'I didn't take him!' Her eyes were wide with shock. 'You must believe me. It was Hex. The whole scheme to get you here was his. I'm pleased it worked.'

He snorted crossly. 'Why do you do what he tells you?' He resumed walking, slowly this time, with Lydia trotting breathlessly at his side.

'Hex is Stephanie's guardian, not yours. How do you think I felt when you disappeared? How could you, Lydia!'

She gasped. He grinned at the sight of her eyes flaring with outrage. 'You!' she uttered scornfully. 'How do you think I felt being trapped on his ship?'

He caught her arm and pulled her toward him. 'You haven't answered me yet. Why? What hold does Hex have over you?' His face was close to hers and he could feel her breath on his cheek.

She was startled, wanting to submit and needing to give vent to her anger. She tugged her arm free and scrambled away along a sloping trail through the bracken to the top of the island.

It was an easy climb for Carlton and he followed her at a leisurely pace to give her the chance to outrun him. Maybe she told the truth, maybe not. Either way, he was offended. He couldn't shake off the feeling that it was because of her that he was being used. How else, but through her, had Hex become privy to his secrets?

He walked slowly, crossing a dry stone wall that encircled a pasture with an odd shaped stone, a menhir, in the center of it. She was leaning against the stone, panting to catch her breath. He approached her.

She turned and ran across the field to a circle of stones. She stepped into the center and turned to watch him strolling after her.

'What's this?' he demanded, coming close. 'Some game?'

'Look at the stones,' she said, her eyes glinting. 'Druids used to live on this island. This is one of their magic circles.'

Carlton felt a chill that had nothing to do with the temperature. He stopped at the edge of the stones. His upbringing by slaves had endowed him with a strong respect for native superstitions.

'I'll not succumb to your spell.'

'You don't believe in it, do you?' She laughed. 'They used to hang pirates here. Look, see those iron rings in the stones. That's where the gibbet was erected. The pirates were hung here in chains so all the passing ships could see.' She waved her arm at the view.

He looked around. This was the highest point of the island. It was clear enough to see across to Jersey with the Cherbourg peninsular behind it. In the distance there were some ships, their sails full in the stiff breeze as they scudded toward Guernsey from the south.

'Come out of there,' he said.

She pouted at him and spun around, mocking his need. She darted to the other side of the circle, daring him to cross.

He did not move. He frowned at her antics, knowing that he desired her above all else. She ran a few steps to the east where there was a grove of trees. He watched her enter and disappear from view.

There was an atmosphere on that island he could not comprehend. Hex and his crew were the sole inhabitants. He and Lydia were the only two walking in the morning sunlight, yet he sensed they were not alone. Perhaps it was the spirits of the executed pirates or ghosts from the druids of two thousand years ago. It was eerie enough to make him want to return to the *seigneurie* and a tankard of Caspar's mulled wine.

He walked over to the grove to call Lydia. It was a small copse about a hundred feet long of sycamores. Their branches were linked together to form an arched roof over a glade. At his feet were snowdrops and violets and bluebells.

Despite the merry splash of color from the flowers, he shivered. It wasn't the cold. The branches of the sycamores kept out the sunlight and threw shadows that gave the glade the stillness and mystery of a sepulcher. The silence brought him to a halt in the middle of the clearing. The roar of the sea, the spray and the rush of the wind were excluded, like someone holding his breath, waiting for him to go.

He peered through the shadows for Lydia. He was in a cathedral of trees. At the north end, where shadows dappled it, there was a tall, upright stone. He stared, overcome by a foreboding that rooted him to the ground.

A cloaked figure drifted across the glade, followed by another. They disappeared. He blinked, and looked again, wondering if they were real or tricks of the light.

A woman, her face hidden, stood before the stone with her back to him. Her cloak billowed although there was no breeze. She turned. Her face was in darkness. The cloak swirled around her and fell open. She was naked and raised her arms to beckon him.

'Ella?' He stepped forward.

'Carlton!'

A voice shrieked at him in panic. He stumbled forward and fell, burying his head in the mass of bluebells carpeting the earth. The distinctive vegetable smell of the crushed stalks brought him round.

He felt a hand on his shoulder, struggling to pull him up. When he opened his eyes, he saw the cloaked figure peering down at him, face still hidden. The roof of branches was dark above her head.

'Carlton?' The voice was soft with hope.

He smiled and reached up. The woman came to him, kneeling beside him in the bluebells. Her lips brushed his. He closed his eyes and drew her to him, pressing his fingers into her naked breasts.

CHAPTER TWENTY-SEVEN

Ella rose from her knees, brushing at the burs and leaves that stuck to her shift. The tall forest trees of gommier and *powyay* grew close together, their branches intertwined overhead, keeping out the sunlight. The glade high up in the Roxborough hills was cool in the shadows.

This was her secret place, a shrine shown her by her mother and known to no other slave. It was a small clearing deep in the virgin forest, with an outcrop of rock in its center.

She faced the rock. The view below her was of the Layou Valley with its magnificent river meandering at the foot of the cliffs that marked the Roxborough boundary. The forest gave way to the provision gardens and the terraced flats of the canepieces. The plantation house was on the brow of a small hill with canefields extending from it to the coast.

This rock was her vantage point over the whole plantation, a place not even Carlton knew about. One day, she vowed, she would bring him here.

Her mother had used that rock to offer obeisance to her special gods. Alone, unsure of what chants would conjure up the hosts of devils to aid her, Ella drew comfort from the solitude. She was sustained by the knowledge that her mother, long dead from heartbreak, was watching over her.

She fell on her knees and worshipped at the rock. An overwhelming communion with Carlton across the sea swelled through her.

Her strength surged and she was invigorated. She gazed out at the sea, inspired by the certainty that Carlton loved her and would return to her some day. It was enough. Now the shame at the indignity she had suffered would cease. Tita's malevolence toward her would lose its effect.

She laughed, letting her happiness be borne away on the breeze so it filled the valley with her omnipotence.

For slaves, an unquestioning belief in the power of obeah – the mystique that lingered from their African spiritual heritage – was the manna that enabled them to survive under slavery.

Obeah was deeper and more sustaining than the religion of the whites. Nothing was stated; it was swathed in mystery. It thrived in the shadows and doubts of the oppressed mind and died in the bright sunlight.

Ella's restored confidence after worshipping where her mother had practiced before her, was no illusion. It was a fact and would enable her to achieve Tita's downfall and her return to status at Massa Hayes's side.

She wondered how to achieve this end speedily. Since the stealing from her of Miranda, she had walked daily to the rock in search of solace. She did not question why it was now that she was rewarded with Carlton's presence. The fact that he was there, in her, was enough.

She swung down the trail through the ferns with the agility born of her enlightenment. She emerged through the trees and waved happily to the slaves working in the *polinks*. They recognized her new mood. The word passed from slave to slave that Ella's powers were restored.

It did not take long for Tita to be informed by Pool who heard the gossip in the kitchen, that Ella was practicing once more. The effect of obeah was enhanced for the slaves when someone they respected gave proof of its ability. Ella's announcement in the quarters that she had a vision that she would reclaim her position in the *cou*, and that Mas Carlton would return, was enough to make her spells *appear* to work.

Slaves who felt they were victims of another's jealousy, came to her for charms and, thus protected, were no longer fearful. Ella had a few weeks grace before doubts about her powers set in. If she wasn't back in the *cou* as she boasted, she would be finished forever as an effective force.

She began to plot her return by trying the methods she recommended to others. One night, she visited the house and placed vials containing her urine and a hair under the eaves in each corner of the balcony.

For obeah to be effective, the intended victim must know that a spell is directed against him. To alarm Tita, she had a vial placed, with Marcus's help, in her room where Tita soon found it.

Tita's reaction was not what she expected. Instead of shrinking into a paroxysm of fear, Tita smashed the vial with a great display of scorn. The gesture thrilled the slaves, and frustrated Ella. It showed she had a formidable adversary.

More practical *obeah* was required. This included the introduction of certain herbs into Tita's food. Whereas occasionally this resulted in Tita suffering a headache, billiousness, or gas, she always had an antidote of her own that brought her back to Hayes's side after a short absence.

Time was running out. Every slave on the plantation knew of the struggle and were impatient for its outcome. She was obliged to try more drastic measures, but what? It was not a problem she could share with anyone because her success must be seen to be demonic, not domestic.

She considered asking Mercury and the slaves to create difficulties so that Massa Hayes would be compelled to seek her aid in controlling them. Yet that would be against Mas Carlton's interests. It was vital that she keep the slaves docile so that any possibility of a maroon-inspired insurrection be avoided.

After two months of failed spells, Ella was baffled. Every night, she trod the path up to the *cou* to stand in the darkness under the giant *saman* tree that grew beside the house. Its huge branches spread over the house like an umbrella. She wished her intentions would somehow rain down on the roof like hailstones and become reality.

Tita, who must have known of her presence outside, brought Laura onto the balcony one night and told her in a loud voice about silly old *soucouyans*, witches who had lost their magic.

'Tita done tell de massa yo' watchin' de *cou* ev'ry night,' Pip reported. 'She say yo' go'n change yuhself into a cockroach an' bite Laura lips.'

Ella looked at Pip scornfully. If she could do that, she would bite Tita not Laura. 'What de massa say?' she asked eagerly.

'He tell her squash de cockroach and hush her nonsense.'

That was no comfort. Thanks to her presence calming the slaves, Hayes was able to run the plantation. He did not need her at the house.

In desperation, she considered administering a potion to Hayes himself. Something similar to the potions she produced for frustrated lovers might work. She did not want Hayes smitten with desire for her, but to be stirred up with yearning for her company, instead of that of the treacherous Tita.

She spent days drying herbs in the sun and pounding them in her mortar. She pondered what combination would produce the right effect in Hayes. She was no nearer the solution when Massa Hayes sent for her.

Marcus brought the message and Ella wasted no time in letting him spread the news around the plantation that she had been summoned to the *cou*. Her powers, the slaves could see, were working.

She hurried to the back stairs. Neither Marcus nor Pip knew why she was wanted, only that Tita was on the balcony with Hayes. She calmed herself before stalking around the corner of the balcony with a brave show of her old dignity. Hayes was holding a paper in his hand, staring at it.

Tita bit her lip nervously at the sight of Ella.

'Good mornin', sir,' she said in her best accentuated English.

'Yo' let dat obeah witch come here!' Tita's squawk raised no reaction from Hayes. 'Ah go'n 'teck mah chil'en.'

'Stay!' Hayes's voice was edged with impatience. He looked frail as he sat in his chair. Ella had the impression that he was able to overrule Tita only because she herself was present.

Tita pouted sulkily at being ordered to remain.

'Read this!' Hayes thrust the paper at Ella.

She took it eagerly, wishing all the slaves in the plantation could see her. She glanced over the balcony and was disappointed that no one was watching from the courtyard. Pip was listening under the gallery so she raised her voice for him to hear.

' "Dear Father," ' she read. ' "You will see this letter is being sent from Jethou in the Eng –" '

'No need to shout!' Hayes glared at her. 'I'm neither deaf nor blind.'

'Sorry, massa.' She ignored the smirk on Tita's heavily painted face.

'Read the end of the letter.' Hayes waved his finger at the page. 'She says it's nothing.'

The accusation made Tita glower. She tossed her head and her long black hair swirled angrily. Hayes silenced her attempt to speak with a stern glance.

Ella sensed her time had come. She scanned the end of the letter to see what caused Tita's discomfort. She wanted to weep with joy.

'What does it say?' Hayes was watching her closely. 'I was right, Tita! It's something good for Ella and bad for you, I'll be bound.'

She read, ' "Why is Ella no longer interpreting my letters for you? With respect, father, I feel inhibited in writing about our affairs if Ella is not the one reading for you." '

'Hah!' said Hayes. He watched Tita triumphantly while Ella read the rest.

' "If there has been a misunderstanding, I beg you to reconsider Ella's position. Roxborough cannot survive without her. She is trusted and obeyed by the slaves. If she turns against us, I dread the outcome. I had these thoughts while walking in a mysterious glade here. It was as though Ella was at my side, as she should be at yours." '

There was silence on the balcony. Hayes wheezed, waiting. Neither Tita nor Ella said anything. He cocked his head on one side and regarded Ella shrewdly.

'That's the truth?' he asked. 'Them's Carlton's words?'

'Yessa!' Ella almost shouted, unable to keep the excitement from her voice.

Hayes clambered to his feet and faced Tita. 'Do you agree that's what's in the letter?'

She scowled and raised her chin defiantly.

'Bah!' exclaimed Hayes in disgust. He walked slowly to the grand steps. At the top, he stood and surveyed the plantation below him.

'Ella,' he called suddenly, 'tell that lazy nigger, Pip, to bring my sangaree.'

Hayes never apologized to Ella. She would have been ashamed if he had. During her period in the nursery with Congo Venus she gained a knowledge of the undercurrents of the plantation. It would help her when Carlton returned. For the present, she could do no more than see conditions remained stable.

Tita took Ella's return to the *cou* with bad grace. She was relegated to minding the children instead of sitting on the balcony with Massa Hayes. She suffered a great loss of face. She was never popular with the slaves because of her haughty ways, and they relished her disgrace.

She fought back through the children. Laura was now ten. She was a spoilt, bad tempered child who doted passionately on Tita, copying the way she spoke and behaved.

Ella was appalled at the state of the *cou* because of her banishment. No one bothered to check Laura's unruly behaviour. There was a disintegration of the running of the house. A slave needs a master,

Carlton often said. Without Ella's control, the house slaves performed their duties apathetically. Tita had shown no interest in correcting them.

Ella set about her improvements. Cleo and Pip welcomed her back to the kitchen. The two housegirls were resentful and Pool was open in his criticism of her. She bided her time.

She arranged with Mercury for a gang to clean the courtyard, weeding, cutlassing the grass and tidying up the area in front of the house. Hayes was delighted by the activity he could watch over. He sat on the balcony, a glass in his hand, drooling as the fine black bodies sweated in the hot sun and the appearance of the courtyard smartened rapidly. Laura watched with him.

'Massa?' said Ella.

He nodded his head for her to continue, alerted by the tone of her voice that some problem was about to be broached. Laura at his side pulled ugly faces at her.

'The slaves working well, *oui*?' she said hopefully.

Hayes heaved and wheezed and raised his head to look at her. 'What now?' he asked warily. 'You have that whine in your voice Tita uses when she wants money.'

'Money?' Ella was appalled. 'Not money, massa. It's the house. The slaves clean it outside but I can't do anything inside. It does be a mess. The house girls been spoiled by Tita. They don't want to work.'

'Tita don't spoil no girls,' said Laura crossly. 'She only love me.'

'There, there, child.' Hayes fingered Laura's bottom and the girl smirked happily.

'With your permission, massa, I want to train two new girls for the house.'

Hayes nodded. 'You're a wily wench, Ella. Those girls gave me good service.' He sniffed. 'Maybe I need a change. Get a black one and a red one. Something pleasin'.'

Ella frowned. Carlton had a rule not to sleep with his house slaves in case they got too fresh. 'I go'n get you a new bed wench if you want,' she said hesitantly. 'I need girls that do the job.'

Hayer was fondling Laura as he held her between his knees. The child's eyes were glazed.

'I need a new house boy,' Ella said. 'Pool good to sell. He's too slow and too rude, massa.'

'Pool got more manners dan yo'.' Tita emerged from where she was eavesdropping behind the drawing room. 'Yo' only vex wid he 'cause he won't pleasure yo'.'

Hayes pushed Laura away from him in a rage. 'I ain't havin' you two bitches quarrelin' on my balcony. Ella, you started this. You can have new girls if you want. Pool stays.'

'Yes, massa.' Ella refused to be harassed by Tita's mocking laughter. She backed off the balcony while Laura watched, her eyes bright with mischief.

'What's pleasurin'?' She heard her ask Hayes.

'Pleasurin'?' Hayes grinned, his anger diverted by the child's question. 'It's what a buck does to a wench to make pleasure.'

'De wench feel pleasure too?' Laura slipped her hand in his and squeezed it. Hayes laughed.

'Why, you're a bright missy, ain't you?' He sounded proud. 'Wenches like to pleasure, I guess, but white ladies reckon it's a sufferin'.'

'Dat why Tita cries when Pool doin' it to her, gran'pa?'

'By the devil!' Hayes wheezed with laughter. 'Take this child away, Tita. She knows too much already.'

Ella walked downstairs sadly. She longed to be able to pry Laura and young Hayes from Tita's clutches before they became as evil as her.

She began by training new house slaves. She avoided Pool, although every night he stole out of his cell and she worried if he was going to meet the maroons or Tita. During the day, she prepared an inventory of stores to send to Carlton for new supplies.

Pip helped her with the task, shifting barrels and crates in the pantry. 'Dis t'irsty work,' he said with a grin. 'Ah does need help.'

'Pool ain't no good.' Ella frowned. 'If he know what here, he steal it.' She patted her cap. 'Where's Marcus?'

'He gone since breakfas'. Miss Laura tell he to 'company her to de school cabin.'

Ella put down her list on a shelf. 'That ain't right,' she said. 'Come with me.'

'Yo' worry 'bout Laura? Tita don't care none.'

'I care 'bout Marcus,' she said, hurrying out of the pantry.

Pip locked up and followed her across the courtyard. Hayes was standing on the balcony with Tita and young Hayes. He eyed them inquisitively.

The school cabin was a few yards from the main house. Since the slaves cleaned the courtyard and cut back the undergrowth, there was a wide path through the trees. Ella hastened along it, not calling out.

'First we see where Marcus does be,' she said to Pip. 'No sense 'larmin' no one.'

She pushed open the door to the cabin and peered inside. There was no one in the front section where Carlton used to do his studying. The door to the back room was closed.

'Wait here,' she whispered to Pip and walked softly across the room. She put her ear to the door.

'You're my buck,' she heard Laura saying.

'Yo' hurtin' me!' a voice replied.

Ella was uncertain what to do. She liked Marcus and did not want anything to happen to him. All the slave children played master and slave games together, pretending to beat each other. Slowly she pushed open the door.

Marcus was lying on the bed, his breech cloth around his ankles. Laura, her naked body as white as tallow against his ebony sheen, crouched over him. Her head was bent to Marcus's thighs. The boy had his eyes closed and thrashed his arms on the bed.

'What's this?' Hayes's gruff voice resounded through the cabin.

Ella backed away from the bed as Marcus squirmed to escape. Laura didn't hear. She clung to him.

'Yo' got to pleasure me, or I tell Tita to lash yo'.'

Hayes reached the partition and stared at the scene. Tita pushed past him and seized Laura.

'Mah darlin'!' she cried. 'What de nasty nigger makin' yo' do?'

Laura howled with outrage. Tita cuddled her and turned to Hayes.

'See what this kitchen nigger done do?' she cried. 'He tryin' to moles' yuh gran'daughter.'

Marcus dropped off the bed. He crawled to Ella and lay trembling and weeping at her feet. She kneeled down and patted his shoulder.

She looked up at Hayes. 'Whatever the boy did, he did because Laura told him,' she said. 'He's an obliging fellow. He does what he's told.'

'That's a lie. Yo' saw it yuhself, massa!' Tita shook her fist at Ella. 'Yo' only tryin' 'teck him.'

Hayes turned away from the room without a word. As soon as he left the cabin, Laura stopped crying. 'He go'n lash Marcus?' she asked hopefully.

'Of co's, Laura. De massa got to punish de buck.' Tita smiled.

To Ella's surprise, there was no retribution. Hayes forgot about Marcus. He returned to the house, sat with his punch, and stared at the sea. Ella and Tita moved cautiously about the balcony, waiting for his decision, but none came.

For Laura, the experience was exhilarating. She discovered how pleasing a black body was. It added to her pride at being able to do what she wanted with the slaves. Marcus was terrified. The word spread around the plantation. He was an object of awe. The older slaves worried; the younger ones were impressed.

A letter came from Carlton the next day and Ella read it to Hayes. It told of Carlton's experiences on Jethou and of the arrival of negroes from Africa.

' "They are miserable specimens," ' he wrote, ' "having suffered greatly on the voyage. I was promised some Batutsi females. Alas, only one survived. She is a most contrary creature. All I can do for the first weeks is see the beasts are fed well." '

His letter continued, ' "I have hopes that my African, Nat, will take to the Batutsi. Now he is inspired by his duties at the *seigneurie* and waits on Lady Lydia and her sister with great industry. I misjudged him for he is proving a very capable house slave. Caspar is as lively as ever." '

Hayes sniffed scornfully. 'Carlton got niggers lively enough here that needs him.'

Ella read the rest of the letter. ' "When the island's owner is away, I am King of Jethou. My kingdom flourishes and my subjects are well," ' he concluded. ' "When I have seasoned this poor consignment, I will return to Roxborough." '

'Humph,' grunted Hayes. 'Sooner the better.'

Ella suspected that Tita was planning some mischief. The woman was vexed about Hayes not punishing Marcus. The slaves were on edge too. Laura strutted about the house proudly. Marcus lost his vitality and usefulness and slunk around the kitchen in dread.

A few days later, Ella tried to wake him as he lay on the mat where he slept on the kitchen floor. He wouldn't stir.

Pool emerged from his cell and laughed. 'He dead,' he sneered. 'Tita done fix him. Her obeah more powerful dan yuh'n Ella. Tita go'n be Mistress here, not you.'

CHAPTER TWENTY-EIGHT

When he began his duties in the *seigneurie*, Nat was unaccustomed to waiting on ladies. Stephanie's presence and her eyes constantly watching him made him nervous. He made many mistakes and Master De Quesnel got impatient with him. When he was close to despair, Stephanie smiled at him secretly so De Quesnel didn't see. He drew encouragement from that smile.

She smiled at him often, when he served her in the parlor or when they met in the passageway as he moved silently about his duties.

In the parlor, Stephanie liked to sit in front of the open windows. Sometimes she sat with a book, other times she had some material stretched over a hoop and sewed designs on it. Occasionally, she sat with nothing in her lap but her hands, one clasped in the other as she stared out to sea.

Nat was troubled when he saw her like that because it meant she wasn't happy. Her happiness became paramount to him. He realized this gradually, for he arrived at conclusions only after a great deal of thought.

He worked hard to please her. It was a new sensation for him and he gloried in the pleasure his work brought him when it made her happy. Mas Carlton noticed the change in his attitude and pronounced himself pleased. He did not know the real reason was Stephanie's encouraging smile.

'That tyro doctor knows a thing or two!' Carlton exclaimed happily to Lydia when they were taking afternoon tea with the sun streaming through the open windows of the parlor.

Nat heeded Gwen's instructions to listen carefully to the whites' conversation so he could recount to her what was discussed. He lingered over the teatray. Stephanie, sitting on the couch beside Lydia, caught his eye. She blushed, and lowered her lashes. His spirits soared.

'Really, Carlton?' Lydia sounded bored. 'Please don't tell us more about those unfortunate blackamoors in the barracoon.'

Carlton ignored her. 'He said Nat needed a change of air. Look at him! He's a new man now.'

Lydia barely glanced at Nat. Stephanie stared at him boldly, since she had been invited to do so. Hex was away in Guernsey so she did not have to fear his reprimand.

'Perhaps it's the change from serving you, Carlton, to attending myself and Stephanie instead.'

'Are you mollycoddling the scamp?' Carlton demanded, his good humor vanishing as he regarded Lydia closely. 'Ruins a slave, that does.'

'Nat is not a scamp,' said Lydia. 'He's very intelligent.'

'He's from a great family in Africa,' said Stephanie, no longer able to keep quiet. 'His father rules a land that extends in both directions so you can walk for ten sunsets without leaving it. Imagine!'

'Stephanie!' Lydia's cup clattered into the saucer. 'Whatever next!'

'It's true,' said Stephanie brightly, oblivious of the stern expression on Carlton's face. 'Ask Nat.'

Carlton stood up. 'Niggers will tell you anything you want to hear.'

'I don't think he lied,' Stephanie interrupted, refusing to be cowered by his scowl.

'What if it is true? It's of no importance. It's how he behaves that counts.'

Nat stood by the tea table, uncertain whether to go or stay. Only Stephanie glanced at him shyly.

Carlton was fuming. 'Blacks get enamored with their own importance. You think he's intelligent, Lydia. Stephanie, to you he has a romantic past. By the devil, Nat's a slave and must be treated as such.' He strode over and raised his hand to strike him.

'Don't be silly, Carlton.' Lydia stiffened. 'Nat's not one of the wretches you have penned down by the shore. He's a man of character and talent and we're both delighted he looks after us so well, aren't we, Stephanie?'

Carlton snorted disdainfully. 'My curse is women who suppose negroes are whites with black skins!'

'Indeed?' Lydia flushed while Stephanie peered at her teacup, biting her lip.

Nat saw her delicate complexion deepen so he knew she was offended. He was sorry; it was because of him.

'If you find our company distasteful, Carlton Todd, perhaps you would be better off in the barracoon. Surely there's a dusky Venus there who would appreciate your animal nature!'

Stephanie hissed with shock at Lydia's outburst and clutched her sister's hand.

Nat, whose understanding was based on the passion with which Lydia spoke rather than the meaning of her words, blinked at his master. Carlton merely raised his eyebrow, nodded his head ominously and stalked out of the parlor.

'Sister!' said Stephanie aghast. 'How could you say such a thing?'

Lydia blushed. 'I don't know,' she said. 'But I'm glad I did.'

'Don't cry!' Stephanie patted her hand, her eyes peering over Lydia's shoulder to Nat. 'Some more tea?'

She took her sister's cup and held it out for Nat. He removed it gently from her hand, his fingers touching hers.

He marvelled at her white skin next to his. In his breast there was a longing to seize that hand and hold it close to his lips. Instead, he put the cup on the tray, poured tea into it and offered it to Lydia. The lady took it with a strained smile.

'I've been wanting to speak to him like that for weeks,' he heard her say. 'He spends every day with those creatures, quite ignoring me.' She sipped the tea and seemed to feel better.

'We hoped, getting him here . . .'

Stephanie interrupted the silence as Lydia's voice trailed off. 'What are the Africans like?' she asked eagerly. 'Hex has forbidden me to go near the stockade. Are there women there too?'

'Three.' Lydia finished her tea and held the cup out for Nat to collect. 'Carlton wants this black Apollo here to . . .' She hesitated and glanced at Stephanie. 'Well . . . to marry one of them.'

'That's dreadful.' Stephanie fell back in the couch, almost swooning.

'It is. To buy and breed slaves for sale. I shall never get used to it.'

'Nat?' Stephanie made an effort to regain her composure. 'Come here.'

He put down Lydia's cup and stepped hastily to her side. His face showed the concern he felt at the worry reflected in her brilliant blue eyes.

'Something wrong?' he asked anxiously.

'Oh no, Nat, not with you here.' She smiled but he saw the glimmer of tears.

'Miss?'

'Oh listen to me!' she said with despair, clasping Lydia's hand. 'What a foolish girl I am. I don't know what I'm saying, I don't know what's come over me.'

'Calm yourself, Stephanie. Why are you so excited?'

She swallowed, fanning herself rapidly. 'Nat,' she said not daring to raise her eyes to meet his. 'Is it true you are to be married to one of those . . . those captive blackamoors?'

'Me, miss?' He gulped at the thought. 'I left my father's land when he tried to force me to marriage.'

'Mr Carlton has such a plan for you.'

He backed away. His sadness was as profound as her own. 'No, miss,' he said looking from Stephanie to Lydia and back again. 'I cannot.'

Lydia clapped her hands. 'Goodness, Stephanie, what have you said? You've quite upset the darling black. Carlton will be most put out.'

'That's nothing to what I'll be if he does such a thing to Nat. It's monstrous. He's just a sweet, innocent boy.'

'Yes, miss.'

Lydia looked at her sister's flushed cheeks and palpitating breast. 'Stephanie?' she suggested, hinting with her eyes because Nat could overhear what they were saying. 'Shall we take a walk in the garden. Perhaps some fresh air?'

'Fresh air, yes.' Stephanie rose to her feet, touching Nat's arm.

'A walk, yes, but talk, no. I know what that gleam means, Lydia. You want to lecture me about Nat. What difference does it make? I shall never be a lady like you. How am I going to meet a man when I have to spend my entire life on this rock guarded by Hex.'

'I don't want one anyway. I'm content to have Nat as my companion.'

'A blackamoor as a *companion*, Stephanie? I hope that's all you are thinking.'

She gasped. 'You're . . . you're heartless, just like Hex!'

'I have your interest at heart, Stephanie. You do not know about blacks, I do.'

'How do you know the way I feel? I'm not like you.'

Stephanie was standing face to face with Nat. Her head reached up to his shoulders. She raised her eyes and gazed into his. 'Don't worry, Nat,' she whispered. 'Carlton won't force you to do anything. I promise you.' She fingered the frills of his stock. For a moment, he thought his heart had stopped beating.

'Stephanie!' Lydia prodded her with her fan.

'Yes, sister.' She sighed and left the room with a backward glance at Nat. He bowed his head and was surprised when Lydia rapped him on his cheek with her closed fan.

'Yes, mistress?' he asked, his eyes blank. Lydia was staring at him.

'I'm watching you, boy,' she said, sounding like Mas Carlton himself. 'If you make my sister unhappy, it's Hex De Quesnel you shall answer to, not Carlton Todd.'

He lowered his head, wondering what he had done wrong.

He waited for Lydia to leave the room and then cleared up the tea cups. He touched the couch where Stephanie had sat, feeling her warmth where the brocade upholstery was dented with the impression of her body. He pressed his cheek to the cushion and sighed.

Only forty of the Africans out of the hundred Hex De Quesnel had shipped to Jethou, survived the voyage. These forty were quartered in a barracoon built close to the landing stage, down wind of the *seigneurie*. There was a stockade with a large area for their daily exercise.

The three females were penned separately, away from the males. Carlton was explicit in his instructions to Hex's seamen, the guards of this precious cargo, that none of the men were to molest them. Such was their discipline, the women remained untouched.

'Aren't they beauties?' Carlton was inspecting the quarters with Prince and gazed at the three females fondly. The Batutsi was tall with splendid shanks and firm thighs with the high rump and full breasts of her race. She was broad shouldered and broad hipped.

'With a conny like that,' Carlton said, drooling, 'it will take a giant to mount her. What a whelp she'll produce.'

Prince took a handkerchief from his sleeve and blew into it pointedly. He still affected the dress of a dandy, even though the only women on the island were Lydia, Stephanie and Gwen, apart from these three black wenches. He eyed them with distaste.

'Do you really consider them beautiful?' He kept his handkerchief to his face.

'Look at her body, Prince!' Carlton put his hand on the Batutsi's breast and squeezed. The female slapped him away. He raised his whip but Prince caught it before he could strike her.

'That will serve no purpose, Carlton. She's lively, be thankful for that. The other two are half-dead.'

It was true. During the time they had been on the island, Carlton had been unable to rouse any response from them. Their eyes showed no emotion. When he examined their bodies, they let him finger them without protest. Only the Batutsi resented his handling of her. Because of her size and strength, he could do nothing unless he summoned Hex's men to help. He was too proud for that.

The females' lack of spirit worried Carlton. They ate little, scooping up the feed with their fingers and swallowing it with expressions of disgust. Sleep and regular feeding improved their condition over the miserable shape they were in when they arrived. Getting them to shake off their lethargy was more difficult.

'The males are the same,' said Carlton as he and Prince walked away from the cabin. He pushed open the gate to the main stockade. A group of Africans were reclining in the shade of the sycamore trees, their eyes fixed listlessly on the sea. There was no sense of excitement when he entered; none of them moved or spoke.

'What do you think, Prince. Are they sick? They have the best feed, Hex is most generous with his rations, and they have a measure of brandy every day. Yet there's no spunk in them. See, not one has the inclination of that Batutsi to resist me.'

He lashed out with his whip, opening a cut on the bare backside of the nearest one. He didn't flinch.

'You sound disappointed. Do you like to whip negroes?'

'Damn you, Prince! Of course I don't.'

'You want docile slaves. You've got them.'

'Ah, but how do I make them work?'

Prince returned his handkerchief to his sleeve with a deliberate sigh. His reluctance to be involved in the slave seasoning had been clear to Carlton from the start.

'It appears to me,' he said, draping himself against the gate post with all the nonchalance of being at one of Helen Witham's *At Homes*, 'that these dandas are neither sick nor contrary. They have no idea what is required of them.'

'By the devil, Prince. They've had long enough to learn!'

'From whom? You? Can you speak their tongue? They're all from different tribes judging by their surly features. They know where to eat and sleep and shit. In Africa, do they ever need to know more?'

'At Roxborough, we creolize new niggers in weeks. Ella's good at that.'

Prince permitted himself a polite laugh. 'Where is your Ella?'

'In Dom –'

'I don't mean that, Carlton.' Prince waved a languid hand at the negroes lying around the stockade. 'I mean someone who can talk to them, tell them what *buckra* – you! – want from them. At Roxborough, you have slaves everywhere. They cut the cane, plough the fields, clean the drains, grow the ground provisions. The dandas can see what to do. These poor brutes have nothing to see and no one to show them.'

'You think I don't know that!' Carlton snapped. He didn't want Prince to see that he was impressed. In a curious way, the weeks together on the island brought back the easy intimacy of their shared childhood. He trusted Prince in a manner he could not extend to Lydia and Hex.

'You damned black popinjay!' he said, brushing past him and marching out of the stockade. 'What the devil am I to do? Throw them in the sea? You must help me!'

'What can I do?' Prince drawled, swaggering along the path behind him. 'I can't speak their tongue any more than you can.'

'You're black, dammit. You could show them.'

'Give me a cutlass, some ratoons and we'll start a cane piece right here.' Prince waved at the pasture and snorted with disgust. 'What do you want them to do?'

'Hex wants slaves for his ships. I want that Batutsi to breed with Nat.'

'Then give Hex the males and pen Nat with that grotesque female. He won't be alive in the morning.'

'Hmm.' He was thoughtful. 'Maybe you're right. Nat's big but he's virgin. You wouldn't care to cover her first, would you?'

'Me?' Prince stopped and flung his arms in the air. 'Don't these clothes, my manners, my *brain* whose advice you crave, mean anything to you? Do you still think I'm your Bondmaster buck to stud at your command?'

Carlton shrugged his shoulder, hurt by Prince's attitude. 'I'll take the Batutsi if you don't think you can tame her!'

'You!' Prince struck out along the path. Carlton couldn't understand why he was angry.

'Are you rutting with Gwen at last?' he asked, hurrying after him. That would explain it.

'No!' Prince despaired. 'Are you still at it? All you can think of is whelps. What about you and Lydia?' he asked sarcastically. 'Shouldn't she be full for you after all this time?'

Carlton's anger stirred and he gripped his whip, wanting to slash it across Prince's smug face. Prince winked and dug his elbow in his waist.

'Come on, Carlton, don't be so pompous. I only asked you the kind of question you keep asking me about Gwen.'

'That has nothing to do with it. I believe Lydia is involved in the scheme that trapped us here. She has her reasons . . .'

'Aha!' Prince nodded his head knowingly. 'She's an attractive woman, Carlton.'

'To hell with that, Prince. I don't want to *marry* her.'

'What an asset she'd be at Roxborough, though. You might even be invited to Government House if you have a titled lady as your bride!' Prince's laughter was genuine and it relaxed Carlton. He slapped him on his shoulder.

'Come on, boy. Let's see if Caspar can mix us a punch.'

'Yes, massa!' Prince grinned as they walked arm in arm along the path to the *seigneurie*.

CHAPTER TWENTY-NINE

Caspar carried the pail of water from the well and placed it on the kitchen floor. Prince was seated at the table, a dish of coffee steaming in front of him. Gwen was busy with the breakfast, transferring eggs from the skillet to a platter already laden with juicy chunks of fried ham. On another plate a boiled chicken, white and bloated, lay on a bed of potatoes with its legs pointing upward.

Gwen indicated it with a nod of her head. 'Take that chicken and tell Nat come quick for the eggs,' she said.

Caspar seized the plate and hurried across the passageway to the dining room. Gwen sighed.

'You tired, Gwen?' asked Prince immediately.

'I should be, with a fancy monkey like you sitting in my kitchen all day.'

'Gwen!' Prince rose lazily to his feet. 'If there is anything you need me for, I'm here.'

'You!' She stood with her arms akimbo and laughed in his face. 'What can you do? Wait on my ladies at table? Oh no, that's beneath you. What about helping me wash the wares? No, your hands go'n get red and rough.'

Prince smirked and put out his hand to touch Gwen. Caspar barged through the door with Nat close behind him.

'I tell Nat yo' go'n box his ears.' Caspar laughed.

'I will too,' said Gwen pushing past Prince and passing the platter to Nat. 'Take that, serve them two eggs apiece, and come back.'

Nat peered at the plate. 'Miss Stephanie, she like her eggs soft. I give her dat one.' He pointed at the eggs. Watching them lovingly.

'Get out, you great *bozal*!' Gwen smacked his behind as he ambled out in a daze.

'You want me for anything, Gwen?' Caspar looked up at the housekeeper eagerly. 'I'm going' ridin' today. Mas Hex say I can take the donkey. I want to see what his men are doing at Devil's Hole.'

'Go on,' said Gwen, ruffling his hair. 'Maybe Prince will help me for a change.'

Caspar winked at Prince and ran out of the kitchen. They heard him shouting the donkey's name, and the animal's answering bray.

'He enjoys it here,' said Gwen, sighing as she sat on a stool at the end of the table. Prince walked behind and laid his hand on her shoulder. She wriggled irritably and brushed his hand away.

He shrugged. He was so used to Gwen's moods, he would find it strange if she didn't spurn him. The more she refused and rejected his advances, the more his determination increased. It was an odd way of love. He did not mind it in London. In Jethou, where there were neither lonely ladies nor whores to absorb his energy, his desire for her was overwhelming.

'Gwen?' He pulled up a stool and sat beside her. 'Carlton has some females in his slave pen. Why don't you ask him for one to help you here? You wouldn't feel so tired.'

'I'm not tired,' she said with a yawn.

Prince's laugh was part of his charm. Women couldn't resist it. He laughed for Gwen.

She stifled the yawn and for a moment her eyes twinkled and she allowed herself a brief smile. Prince's heart missed a beat.

'If you have a helper, you'll have time for me, won't you? We can take walks together. I'll show you a magic wood where you walk on a carpet of flowers . . .'

'Where's Nat?' Gwen's bluntness distracted Prince.

'Serving, of course.'

'That *bozal* is mooning over Stephanie! All day he talks 'bout her. I've told him to take care.' She sighed and laid her hand on his arm. 'Prince, it ain't good. Stephanie's only playing with him.'

He tried to squeeze her hand but she withdrew it rapidly. She looked dismayed at her own weakness.

'Nat's luckier than I am,' he said.

'Don't be foolish, Prince. Nat knows nothing. He's a *bozal* with a sharp cutlass that's never cut cane. Speak to him, Prince. Tell him white ladies ain't for the likes of him.'

'They ain't for the likes of me either, Gwen.'

'Shut up and take your sweet talk out of my kitchen.'

'Gwen?' He tried one last plea, rising to his feet. He caught her arm but she slipped away.

'You used to want me, Gwen. Don't you remember the love we shared in Antigua? I'm still hot for you, even though you're fat and ugly.' He ducked as an iron cooking pot whistled over his head.

'Hah!' He laughed. 'Now you take notice? What do you say, Gwen? There's no one else but you. There never has been. Not here, in my heart.' A cup crashed against the wall beside his ear.

'You don't have to say you *love* me, Gwen.' He opened the door to the fruit garden and dodged behind it, poking his head around to finish what he had to say.

'Just give me a chance to show how much I *love* you!'

A plate smashed against the door sending shards flying in all directions. He left her and walked to the mulberry tree with a bounce in his step. He was happy. It was the first sign of affection he had had from Gwen for weeks.

He sat under the boughs of the tree to think. Perhaps the fault was his own. In London, he had no time to woo Gwen; he was too busy with his conquering of the court ladies and roistering with the young blades. Besides, he expected that when he took no notice of Gwen, she would be weakened by passion and beg him to return. Yet she remained abdurate.

He sighed. He would have to start again, pursuing her as though she was a young virgin. It was amusing thought.

'Oh!'

The cry startled him. He rose to his feet and bowed.

'Good morning, Miss Stephanie.'

'I didn't see you there.' She was blushing furiously. 'I was taking a walk around the garden.'

'It's a lovely day for it.'

'Yes . . .' She hesitated, glancing back at the windows of the dining room. Prince wondered if Hex could see her from there. He never let Stephanie out by herself. She read his thoughts.

'My brother is in the drawing room with Mr Carlton,' she said nervously. 'My sister is just coming.'

Prince indicated the bench. 'Would you like to sit while you wait?'

'Oh . . .'

It meant nothing to him whether she sat or not. Yet she was a pretty young thing, nervous as a humming bird, with large blue eyes and the soft vitality of innocence. He preferred the maturer beauty of her sister although he could see how the girl could captivate a simple soul like Nat.

To his surprise, Stephanie did sit.

'Please sit down too, Prince. You look far too superior standing over me like that.'

'Me? Superior?' He laughed, his teeth flashing in the sunlight and his eyes glinting. 'No one has ever said that to me. Actually, most women find me adorable.'

'I'm sure they do.' Stephanie giggled behind her hand. 'I'm not like most women. You see, I'm not sophisticated. I've been to London once. I've spent my short life since leaving convent school, here on this island.'

It was the first time Prince had heard such a long speech from her. He wondered how she kept such a lively spirit in check when she was with Lydia and Hex.

'I assure you,' he said gallantly, 'that you are at no disadvantage.'

'You are wrong,' she said, sighing. 'I know nothing.'

'Nothing?' He felt the warning tightness in his chest and the tingling in his loins. He swallowed. This was Hex De Quesnel's prize bloom; not to be plucked without permission. He pulled out his handkerchief to gain time, mopping his brow elegantly.

Stephanie was gazing at the house. 'I must ask you,' she said with a rush. 'Lydia will be here in a minute. It's about Nat. Does he . . . has he . . . oh dear! I don't know what I mean.' She covered her face with her hands.

Prince smiled and touched her arm. She leaped away from him, then settled when she saw his warm smile. 'I understand,' he said gently. 'Matters of the heart can be difficult to speak of.'

'The heart . . .?' She gasped.

'You're fond of Nat, Stephanie. It's only natural. He's a young man, rather mysterious and quite good looking. As to "does he, has he", I'm sure the answer is No. He comes from a very good family.' He hoped he didn't sound sarcastic. He wanted to be helpful.

'Thank you, Prince.' She rose to go.

'Stephanie?' He stood up with her. 'Do not worry. Your interest in Nat is curiosity, nothing more. That is so, isn't it?'

'Oh . . . oh yes, of course.' She blushed.

'I'm glad.' He looked serious. 'It could be disastrous for Nat if it was anything else.'

'Stephanie!' Lydia hurried along the path to the mulberry tree. Her lips tightened with disapproval at the sight of Prince. He bowed gracefully and grinned.

'My lady, what a lovely day! I was complimenting your sister on her likeness to you. She is so young looking, you could be twins.'

Lydia tittered. 'Prince,' she said with a sigh. 'You make me realize how I miss the season. Flattery never did a woman harm. There's a dearth of it here.' Her eyes gleamed.

'I am here, Lady Lydia, should you want a guest for a *soirée*.'

'What a wonderful idea! Let us have an *At Home* this very afternoon.'

'What about Hex?' asked Stephanie.

'Hex,' Lydia said in a voice husky with excitement, 'will be in Guernsey. He's taking the slaves with him to place in his ships. We'll be left to our own devices for tonight.'

Carlton counted the slaves being led from the stockade to the beach. He whipped them occasionally so they trotted briskly. He understood no more about them now than he did the day they arrived. Yet, by dint of judicious use of the bullwhip and brandy, and aided by a stout, loud-voiced bosun from one of Hex's ships, he had managed to train them to respond to commands.

'Damn fine job!' Hex was standing at his side while the line of negroes trotted out of the stockade. 'You fattened and subdued them. They'll be grand boys on my ships. The crew will teach them the ropes.'

'They don't have the zest I'd like to see. At Roxborough, my herd are lively, pretty bucks. These are mindless brutes.'

Hex chuckled. 'That's what I want, Carlton. I've ordered another consignment.'

Carlton groaned. 'I've had enough, Hex. Anyone could train *bozals* for you. It's time I went back to Roxborough.' He gazed past the slaves waiting on the beach, to the schooner anchored a few yards off shore. On such a vessel he could be home in Layou in a matter of weeks. How he longed to see Ella, his father, and Roxborough again.

'To Dominica, Carlton? So soon? What about Lydia? She tells me you've said nothing to her yet.'

'Does Lydia govern the date of my departure?' He drew himself up to his full height. He was inches shorter and much lighter in weight than Hex. The man's thick neck was like a bull's, his chest massive and his body built like a fighter's.

Hex had the allegiance of five hundred tough seamen – whites, not blacks controlled by lash and shackle – and carried himself with the confidence that power gave him. He was eyeing Carlton balefully.

'Lydia has expressed no wish to go to Dominica, Carlton.' He spoke softly, his voice heavy with menace. 'She wants your company here. Perhaps were she to be married, her husband's wish would be paramount.'

Carlton stepped away. Hex's hand fell on his shoulder and pulled him back. His fingers squeezed the side of his neck with a grip that paralysed him. He bit his lip to stop crying out at the pain.

'The Batutsi wench, Carlton . . .' Hex began to laugh. 'I shall have her myself when I return.' He released him and strode rapidly down to the bench, his deep-throated guffaw echoing around Carlton's ears.

Carlton had built up a kind of relationship with the Batutsi. Bella was his name for her, after the poisonous herb – belladonna – that grew with its deadly purple flowers and black berries among the trees on Jethou's heights. He was fascinated by her. She was more like a wild animal than any slave he had known. She was as fierce as Nat was placid.

Many times he ventured into her cabin alone, trying to win her confidence. He took Prince's advice and refrained from beating her. When she slapped his hand away each time he tried to touch her, he fought back his temper, smiled and tried again. Gradually – and this he regarded as his real triumph over these savage *bozals* – he began to tame her. She let him stroke her.

His aim was to get her malleable enough to put her with Nat. He had been unable to discover if she was a virgin and he could only guess her age. He placed her under twenty, probably a warrior by her massive size.

He was planning to bring her together with Nat over a period of weeks so that Nat could find his confidence with her. If Hex's threat was real, he only had that night to mate Nat with Belladonna.

'Come, wench,' he said, patting her playfully on her muscular rump. She was wearing a cambric shift that was so short it hardly covered her huge thighs. Her mouth hung open.

'Have to chain you, Belladonna,' he said. 'We're going for a walk.' He knelt down and snapped a fetter around her ankle. She was used to that. There was a short chain attached to it and he held the end in his hand.

'Look lively now!' He jerked the links and Bella followed him passively out of the cabin. 'We're going to the *cou.*' He grinned to himself at his use of slave patois. If Ella saw him with this fine female on a chain, what a ruckus she would make.

Belladonna sniffed the air, her eyes darting from side to side, as he led her along the trail to the house. Suddenly, she plunged into the ferns at the side of the path, dragging him with her. She was trembling. She raised one leg and stood motionless on the other, refusing to move.

'Bella!' He was perplexed. 'I'll have to beat you.' He realized that he couldn't hold her if she decided to run. That would mean flushing her out of the Jethou woods with the dogs. Chasing her would be fine sport for the huntsmen who came from Guernsey to shoot the island's rabbits. He didn't want that to happen.

He touched her shoulder gently. 'Why are you nervous? You must walk with me.'

She shied deeper into the ferns, pulling him with her. There was a clatter of hooves on the path and a shout as Caspar rode into view on the donkey. Belladonna tried to run but the bracken restrained her. Caspar was laughing.

'You have a wild cow there, Mas Carlton?' he chuckled, reining the donkey to a halt.

'You scared Bella,' Carlton chided, trying to soothe the wench by stroking her brests. 'This is Caspar,' he said softly. 'You've seen him before.'

He stepped back on to the path and persuaded her to follow him. 'She's very skittish.'

'What are you going to do with her?' Caspar got off the donkey.

Carlton was grateful for his company. Bella's animal strength and the proximity of her buxom body in the ferns had disturbed him.

'Put her to Nat,' he said blithely. 'Time that colt had a filly to mount.'

Caspar sniggered.

'What's wrong in that?' He jiggled the chain to keep Bella walking with them. She was watching the donkey anxiously.

'You might persuade the filly,' said Caspar. 'Not the colt. Nat's not interested in wenches. Not like me.'

'You!' Carlton snorted loudly. Bella reared back and he tightened the chain to restrain her. 'You'll have to wait until we get back to Roxborough, boy, for me to find a chit your size. You couldn't satisfy this gigantica.'

Caspar looked at Bella in awe. She towered above him and walked with the bounce of savanna negroes, her eyes restlessly searching the woods and path ahead for danger.

'Are we going back to Roxborough soon, da'?' he asked, taking advantage of Carlton's preoccupation with Bella to refer to him familiarly.

'Aye, boy. Soon as I've dealt with De Quesnel.'

'We taking this black sow too?'

Carlton shrugged. He had yet to devise how they would return, let alone who would go with them. From Hex's threats, he was aware of the intrigue spun around him. The man's remark that his departure depended on Lydia's willingness was infuriating.

He looked at Bella, a fine creature without a devious thought in her head. A way to escape Lydia's machinations occurred to him then. He halted, amazed at the audacity of it. Belladonna waited, her flat nose flaring with curiosity.

'By the devil,' he said loudly. 'We *will* take Bella! And a quantity of Hex's brandy that he's got hidden in the cave at the *Creux*.'

Caspar was astounded. 'How do you know about the Devil's Hole? Did Mas Hex tell you?'

'You question me! I'm supposed to know everything. D'you think I haven't seen ships landing kegs at the secret landing? That's why he needs slaves, to tote his contraband.'

'Da' . . .' Caspar peered up at the house nervously. 'I found a gun at Devil's Hole today. I have it here.' He patted the saddle bag.

Carlton smiled. 'You're a good boy. Keep it safe in my room. We may need it.'

Belladonna's arrival at the *seigneurie* caused a stir. It was late afternoon and Lydia was holding her mock *At Home*. Carlton saw the note inviting them when he reached his cottage. He screwed it up angrily, annoyed by her games, then he thought for a moment. This could be the opportunity he was waiting for.

'Belladonna,' he said with a grin. 'I'm going to introduce you to society.'

'Are you taking her to the house like that?' Caspar asked in amazement.

'Why not? She's better dressed now than she is usually.'

'Mistress Lydia will have a fit.'

'I hope so.' He led Bella through the fruit garden to the house. She gazed at the mulberry tree reverently but seemed unimpressed with the *seigneurie*. She lowered her head to enter the house and padded meekly along the dark passage to the reception room.

'Announce us,' said Carlton, winking at Caspar.

The boy opened the door. Lydia and Stephanie, in their best afternoon gowns, were seated primly on the couch. Gwen, in a dress given her by Lydia and hastily let out at the waist to accommodate her ample figure, sat on a chair opposite.

Nat, in one of Prince's suits, was uncomfortable in a corner where he sat, his eyes fixed on Stephanie. Prince lounged against the fireplace, a glass of sherry in his hand.

'Mister Carlton Todd, the Bondmaster of Roxborough,' sang out Caspar, 'and Mam'selle Belladonna, late of Africa, and Master Caspar Todd, that is myself.'

'Bravo!' cried Prince, clapping his hands. He stopped abruptly when Carlton stepped into the room, jingling the chain. Lydia and Stephanie stared with horror as Bella, nose twitching nervously, followed him.

Carlton gave the end of the chain to Caspar who hooked it over a chairback. He stroked the back of Bella's neck gently. Within moments, after he glanced around the room and its occupants, she was at ease.

Stephanie clutched her bosom and fell back to the couch. Nat rushed over to her.

'Miss Stephanie . . .?' His concern was cut short by Lydia's outraged voice.

'What is this, Carlton, a joke?' She rose to her feet and stared hard at Bella, then at Carlton. 'You could have dressed her more suitably, couldn't you?'

'No time,' he said. 'Been busy. Thought you'd like to meet Bella.'

'Is she the new kitchen helper for Gwen?'

Carlton ignored the mockery in Prince's voice. 'That's an idea. Would you like her, Gwen?'

Gwen turned her back on him without a word. Lydia was fidgeting, trying to adjust to the situation.

'How charming she is,' she said, crossing the floor to embrace Bella. The girl shied away.

'Not yet, Lydia. She ain't tamed yet. Nat!' Carlton's voice cut across the stillness in the room and Nat raised his head reluctantly.

'I'm giving you this filly. She's your breed. Take her to your quarters and start rutting. She's clean, no disease.'

He caught Bella's shift by the hem and raised it, exposing her huge black thighs and bulging pudenda.

Stephanie swooned. Lydia stared dumbfounded.

'She's ripe for you, Nat. Ride her well and get her full.' He let the shift fall and winked at Caspar who was trying to stifle his giggles.

'Come on, Bella,' he said, taking her chain. 'He's your buck. Caspar, fetch Nat to the cottage and see he shucks off them fancy togs.'

He led Bella out of the room, delighted at the furore he knew would erupt when his back was turned.

'I ain't goin'.'

'Very wise,' said Prince. 'Those laps of hers will crush you.'

'Don't be coarse,' said Lydia. 'We have to think of this sensibly.' She was cradling Stephanie in her arms. The girl had recovered from her swoon and gazed unseeing at the sea.

Prince paced the length of the room and back again. He was wondering what was the reason for Carlton's behavior. He knew that Carlton never did anything unless he had an ulterior motive.

'Surely he doesn't really expect Nat to go to that . . . that creature, does he?' Lydia was appalled.

'He does!' wailed Stephanie. 'You told me Nat was to marry a wench. That's what you really meant, isn't it? He has to do that dreadful wickedness to her.' She burst into tears.

'Hush, child.' Lydia patted her shoulders, her eyes pleading with Prince for help.

He turned to Gwen. 'Can't you do something?' he begged.

'Smelling salts,' she said casually. 'Isn't that what ladies use when they're upset?'

Her scorn shocked him. 'Comfort Stephanie, Gwen. I can't.'

'Why not? Ain't you the expert in coddling white ladies?'

'You're a woman. I have to tend to Nat.'

'Ah yes.' Gwen gave a mock curtsey. 'Milady,' she said. 'I enjoyed your *At Home*. Perhaps you'll visit me sometime? My abode is a modest closet under the stairs. I don't complain.'

'Get out!' said Prince. 'There's been enough madness for today.'

Gwen rewarded him with a stare of contempt, tossed back her head and made a proud exit.

He wondered how long it would be, once the door was closed, before Gwen burst into tears too. He had never seen her so agitated, nor spoken to her so harshly. Dammit! he thought to himself, what was Carlton up to?

'Nat?' It was Caspar who broke the silence in the room. He was grinning cheerfully. 'Are you coming, like Mas Carlton said?'

'No!' shrieked Stephanie.

'Of course he ain't,' said Prince. 'See the boy, he's in shock.'

'Bella's a Batutsi like he is,' said Caspar. 'They can talk to each other. They don't have to *do* anything.' He giggled. 'That's how it is at Roxborough. Mas Carlton puts a colt to a filly but she lies with her man and the buck ruts with his wench. Mas Carlton never knows.'

Prince watched the appalled expression on Stephanie's face. Fortunately, she had been so shocked by the sight of Bella's nakedness that she couldn't comprehend all Caspar said. Lydia was fascinated.

'What a remarkable life you lead at Roxborough, Prince,' she said.

'Not me,' he replied quickly, avoiding the gleam in her eye. 'My home is Antigua.'

'Yes . . .' Lydia smiled. 'Helen Witham told me all about you.'

'Everything?' He felt the heat in his breeches. The atmosphere in the parlor was charged. Even Nat was roused by it.

'I ain't goin', Caspar.'

Stephanie sat upright. 'You heard him, Caspar,' she said drying her tears. Lydia rose from the couch and stood close to Prince at the fire place.

'Tell Mas Carlton,' said Stephanie, 'that we will not permit Nat to be involved in this disgusting practice. Will we, sister?'

'No, of course not.' Lydia smiled at Prince. 'That was a disgraceful display. I shall tell Hex.'

'He'll only laugh,' Stephanie said with a sigh of resignation.

'Mas Carlton won't laugh.' Caspar shook his head. He looked at Nat again. There was a fierce gleam in the African's eye that he hadn't seen before.

'Very well,' he said, ever cheerful. 'I'll deliver your message. Maybe I'll have to service the wench myself.' He nipped out of the door smartly, before Prince could cuff him for his rudeness.

Caspar sauntered along the passage and out into the walled garden that divided the cottage from the *seigneurie*. The days were getting shorter with a long twilight before the descent of night. Not like

Dominica where the sun was not so lazy to slip under the sea.

He hoped Mas Carlton was serious about returning to Roxborough soon. It would be better for both of them. He believed Carlton was pining for Ella. He had a lovely white lady in love with him and he only had to say the word for Gwen to be back in his bed.

Yet he did nothing. Perhaps, thought Caspar gravely, Carlton was getting old.

He stopped outside the door to the cottage. The only means of light was the *crâsset*, a primitive fish oil lamp with a wick of twisted rag that floated in oil from the liver of cod or conger eel. It was so dim inside the front room where the *crâsset* burned that he could hardly see. A sixth sense made him peer through the window before he pushed open the door.

At first, the shadowy shapes rolling across the earth floor made him think two dogs were fighting inside. He was about to bang on the window when a flash of white flesh made him pause. He pressed his nose to the glass and looked again.

'Oh lord!' he said and backed away. He turned and ran across the garden to the house. He rushed along the passage and threw open the door to the drawing room. Prince was sitting on the couch with his arm around Lydia's waist. Stephanie and Nat were standing side by side at the window watching the twilight descend over Guernsey.

'Prince!' he called. 'Come quick!' He turned and bolted out of the room without waiting to explain. He remembered the gun stowed in his saddlebag hanging on a nail in the stable. He raced for it, grabbed the bag and ran back to the garden as Prince and Nat reached the mulberry tree. Lydia and Stephanie were close behind them.

'What is it?' cried Prince, catching hold of his shoulder and shaking him.

'Belladonna!' Caspar shouted. 'She does be killing Mas Carlton.'

CHAPTER THIRTY

Prince released Caspar and stared after him as he ran to the cottage. Lydia was at his side.

'What's wrong?' she demanded.

'Go back to the house,' he said, brushing her hand away. 'Shut all the doors. Open them only when I say so. Nat, come with me.'

Without waiting to see if she and Stephanie did what he said, he dashed through the gloaming after Caspar. The boy was peering through the window. There was a loud crash from inside the cottage.

'They wrestlin',' Caspar said. 'Mas Carlton bang 'gainst a chair.'

'Stay here!' Prince bounded to the cottage door and pushed it open. He had no plan of what to do. Nat hesitated on the threshold while Prince plunged into the parlor.

In the darkness, he saw an enormous shape like a lumbering bear roll across the floor, bumping against a table sending it spinning across the room and the *crâsset* smashing to the ground. The oil spilled on the dry bracken covering the floor and the wick ignited it. The pool of fire revealed an odd sight.

Bella was naked, her sweating body sparkling darkly as the fire flickered. Her shadow loomed over the walls and ceiling, adding to her formidable size. She was straddling Carlton, pummeling him with her huge thighs. He was writhing beneath her, his lips and long white legs bucking and thrashing.

The flames brightened, catching more of the dry bracken. In the light, Prince saw clearly. Bella was churning her hips and Carlton, trapped below her, was responding manfully.

Prince laughed with scorn. 'You've met your match now, Carlton.' He stamped on the flames until they were extinguished. Faces, white with shock, pressed against the window pane. As the fire died, the faces disappeared. He left Bella and Carlton humping and heaving together, and closed the cottage door.

Lydia and Stephanie waited outside, their arms clasped around each other. Caspar was holding the saddle bag at his side, his eyes fixed on the darkened window. Nat was watching Stephanie shyly.

'I told you to go to the house.' Prince was cross.

'I'm glad I didn't.' Lydia pushed out her chin. Her lower lip quivered. 'I wish she'd kill him.'

'Mistress Lydia!' Caspar was shocked.

'Shut up!' Prince cuffed him. 'Next time you trouble people make sure you know why.'

'I saw Bella throw Mas Carlton on the ground. That ain't right. They weren't doing *that* then.'

Stephanie uttered a cry of anguish. Nat moved closer to her.

'You got plenty to learn.' Prince put his arm around Lydia's shoulder and drew her away from the cottage. Night had fallen, and with it came a chill from the sea. He led the two women gently back to the house. Nat followed, his shoulders drooping.

'What are you so put out for?' demanded Caspar. He was smarting under Prince's rebuke. 'If you'd done your duty by Bella, this wouldn't have happened.'

Nat looked at him forlornly. 'Cas, I love that girl.'

'Bella?' He stopped in amazement.

Nat didn't hear. 'She's suffering so much. She's a bird in a cage. She longs to fly but how can she?'

'No,' said Caspar with a grin. 'You don't mean Bella. She's a cow in heat, not a bird.'

'I can't tell Stephanie how I feel, Cas. That will only make it worse.'

'Damn right it will.' Caspar realized the enormity of what Nat was saying. 'Keep your feeling to yourself. You don't know what white men do when they catch a nigger so much as thinking about their women.'

'She's fond of me, Cas.'

'Of course, she is. You're a handsome buck when you're not moody. Forget her, Nat. Rut with Bella like Carlton wants. She'll drain you and take off the pressure.'

Nat's face showed his disappointment. He sighed and loped away through the trees into the dark. Caspar hunkered down under the mulberry tree, waiting for Mas Carlton to finish.

The thought of what was happening on the floor of the cottage thrilled him. He rubbed himself without being aware of what he was doing until the strain of his flesh against his breeches made him stop. He felt warm inside and swayed on his haunches. He stood up, scarcely able to walk.

He caught sight of a shape moving across the garden in the faint light from the moon. His strength died and he patted the saddlebag under his arm for reassurance. He was not sure if he would be able to use the gun but he would try. The shape glided toward him.

He struggled to withdraw the gun from the bag. Instead, he drew attention to himself with the noise.

'Caspar?' a voice whispered. It was Gwen. She moved soundlessly toward him.

'I thought you were a jumbie,' he said, sighing with relief. He sat down on the bench under the mulberry tree and made space for Gwen to sit beside him. He told her what had happened. She seemed sad.

'You hot for Mas Carlton?' he asked.

'No.' She shook her head emphatically and patted his knee. 'Those days have passed. He used me, the same as he does any woman. I thought I could win him but I didn't have a chance. I'll always remember the voyage to England. I was happy then.'

He was acutely aware that Gwen's hand was on his leg. She squeezed it. He flushed in the darkness. His crotch stirred and he shifted away, almost toppling off the bench. He caught her arm to steady himself. She turned to face him.

The moonlight flattered her, softening her features to those of a young girl. Her fingers curled around his waist and he found his lips nervously touching her cheek. She was trembling too. He closed his arms around her shoulders and nestled his nose in the soft flesh at her throat.

He was confused by the emotions tearing through him. Gwen pushed him gently away so he was sitting with his back against the trunk of the tree. He grasped her shoulders, panic stricken lest she was treating him like a child and rejecting him.

He struggled to sit up. Her head rested firmly on his chest while her fingers tugged at his breeches. He closed his eyes with shame when he leaped out into her hand.

Images of Bella astride Mas Carlton, and of the couplings he had seen in the slave quarters at Roxborough, flashed through his mind. His legs jerked in spasms with a life of their own and his body moved out of control. He writhed under Gwen's expert touch, thrusting himself into the velvet night that engulfed him.

He squirmed, beating his fists on the bench, seized with a joy that rushed through him until he cried out with relief. He fell limp as Gwen rose from her knees.

'Next time,' she whispered, wiping her mouth. 'We go'n do it 'nother way.' She grinned and was gone, vanishing into the shadows as mysteriously as she came.

Caspar tied his breeches and stood up. The door to the cottage banged open. He flexed his knees, took a deep breath and walked over. Mas Carlton was clinging to the door jamb and panting. Blood streamed down his chest and back.

Caspar stared at him, too nervous to speak in case Mas Carlton knew what he had been doing.

'What, son . . .?' Carlton sighed and shook his head. 'Am I such a sight?'

'No, sir.' He grinned weakly. 'You're bleeding.'

Carlton looked down at his crotch and fingered himself gingerly. 'Damn lucky I still got it!' He laughed. 'Did she see?'

'Who?' Caspar took a step back, wondering what he had forgotten to do.

'Lydia, of course.'

He frowned, recalling the events of the night in his mind. 'I don't know.'

'Was she here?' Carlton was getting cross. 'Did she come with Prince?'

'Yes.' He was worried, uncertain what Carlton wanted to hear. 'Mistress Lydia came when I called Prince. I thought Bella was killing you. I'm sorry.'

'By the devil, she was!' Carlton's laugh was stronger this time. 'She did see? Lydia really saw me pleasurin' Bella?'

'Did you want her to?'

'Of course, Caspar. I told you I had a plan.'

'I don't understand.'

Carlton leaned over and patted his shoulders 'Thanks to you, the ruse worked. Now Lydia's seen the slave side of me riding a nigger, perhaps she'll forget the idea of marriage. We'll be on our way back to Dominica soon.'

His hand slipped from Caspar's back and he sank to the ground exhausted.

The days that followed were tense ones. Carlton stayed in his cottage, recovering from his bout with Bella. She was taken to the kitchen by Gwen and proved to everyone's astonishment to be a rapid learner.

She was soon shouting stirring African choruses while she washed the wares and helped Gwen prepare meals. Nat treated her with disdain, performing his duties with an air of preoccupation.

Prince viewed Bella's transformation with amusement. 'It's Carlton's method of subduing slaves,' he explained to Lydia. They were walking across the upper field together reveling in the fresh breeze that cooled them in the hot sun. Stephanie trailed behind picking flowers.

'He's branded her with his body instead of an iron. It's an old slaveholder's trick to break the maidenhead of their females.'

Lydia gasped. 'I don't believe it.'

'Do I shock you?' Prince's lip curled in a mocking smile. 'A slaveholder's wife has to put up with such things.'

'Did Carlton tell you to speak to me like this?'

'No, why should he?' Prince stopped and looked back for Stephanie. She was standing with a single flower in her hand staring across the small channel that divided Jethou from its neighbor, the much larger island of Herm. She was watching the ruin on Pierre Percée reef between the two islands.

'I think he's testing me.' Lydia giggled. 'That disgusting display with Bella . . . the way he's ignoring me . . . your remarks about the odious life on his plantation. He wants to see how I'll react.'

Prince scratched his head. He was growing close to Lydia. There were signs that, given the right mood, he could make love to her. The idea thrilled him; it was a challenge. She shared a room with Stephanie; Hex was ever vigilant and Carlton possessed a knack of knowing his intentions before he did.

He glanced around at Stephenie again. She was still engrossed in the sea.

'Shall we sit?' He took Lydia's arm and led her to a boulder that was surrounded by a circle of stones at the peak of the island. They sat on it close together, their thighs touching.

'Carlton is a strange man,' he said. 'If you believe too much in him, you may be disappointed.' He put his arm around her.

'He told you to tell me that!' Her eyes gleamed and she tapped the tip of his nose with her finger.

'No, I assure you.' He looked hurt. 'It's true.'

'I don't care,' she said, throwing back her head so that the breeze caught her long hair and ruffled it.

'I've made my decisions. Nothing he can do will put me off. I want to leave here. To feel free, to be the mistress of a grand plantation with slaves to serve me. I'll even get used to the slave breeding.'

Prince looked crestfallen. He withdrew his hand and turned on the stone to face the other side of the island. Lydia laughed, reached around and tweaked his nose.

'Don't play with me,' he warned. 'My savage blood gets hot.'

'I get wild, too,' she said softly.

He swung back and gripped her shoulders. He was overwhelmed by the desire smoldering in her eyes. 'When?' he said, shaking her gently. 'When?'

'I don't know . . .'

'If you're going through with this, going with Carlton, you'll need me. I understand you. I care about you. He doesn't. He's an evil brute, Lydia.'

'So's my brother,' she said simply. 'Hex wants me to marry Carlton. So do I. It's not only the money or the influence Hex will have in the Caribbean through the marriage. I like Carlton. He's searching so desperately for something.'

'I'm desperate for you, Lydia,' he sighed. 'My heart leaps every time I look at you. I long to smother your body with kisses, to –'

'Prince, I've heard it all before! I'm not an innocent like Stephanie.' She raised her eyes and glanced across the fields.

'She's coming. Let me go. She's so confused, she's likely to tell Hex everything. Where would you be then?'

He released her and stood up, facing Lydia so she could see the bulge in his breeches. He stretched, emphasizing the outline of his body and the firmness of his thighs.

When he lowered his head, he was surprised that she wasn't watching him, as he expected. A vessel was rounding Crevichon, the small island that sheltered the landing beach.

She turned back. 'Meet me tonight,' she said in a whisper.

'Where?'

'The stable. I'll come when Stephanie has gone to sleep.'

He nodded, satisfied. He was undetered that the ship was bringing Hex from Guernsey. He escorted her and Stephanie down the slope of Bull's Hill to the beach to meet him.

Hex hugged Lydia and Stephanie, hailed Prince, and marched briskly up to the house. What Lydia told him when they were alone, Prince didn't know. He stayed in the kitchen, trying to raise a smile out of Gwen. She scolded him for troubling her, then ignored him while she showed Bella what to do.

Nat drifted in and out, serving dinner in a daze, only brightening to tell Gwen that Stephanie had smiled at him again. In despair, thinking nightfall would never come, Prince strolled over to the cottage to see Carlton. He found him writing a letter.

'To Ella,' Carlton explained. 'It's addressed to Hayes but Ella reads it to him. She added a note in his last letter so I know she's caring for him again. He's an amazing old man, Prince.'

He flung himself in a chair while Carlton sat at the trestle table, biting the end of his quill. 'Are we going back soon?' he asked abruptly, unable to wait for Carlton to finish writing.

'What makes you ask that?' Carlton set down the pen, only the twitching of a muscle in his cheek betrayed his annoyance at the interruption. Had it happened at Roxborough, Prince would have been bawled out of the house and shamed in front of the house slaves.

'The way you're treating Lydia.' Prince challenged Carlton with his eyes. 'You're trying to make her hate you so she won't feel bad when we go.'

'Does she hate me?' Carlton's eagerness confirmed Prince's suspicion.

'You'd like that, wouldn't you?'

Carlton shrugged. 'It would help, yes. I want to go home. Without Hex's approval, I'm trapped. He won't give his consent until Lydia agrees.'

'You don't care for her any more?' Prince sat up straight. How ironic, he thought.

'Why is it important to you?' Carlton's voice was soft and menacing.

Prince, excited by the prospect of seeing Lydia later, didn't notice his tone. 'It's not. It's just that I'd like to return to Roxborough too.'

'Can you remember it after so long, Prince? Nearly twenty years since Captain Loring took you away from me.'

At last he realized from Carlton's scathing tone that he was on dangerous ground. 'Not much,' he said pleasantly to deflect Carlton's temper. 'Massa Hayes, yes. He was a fine old boy.'

'I hated him for selling you. I vowed then that when I became the Bondmaster no one would deceive me.'

'Deceive you? I did belong to your father, Carlton. He had a right to sell me.'

'No, he didn't. You were *my* playboy.' There was a gleam in Carlton's eye that worried Prince. He tried to change the subject.

'You must have fine stock at Roxborough now, Carlton. Nearly five years since you left.'

'Aye.' Carlton's mouth was mean. 'Why did you let Captain Loring take you, Prince?'

'Me? It was nothing to do with me.'

'Of course it was. You were as sly then as you are now. You could wheedle anything out of me. You *wanted* to go with Loring, didn't you? You wanted to get away from me!'

'No, I didn't!' Prince stood up, thoroughly alarmed. 'I was twelve years old. Who knows what I thought?'

Carlton snickered. 'No one defies me, Prince, even you.'

'Of course, Carlton.' He smiled to humor him. There was a wildness in his manner he did not understand. 'Please say hello to Massa Hayes for me.'

'What?' Carlton stared blankly.

'In your letter. Say I'm coming back with you soon.'

'Are you, Prince?'

Caspar entered the parlor with a tray of *crâssets* and placed two on the table, one on either side of the letter. 'It will be dark soon, sir,' he said unnecessarily.

Prince bit his lip, annoyed at Caspar for interrupting at that moment. He was at a loss to understand the venom in Carlton's voice. He wanted to ask what was wrong but Carlton turned his back and picked up the quill. The muscle in his cheek was twitching. Caspar touched his arm and nodded at the door. Prince sighed.

'Goodnight, Carlton,' he said. 'I'm going for a walk. The moon's full.'

Carlton didn't lift his eyes from the paper.

'How long's he been like this?' Prince asked Caspar outside the cottage.

'Like what?'

'Full of doom.'

'That's nothing.' Caspar laughed. 'Bella showed him he's not young any more. He's been sulking ever since.'

'Hah!' Prince laughed too, his spirits restored. 'He frightened me.'

'Take no notice. You know how white men does be, *oui.*' Caspar's smile reassured Prince. He punched him lightly on his chest and walked with a spring in his step toward the stable.

Caspar slipped back inside the cottage to tell Carlton.

The stable was not the place Prince would have chosen for his tryst. He regarded himself as an artist in matters of the heart. If a bed wasn't available, a couch was the minimum. A pile of hay shared with a donkey indicated a decline in his standards.

There was no time to think more. He no sooner reached the stable, pushed open the door and murmured noises of assurance to calm the donkey, than Lydia seized him around his neck.

'Prince . . .' she whispered eagerly.

He held her waist, pulling her toward him. He searched with his lips for hers. She twisted away.

'My dear Lydia,' he said. 'You don't know how much I desire you . . . to kiss you . . . to have you! I have yearned for this moment, since –'

'I know, I know,' she said harshly. Her fingers were at his waist. 'Do it now, I beg you, before we are discovered.'

'Who can –?'

'Hush, my darling.' She trembled in his hands.

He fumbled to raise her skirt, sliding down with her in the hay. The donkey backed away in alarm, giving vent to a long snort of protest that sounded like a swinging door in need of oiling.

'My god,' she said. 'They can hear that in Herm.'

'Lydia,' he crooned. His instincts were blunted by his desperate desire to possess her. He was overwhelmed by the piquancy of penetrating this woman who thought she was cheating Carlton.

That Carlton wanted nothing to do with her gave him licence. He thrust into her without love, and she whimpered with pleasure at his brutality.

Was this revenge, he wondered, as he ran his hands over her thighs, feeling her rise to meet him. He toyed with her as long as he dared, bringing her close then releasing her. He brought her back again so they both teetered then tumbled over the top together.

The ecstacy was heightened by the feel of her finger nails raking across his buttocks like a whip slicing into his flesh. He lay, spent, on top of her and the pain cut through him again.

The donkey sawed, lanterns flashed around his head, his buttocks stung. He opened his eyes; too late. Lydia lay petrified beneath him. The whip cut into his skin. He jerked out of her and tried to stand. His breeches caught around his ankles, toppling him back on top of her.

Carlton used the whip deftly, gouging another strip of blood across his thighs.

Prince cried out at the slash of pain but his voice was drowned by the donkey's screeches of protest.

'Enough!' said Hex.

Prince raised his eyes and the first inkling of doubt assailed him. He could handle Carlton, but Hex's presence was a complication.

'Lydia,' he hissed anxiously in the respite when the whipping stopped. 'Tell Hex . . .'

He was dismayed when Lydia rose, shook down her skirt and brushed hay from her bodice. She looked scathingly at him, ran her hand through her hair to remove the bits sticking in it and stepped over him. Carlton and Hex stood aside to let her pass and she left the stable without a word.

Hex was frowning and his eyes glinted. Carlton's anger seemed strangely muted. Caspar was standing with them.

'You!' Prince shouted at Caspar now he realized how he had been betrayed. Caspar grinned brightly.

'I can hardly marry Lydia now, can I?' said Carlton as though he was continuing an earlier conversation that Prince had not heard.

'Your nigger.' Hex spat in the hay. 'Not mine.'

'Your sister . . .'

'Yes.' The two men were silent.

Prince sat up, drawing his knees up to his chin and trying to untangle his breeches. As long as they were talking, there was a chance that he could get away with some token punishment like . . . like what? Why should he be punished at all?

'I didn't force her!' he cried angrily. 'It was her idea to meet me here.'

'You hear?' said Carlton looking grave. 'She's hardly fit to be a slaveholder's wife when she freely lies with slaves.'

'You've shared whores with your nigger before.' Hex chuckled.

'I don't want a whore for a wife.'

'What woman isn't?'

The two men were silent again. Only the donkey commented, its raucous noise like snorts of mockery in Prince's ears. He was uneasy, sensing he was the victim of a charade they had planned between them.

'Shall I?' said Hex.

'You have the right,' said Carlton with equal politeness.

'So have you.'

'She's *your* sister.'

'Ah yes.' Hex leered, driblets of spittle trickling into his beard.

Carlton's whip whistled through the air and struck Prince on his cheek. He let go of his breeches and covered his face.

Carlton was at his side, tugging at his wrists. 'Hands behind your back, Prince,' he said, his voice as hard as granite.

He obeyed immediately, trusting Carlton even then.

Carlton took a length of rope from his pocket and bound his wrists together. Prince assumed Hex was going to whip him.

'Lie down on your back,' Carlton ordered, pushing him in his chest. He fell back. He couldn't move his feet because of the breeches around his ankles. He was surprised to feel a weight on his legs and glanced down to see Caspar sitting on his shins.

Carlton placed his boot on his chest, pinioning him to the floor of the stable. The whip was dangling in his face, ready to strike him if he moved.

His curiosity at what they were going to do lasted only seconds. Caspar, at a word from Hex, produced a small, sharp knife. It had a wooden handle and a blade about six inches long, curving at the end to a point. It was the type used by thatchers for cutting reeds, or by stockmen . . .

Prince summoned up his energy and gave an enormous leap. Caspar was thrown off his feet but Carlton fell across his shoulders, pushing him back to the ground.

All he could hear was Hex's laughter and the donkey's jawing.

Carlton's shoulder was across his throat. He felt hands lift his testicles, pulling them until the skin of the scrotum stretched. He was blinded by agony. He shouted but Carlton rammed the stock of the whip into his mouth he bit on it, tasting the leather.

'Make it clean,' Carlton said.

'I always do,' Hex replied.

Prince grit his teeth at the pain as the knife cut through his stretched skin.

'Damn you!' shouted Hex, tossing the handful of flesh at the donkey's nozzle to quieten it. The animal stepped back in surprise and squashed Prince's testicles under his foot.

Gwen, who had been watching by the door, rushed in with a bowl of water and a jar of unguent. Carlton and Hex left her to it.

She bathed him and rubbed him with the salve to stop the bleeding. Caspar untied his wrists. She took him in her arms, kissing him warmly on his lips.

He opened his eyes.

'I love you, Prince,' she said solemnly. 'Now you'll never be anyone's but mine.'

CHAPTER THIRTY-ONE

The rain beat down on the shingles of the *cou* with the incessant noise of a dozen *tambous* patted at a fast, African tempo. It echoed throughout the house with a lusty resonance, drowning conversation and isolating the occupants with their own thoughts. It brought relief from the airless heat that had hung over Roxborough for weeks. The soil needed the rain and so did the slaves.

The clouds, dark and threatening, were welcomed by Ella. She was exhilarated by the gloom for she knew the rain cleaned the plantation, made the earth smell sweat and doused the choler of the slaves.

Pip stood by the open half of the kitchen door watching the rain. It pelted down, splashing the mud and stones of the courtyard and forming rivulets that twisted like snakes racing downhill into the grass. His shirt was sopping as gusts of wind blew into the kitchen. He laughed, letting the drops cool his brow and trickle down his cheeks.

'Shut dat dam' door,' grumbled Pool.

'Ah like de rain,' said Pip with a grin. 'Yo' can't see de quartahs from here, it so dark.'

'Yo' ain't like it if yo' livin' in it.'

Pip frowned. 'We livin' it it, ain't we?'

Pool stood up with a chupes of annoyance. 'Ah mean de bush, *makak*. Not ev'ryone does live in a fancy *cou* like yo', monkey.'

Pip turned away from contemplating the rain and stared sternly at Pool. 'Massa give slaves shelter. Ain't no cause for niggers to live in de bush.'

'Hah!' Pool sat down again. 'Dat's yo'! Always relying' on massa. Massa day done! Some niggers see sense. Dey free.'

'Dey wet, dough!' Ella moved around the kitchen with a great show of energy. 'Pool, take this 'canter of rum to Massa Hayes.'

The slave's mouth dropped open and he looked at Ella with disbelief. 'Ah ain' go'n catch mah deat' in dis rain.'

Ella sighed. It was just what she expected from the troublesome boy. If Marcus was alive, his eagerness to help would have shamed him. She pulled up her skirt and tucked it in her waist band so her ankles and legs were free.

Pip looked surprised. 'Where yo' go'n?'

'See Massa Hayes. He bound to be lonely in the rain.'

'Ah go,' said Pip holding out his hand for the decanter. 'Mah shirt wet a'ready.'

She smiled gratefully. 'You good, Pip.' She shot a mean glance at Pool but he was resting his head on his arms on the table, pretending to be asleep.

'I go, lest Tita troublin' de ol' buckra.' She winked at Pip as he opened the bottom door. The rain splashed her as she lowered her head and dashed out.

There was no way to enter the house from the kitchen without getting soaked when it rained. Dominica, with its mountainous interior, was a wet island. It had more than three hundred rivers and rain forests covered most of the country.

When she reached the shelter of the balcony, Ella paused to recover from the rain's cold sting. She was drenched and the rain found her as it blew under the eaves. She pulled open the door to the dining room and darted in. The room was empty.

Next door, she heard the shrieks of Laura and young Hayes as they played with Sophie and Mingoson. She crossed the floor of the dining room, listening to the patter of the rain on the roof. It was warm and dim in the house with the shutters closed.

She expected to see Hayes in the drawing room. Instead, she surprised Tita standing by the bureau. 'What are you doing here?' she said, more to make conversation than to pry. 'I'm nearly drowned. So much rain!'

Tita spun around guiltily. From her expression, she clearly wished Ella had been drowned. She kept her back to the large wooden cupboard.

'Where's Massa Hayes?' Ella asked, amused by Tita's discomfort. Tita nodded her head in the direction of the bedroom.

'What *are* you doing, Tita?' She tried to sound natural as she asked the question again but her suspicions were roused by Tita's odd behavior.

'Ah . . . er . . . Ah done drop a sovereign. Ah tryin' find it.'

'A sovereign?' Ella's voice thickened with doubt. 'Who gave you a sovereign?'

'De mistress . . . before she die.'

'Oh.' Ella felt cold and wet. She dismissed Tita from her mind and knocked on the bedroom door.

'I said go away!' shouted Hayes in a shaky voice.

'I've brought rum, massa,' Ella sang out brightly. She opened the door and walked in, curious why Hayes wanted to keep her – or was it Tita? – out of his room.

The shutters were ajar to let in the light. Spray from the rain was seeping in. Hayes lay on top of his bed, fully clothed with his boots on. Ella pushed the door closed to keep Tita out.

'Damn rain,' he said. His voice was quavering. 'I wanted to go riding. So restless . . .'

She put the rum on the dresser, noting that Hayes's keys were in place. At least Tita had not taken them.

'I've brought rum with peppers,' she said soothingly, pouring a glass and handing it to him.

He sniffed it suspiciously. 'You're a good wench, Ella.'

She smiled, relieved to find Hayes was not in a vile mood, despite the rain. He was eyeing her inquisitively as she moved about the room, folding clothes and tidying up. She was conscious of her wetness. Her skirt was still raised to her waist and the thin cotton material of her bodice clung damply to her breasts.

'Aye,' he said weakly after he drained the glass and held it out for a refill. 'You ain't as trim as Tita and you're as black as sin itself but, by the devil, a man could pleasure himself with you, Ella!' He broke off into a wheezing cough.

Ella patted his back. His face turned livid at the energy required to get himself under control.

'I'll make you a remedy for that.'

'No more slave remedies,' he said. 'I've had enough of Tita's potions already.'

'Tita don't know nothing about herb teas.'

'You're right,' said Hayes, taking the full glass from her. 'Sit here and have a rum, Ella. I'm in the mood to talk and it does me good to see you so lusty.'

'What did Tita give you?' She was anxious about Hayes's trembling.

'A nightcap. Made me sweat the whole night. God, I feel weak this morning. That's why I wanted to ride, to get it out of my system. Drat the rain!' He gulped the rum and fell back on the bed.

'Listen,' said Ella, taking the empty glass from his hand. 'Don't drink anything that Tita prepares for you.'

'You think she's trying to poison me?'

'No!' Ella scoffed at the idea. 'Why should she?'

Hayes lowered his voice to a whisper and beckoned her closer. She brought her ear down to his lips. 'She wants my treasure.'

She drew away slowly. Had Tita discovered the money in the bureau cupboard drawer? Was that why she was skulking beside it?

'Thought that would surprise you.' Hayes chuckled. 'Didn't know I have a treasure, did you?'

Ella shrugged. It was of no interest to her. 'No, massa,' she said indulgently.

Hayes seemed so frail. Stretched out on the bed, wheezing and spluttering, he was a pathetic creature. She was worried.

'Don't tire yourself. Let me take off your boots.'

'My boots?' His eyes were glazed. 'Oh, aye.' He had forgotten he wanted to go out.

She removed the boots with difficulty, disturbed by the frailty of his limbs. He was mumbling so she bent her ear to him again, grateful for the pounding of the rain on the roof that made his words hard to hear. She was certain that Tita was listening outside the door.

'She gave me a remedy, Ella.' His mind was wandering. 'It made me say things . . . about my treasure.'

'Did you tell her where it's hidden?' His hand lay limply on the sheet and she took it up and squeezed it. He opened his eyes and smiled at her triumphantly.

'No! I don't want her to have it. That's for Carlton. Remember that, Ella, if I die before he returns.'

'Of course.' She straightened. 'Sleep now.' His palor frightened her. Whatever Tita gave him, it hadn't finished its work. He looked every evil day of his age.

'I can tell you . . . where the treasure is.'

'No!' She covered him with a sheet. 'You tell that to Mas Carlton!'

She opened the door quickly. Tita was nowhere to be seen. A movement on the balcony caught her eye. She peered through the drawing room shutters in time to see Tita moving away from Hayes's window where she had been listening to everything the old man said.

* * *

While the rains fell on Roxborough, four thousand miles away to the north east, a ship set sail from Jethou for the Caribbean. It would take many weeks to complete the voyage, sailing by way of Madeira, the Canary Islands, and the Slave Coast of Africa before embarking on the Middle Passage across the Atlantic to the West Indies.

A small group stood on the beach and watched the vessel filling its sails as it tacked out into the open channel between Jethou and Guernsey.

Lydia was sobbing into a handkerchief. Hex was thoughtful, calculating the risks of the voyage and the months it would be before he would see a profit. Stephanie was not watching the ship; her eyes were turned toward the Pierre Percée reef partly submerged in the unusually high tide.

'Go back to the house with Lydia,' Hex shouted at her. She started.

Nat touched her gently on her arm. 'We go now, miss.'

Hex scowled as Stephanie, still engrossed in her thoughts, followed Lydia up the path with Nat.

'Go on, young fellow.' Hex booted Caspar playfully in his backside. The boy beamed, his eyes flashing mischievously.

'I want to talk to your father. Get the wine mulled.' Hex pulled his coat around him as a gust of wind buffeted him.

His gruff voice roused Carlton from his reverie. He took a last look at the schooner and trudged up the beach after Hex. He wondered if he would ever see Prince again. He had given him and Gwen a letter for Hayes so that if the ship touched at Dominica, they would be made welcome. Gwen said they planned to return to Antigua and Clothilda Harkness.

It had taken weeks for Prince to recover from his castration. Bella scoured the island for plants similar to those she knew in Africa to make teas to revive him. Gwen devoted herself to comforting him.

Prince lost weight and vitality and seemed on the point of expiry. Then Hex decreed he could sail on one of his ships bound for the West Indies, and Prince began to revive.

'Good thing he's gone,' said Hex. 'Troubled Lydia having a eunuch here.' He slapped Carlton on his back and urged him along the path out of the wind that blew across the shore.

'A neutered nigger is worth plenty,' mused Carlton aloud. 'Safest there is.'

'I'll give you his value, Carlton. Name your price.'

'You can't buy me. I should have been on that ship with Prince.'

'Not gelded too, I hope?' Hex's laughter bounced over Carlton with a rush of foul breath. He stopped for a moment pretending to think of something, then changed sides on the path so he was not downwind of Hex.

Carlton doubted if Hex knew how much he hated him. The man treated him as his bosom comrade, unaware that his hearty behavior disgusted him. Hex looked upon their caponizing of Prince together as the bond that proved Carlton was a man of his own mettle.

Until the moment was right for him to exact his vengeance, Carlton was forced to suffer Hex's vulgarity.

'You can sail as soon as you want, Carlton,' Hex said, putting his arm on his shoulder and leering obnoxiously. 'Just make me your partner at Roxborough. Take Lydia with you as your wife. In exchange, give me the monopoly on your rum and sugar output.'

'You put such a high price on used goods?'

Hex withdrew his arm and his brow clouded with anger. He stared at Carlton until he decided it was a joke and roared with laughter. Carlton held his breath.

'I'll finance your breeding program for the next five years in return for fifty percent of what you receive for every slave you sell. Guarantee me a hundred head every year at fifty percent of market value and I'll give you a ship with a full cargo of provisions to sail you home.'

The wind howled about Carlton's ears as he pretended to digest Hex's offer. It didn't take him long. 'No deal,' he said brusquely, striding up to the house. 'I don't need capital and I have a market in Dominica for every slave I can breed now that the trade ban's in force.'

'Where's your vision, Carlton? You could spread the Bondmaster breed throughout the Caribbean with my ships . . . to Cuba . . . to America. You'll make more money. I could even send you fresh stock from Africa that you'd tame in your barracoons.'

'No.' Carlton branched off at the mulberry tree to return to the cottage. 'I don't want a partner, Hex.'

'Think of this, Carlton, boy.' Hex glowered. 'In a few years, slavery will be abolished. Where will you be then? With me and my ships, you have five years to make a fortune then get out. You and

Lydia could return to England. Have a fine mansion and live like a lord.' Hex punched him on his shoulders.

Carlton gripped his fists to restrain himself.

'Think of it. I'm going to Guernsey tomorrow. When I return, we'll talk.' It sounded like a threat.

Hex was away longer than expected. During his absence, Carlton gradually assumed the demeanor of one who had changed his mind and was willing to accept his plans. He dined daily with Lydia and Stephanie and joined in their domestic charade without protest. He burned up his ardor in twice weekly sessions with Bella who was now the *seigneurie's* cook, with Gwen's departure. Nat, who considered Bella an inferior, showed no interest in her.

Carlton kept occupied studying the layout of Jethou and the routine of Hex's crew of sullen heavyweights who were the island's guards. He knew that Lydia was the one to set him and Caspar free when the time came to escape. He was affable with Lydia but could not bring himself to the intimacy she wanted.

Every evening, he retired early to his cottage, reading by the light of the candle until Nat and Caspar came, after Lydia and Stephanie had retired to bed.

'Mas Carlton?' asked Nat one evening. He hovered nervously in the parlor, his eyes cast down.

Carlton laid aside his book. 'Yes, boy,' he said harshly, beckoning him into the room to stand in front of the fire. He studied Nat. He had grown to a sturdy young colt in his prime. He still had the shyness of a virgin which Carlton attributed to his royal breeding. That would change as soon as Bella got to work on him.

Nat stood on one leg, lowered it, and stood on the other. He moistened his lips and passed his hand across the furrows in his brow. 'Sir, in my tribe, a king must be pure until his first wedding night.'

'Yes, yes,' said Carlton, losing patience. 'We're not in Africa now.'

'In my mind I am, sir. In my body, too.' His eyes were bold. 'I've never known a woman,' he announced proudly. 'Now I am ready.'

'By the devil, that's a relief! I could use some help. She's a warrior in bed, Nat, as well as on the plains. You'll be sorry you waited so long to get to grips with her.'

'You misunderstand me, sir. I'm ready to be wed.'

'Jump the broomstick, you mean? Sure, we'll arrange it tomorrow. I'll tell Bella when she comes tonight. When you get her full, Nat, I'll give you a sovereign. Heh, heh!' He rubbed his hands together. 'What a whelp that will be.'

Nat shook his head and fled from the room without another word Carlton was momentarily puzzled then dismissed Nat's odd behaviour as being the result of his highly strung nature. He had come a long way since Caspar had fished him out of the sea . . .

Someone was shaking him awake. He jerked up his head. The fire was dying down and his book lay open on his lap. 'What . . .?'

'Mas Carlton!' Caspar cried in his ear. 'Mistress Lydia said to come at once.'

'Dammit!' He stretched himself lazily. 'Is this one of her ruses? Tell her I'll come in the morning. Time for bed now. Where's Bella?'

'You must come, sir. She's at the door.'

'Here?' He pulled himself out of the chair. 'Put her in my bed.'

'Miss Lydia?'

'Not her! Bella.'

'It's Miss Lydia who's here.'

'Carlton!' Lydia burst into the room. 'You must do something quickly. I warned her but she wouldn't listen. Hurry, before it's too late. Hex will be here in the morning.' She started to weep.

'What the devil's going on, Caspar?'

'Miss Stephanie, sir.'

'She's gone, Carlton.' Lydia's tears increased.

'What do you mean? Where can she go?' He looked from one to the other, cross at being disturbed and wondering how soon he could get Lydia out of the cottage.

'I don't know.'

'Shut up, woman!' He slapped her across her face in his rage. Lydia stopped weeping and stared at him with disbelief.

'It's your fault,' she spluttered. 'He's your slave.'

His heart sank with foreboding. 'Who is?'

'Nat, Mas Carlton. Miss Stephanie isn't in her room and I can't find the *bozal* anywhere.'

'He went to bed. He was talking to me before I dozed off.'

Lydia wailed. 'She's run away with him, I know it!'

'They can't get far.' Carlton walked to the door. There was a bright moon throwing its pale glow onto the sea. The wind had dropped and the tide was out.

'They are together somewhere without a chaperone,' pronounced Lydia. She made it sound like a death sentence. 'If she isn't here before Hex returns . . .'

Carlton knew what would happen. Somehow he must find Nat. That boy was too precious to sacrifice to Hex's madness. 'Damn the girl!' he shouted, pulling on his coat. 'She bewitched him.'

'He put a spell on *her*!' Lydia cried. 'Where are you going? You can't leave me here alone.'

'Like hell, I can!' He lifted his whip off its hook. Caspar had disappeared. 'Where's that boy?' he shouted.

'Here, sir.' Caspar ran back into the room, wrapped in his bulky Guernsey vest.

'Get a *flambeau*, boy. Lydia, go to the kitchen with Bella. Have you searched the house?'

Lydia nodded, gulping back her tears.

'The stable?'

She shook her head.

'Come on, boy.' He raced out of the cottage with Caspar at his heels. Lydia followed him to the stable. There was no one there except the garrulous donkey who started to bray indignantly.

'What a crazy thing to do,' said Carlton. 'I should have known.' He scratched his ear. 'Where should we look?'

'If we wait until daybreak, won't they come back?' Caspar asked. 'They can't go anywhere without a boat. Nat's not a sailor.'

'You don't understand,' Carlton snapped impatiently. 'By then it's going to be too late. Maybe it's too late already. I'll wager they've planned this for weeks, just waiting for the full moon and Hex to be away.'

'They're in love . . .'

'Niggers rut, boy, not love.'

'Yes, sir.' Caspar agreed readily.

'Hey!' Carlton caught him by his ear and twisted it. 'You know something, don't you?'

'No,' he cried. 'You're hurting!'

'He hasn't done anything.' Lydia clasped Bella's hand for support.

'Let him go.'

'Maybe he hasn't done anything, Lydia, but he *knows* something. Where have they gone?' He twisted his ear until Caspar begged him to stop.

'The chapel, sah,' he said in slave patois.

'The chapel? Where's that? There's no chapel here.'

'Nat didn't say.' Caspar rubbed his ear and frowned ruefully.

Carlton remembered the cathedral of trees he discovered with Lydia soon after he arrived on the island. There was a druid's stone, like an altar, there. Perhaps Nat would see that as similar to a wedding place in Africa. He glanced up at the sky again. It was cold but the night was still clear with plenty of moonlight. It would take Nat and Stephanie an hour to reach the wood. Maybe there was a chance to get to them before it happened.

'We'll go to Devil's Wood,' said Carlton. 'I think they'll be there.'

Lydia clung to Bella's stout arms as he set off up the path followed by Caspar bearing the *flambeau.*

Carlton tucked his whip in his belt under his coat. He would have preferred more adequate protection. Hex kept guns in his armory, a locked cupboard in the *seigneurie*. It was too late to go back.

'Caspar,' he said, remembering. 'Where's that gun you found? I'd like it in my hand now.' He stared into the darkness around them, listening to the eerie silence of the night. 'Well, boy?'

Caspar dipped the *flambeau*. 'I looked for it, Mas Carlton, but it gone.'

'Gone? Who took it?'

'I thought perhaps you did, sir.'

'Dammit, boy. Would I steal from you?' Caspar didn't answer. 'When did you see it last?'

'I check it every night, sir. In case . . . well, it was there yesterday. Perhaps Nat . . .?'

They trudged on in silence. Carlton hated a slave to be disloyal to him. At Roxborough, he punished offenders then sold what was left of them. Prince had got his comeuppance even though it took twenty years. Nat? Why had he done it? The boy was always well disciplined. Stephanie was no flibbertigibbet. What could the pair of them gain by running off together? Had they run, or was it a moonlight tryst?

'By the devil!' he muttered aloud, startling Caspar. 'When we find

Nat, we've got to get him away from here. Hex will kill him for bursting Stephanie's maid.'

They entered Devil's Wood cautiously. Caspar was wide-eyed with fear at the atmosphere of the glade, darker than night with boughs keeping out the moonlight.

Carlton shouted Nat's name. His voice was swallowed up by the trees. He walked briskly from one end of the glade to the other. The druid's stone loomed out of the darkness and the light from the *flambeau* dimmed and flickered although there was no wind.

'Dey ain't here, massa.' Caspar's voice squeaked. 'Ain't no one here 'cept de jumbies.'

'Aye!' Carlton squeezed Caspar's shoulder and spoke boldly to give himself courage. 'Then where the devil have they gone?' He followed Caspar out of the wood without looking back.

They crossed the upper field and cut down from Bull's Hill. Dawn was an hour away. 'Don't want to wake Hex's men,' said Carlton. 'We'll return home behind the barracoon.'

As they walked along the lower path, Caspar spied a light. They doused the *flambeau* and crouched down in the ferns. The light bobbed toward them.

'You take Nat's feet,' whispered Carlton. 'I'll go for his neck.'

As the light approached, they saw the outline of two people and their cloaks billowing in the darkness.

'Now!' said Carlton.

'Murder!' a woman's voice screamed.

Caspar yelped, felled to the ground by a knee in his crotch. Carlton felt his arm being seized and twisted behind his back. The torch dropped to the ground.

'By the devil . . .!' he exclaimed.

'Carlton?' It was Lydia's voice. 'That's you?'

'Of course it is.' Bella released his arm and he picked up the torch. Caspar clutched himself, watching Bella with awe.

'What the hell are you doing here?'

'I couldn't sleep.' Lydia looked haggard with her hair in disarray and eyes red from crying. 'Bella says when a Royal Batutsi set his mind on an idea, only death can stop him.'

'I ain't lettin' Nat die for a white wench!' Carlton slapped his brow and cursed Nat under his breath. 'If only we could find him . . .'

'Hundreds of years ago,' said Lydia. 'Herm and Jethou were

joined together. There was a chapel built by the monks . . .'

Carlton stiffened. 'Where?'

'On Pierre Percée reef. It's a ruin now. You can walk there at low tide. A spring tide covers it.'

It was dawn when they reached the east side of the island just above the landing beach, opposite Crevichon. The sky was lightening with myriad shades of blue as clouds scudded across it and darkness rolled away. From the north, behind Crevichon, a vessel gently sailed into the bay.

'Hex!' Lydia waved wildly as the ship dropped its anchor and a dinghy rowed toward the shore. She ran down to the beach to meet him.

Carlton was peering across the rocks to the reef. The tide was rising now. In the dawn, as the sun rose, he saw the silhouette of the old ruined chapel. The sea was lapping the rocks around it.

He stared while the light brightened and he made out the shapes of two people huddled together on the reef. Bella screamed when she saw them too. She fell to the ground and thumped the earth with her fists.

'Stop her damned row, Caspar!' he shouted, wondering what to do.

Caspar beat Bella's backside and rolled her over on the ground. She swallowed her screams and whispered in his ear. She raised herself to a squatting position and keened softly; it was a dirge with mournful tones of the Africa she would never see again.

The dingy reached the shore, borne in rapidly by the tide. Carlton was surprised how high it was getting until he realized that this was the highest spring tide of the year, nearing its peak. Just as it ran very high, it also ran very low and that's how Stephanie and Nat had got to the reef.

He could see them clearly now. Nat was standing straight and proud with Stephanie clinging to him, her blonde hair blowing around them in the wind. They were both fully clothed.

Carlton shook his head in despair.

'Bella says its a Batutsi rite.' Caspar touched his arm.

'I hear you, boy.' He stared at the reef as the sea washed over it, lapping around the couple's ankles. Neither seemed to notice. They were both facing the sunrise, away from Jethou, and didn't see the rowing boat with Hex at the prow bearing down on them.

'He go'n save them,' said Caspar. 'He a sailor, *oui*?'

The waves pushed the boat. The coxswain steered uneeringly between the rocks right up to the side of the reef.

'Nat!' Carlton shouted but his voice was tossed back at him by the seaspray pounding the rocks.

Nat stood still, a black shadow in the sunrise, with a white sprite beside him.

Hex was gesticulating from the dinghy. He was unable to get close enough for him to grab Stephanie. Carlton watched as Hex waved at the couple, trying to attract their attention.

'Why doesn't Nat do something?' cried Caspar.

'He is.' Carlton gripped his son's shoulder as a chill seized his heart.

They watched Nat turn slowly, his head upright. Stephanie kept her cheek against his chest. Nat raised his arm and pointed at Hex. On the shore, too far away to hear the sound of the gun, they saw the explosion of flame and the puff of smoke.

Carlton saw Hex spring out of the boat as he took the full force of the charge in his chest. It lifted him up as the dinghy fell into a trough. He smashed down onto the reef in the shallow water at Nat's feet.

Nat rolled Hex off the edge of the reef with his foot. The waves washed him away.

Nat smiled, his eyes at peace now. He turned to face the sun and his ancestors.

Stephanie raised her lips to his and they kissed, lost forever in happiness as the waves roared in and swirled around them.

CHAPTER THIRTY-TWO

The arrangements were complete for Carlton's departure. He stood awkwardly in the parlor and faced Lydia. She was dressed for the cold with a bonnet tied securely under her chin and her thick cloak wrapped around her.

The room, which minutes before was full of people making forced conversation, was empty. Caspar closed the doors after ushering everyone out, and left Carlton and Lydia alone.

Carlton was wearing his traveling clothes and clasped his hat in his hand. He spun it and wondered what to say. 'By the devil . . .'

Lydia giggled.

He glared at her. 'What's funny?'

'Nothing.' She dabbed her eye with a handkerchief. 'I don't feel to laugh. I'll always remember you whenever I hear that oath. Everything is *by the devil* for you.'

He punched his hat. 'Dammit, Lydia! You know it would never work. I must go.'

'Yes, you must.' She didn't sound convinced.

'Stay here . . . Hex's ships . . . you're a rich woman, Lydia. You can sell them or trade. When this war's over, the world will be clamoring for goods. They'll be such a trade boom and a new demand for merchant ships.'

'We could run the fleet together, Carlton . . .' She walked over to him and laid her hand gently on his, staying the destruction of his hat by his nervous fingers.

With her standing so close, he saw her gray eyes glistening as she blinked back her tears, the petite nose and the trembling lips of the woman he once thought he loved. He lowered his head and kissed her, not on her mouth as she wanted, but on each tear-damp cheek.

She gripped him and pressed her mouth on his, her tongue fighting to plunge between his lips. He raised his battered hat between them and pushed her away.

'You don't need me,' he said. 'By the devil, you don't.' He watched her weak smile and patted her arm. 'I'm going to leave Bella here.'

'She's mine anyway. She's part of Hex's estate and he left me everything.'

'Except me!' Carlton sighed. 'No man, or woman, Lydia, can own me. Hex tried, and so have you. I'm grateful for the ship. I'll return it full of cargo, the best rum from Roxborough, sugar, slav –'

'No slaves!'

He frowned at the interruption. 'They can pass as crew. You can use them on this island. I'll find you a lively lad like Caspar . . .'

She shook her head. The moment of farewell seemed to have passed and they were quarreling with ease again.

'Dammit,' he said, 'my slaves are the finest in the world. My nursery is packed with whelps that will make the Bondmaster breed famous. Not like the wretched *bozals* Hex penned here. I'll send you a dozen, a gift.'

'Can't you understand, Carlton? When I say no, I mean no.'

He arched one eyebrow and grinned. 'You see, you don't need me. When I say yes, I mean yes! You can handle Hex's fleet with ease. Did I ever tell you,' he added as he walked to the door, 'how beautiful you are when you're cross.'

'By the devil!' She blushed at her oath.

He smiled broadly. 'Look after Bella.' He opened the door where Caspar was waiting. The wellwishers and the curious acquaintances who had been visiting the island since Hex's death, were already strolling to the beach to see his ship depart.

'We must hurry, Mas Carlton.'

They walked arm in arm down the path as Caspar skipped in front of them. It was the time for inconsequential chatter. He longed to be free of her now and yet . . . he couldn't help thinking how he would fare if he did stay. He looked out to sea where the waves were surging with a monstrous energy. No. He preferred the undemanding life of Dominica; the lazy routine of Roxborough with Hayes in his chair grumbling, Ella conjuring her spells and slave whelps gamboling naked in the paddock.

'I'll miss you.' He lied to make her feel better.

She glanced at him suspiciously.

'Do you remember that medical student we met at Almack's. He'll join the ship in Bristol. I need a doctor for my slaves.'

'That's nice.'

The *Sir Godfrey Webster* was pitching at her mooring off Crevichon. She was a fine ship. She was bound for Bristol for provisions, then to make the voyage by way of the Canaries to the Caribbean.

'I'll be home in under three months,' he said happily.

She did not comment. Her relatives and friends were waiting at the beach. Carlton strode up to them and shook hands briefly with some of them.

Bella stood alone where she could see over the bluff to Herm. The Pierre Percée reef was half-submerged, the ruined wall of the chapel sticking up like a lone dead tree on the great plains of her homeland.

He left the group around Lydia and walked up to her. She didn't turn as he slapped her buttocks. 'Dammit, Bella! You're a buxom wench.'

'Mas Carlton,' she whispered. Her hand touched her belly. 'I have you. Here.'

'Aye,' he said. 'We had some grand rutting. I'll miss that conny.' This time he didn't lie.

'Your son . . .' She rubbed herself. 'Here!'

'By the devil!' He slapped her buttocks again. 'Pregnant, are you? Get me a buck and I'll tell Lydia to give you a bolt of cloth.' He spun around on his heels and walked back to the group on the beach.

Bella held her head proudly for all to see her profile outlined against the sky. She was the one who bore the Bondmaster's heir. His name would be Nat.

Carlton stood with Caspar at the taffrail and waved as the sails filled with a stiff breeze and the ship drew away from the island. Lydia was alone on the beach and above her, on the bluff, was Bella.

Behind them both, on the crown of Jethou, was the grove of trees with its mysterious glade. To the east, washed by the sea, was the Pierre Percée reef.

'Goodbye,' whispered Carlton sadly. He wondered if Lydia would accept Bella's son like her own. Perhaps one day the buck would become the Bondmaster of Jethou and rule a fleet of fine ships and stout-hearted men . . .

'By the devil, son!' he muttered under his breath, gripping Caspar's shoulder.

'Yes, da',' the boy said happily.

* * *

Hayes no longer sat on the balcony where the slaves were accustomed to see him every day. His absence began the decline of the plantation. In vain, Ella tried to bully him out of his bed each morning.

As the word spread that the massa was fading, the slaves abandoned their tasks. Who was there to make them work? Without Hayes on the balcony, Ella discovered to her chagrin that she had no further influence on them.

She pleaded with Mercury to set the slaves to work. She even brought him to see Hayes in his bed. The driver could do nothing. The slaves needed to see a white face to be reminded of their Bondmaster. Without a white presence, they drifted to apathy performing only simple tasks necessary for their own survival.

Ella fought to keep Hayes alive. She administered every antidote she knew to combat the poison Tita must have slipped into his nightcap of rum. She had no proof. Tita herself remained aloof, saying that if Massa Hayes was dying, it was Ella to blame, not her. She had no part in his care.

The old man had his lucid moments. He would pull himself upright and gaze at her fondly. Sometimes he reminisced about Carlton as a boy. At other times, he ranted about the duplicity of slaves.

Ella encouraged him, planning that the next day she would get him on his feet and out onto the balcony. With him in his chair, she would order the slaves back to work. Alas, the next day he was always worse.

He lingered for weeks. Tita fumed at not being able to see him alone. Ella slept on a mat in his room and during the day, posted Pip or the new boy, Dontfraid, to watch over him. She didn't trust Pool. In fact, Pool was seldom to be seen. She knew he was consorting with the maroons and that they, like the slaves, were waiting for Hayes to die.

Each day, she compared Hayes's condition with the day before. He was wasting visibly. She was puzzled; it was almost as though he was willing himself to die.

She prepared all his food, and fed him, herself. He was never alone. She was sure there was no way that Tita's influence could make him die before her eyes. Yet Hayes showed no interest even in waiting for Carlton's return. He seemed to be hurrying to die before Carlton reached home.

The end came at night. Ella was lying on the floor, listening to his shallow breathing. She was startled when he called Carlton's name. She rose immediately and put her ear to his mouth.

'Carlton,' he said. 'I'm sorry . . .'

'Don't go, massa! Wait for him.' she tried not to cry.

'I see him . . .' He sighed. His fingers clawed over the sheet to find her hand. 'Ella . . . below the bed . . . under the floorboards . . .'

'Hush, massa, sleep now. Tomorrow.'

He gripped her hand. 'Shut up, wench!' he said with great effort. 'The bureau . . .'

'I know,' she said. 'I'll keep your gold safe for Carlton.' She stroked his brow and he slept peacefully. She stayed with him until his gentle snore changed to the rattle of death and he croaked his life away.

She hurried to the shutter of the window and flung it open for his spirit to fly out. Outside the sky was clear. There was no moon.

She turned back to Hayes and kissed him on his mouth. Slowly, so as not to wake Tita, she opened the door and tiptoed out of the house. As she descended the grand steps, she became aware of another shadow moving in the dark below the balcony. She sniffed the odor of the bush.

'Pool!' she whispered into the darkness. There was a strained silence. She imagined how frightened he must be to hear his name called so boldly.

'Pool, come here. I need you.'

The slave emerged from the gloom and stood beside her on the lowest step. He was naked and smelt of woodsmoke and damp grass. He put his hand on her waist.

'Yo' does want me?'

She lifted his hand away. 'Later, Pool. De massa done die.' If yo' help me we can share his gold.'

'Yo' gib me half?'

'*Oui.*' Ella beckoned him. 'Walk softly.'

Together they lifted the bed without a noise. Ella held the candle while Pool located the loose floorboard. There was a leather sack in the space underneath and he hauled it out carefully. His eyes gleamed in the flickering light from the candle.

'Dere be more,' said Ella. She took the keys and opened the bureau, feeling for the secret catch she had once discovered by accident. The drawer slid open soundlessly and she lifted out the pouches and carried them to the balcony. Pool dipped his fingers in the gold.

'We rich, Ella,' he said, his voice husky with greed.

'No we ain't.'

'We got to hide dis money while we make plans. We can't 'scape with it now.'

'Ah go'n call de maroons help me.'

She shook her head. 'No time. Dawn conch go'n blow soon.' She waited while Pool considered the matter. 'Dere does be a cutlass in de kitchen,' she said. 'Go for it. Don't wake no one. Dis be our secret.'

Pool's excitement at the sight of the gold confused him. Ella was grateful for his training as a slave for he did what she said. Yet there was nothing to stop him seizing the sack and toting it off to the hills himself. Instead, he found the cutlass and returned to help her carry the bags of gold down the steps.

Years before, when she was Carlton's bedwench, Ella helped him bury the proceeds from an auction of stock. Carlton chose a spot close to the northeast corner of the house, paced out equidistant from the trees. She measured the distance carefully while Pool watched her.

'Dig a hole here,' she said, crouching down and scratching in the soil. 'We go'n bury de gold so it safe 'til we come for it.'

She relied on Pool's greed to prompt him to think that such an idea was to his advantage. What was to stop him returning the next night with the maroons and retrieving the treasure himself? He dug with a will, chuckling to himself.

When the hole was deep enough, they rolled the sack and the leather pouches into it and kicked in the earth. Pool stomped it down to disguise the digging. Ella squatted over it and urinated. They were both satisfied it was safe.

Pool caught her arm. 'Yo' more evil dan Tita,' he said.

She nodded at the compliment and led him to the kitchen. 'I get yo' a rum,' she said. 'Den we go to my chamber and I *show* yo' dat I better'n Tita in dat too.'

He sat down at the table and began to pull himself in anticipation. Dontfraid was asleep before the fire.

Ella moved swiftly. She unlocked the pantry, found what she wanted and stirred it into a glass. She added rum and molasses and lime and brought the concoction for Pool.

'A punch,' she said with a wink. 'It special.' She held a glass herself and raised it to her lips.

Pool drank thirstily, touching Ella with his free hand as she stood beside him. He gathered up the hem of her skirt and slid his hand underneath, rubbing it slowly up her thigh. He fingered her as he drained the glass and put it down on the table.

His eyes shone and he pulsed with excitement. 'Dat sweet . . .' he said, then hesitated. He tried again. His head swayed. Ella waited.

His hand slipped slowly down her leg and he pitched forward across the table, his head banging against the glass which rolled off and smashed on the floor. Ella reached for the cutlass at his side. She had a lot to do before daybreak.

When Pip peered into the kitchen an hour later, she was cooking. Dontfraid was washing the floor with a cloth. The windows were open and the dawn's early light filtered into the room where a lantern still glimmered from its hook in the rafters. Pip was surprised she was up so early.

'De massa done die,' she explained without emotion. 'I send for Congo Venus to wash and lay him out.'

'Oh lord!' Pip sat on the edge of the table.

'No time for misery!' Ella bustled around him. 'Go'n wake Tita. She want to pay her last respects.'

Pip blundered out of the kitchen, still half asleep. Cleo the cook, and the house girls, woke next and Ella gave them instructions. Soon the house was alive with activity. She could hear Tita and the children running across the floor above her head. There were no cries of sorrow only Tita's shouts as she told Pip and the children what to do.

Pip was down cast when he descended the stairs. 'We got a new mistress,' he announced gloomily.

Ella, who had been on her feet since Hayes died, took no notice.

'Tita say dis, Tita say dat.' Pip walked to the pantry and removed a bottle of rum. He poured a gill in a glass and downed it quickly. 'Dis eye-opener,' he said grimly. 'Pity 'bout Massa Hayes. He look peaceful, dough.'

'He was.' Ella sighed. 'He see Carlton comin'.'

'Lor', ah sure hope so. Ah don't want Tita for de mistress.'

Ella walked up to him and placed her hand gently against his cheek. 'Yo' a good man, Pip,' she murmured. There was silence in the room. Dontfraid and Cleo were watching her curiously.

'We got to work together, all of us, 'til Mas Carlton come.'

Pip shrugged. 'Tita say she want breakfast at de Massa table. She an' Laura an' Hayes an' Mingoson. Dey all a' de table.'

Cleo wailed. 'Why! She ain't even wait 'til Massa cold.'

Ella took the cloth from Dontfraid. 'Go'n set the table,' she ordered in a tired voice as she wrung the cloth over a pail. The water was a scarlet color. Pip looked mournful.

'She say she want dis, she want dat,' he grumbled.

'Miss Ella done prepare a soup,' Cleo held up a ladleful and let it spill back into the cauldron.

'Serve them, Pip.' Ella yawned. 'Ah go'n see Massa Hayes.'

'Where Pool? He should serve Tita, not me.'

Cleo snorted scornfully. 'He serve Tita plenty a'ready. Ain't he her buck?'

Pip nodded his head knowingly. 'He runnin' wid dem maroons. He come when he hear Massa Hayes done die.'

Ella smiled enigmatically and walked out of the kitchen. Slowly, she ascended the grand staircase, her back straight and her head held high. Tita was waiting for her at the top, her fists bunched like a fighter's.

'Yo' ain't won!' she screeched. 'Wid Massa Hayes dead, Miss Laura does be in charge. She tell yo' haul yuh black ass ou' de *cou*. Go back to de quartahs where yo' belong!'

Ella ignored her and settled herself in Carlton's chair.

The shouts of the children as Pip put the tureen of soup on the table drifted through from the dining room.' 'Wait for me,' Tita warned them with a shout. She turned back to Ella.

'After we bury Massa Hayes,' she said, waving her fist, 'yo' go'n quit dis place. For sure!' She stood in the doorway, distracted by the noise of the children. She gloated at Ella then hurried to the dining room, took her seat at the head of the table and picked out the best lumps of meat from the soup for herself.

Ella leaned back. The sun was surmounting the ridge of hills in the east and casting its brilliance across the plantation to the sea. A ship tacked around the headland that jutted out like a sentinel guarding the Layou River. It was a big vessel, with all sails filled.

Ella raised her head. Pip was standing beside her. He sighed. 'Tita like dat soup plenty,' he said bitterly. 'Why yo' spoil her so?'

She reached for his hand. 'That's Pool in the soup. She done eat her own lover's lights.'

Pip stared.

'You see that sail?' Ella squeezed his fingers, fighting to keep back her tears. 'Carlton and Caspar. They've come in time!'